GW00792799

Four Kinds of Shipwreck

Jill Anabona Smith

Published by New Generation Publishing in 2022

Copyright © Jill Anabona Smith 2022

First Edition

The author asserts the moral right under the Copyright, Designs and Patents Act 1988 to be identified as the author of this work.

All Rights reserved. No part of this publication may be reproduced, stored in a retrieval system or transmitted, in any form or by any means without the prior consent of the author, nor be otherwise circulated in any form of binding or cover other than that which it is published and without a similar condition being imposed on the subsequent purchaser.

ISBN

      Paperback   978-1-80369-280-7
      Ebook   978-1-80369-281-4

www.newgeneration-publishing.com

New Generation Publishing

Should you choose a man you look up to?
Or one who meets you eye to eye?

For Raphaella … and with thanks for the invaluable support
of the Pen to Print Book Challenge team, in particular,
Anna Robinson
and of my husband – as always, a rock.

The members of IsleWrite have nursed and nurtured this
manuscript through its lengthy gestation
period. I will always be grateful. We are writers.

Cover photo: grahamward62
Design: graemecampbell.design

The **Book**Challenge

WHAT'S YOUR STORY?

This book was published through
The Book Challenge Competition part of
The London Borough of Barking and Dagenham
Pen to Print Creative Writing Programme.

Pen to Print is funded by Arts Council, England
as a National Portfolio Organisation.

WHAT'S YOUR STORY?

Connect with Pen to Print
Email: pentoprint@lbbd.gov.uk
Web: pentoprint.org

Supported using public funding by
**ARTS COUNCIL
ENGLAND**

**Barking &
Dagenham**

Contents

Flotsam

the wreckage of a ship or its cargo found floating on or
washed up by the sea

Trapanning. That's the word.

She should take that old auger that's up the garden and bore a hole in her husband's skull, whirring away until his secrets are exposed.

How else will I ever know what he did with it?

He must have put it somewhere.

One thing's for sure, he won't tell her and soon Halcyon, this awful barn of a house will be rubble. She's running out of time.

So … she'll very carefully ease off the plate of bone (about the size of a saucer, she saw it in a film) scrape back the meninges and poke around the relevant bits.

How will I know they're relevant?

Well presumably they'll be tidily marked – this is after all, the famous head that effortlessly found fraud.

Among the yards and yards of something like cod roes (blame YouTube – the patient was still awake, for goodness' sake) she'll find files marked with pound signs in carefully pencilled handwriting. Why pencilled?

Erasable, that's why. To leave no trace-

'Are you all right?'

'Oh.' Ava drops the armful of towels she's carrying. 'Fay. Sorry, sorry, miles away.'

'You look a bit green.' Bracelets jingle as her neighbour pushes back the sleeves of her jumper. For a moment, it looks like she's going to help but this of course is Fay, who simply slides to the floor and hooks her feet into the lotus position. 'Don't mind me,' her hands meet serenely under her chin. 'Go on.'

Green is a good word for it. I was greenly gullible. But now I'm red. Crimson and scarlet and deep blood red with shame.

'Just worn out. This is taking longer than I thought.' Ava reassembles the towel pile and her mental stability.

Around her, Halcyon is resuming the look it had on that first heady night here. Mostly empty, the rooms echo again as she works through, scouring them for clues. The ridiculously impossible dream she had of the two of them moving into it came true – but lack of funds defeated all the house's potential; everything from the mile-long wallpaper drops down the staircase to the cost of carpeting the ground floor – acres of it - in the same carpet. All the promise it held has, despite her best efforts, evaporated. Perhaps it was all a myth, like the bird it was named after.

'So are you going?' Fay squints at the invitation half-hidden under bedding on the coffee table.

'It's Saturday fortnight, that thing, the wedding. We move the Wednesday before and I've got to get the place straight. He gets really upset by anything out of the ordinary and a whole new …'

what is this going to be? Not house, not flat. Home then, although the word seems incongruous given the circumstances ...

'… new place.'

'I know when it is, Ava. I know I don't see things the same way as you, that's true. But I can read a calendar.'

She must have heard me calling her Flakey Fay. Ava channels her embarrassment by jamming towels into a cardboard box that's already full and putting all her weight on the flaps to try and secure it. 'Sorry. I'd only be going because some of them are relatives. They've not met Daisy and she's two now.'

Fay peers at the pink-edged invitation. "*... and afterwards at The Blazing Beacon...*" So are you going?' She unscrews her eyes to focus on Ava.

She really should have her eyes tested. I wish she'd clear off. I haven't got time for this. 'Well I'm not sure – Daisy's not used to being with a lot of people. The childminders won't know that.'

'They're professionals. They'll cope.'

'And me?' She re-folds the sheets. 'A wedding's about, no *is*, the last thing I feel like going to.'

'You'll enjoy it once you're there with a drink in your hand. You see. I've got a good feeling about this. You're turning the corner, Ava. Your karma's coming full circle. It's been a long time, but you're on your way now. Look, you're under pressure, let me help. You said there was going to be childminding, didn't you? So leave the little one with them and the big one,' she nods at the thin figure dozing in his chair, 'with me and Kris for the night. Simple.'

It's a kind offer. Ava threads between packed boxes to go over and tuck the duvet round him again. 'He feels the cold so badly ...' She tries not to dwell on his blue-veined skull. *Where exactly would I place the bit? You'd think all those CT scans would have shown something up, like a cross marking treasure on a map.*

Sometimes I think dementia's contagious.

As if stroking a dog, she runs a hand softly over the top of his head. Silvery hairs form a halo when the light catches and his ears are sprouting.

'I must get the buzzer out and whizz over this. I used to love looking down at this head when he was concentrating, poring over annual accounts, analysing, picking up the details no-one else noticed, then turning up to look at me. "Here. See Ava?" And I'd blush knowing he knew I'd been staring at him.'

'Hmm.' Fay's eyes are closed.

Ava's tried to keep him looking like himself despite not knowing who that is any more. Or who she is, for that matter. His long dry fingers move, stroking the duvet as he naps, the way his granddaughter touches her blue rabbit as she drifts into sleep. Who taught who?

'I *know* he gets cold,' Fay's awake now and unrelenting, 'but we've always got the heating on at The Retreat with people having treatments and zenning out all over the place. He'll be fine.' She remakes her pose and closes her eyes.

Envying her suppleness, Ava goes back and picks up the next carton, the top one off a teetering pile. It's been resting against a mirror firmly screwed to the plaster - no seven years of bad luck here, it says. The dresser covering it sold for £30 to a new vintage shop in the High Street last week.

4

These properties are the modern-day wreckers on the south-east coast, but rather than luring with clifftop lights, they seduce buyers onto their rocks with period features and characterful quirks. Empty for years, the shop had been stripped out, revealing green tiles on the walls proclaiming its origin, International Stores, where butter was once patted into blocks and bacon sliced on a whirring blade.

The new chalk-painted frontage meets with nods of approval from passers-by pleased to see Turner Contemporary's regeneration effect seeping round the North Foreland to Broadstairs. Everyone hopes the Trustafarian funds will hold out and International Vintage Furnishings (it's presumed the logo, IVF, is a sort of in-joke) will flourish. Either way, the locals - the landlord, plumbers, chippies and sparks - have already shared the spoils from the lot lured onto these rocks.

Ava was assured the dresser would be upcycled, repurposed, and sold in their London shop leaving her bemused that they can afford one as well as this new venture. Clever of them to retain an escape route. She should have done that but love blinds doesn't it?

The dresser's drawer had always stuck and if you yanked it hard, would come out in a clatter of Edith's rusty knives and graters and whisks, but still, out of loyalty, Ava wouldn't have wanted to see the thing on the pavement in the seaside rain.

Overall though, she's been too close to burning furniture to keep warm over the last winter to mind.

Shocked by the grimness of her own reflection in the blemished mirror, she shakes her head and the clip loosens and clatters onto the floor. 'Bugger. I don't think so Fay. It's good of you but … sorry - what were you saying?'

'Take advantage of us while we've still got The Retreat.'

'You're not selling?' *I should be used to standing on shifting ground by now.*

'Kris says he needs a new direction.'

'But you've only been there a couple of years.'

'Four actually, almost. But it looks like it's going under. He loved it to start with, now he's always moaning about it.' She stands and drawing her left leg up effortlessly becomes a Tree. 'He's driving me mad to be honest. Oh. Sorry.'

We always apologise, don't we? Women. I'm the one going round the bend. Trapanning indeed.

She could see though that perhaps Broadstairs wasn't quite ready for administered wellness at a price, after centuries of quietly assured self-sufficiency – gulling the Excise men, getting by on no discernible income. 'Oh I see. Sell it now it's a going concern then take on something else …'

'Something like that'- but unbalanced by a wail from the cot in the front room, Fay has to quickly plant both feet on the floor.

'I'll get her,' pinning her hair back up, Ava makes to fetch the child. 'She'll be hungry.'

. 'So. You'll go then?'

As much to get rid of Fay as anything else, Ava commits. 'Yes.'

I should have said thank you. And another wave of guilt washes over her as the front door closes behind Fay.

The boxes run out. This is the last one and it won't take everything that's left. Folding over the flaps, she heaves it out into the echoing hall. Only when she returns to check if he's stirred does she see the book that had been under the boxes and before that, under the dresser. She knows it's a dictionary because she toed it, skidding over the floor and under the cream-painted edifice to hide it from one of his rampages. He has systematically wrecked all the books that were in his mother's rooms, tearing and sometimes, when she's not looking, burning them which is a worry because she hasn't been able to have the sweep in for a while. And

Jon doesn't in any case always use the hearth. These are heart-stopping days.

But a dictionary, now that's sacred. You can look something up online, but in these systematic lists, the pleasure is in not simply finding the word you were thinking of but allowing your eyes to scan the ones nearest to it, like contemplating a box of chocolates. So she had saved it.

What does it say about trapanning then?

Flicking over the foxed pages, she's puzzled. The word that's whirred in her mind all morning means something else. The exploration of a skull by means of an auger and careful probing is spelt tr*e*panning.

Tr*a*panning means something quite different.

How ironic. Because she is fairly sure now, had she searched the contents of his skull, she would have found this was his intention all along.

A stratagem. An entrapment.

No, she stops herself. Be fair. The stratagem – yes, that was him, snaring green little Ava.

The entrapment, that was you, scarlet Ava.

She stares as a charred leaf flutters down from the dictionary's sleeve.

In his chair, he stirs.

It isn't a leaf. It is the scorched corner of an old twenty-pound note.

1995

Jetsam

unwanted material or goods that have been thrown
overboard from a ship and washed ashore, especially
material that has been discarded to lighten the vessel

The office was stifling with June heat you could touch. Outside was no better, the narrow Canterbury streets jostling with students and tourists and locals vexed at being held up. She should have worn something lighter than this suit, but it mattered to look business-like.

These shirt buttons gape a bit, but the jacket'll cover that ...

At least Caldwell's off today, not brushing up past me every chance he gets. I won't miss all the suggestions in every conversation with him. It's well worth doing two people's work not to have him around ...

The client accounts don't take long these days – there's so little going on in this downturn. On a good day, I can run this branch on my own with my eyes closed ...

She should use this time. Study, get more qualifications. Why not?-

'Oh. Good morning.' She looked across the desk seeing nothing but the sandy-haired man the receptionist had ushered over.

'So you'd like to view these properties sir?' She shuffled through the particulars he'd chosen. Interesting. And not just the properties.

'It's Ted. King. And yes,' he took the chair she offered. 'Please.'

He lived in the city. He was looking for anything really. An opportunity. He smiled and it was like there was a secret between them. She supposed he made all women feel like that. 'This one in particular,' he pointed at one place, out of the way and right on the shore. 'How about today?' His voice was a deep, dark brown. 'Now?'

'Yes. Oh god I forgot. No. My car's in for service.'

'Well mine's outside …'

That's how it happens. Chance upon chance. They pile up and suddenly you're somewhere you never imagined you'd be.

'I just need to fill in the book – say where I'm going – the rules,' she shrugged apologetically. 'Suzy Lamplugh and all that.'

'Oh. Rules. Who are they to set the rules? Trust your own judgment.' The deep-set grey eyes were teasing her now. 'You're safe with me.'

'Well anyway,' she took up the challenge. 'OK then, well I'll just do that and we'll be off.'

He stood, collected the leather jacket from the back of his chair, keys from a pocket and said, 'Let's go.'

She saw he was only a little taller than she was and about her age, but the very squareness of him, the wide shoulders, his manner of standing feet apart, made her breathe faster. He was tanned, too, the way people are when they're not tied to a desk for a living. *So not my type. Just goes to show.*

The last time she had brushed her hair was, she realised, this morning. Still, it hung, honey-coloured and smooth as usual and since it would never do anything else, there was no point in wishing for the moon. As Ava and Ted King walked through the office, the receptionist hurriedly dropped her tabloid *Spice girls to split?* into the bin.

'Off to see a few houses,' Ava told her. 'Be back about five.'

She'd told him they had all afternoon.

He was a rough diamond, too big somehow for this claustrophobic office and a mundane afternoon was suddenly becoming something else, a sort of parallel place to the well-structured one she normally lived in, a place where risks could be taken, a bit like the first time you rode a bicycle and didn't fall off.

The agency handled high-end properties and sold to customers who did not expect to use the multi-storey and walk for five minutes, so the firm had invested in a plot of

'And Mum fancied Sinatra.'

'Perfect,' he grinned back.

'Well I think it was the last thing they agreed on actually.' She shook her head then got back to thinking about work. 'I've saved the best till last.' She spoke keeping her eyes on the narrowing lane. 'It's the end of a row of three – the others are holiday homes at the moment, so you wouldn't be disturbed.'

'Might they be for sale too?'

'Oh, well I'd be willing to find out for you. First things first, let's see Number 1 Coastguard Cottages, Seasalter.' As she took the corner from the road down to the sea, she dropped down into third.

'Now down again,' he nodded. 'Now put your foot down, take it out of the corner …'

The car clung to the road, exactly where she put it and very, very fast. A smile flitted over Ava's face. 'That felt good.'

'Some things do,' he laughed.

They turned off at the line of trees planted a long time ago to shelter the cottages from the north wind. He followed her as they moved from room to room, Ava talking up the possibilities each offered. It seemed to be the garden that clinched it though.

'Not overlooked at all,' she pointed out 'and with that view.' The Thames estuary stretched away looking much as it must have done when Dickens gazed out over it. In the distance, shelducks paddled and beyond the mudflats the tide rippled in like molten silver.

On the shingle beach below the cottage a dilapidated jetty pointed to the water. 'Great. I could keep my boat there,' he said.

Ava must have looked doubtful. 'It's just a dayboat,' he assured her, 'not the QE2. For when the boys are here.'

So he has sons. Or did he say *when the boy's here?*

'It's a fair price,' he nodded. 'They'll take it off the market if I go ahead?'

Ava thought of the vendor, anxious to sell. 'You could try an offer …'

'No,' Ted shook his head. 'Just holds things up. I'll take it,' and shook her hand leaving it branded forever. 'You've got my details. I'll get onto my solicitors.'

He drove back to the office chatting easily about the chances of an early exchange of contracts. His lawyer, a friend, would see to it.

Without the car to hold her concentration, Ava was left to gaze at the strong square-tipped fingers on the gear lever. Surely, he must be able to read her like a book – he would have had a lot of practice.

When the car roared off, the exhaust note reverberated from the overhanging timbered shopfronts. On the pavement, Ava knew something had just happened and that corner of Canterbury would always remind her of it. Every time she walked into the office, there it would be.

'Oh,' she said aloud.

A slippery, confident wheeler-dealer in a fast car. Had she no sense? As she headed back into the sweltering office, she could still feel the tingling heat of his palm gripping hers.

By late autumn, she'd heard nothing further from him. The sale had completed without a hitch. No doubt he spent any time he wasn't making a profit shooting round the country impressing women.

'No trouble at all,' beamed Caldwell. 'An ideal client, Mr. King is.'

Ideal. From now on, Ted King would always be here, right here, beside her, inside her head.

Except he wasn't.

And cursing herself for an impossible romantic, she recognised instantly that no-one else would ever occupy this place in her soul.

But *coup de foudre* or not, Ava had other things to concentrate on.

'You'll soon like it here Mum.'

Ava's mother sat in her usual chair, her father in his. Ava might have teleported them out of the draughty front room in the crumbling semi which had been their home, then re-materialised them in this 'cosy living room with integral kitchen' on the sheltered scheme she'd found for them.

Her father made a good job of sounding grateful. 'I'm sure we will dear.'

But her mother, as ever, found fault. 'I'm not sure a fringe suits you now, at your age,' her mouth turned down.

It had taken Ava a lot of time to find this place, sunny and well-run. Then she'd started thinning out her parents' possessions ready for the move and her first exams last week had meant she'd no choice but to turn down Ted's offer of an afternoon at the cottage. He hadn't seemed too worried. *Maybe he realises he can't have all me any time he likes. After all, he's away a lot.*

Ava had known for a long time that nothing would be good enough for her mother but the three had long since crossed the line from Ava being the child and they the parents. It had taken a year of hard talking to get them out of the house and pulling every string she could at work, she had finally found a flatlet that they couldn't argue with. Small yes, but with a postage-stamp garden leading off what her mother called 'that kitchenette.'

Tired of the same old arguments, Ava bit back the comment that her mother hadn't cooked anything edible for quite a while now.

'The food in the dining room here is lovely Mum. Isn't it Dad?'

'Lovely. Bangers and mash and onion gravy ...'

'Oh *that,*' her mother's nose had wrinkled. 'Common, that's what that is. Now where did I leave the teapot? I can't find anything since you put us in this place Ava.'

'Found it in the fridge yesterday,' her dad whispered.

Considering all the work it needed, Ava had got a good price for the old home and invested the proceeds in an account in all their names.

'It'll be yours one day dear, you know,' her father had patted her hand. 'Why not have it now?'

'It's still your money Dad. You might fancy a cruise,' she laughed.

'Oh I don't think it's your mother's sort of thing, that.'

'Probably not.'

So she'd hardly had time to pine for Ted King. In the midst of bundling her parents' surplus things into black bags for the tip, it occurred to her this would be the perfect excuse to ring him. Would he like to see if anything here was of interest? Such a cliched come-on and she could do better than that surely? If she was interested in him. She could still feel the strength of his handshake and the impression of his palm on hers.

And then, on top of her files on her first day back from the week she'd taken off to move her parents, there was a hand-written note.

Mr. King rang. To do with Coastguard's??? Pl ring him.

'When was this?' Ava showed the receptionist the slip of paper, trying very hard to keep her voice disinterested.

The girl's face wrinkled with effort. 'The day after you went off I think. But Mr. Caldwell said it wasn't important 'cos the sale's all gone through.'

'Yes, the sale's completed. That's right,' Ava remembered how disappointed she'd been when the keys

16

had been collected not by Ted King but by the solicitor's clerk. 'Not important. Try and remember to date notes though in future.'

The morning dragged on, Ava mechanically dealing with things, the usual ebb and flow of customers making no impression on her. At last, people began pulling on coats, taking orders for the sandwich bar. Ava called through that she'd be staying in and the girl, still smarting at being told off for her note's deficiency, tossed her hair and pulled on her jacket before stamping out, the door slamming behind her.

Ava closed her office door and taking a deep breath, dialled the number.

'Lo?' the man's voice was young.

'Oh. I was trying to get hold – *oh I was so trying to get hold of* – of Mr. King. Ted. Is he there please?'

Had he yelled Dad? Or Ted? Unnerved, she jumped when the dark voice said, 'Yes?'

Ava swallowed.

He'd just moved in he told her. 'Number 1, Coastguard's.'

I know that, you've forgotten I sold you the house.

'But you know that,' he sounded contrite. 'Sorry. It's manic here. Done most of the work on it. Come and see.'

So simple. A risk possibly, but the only way to find out what she wanted to know... Telling herself she was just going on a re-valuation call, she said she'd be there at one o'clock. On the other end, he sounded as if he was dealing with someone.

Then he was back. 'I'll collect you.'

'It's out of your way surely?'

'I'll collect you.'

'Right then.'

Who had he been talking to?

17

It was a different car. Red, this one, as low but faster. 'Drive?' he offered the keys.

'Maybe later.' She just wanted to watch him as the exhaust burbled then roared.

But when he pulled round the corner to where the three cottages stood, the lane was cluttered. There were a couple of builders' vans and a heavy delivery lorry was offloading fence panels, the crane flying them through the air to the garden's edge where a young lad was guiding them down to earth.

'All right Owen?' Ted called.

'Yup. Nearly done mate.'

'They'll be gone soon,' Ted guided her round the diggings for the foundations of an extension which would run along the whole flank of the building. 'Careful there. Come in.'

The front door was open and the house had changed radically from the one she'd been daydreaming about.

'You're extending. I see.' Ava tried to hide her disappointment. All the way here, she'd thought he'd let her in to the empty house and kiss her, not able to wait a moment longer. Stupid. Why would he?

'Mm. This is working out for me, but a bit more space will make a lot of difference. More stock in means more to sell.'

The smell of still-drying plaster and fresh paint made this a different house. Now the two small ground floor rooms had been opened up. A simple kitchen with an Aga had been installed along the back wall with an island separating it from what had been the front room where a long table surrounded by mis-matched dining chairs stood, the sea beyond them below the garden.

'Drink?' he indicated one of the stools at the island and she sat, taking in all the changes. 'There's a Chablis chilling. I've been saving it.'

'Sounds lovely, but what's the occasion?'' She was starting to get her thoughts together.

'You're here,' he grinned, uncorking the bottle.

'To talk about re-valuing the property?' she ventured.

'That too.' He poured pale wine into two glasses and pushed one towards her. 'If you like.'

The lad he'd called Owen stuck his head in from the garden. 'Off now. See you in the morning.'

'Half day?' Ava asked.

'No, he's working on another property for me, down in the village. The fencers will be in tomorrow, then it'll be all go on the extension.'

'Another property? Don't remember selling you another one?' she feigned indignation.

'Don't get uppity,' he took a drink. 'I already owned it. Had tenants. They went so it's going to go back on the market when it's been refurbed. Then,' he emphasised, 'I'll be back to you for selling it.'

'Great. Well here's to a good purchaser,' she raised her glass.

'Let's look upstairs eh?'

As they toured the bedrooms, Ava had that giddying feeling of the closeness of him again. His physical presence in the room was impossible to ignore, heat and the sound of his breathing when he was listening to her, the deep-set eyes watching her.

'What's behind the door?' she asked as they stood in the first of the two bedrooms. Sun streamed in through the windows and the sea shone below the beach. Her words echoed in the empty room, devoid of furniture, curtains, making her wonder how it would look with a bed in it.

'En-suite,' he nodded. 'Wetroom. Come and see.'

It was a tight space so now they were so close she could smell him again, caramel and musk. To sound professional, Ava admired the finished work. 'The tiles and suite are top quality and the workmanship's very good,' she said, aware of him standing there and her mind took a picture of a moment in time.

'Good. Come and see the other one,' he gestured for her to follow him.

The other bedroom was larger and this one did hold a bed. A single folding one though, not likely to stand the weight of two.

'And another en-suite,' he opened a door again. 'This one's big enough for a bath and you can see the sea when you're sitting in it.'

'How lovely.'

'More wine?' he took her empty glass. 'We can sit outside. They've all gone now.'

She followed him carefully down the narrow staircase which wound round the back of the inglenook in the sitting room and then, glasses replenished, out into the warm soft air of the September afternoon.

'Garden's a mess now, but come the spring, it'll be good. Going to make it into a real sea garden, plants that don't mind salt and wind. Eryngium, valerian, that sort of thing?' When Ava shook her head, he went on, 'Just natural seashore plants.'

'Oh and driftwood?' she warmed to his idea. 'Flotsam and jetsam?'

'Derelict and lagan,' Ted smiled.

'I don't know lagan,' Ava acknowledged.

'It's *Laga maris,* the law of the sea. Flotsam, jetsam, derelict and lagan. Lagan is something sunken but marked by a buoy for retrieval by the owner. I reckon it's how they made their living round here, back in the day,' he laughed, 'one boat bringing in then sinking the contraband, like barrels of brandy, another from the village collecting them.'

Turning, he nodded to the highest point of the garden, 'And decking over there for drinks in the evening.'

'You'll have great sunsets here,' she nodded, on safer ground now. 'That's due west. Turner's 'loveliest skies in Europe'. And the light's magical.'

'He was right. I like this corner of England best. It's close enough to London and Europe for business but overlooked. Quiet.'

A thought occurred to her. 'The new fences won't block the views?' Beyond the boundary, steep shingle slopes made it unlikely anyone would intrude.

Ted stood, hands in his jean pockets and flexed his back. 'No. The ground drops enough. They'll make it private but not shut in.'

'Do you need them?'

'They make good neighbours,' he smiled.

'Oh what *is* that from?' Ava fretted, trying to recall.

'Frost. *Good fences-* '

'*-make good neighbours* – of course,' she joined in.

'It's not my favourite though.' He finished the Chablis into their glasses.

'Oh?'

'Hang on,' he ducked into the house and came back with a book in his hand. 'First edition this. Signed. Quite valuable …' he flicked through the pages, then read:-

'Two roads diverged in a yellow wood,
And sorry I could not travel both
And be one traveler, long I stood
And looked down one as far as I could
To where it bent in the undergrowth;

Then took the other, as just as fair,
And having perhaps the better claim,
Because it was grassy and wanted wear;
Though as for that the passing there
Had worn them really about the same,

And both that morning equally lay
In leaves no step had trodden black.
Oh, I kept the first for another day!
Yet knowing how way leads on to way,
I doubted if I should ever come back.

I shall be telling this with a sigh
Somewhere ages and ages hence:
Two roads diverged in a wood, and I—
I took the one less traveled by,
And that has made all the difference.'

She stared, astonished. 'I don't think I've ever heard anyone recite poetry. That was beautiful.'

'Well, I can't claim the credit,' he laughed. 'But it's always appealed to me, that thing about taking the outside chance. It's done me all right.' He took a gulp of the straw-coloured liquid.

'And *ages and ages hence*?'

'I deal in antiques Ava. Things that have survived long after the folks who originally decided to buy them. What someone won't buy today because it's not in fashion, will be worth plenty when its time comes.'

He was full of surprises.

They talked on, watching the sun sink through pink ribbons of cloud until, for a moment, the horizon looked as if it were on fire.

She felt the same.

Ted stood and held out his hand. 'Shall we?'

But there was no question really, was there? This is the moment when that parallel world became the real one ...

He takes her hand and leads her indoors. The sofa in the living room has been unfolded. He shrugs, pulls a bedroll out and with a flourish, there's a bed.

The very last of the sun is low and shafting right into the room.

'Undress Ava. If you want to.'

So she does. In the future, this comes into her mind over and over again.

'Be comfortable.' So close she can feel his voice growl in his chest, he kisses her neck, biting the curve where it meets her shoulder and she kneels on the softness of the duvet, watching him.

His body is firm, moulded and looks toasted and scented with warmth. Turning away from her, he pulls his shirt over his head and when he turns back he is ready for her.

He has made her wait for this. It will be worth it.

This is the refuge Ava revisits, time and again, when she's at a low ebb. A sunny day, a car ride to the sea, the scent their bodies made, tangled together. And everything that followed. The memory fills her with warmth.

My body doesn't look like that these days though. They say you should never go back to where you were happiest. There should be a law against it.

Maybe they're right.

But, as he said, who are they to set the rules?

'Why is the pub called that?' she asked one day as they drove past the low, white-painted building. 'The Seasalter Company? Were they militia?'

'Seasalter is a liberty – an area bonded together although there are no obvious boundaries – and that makes – *made* – the people look after one another.'

'What is a liberty exactly? Sorry to be ignorant.'

'Probably you could say land no one else wants. There were salt marshes, it was isolated … the Crown wasn't interested, nor the Church, not in the Domesday book.'

'It sounds wonderfully romantic,' Ava was wistful. 'So they all stuck together, looking out for one another.'

'In a way,' he laughed. 'The Company were supposed to be about fishing, oysters. But the boats had other uses sometimes. They say they were all smugglers.'

'That was what you meant about … lagan?' she remembered.

'I reckon everybody in the liberty knew what was going on, so everybody kept quiet and everybody profited somehow.'

'Like Broadstairs – Defoe said that most of the people had no visible means of support'-

'-and not to ask questions about how they survive or else,' he menaced.

In the laughter, a tiny question scuttled like a rat across Ava's mind.

'Is it nice? The pub?' She shooed the rat away with a yardbroom.

'I hope so. It's mine. Well partly.'

'That must be interesting.'

'The other half wanted something to do when I'm away. Fair enough I suppose. I could make it better but Sal has her own ideas.'

'Your wife?' *Oh god that word you said you wouldn't say.* It plummeted like a rock into the space between them.

After a second Ted said, 'She runs three around Kent and Surrey. Always away in one or other of them, bossing everybody. Not achieving a lot by it.'

'That's a shame.' *So I can only come here when she's away. I wonder where the others are. I could go in. Look at her. Just to see. While he's away, travelling.*

For a year or more, weeks would go by when they made no demands of each other, then Ted would ring to say he was free, could she come to the cottage? If she wanted to. Testing the water to see if anything had changed and finding it hadn't. Each time, Ava shoehorned him into her diary, with work, the degree course she'd started, the appointments she had to take her parents to. She found time and each time, Ava was left spellbound by him and the effect he had on her body. More than that though, he made her feel … she searched for the right word, driving back from the cottage, the scent of his skin still, just, on her hand. More *loved*. Although he had never said the words.

The refectory was filled with noise, voices and clattering plates. Ava took her tray to one of the tables near the open doors. Outside, students sat and lay on the grass in the sunshine. One of them, a lad named Joshua had shadowed Ava for weeks. He'd been kind, offering to help with an assignment she'd had to miss because of work, phoning in the evening to talk her through the modules.

He detached himself from the others and loped over to her, beanpole legs in skintight jeans. 'All right Ave?' He sat down. 'You doin' anything this weekend?'

No, she said, she wasn't, realising too late that was a mistake.

'Only – I thought – come out for a drink with me? Down by the river, that new place?'

'Josh, it's kind of you but …' He seemed such a child. Nearly a foot taller than her as all the youngsters seemed to be. But so thin. Unformed almost, his face nearly as pretty as a girl's – no beard to speak of and the rosy lips of a putto. Quite possibly, he had a body that could go on all night but what use was that without knowing how to use it?'

'No?'

'No.' She came back to the refectory in a hurry. 'Sorry.'

He coloured up. 'Sorry Ave – are you with someone then?' He glanced at her bare left hand as if to check she hadn't suddenly started wearing a wedding ring. 'You never come to any of the parties this lot have.'

'No. And yes, I am with someone – sort of.'

'Oh. Married then?' He shook his head. 'My sister did that. No future in that Ave. Come out with me. I know I'm a bit younger than you but I'll give you a good time, promise.'

'Thanks for the advice but the answer's still no.' The salad on her plate looked tired. She drank the water in the plastic cup and stood up. 'Thanks Josh. Sorry.'

And he shrugged and loped back to the gang on the grass.

'Can you get away? Friday night?'

'This Friday? Where to?' It made her feel giddy.

'You say.'

Her brain pulsed with adrenalin. 'Maybe Suffolk?' She could already feel him – as if he was there now in the office, in her hand.

'Sounds perfect. I'll book a hotel.'

'My friend has a cottage. On the beach. I could see if she's going to be away …'

'Even better. Let me know. Have to go. Looking forward to it. I could pick you up after work … I'll be in a Merc. Don't bring too much luggage,' there was a burst of laughter. 'No room.'

How stupid am I being? A married man and he hasn't even got to pay for the hotel? Come on.

'Course you can mate.' Corinne was expansive. 'I'm in town, so take all the time you want.'

'What are you doing?'

'Jamie and Nick are back – really looking forward to seeing them.'

'Oh.' For a moment, Ava did want to be with her friend and two of her siblings, Ava's surrogate brothers. But this was time with Ted. 'Thank you Corinne. It'll be perfect.'

'Key's under the mat. You know.'

'Yes. I know'

Oh what he did for her, driving up in that low black convertible, pulling up outside the office just as Caldwell was going home. 'Mr. King isn't it? Can I help?'

'No. Thanks. Ava will be going along for the ride. I'll rely on her.'

Silenced, Caldwell huffed off and Ava slipped down into the car's leather interior. 'How beautiful.'

Ted smiled. 'Let you drive later. Just relax for now. It's Friday. You can.'

'Oh *yes.*' Behind closed eyes, she listened to the engine's pull. 'Think it'll take long? Couple of hours maybe?' She'd spend them looking at him driving – pure pleasure.

They made it in an hour and twenty and Ava, eager to go to the pub, have a meal, walk, do everything, began to spot places as they drove into Lowestoft.

'Yes we'll go there,' Ted nodded as she pointed out a place on the beach. 'But an early night tonight.'

'Well of course,' she smiled. Food could wait.

'No I mean it. This is the first place in England to watch the sun rise, then we'll walk up the Scores and get breakfast. Then we'll come back to bed, then we'll have lunch. I thought we'd go into the Broads for that?'

'I'm worn out already.'

'Well what would you like to do?' He indicated and overtook three cars.

She thought for a moment. 'Just sit - and watch. The light and the sea and the birds ..'

'Oh, so not me?'

'I never stop watching you.'

He seemed pleased. 'Well there are steaks in the coolbag. How about we start with a quiet night in?'

But a night in with him was never going to be quiet.

As she dressed the salad leaves he'd brought, Ted came up behind Ava and his big, warm hands on her waist reminded her of every pleasure he'd already given her. 'Oh,' she laughed. 'That's wonderful.'

'Is it?' He slid his hand to the front of her jeans and unzipped them. Soon, his fingers were inside her pants. 'Is this?'

'Oh God yes,' she bent forwards, pushing back into him.

'Good. Oh Ava. Come *on.*'

She made him stay where he was, exploring and teasing, as she wriggled with pleasure.

And then it was her turn. 'This?' His jeans were open now, her hand inside. 'And this?'

'Oh definitely yes.'

'Good. Now,' she stretched over her shoulder to kiss his face. 'Steak? Or more starter?'

'Steak'll still be here in an hour or so, I reckon …'

But when they woke for the sun rise, it was rain that greeted them. Ted closed the curtains, brought Ava tea in bed and said, 'Fancy a bit of shopping?' He pulled the covers up around her. 'After.'

The High Street looked as if it was mainly filled with the usual multiples, so she wasn't unhappy when he turned out into the countryside beyond Oulton. 'Mind if I combine business and pleasure for a bit?'

'Fine with me,' she grinned, happy to be beside him in his car.

'When you said Lowestoft, I thought of my old mate Steed. Dealer, like me and he's got a big place, a barn out here.'

'Oh. I'll make myself scarce shall I?'

'Whatever for? No I've told him all about you.'

Ava, used to being kept secret, tried not to show how pleased she was.

In the car park, Ted opened the boot and took out a canvas bag. As a golden Labrador bounded out of the oak barn's door, sniffing and tail-wagging, to investigate them, Ted reached in and found it a dog biscuit which disappeared immediately.

A voice boomed 'Tinker! Here you silly bitch, it's only Woody.'

'Hello darling.' A bulky, silver-haired man in a leather waistcoat swept up Ava's hand and shook it. 'You're Ava. Least I hope you are or I'm in the deep stuff.'

'No, you got it right Steed, here she is. Told you she's a stunner didn't I?' Ted was grinning broadly. 'Ava, meet Steed.'

'Hi,' she smiled then bent to stroke the dog, enjoying the feel of the shiny coat.

'You in our line of business Ava?'

'Ava,' Ted said with some pride, 'is an estate agent. A very good one.'

'That right?' Steed reappraised her. 'Are you now?'

'And I'm studying. For exams. Financial analysis.'

'Well good luck with them. Now, come on in for coffee you two.'

The barn soared up into the beams, birds darted between haphazard floor levels built up into different corners, each one filled with stock. 'What you brought for me Woody?'

As the kettle boiled, Ted knelt to the bag and carefully drew out a square mirror, the frame handbeaten copper. 'Newlyn. It says, look on the back.'

'Oh that's nice mate.' The two men were engrossed.

Feeling a bit left out, Ava offered to make the coffee.

'Yes please love,' they both said at once then went on talking.

'Like a drop of something in it?' Steed offered, reaching down to the bottom drawer of his desk when she gave them their mugs, and splashing Scotch into his.

'A drop, not one of your specials,' Ted grinned, nodding out to the Merc, rain channelling down its glossy black paintwork. 'That car's a proper bluelight magnet. I'd be invisible in the truck.'

Ava warmed her hands round her mug and took it with her, strolling around all the pieces of furniture and china and silver and paintings. Some reminded her of the things she'd salvaged from her parents' old house. There was no room in the flat, so she'd pulled out the best ones and put them into sales.

The truck. There was so much of Ted's life that was a mystery to her yet he was sharing his friendship with Steed – she couldn't complain.

'This is lovely,' she said aloud, stopped by a watercolour in a deep gold frame. '*Lowestoft Pier, 1898,*' she read from the label, gulping at the price. 'I love how the waves are breaking along it.'

Steed's voice made her jump. 'You've got a good eye, Ava. Some people like bigger, busy subjects like this one,' and he pointed out a ship anchored off with tenders busy ferrying to and from the shore. 'But simple's better and this will sell because it'll remind someone of being on the pier, even now.'

'Ages and ages hence,' she smiled at Ted.

'Tell you what Steed. Straight swap? The painting for the mirror?' Ted held out his hand and his friend shook it enthusiastically.

They stayed chatting a while longer, then Ted put his arm round Ava's shoulder. 'We must be off.'

'Don't hurry, if you need to chat more - I'm happy looking around.'

'I've got plans.'

The watercolour disappeared into the Merc's boot and they waved goodbye to Steed and Tinker, just as it started to rain again.

'Why does he call you Woody?'

'Oh, that came from my little brother. He couldn't manage Edward so he just said Woody. I wasn't Ted until I was older.' Another piece in the jigsaw of her knowledge about him to cherish when he wasn't there. At Oulton the rain stopped and they parked to look at the boats then strolled until they came across a pub for lunch.

'How beautiful this all is,' Ava looked around her. With the sun out, the water glittered and danced. 'Is it tidal here?' she frowned watching the flow and thinking about the Broads.

'Yes, but not like the coast. Smaller.'

'Safer that way?'

'You bet. I learnt to sail here, with my brothers when we were little,' Ted smiled at the memory.

'Sounds like Swallows and Amazons. Tell me about them?'

'Oh no. We were always fighting,' he laughed. 'Knocking each other about over some squabble or other. Now one's in America, the other's on a ship somewhere in the world, Navy man.'

'So you don't see them much.'

'No. We catch up when we can. Shame but there it is. Great memories of holidays though. Better than the East End.'

'Where you grew up?'

'Yeah,' he finished his beer. 'It was real then. Real people.'

Then it started to rain again and they ran for the shelter of the car.

As they drove back to the cottage Ava thought about what Ted had told her. Her own childhood held no such memories.

'All right?' The warmth of his hand on her knee brought her back.

'Very.'

The cottage was chilly and she shivered as soon as she took her coat off. 'You've caught a chill,' Ted frowned and made up the fire, insisting she sat there under a duvet while he nipped out.

A familiar, delicious smell woke her. The room was lit by firelight and candles on the table.

'Oh good. You're awake. Chicken's done,' Ted said from the kitchen. 'How are you feeling now?'

Ava's head was pounding. 'I think you might have been right about a chill. How long have I been asleep? I should take paracetamol – there's some in my bag.' *What a waste, to come all this way, then sleep.*

She rummaged in the bag he brought her, tipped two down with some water and ran a brush through her hair then threw the brush back, on top of the postcard she'd bought to send her parents.

'Your hair is beautiful,' Ted smiled. 'I was looking at it when you were asleep. The firelight made it shine.'

Fairly sure no other man had ever paid her a compliment like it, Ava reached up to him for a kiss but then he pulled away to check the oven.

Quiet weekend at Corinne's cottage Ava wrote on the card, hoping they'd assume it would be with Corinne herself. She stuck on the stamp she'd bought and promised to post it in the morning.

Ted brought her a glass of red. 'Feel up to eating now?'

'Yes, it smells wonderful,' she smiled, so he jointed the chicken and they ate, like lord and lady of the manor, with fingers, throwing bones into the fire while he made her laugh about his brothers.

'Your parents – aren't still alive?' she guessed.

'Mum's been gone a couple of years now. One of those things, cancer. But Dad's still hale and hearty – comes out on the boat with me sometimes for a bit of fishing.'

'He sounds like fun.'

'Oh Pete's fun all right,' he nodded. 'A good Dad.'

With a crack, a log settled into the ash and the bones whitened and crumbled. Ava stood. 'If I sit here much longer, I'll fall asleep again.

'And that would be a shame.'

Minutes and hours slid by, lulling them away from reality but soon the clock couldn't be ignored and they had to pack up and head back.

As they crossed the boundary into Kent, a wave of melancholy broke and Ava couldn't stop a sob blurting out. 'It's over, isn't it? Oh Ted,' the tears flowed down her face, no matter how hard she tried to stop them.

'Here,' he pulled into a layby. 'You mean the weekend, right? It was always going to be, Ava.'

'I *know* dammit. My exams start in a fortnight. I just *forgot.'*

'Thank Christ for that,' he breathed out. 'I thought you meant us for a minute.'

'You didn't have to do that,' Corinne rang, eager to find out how it had gone.

'Do what?'

'Leave me the painting, the thank you note.'

'I've literally no idea what you're talking about. Oh – not the painting of the pier?'

'It's gorgeous. In pride of place already. It's really kind of you, there was no need to thank me if you had a good time. I posted the card to your parents by the way.'

'Oh god – forgot all about it. Thanks.'

'Too much else to think about?'

'I had my hands full.'

'And did you? Have a good time?'

'Better than.'

'Make it work for you.'

Ava hung up. *How?*

But then she had to concentrate on her exams.

On the day she said it, Ava and Ted had worked in the shingle garden all morning. It had been almost two months since they'd been together but on this, one of the rare occasions when she could stay overnight, it seemed a mutual decision to postpone the moment when they'd fall on each other in their familiar, delicious, stepless dance, building the tension of longing.

The spring sunshine made the rivulets of low water on the mudflats flow silver. The Chancer, the dayboat Ted and the boy as he called him, had been sailed round from Sheppey and leant against the jetty as if resting after the journey.

As Ted swung the billhook, the muscles in his back formed an intricate pattern, sweat glistening over his tan. This side of the cottage, the farthest from the road, was entirely private and in any case, the other two houses were holiday homes and this was too early in the year for them to have visitors, so Ava and Ted were able to be out here quite alone.

'You've never been married?' He knew she was on her own now.

'Not me,' she shook her head. 'Why would I? Why does anyone?'

'Good question.'

Later, after making love, she said, delighted, 'I love you,' and her words fell into the stillness of the sunlit room.

'That's bad,' he observed.

'No – Oh. I didn't mean anything,' she hurried. 'Just that this is so … I love it.'

It didn't seem to upset him too much. 'Well make the most of me while you've got me. I'll be away again for a bit.'

'How long?' She wished she didn't want, so badly, to ask.

He shook his head and shrugged bare brown shoulders. 'No way of knowing …'

She knew she had broken it. By saying three simple words, she had changed their relationship from the free and easy thing they both enjoyed. Unintentionally, she was sounding like a woman who could threaten his marriage. Pointless to go back and try to unsay them.

And it struck her that once he was away buying, other women would cross his path. She hadn't thought of that before.

It was a long summer, the dusty streets full of families and tourists, clicking one another at the cathedral gate and in its surrounding overhung streets.

At Coastguard's, where the air would be cooler, there would be visitors too in the other cottages and, probably, Ted's wife at Number 1.

The last time she'd been there, Ava had been washing her hands at the kitchen sink. A pair of yellow Marigolds lay on the drainer. She was a real person, his wife, doing housework in the cottage where Ava and Ted made love. Ted had described her as difficult, probably to make Ava feel what they were doing wasn't wrong. Well any married man would say that, make his excuse that way. There was, she suddenly saw, no real room in his life for Ava, burning longingly for him.

The postcard arrived at the office and so, open for the world to see, it was neutrally phrased. *Look who's in Lithuania.* No darling, no missing you, no can't wait to get you into bed as soon as I get back. He'd probably sent the same thing to his wife.

Soon the schools would be going back, the melee in the city would reshape into more organised, silver-headed groups of travellers and then Ava's final exam results came through.

A First. If she could achieve that, all that work mixed and muddled up with all the disquiet of an affair with a married man who didn't really need her, how much more could be achieved if she just concentrated on her career? A First wouldn't make him make space in his life for Ava. The argument went on in her head for weeks. If he'd been there to talk to might he have been persuaded that they could work as a couple? But how? What could Ava offer such a self-contained operator, to whom even his existing wife and young son seemed peripheral? He had it all, just the way things were.

I've become lagan. Marked by my owner for retrieval whenever he can fit me in. Infuriating. It made her burn. She would end it, never get involved like this again. But the lesson left a void in her life.

In the quiet spell, towards the end of the autumn, sales were dropping still further, recession was biting deeper every day. The last golden leaves dropped from the trees to race along the River Stour the morning Ava walked between the Westgate Towers towards the office, knowing that this could wait no longer. As she pushed the post on the door mat back the door was wedged by the local free paper.

'I'll just check our sales ads in The Recorder,' she handed the opened post to Caldwell hoping it would keep him busy, but he wasted no time trundling over to read over her shoulder, glancing down her blouse at the same time.

The headline stopped her hand from turning pages.

Local antique dealer helping police with their enquiries.
After a spate of burglaries at high-profile addresses in
the Swale area, a local man known to own several antique
outlets in the Kent and South London areas has been
helping police with their enquiries.

She screwed up the paper, old Caldwell protesting that he hadn't read it yet. Really, how rude. What was she thinking of?

She ignored the blustering, aghast at the thought of Ted, a free spirit, on the run or worse still, locked up.

It couldn't be him. He was clever and fast and better than that. Her heart wept for the warm, loving person she thought she knew. But this was out of her hands.

She obviously didn't know him, he was just a fantasy and he didn't care about her, just a willing woman for days when he had time to spare. As much fun as it had been with Ted, she had to face it. She'd let herself be used for long enough.

The following week, buoyed up by exam success, she applied for a job in London. If he missed her enough, perhaps when he got out, he'd come looking for his lagan, marked by the imprint of his palm, not declare undying love but at least, just maybe, that she belonged somehow in his life.

It wasn't very likely though.

She wouldn't be there. Lesson delivered.

***

It caught at his throat, wondering again about Ava. Had she meant it, about loving him? But then she disappeared. Funny things women. You could never be certain – although he thought he had been about Ava. First things first. There was a lot to deal with. And then there was Sally.

August 1998

Derelict

a ship or other piece of property abandoned by the owner
and in poor condition

Always enjoy the first few days of an audit. There's the chance someone won't be able to keep his mouth shut and we'll clear it all up in no time. The ones that drag on eat into the fees. But I can usually spot what's going on. Well I will do when this bloody train comes. *Incident* the tannoy says. Some silly sod's gone under a train. Inconsiderate.

Make the most of the delay, go through the papers again. Careful. Don't want them blowing all over the platform.

Frogs and Toads, son Father used to say. Make both sides balance. If you look carefully enough, you'll see where they don't and that's where to dig a bit deeper. I learnt more from him than I ever did at Lancing – heaven knows why they sent me to the place. Hateful. Makes me shiver thinking about it. Always cold, always hungry. They didn't want me at home, that was crystal clear. Wouldn't like that for Syd. Anyway what else has Margaret got to do but look after the child she saddled us with? And there's the fees … Won't your father start a trust fund I said at the hospital. What with she said. That was the first I knew of it – who'd have thought it? Long-established business, so nothing much in the way of overheads like premises. All paid for long since. Nothing much in the way of turnover either, it transpired. He kept that quiet when I went to him about doing the decent thing and marrying his daughter, I can tell you. She was all over me, right from the first date, I really wish I hadn't bothered – here's the train at last.

It's quite obvious someone's on the take. So that's what we'll do, exploit the weakness, pick it like a scab and see what transpires. My money's on Gibbs, the founder of the firm. He was defiant, but wavery on the phone. Have to take care he doesn't keel over while I'm grilling him. Poor PR. But if he's got any sense …

Scott and Hatton have agreed this one's mine. They owe me those two, had the pickings of the last case, I was just a minority shareholder - but this one … well not to get ahead of oneself …

I have got the wherewithal at the moment though, so let's get on with it … Now, escalators.

Northern Line's all to cock as usual but I'm not late. Benefit of allowing an extra ten minutes for any journey.

I spot her as soon as I walk in the office. You couldn't miss her. Hair that swings when she walks, folds onto her shoulders when she stands and then, when she looks down at something in a file, it falls in a smooth curtain so you can't see her face, see what she's thinking. Although that seems perfectly obvious to me and all the other men in here. And to be honest the Equal Ops brigade are baying for more women at the higher levels in the firm – although I'd give her the job anyway just to have her around.

I've got to interview everyone on the list so I'll make a go of it, but it's a waste of time. CV says she's 33.

But those legs …

Each candidate was told to put in a report of their role, the firm's positives and negatives, include any recommendations for the future, usual sort of thing before I got here. She must have been up all night because hers was emailed first thing next day. Even included something about *I thought the firm was taking on too many new clients. A lot of their details were not what one might wish.* What young woman talks like that nowadays? With those legs? Jolly good. Some of it was just plain wrong of course but then she couldn't know what we were thinking – or at least if she did, she'd have been in on it and there's no evidence.

Looking through all the reports at home last night I said to Margaret, this one's a potential. She's young, but she's got a handle on where things could be improved all right. Oh says Margaret, a handle is it? And not making a joke of it. Christ, women are hard work.

You'll be working late again, no doubt, Margaret says.

Probably. Might stay over for a couple of nights, not waste time on trains that don't come and all that grind.

The office was awash with anxiety.

An audit was a normal, necessary evil. No-one would come out of it smelling of roses because that wasn't the point, was it? Especially with the new owners' team of assessment auditors set on making a name for themselves.

Everyone was long-faced with fear, tight-voiced, but Priti, Ava's diminutive intern, said 'That tall one. Silver fox type in the navy suit. He's nice,' until Ava told her, rather sharply, to concentrate on her work. He had presence though, she'd give him that. Tall like that boy at college had been – what was his name? Didn't matter - but so much more … well, be honest … sexy. Something, *everything* to do with raw power, your entire future in those long, slender fingers.

The green phone on her desk rang and Ava could see from the extension list it was coming from his office. She picked it up, guessing correctly that it was her turn for a grilling.

Priti was right. He was good looking, this Jon Wilkes, she thought, watching him sort papers before he began. Slim fingers that didn't look as if they ever got dirty. He'd certainly made himself at home here in the few days since he'd been parachuted in on top of them all. There was a pot plant she didn't remember being there before and a photo in a frame of an ordinary-looking woman holding a baby girl on her hip. The child was scowling into the sun, as they always do.

'Your wife?' Ava nodded to the picture making small talk.

'Eh? Oh,' he caught her meaning. 'Yes. And Syd.'

'Sid?'

'S.y.d,' he spelt for what Ava knew wasn't the first time. 'Her mother's idea. Couldn't talk her out of it. Now I can't talk to her at all,' he muttered, head back in his files.

'Oh, she's a fan of the Mitford girls? That was Muv's name.'

'No idea.'

Recognising a conversational dead end when she saw one, Ava fell silent. Eventually Jon Wilkes looked up and sighed. 'It's a bloody mess this place isn't it?'

'Sorry?'

'The client accounts are as good as empty, there's petty cash running out of every door and window with no authorisation, commissions are paid out without any paper trail at all far as I can see'-

'-Mr. Gibbs has always worked this way. Trusts his employees …' Ava's voice faded, picturing the small, rotund founder of the firm. 'Did you say empty? The client accounts?'

'Fraid so. Head Office started looking at the accounts a while back. There's been quite a bit of investigation going on the QT before I got here.'

'Well if it's that bad, why did they buy us up lock, stock and barrel? There won't have been any goodwill if things are as bad as all that,' Ava defiantly tried a rearguard action.

Jon Wilkes looked at her. 'The premises. We bought the freehold. It's worth ten times more than the business would be even if it was being run properly.'

Asset-stripping. It wasn't necessary for him to say the words, the implications fell into the room like shards of ice. It was beginning to look as if a change of job was on the cards whether she liked it or not.

Over the next few days, the office looked as if a death had occurred. People scurried, papers in hand, heads down, not making eye contact.

It was lunchtime. In the busy kitchen corner, Ava had filled the kettle and was retrieving her salad from the fridge when Jon walked up and, since she could hardly ignore him, she offered to make him tea too.

'Thank you Ava,' He leant elegantly against the wall, looking down with hands in his pockets as she found the teapot. Everything about him was long – legs, hands, fingers. *Concentrate.*

'Milk?'

'Thanks.'

'Sugar?'

'No.'

'Right, well here it is. Strong enough?'

'Oh yes.'

I bet you are. He was gone. *He didn't say please. Thanks, but not please.*

In the opposite corner, two men drinking coffee began grumbling about him.

'No wonder he's JC Wilkes, thinks he's the son of God.'

'What is the C for?'

'Rhymes with punt mate.'

Ava worked with Jon untangling the labyrinthine accounting system. She was happy to use her recall of deals and customers where she could to darn up holes in the books, but unable ultimately to disagree with Jon's analysis. It was a bloody mess. By the end of the week, empty desks were beginning to outnumber filled ones. Gibbs himself, it was rumoured, had agreed a deal. An early and quiet exit in return for no further questions. And now Jon Wilkes wanted to see Ava again.

It must have felt like this going to the guillotine Ava thought grimly as she made her way up the stairs to him. *I'm next for the chop.*

He was very good at his job, picking through figures like a forensic stork, spotting flaws in balance sheets that everyone else had missed. He smoothed each page as he turned. Every margin had lead-grey pencilled notes in his careful hand, some with references to other entries, one or two in capitals, illegible upside down and at a distance. He beckoned her round to his side of the desk and she could feel her cheeks burning but now she could make out the notes. It made her stomach churn with sudden realisation.

'Here, you see?' he pointed with a pencil at an innocuous write-down. 'They can't have it both ways. The same machinery is here …' he flipped through to the page listing depreciating assets.

'Why didn't I see that?' Ava was embarrassed

'When you've been doing this as long as I have you will,' Jon had said, quite kindly and making her heart flip. So how old was he?

She couldn't help herself. 'When did you qualify? After university?'

'No,' he laughed dismissively. 'Missed that. Just went into the family firm, compliance-qualified.'

So he was what? Fifteen years older than Ava? More?

She shook her head. 'So much better than years of book-learning I bet.' All the years of life – and women - he had had while she was slogging through exams and boys like ... Josh, she suddenly remembered.

She couldn't wait to get in each day, commuting even earlier to avoid some of the delays. Slipping into the ladies as soon as she arrived to put right the damage caused by sweaty tube carriages or rain-drenched streets. Looking for any chance to be near him – she was like an infatuated teenager. His tall slim body seemed to radiate electricity whenever she stood beside him and felt the static, crackling between them. And he felt the same way, she just knew it.

Why him?

He's really not my type. Ted was warm, chunky ... wonder where he is now? He'll be out of course. Perhaps, just perhaps, being him, he avoided prison altogether. Can't imagine him locked in. He belongs in the sunshine, those deep-set eyes crinkled up with laughter.

See? That's another thing. Jon Wilkes is pale, smooth. I shouldn't do this, it's just a physical urge. I should have more self-control. But the way his hair curls slightly on that blue-striped shirt collar ... makes me want to bite his neck.

It was a Monday – she would always remember that. In a slim tight dress bought that weekend, she watched the girls' heads turn as he stalked through the office towards her own glass-walled room. The prickle of desire made her sit up straight but he didn't close the door behind him for privacy.

With his back to the others, he smiled down and put the file open in front of her. The page was marked with a post-it.

Will you come out to dinner with me tonight Ava?
Finally.

For something to say, to maintain the pretence this was work, she shook her head, flicking through her diary and when she looked up at him was rewarded by the disappointment on his face.

She reached for a biro and scrawled *Only joking. Would love it.*

He took the note in his long fingers and folded it, slipping it into his pocket then turning over a few more papers in the file.

Another post-it. *I'll meet you in the pub at 7. We'll go on.*

This time, Ava removed it, folded it gently and dropped it into her bag on the floor. 'I'll look into it for you,' she said a little too loudly as he tucked the file under his arm and left.

The Lion, on the corner of St John Street, was popular with all the staff at lunchtimes, but it would be deserted by seven, closing early like the City pubs. All afternoon, work floated in front of her eyes, columns of figures, reports, spreadsheets. Perhaps she'd got this wrong. Perhaps he'd be mature about it, tell he fancied her of course, but he was married and couldn't betray the rather bland-looking woman who smiled limply at Ava from a photo frame on his desk whenever she walked into his office.

Betray sounds Victorian. Whether or not this is the right thing to do, we could power the National Grid. Simpler to just get a room and hope no-one ever finds out, surely? I'm not even sure I can keep my hands off him through dinner once it's just the two of us. Surely, surely, he feels the same way?

The afternoon ground on and at last it was time.

In the mirror over the hand basin, she could see the expectation in her face, so presumably everyone else could too. Tough. She re-did her lipstick. then made her way down in the lift and out into the warm night air and traffic fumes at Angel, skirting the hoarding round the hole in the pavement. Two workmen, making the most of the overtime, sat with their legs dangling into it and one said, 'Cor she fancies 'erself, that one. I'll have some of that darlin'.'

And it was true. Something in the anticipation of intimacy made her hold herself upright, tuck in her hips, smile slightly to no-one in particular.

She turned off the narrow side street into the Saloon Bar, a gale of laughter making her stop in her tracks just as she spotted Jon who'd come in the other entrance.

It was someone's hen-do, judging by the inflated phallus bobbing above the crowd. Oh yes, Hutton's secretary. He'd be expected to put his hand in his pocket. And be expecting to put his hand in a lot of other places as the evening wore on.

'Jon! Didn't know you were coming,' a voice boomed from the snug. 'Good, good. Come on through.'

Hutton, one of the senior directors, was surrounded by a dozen or so of the accounts girls, some in pink sashes, some wearing bunny ears and one a lurid pink net veil and plastic tiara. Everyone had obviously been there a while. Perfume and wine swirled in the fetid air. They formed a triangle, Ava in the side door, Jon across the bar and the party in the snug.

Shiny-faced, Hutton peered through the crowd. 'Ah. Oh. Ava too, everyone. Do join us.' He turned his back and muttered something to the others who'd fallen silent.

'Yes. But no,' Jon shook his head. 'Afraid Ava can't. You have to be off I think now?' he looked at her crestfallen face.

She took his post-it note from her bag. 'The number you wanted.'

'Great. Well see you in the morning Ava.'

But as he held the door open for her, he murmured, 'Another time then. Soon.'

It was as well, she thought somehow making her feet walk her out and down to the Tube, that the men in the hole had gone or it might have been their lucky night. When she got in, her body was still on fire …

There had been an enthusiastic English teaching student at school who had spent a couple of hours one summer's afternoon enlightening Ava's class on Shakespeare's sonnets but when it came to 'Traffick with thyself alone' had glossed over it.

'Then does that mean what I think it means miss?' Ava had asked, stifled giggles breaking out in ripples around her…

… in her wardrobe mirror, her flushed cheeks looked back at her. No substitute for the real thing, but that wasn't here. Traffick it had to be then. She reached over to the bedside drawer.

Bugger and bugger. Just bad luck. Try again.

He wasn't around in the morning – gone to Bristol, Priti thought and for a few weeks after, their paths only crossed at meetings. Now and then she'd watch him across the floor and think *Silver Fox type* feeling a prickle at the back of her neck. Anyway there was so much to do as the numbers of vacant desks grew, Ava's workload burgeoned and she hadn't time to languish over him.

In board meetings, Ava found she was transfixed by Jon. He had a quiet way of watching and listening until all the hot air had been spent, then summarising, showing them his grip of the salient points. She'd learned a lot by being in his shadow.

Then someone said there'd been an urgent meeting that morning and everyone from her grade up had to be in the conference room at two. On her way, she turned the corridor corner and nearly walked straight into him, deep in conversation with a couple of others.

'Oh! Sorry,' she muttered, instantly aware of his physicality.

'No harm done Ava,' Jon was solicitous. 'Are you okay though?'

There only seemed to be the two of them there, the others had become invisible.

'I am. Yes. Thanks.'

'Good, well, see you soon. There's a bit of news – I should take a front row seat if I were you.'

She managed to make her legs work, walking away from him again and wondering what the news would be.

In the overheated conference room, they listened as Jon Wilkes told them the Board was to be re-structured, with Jon moving up to very near the top.

And that would leave a vacancy.

And that vacancy, Ava thought as she listened, has my name on it.

'Bloody hell,' the man in front of her on the way out muttered, 'That Wilkes knows his stuff. You won't get one over on him.'

She smiled to herself.

'Miss Hanson! Ava! Could we detain you for a few moments? If you don't have to be somewhere else?' Jon's voice cut through the shuffling crowd and heads turned to see what was going on.

She forced her way against the tide with one or two people holding others back for her to make progress. At the stage, she congratulated Jon. 'I'm sure the firm'll be in good hands. What will happen about the vacancy on the board?' No point in messing around, go for it girl.

Hatton harrumphed. 'It'll be some time before that's decided I'm sure.'

'No,' said Jon and a couple of the others nodded. 'We feel that Miss Hanson's skills are what is needed as the firm moves into this new phase.'

They were alone in the conference space now except for a cleaner making slow, methodical progress through the rows of seats, collecting coffee cups in a black plastic sack, tutting at a forgotten file under a seat at the back.

'Miss Hanson,' Jon looked at her. 'I hope you'll accept our offer to join as a junior member of the board. We're fairly sure it won't be long before you move up from there. And here,' he handed over a file, 'is the data you asked me for yesterday.'

At her desk, she unfolded the sheet of paper inside.

I am so sorry we weren't able to make a night of it. How about later? Let's celebrate your promotion. I've tickets for Covent Garden, so I'm booked in at the Piccadilly afterwards. I hope you like Tosca – this is a good production I'm told. I do hope you'll come…
J

The Opera House. The perfect place for a seduction. Each gold-brushed box a potential snug love-nest. Crimson velvet, chandeliers, the indefinable sense of being above the average and, as the lights dim and there's a hush, that undeniable intimacy in the dark. Beside her, his body is alive, sparking. But this is no back row of the movies. They are mid-row, three rows back. He is apparently happy to be seen with Ava. As if aware that champagne is making her float upwards, he reaches for her hand to anchor her beside him when the lights go down. And who seduces who?

As always, Scarpia is the focus. Manipulating, voracious and infinitely more attractive than Cavaradossi. The pulses of the Te Deum, rhythmic and visceral heighten Ava's willing senses. *Nesting in my heart* indeed.

'Home Ava. Where is it?' In black tie, he filled her glass without spills from the bottle in the ice bucket waiting on the bar for them in the interval. 'I don't mean the flat, but where are you from originally? Did I say, by the way, that velvet is a favourite of mine?'

She had dived out in the hour between work and here and snapped it up, not even asking the price, just knowing it was perfect. He'd noticed.

'South London – different parts. My parents were from Sutton originally, but after Uni I was offered a job in Canterbury so I bought a place with Mum and Dad. Studied in the evenings. I moved up to town when I got this job - rented. It's so much easier to do now since the legislation changed – shortholds, you know? Then low interest rates meant I could afford a shoebox in Clapham. It was a tough choice. Renting's so much easier but … it's an investment.'

'Yes I've a couple of tenanted places myself – they're producing quite a good return.'

All right, I get it. You're well off. I saw your salary package in the Standard article I cut out to keep. This isn't about work though. Lighten up Ava. 'But home?' she mused. 'Well I try to get to the sea when I can. I like Suffolk and Kent.'

'Know Broadstairs? I've a place there – it's mother's. But she's in a home just along at Herne Bay. So it's not far from Whitstable to go and keep an eye on her.'

'Oh it's a great stretch – unspoilt, isn't it? We used to go to Broadstairs when I was little.'

'Really? Ma's house is just back from the clifftop – on the North Foreland side. Empty of course. We keep it on though. Great little town.'

Wondering what it was like to keep a house you didn't actually need, Ava went on, 'It's ages since I went. Suppose it's changed.'

'No, no. Not really'- The interval bell rang. 'Better be going back to our seats.'

His hand hovered around her waist, for everyone to see. Once the lights dimmed though, Ava's mind wandered over the fields, the short journey from Whitstable to Seasalter. *Oh concentrate. Are you never satisfied? A really big career step and being here with him – come on Ava.*

The anonymity of a luxury hotel is another seductive environment. As Jon collected the room key, Ava looked around, calculating that roughly half the couples she could see in the overheated foyer and the glittery bar beyond were with someone they weren't married to. It made for a compulsive atmosphere, unspoken promise in every breath of the warm scented air.

With the key in his hand he stood beside her in the lift and she looked up at him, enjoying the way his height dominated the small space, the Te Deum's pulse in her head. *Made me forget God indeed.*

As he unlocked the room, she longed to throw her arms around his neck, her legs around his waist, but first, it seemed, there was more champagne to be drunk. It waited in the bucket with two glasses and a red rose. *He's throwing everything at this.* Seduction by numbers. Tick all the boxes and he'd be assured of sex.

He really didn't have to bother, I'd have had him in the office the first day, but still, it's good to be the centre of this sort of attention.

Then, finally, at last he kissed her.

Oh my Christ. Expensive but worth it.
Margaret's never done that.
And she's got a place near here. That'll save
some hotel bills. Keep everything quiet and
should still be able to manage overnight
claims. Jolly good.

The pattern was set. Monday and Thursday nights, most weeks, Jon made his way to the tiny flat, leaving work later than Ava who would have shopped for wine and steaks in her lunchhour, then dashed home to shower and tidy up.

Somehow, he'd left a shirt behind one night and she laundered it then slipped it on with nothing underneath when she answered the door. He approved.

Six months later, Jon closed the door to Ava's office (something she hated because she knew the staff would speculate) walked past Priti's empty desk and over to her. 'No er, whatsername?'

'Priti? No. Sick leave. Endometrio- oh, never mind.'

It was dismissed with a nod. 'Ah. Anyway, I'd like you to meet Mother.' His voice was low for obvious reasons, so she had to strain to hear him and didn't catch his words at first, so puzzled at the file he held in front of her.

'Sorry?'

'My *mother*. Next weekend. Margaret's going up to Yorkshire to see an old school friend, so I thought you and I could have a weekend – well, Saturday night anyway – by the sea. How does that sound?' He looked as if he'd played a trump card.

'Well I…' Her New Year resolution had been to give the flat a thorough springclean, throw out lots of things, then go to the sales, treat herself to new bedlinen and towels, curtains for the living room. And Ava found herself taking Priti's side. It was a beastly thing – Ava had seen her in tears often enough to know that - to contend with and most likely would rob her of the chance of a family which mattered to *her* family. He'd brushed it aside. The condition had made Priti's decision for her. She would study, she had told Ava because she admired everything Ava had achieved. There were enough daughters in the family to give her parents the descendants they so badly wanted.

I'm so lucky – never had any gynae problems. It's like my body knew it wasn't going to bother with all that.

'I …' The offer of a Saturday night with a married man isn't dismissed lightly. 'Sounds marvellous. It's Herne Bay, isn't it?'

'We'll only have to spend an hour or so with Ma …'

Then Ava's phone rang. 'Ava Hanson.'

'Only me, mate. Can you talk?'

'Corinne! Hi'- she motioned to Jon that she should take the call and he turned on his heels, closing the door behind him.

Well she didn't seem that keen – looked like
she'd rather chat with her girlfriend. After
the hoops I've had to jump through to get
out of going with Margaret to see that
bloody awful pal of hers. Had to make up a
whole pack of lies about working over the
weekend …

'So tell me about this old man Ave?' Corinne poured another glass of chardonnay. 'I mean is it a father thing? Daddy's girl?'

Tonight, they were in Battersea, at Bar Oz, a double-fronted shop divided into a deafening half where people still untrammelled by a relationship displayed themselves and to the right, solemn-looking couples sat and ate in silence, numbed by the demands of the week past and the weekend ahead when children would take over their time.

'Not Daddy's girl, no,' Ava was emphatic. 'He's awesome.'

'In bed?' Corinne's eyebrow arched.

'I meant at work. Though … that too. But honestly Corinne he's fantastic with numbers – can make them say anything. The last report he did on this company we've bought well, it was a bit unclear whether it was the right thing to do but he saw the assets, re-wrote the balance sheet for the Board and it was a done deal. We bought them, sold off the land, made a mint.'

'And a lot of people lost jobs I guess? Sorry I know it's business. Like in Pretty Woman, when Richard Gere decides not to sell the shipyard …'

'Exactly. But he's a lot taller than Richard Gere,' Ava hooted with laughter.

The girls were perched on bar stools at the small high round table, their elbows propping them, eyeball to eyeball, over glasses. The bar around them thudded with sound.

Thursday night was their night, ever since they'd been at UKC together, whenever there weren't better fish to fry. Odd, when you thought about it, that a new man might take precedence over a long-standing friend. Often, one or more of Corinne's three younger brothers would be there with his mates and a buzzing atmosphere would develop, where success and woes were laid bare for therapeutic drinking and later on, dancing. Ava loved that none of them ever made a serious pass at her, but treated her as another sister.

Corinne was off to the Middle East soon, where her oldest brother had landed a peach of a job and wanted her to go. 'Don't you want to come too, Ava?'

It felt like her surrogate family was dispersing. There was a time, Ava thought, when she'd have grabbed at a chance like that, but now she just longed to see Jon again, to have grown-up conversation before falling inevitably into bed. He might be inclined towards tragic operas, but father figure? Not likely, she giggled.

'Wha's funny?' Corinne demanded.

'Not a father figure,' Ava spluttered. 'Definitely not.'

'So how much older than you is he?'

It was just numbers. 'Twenty-two years. But that's what makes him so … clever.'

'With a liking for Ovaltine at eight pm?'

'He's just on his third G'n'T by then.' Ava laughed. 'It's more than that.'

'What then?' Corinne challenged.

'He's smooth. No raw edges. Always says – does - the right thing. It's like riding in a Rolls Royce. I imagine.'

'Smooth.' Corinne thought about it. 'Was the one you had the weekend in Lowestoft with smooth?'

Caught out, Ava sobered quickly. 'No. Rough diamond.'

'Well there you are then. Did I tell you I saw that bloke from Sales? The one I was talking about.'

'You said he was about a foot shorter than you!'

'Well he is a bit. Not that much though. I've never done it with someone I was taller than.'

'Well they're all the same lying down, aren't they?'

'Actually,' Corinne looked around her. 'I think their youknowwhats are all the same size – they just look bigger on a short bloke. Different proportions, know what I mean?'

'I hadn't thought of it like that,' Ava laughed.

'So how tall is this Jon then?'

'Six foot three,' Ava collapsed into more giggles.

'Well you have a look, next time. Same again?' Corinne waved the bottle.

Ava watched her weave her way to the bar. She was right in a way. Suppose all men got the same amount of … man-ness … but it was spread more thinly in a tall man, more condensed in a shorter one. And for the first time in a long time, she thought about Ted.

'Here we go,' Corinne splashed the wine into their glasses.

'-Lo girls. You look like you're 'avin' fun.' The City boy – pink shirt, silk tie loose and beer-stained, pushed between them on the table top. Glasses clashed, wobbled and settled. 'Lookin' for company?'

'No.' Corinne and Ava said in unison and laughed, setting the glasses jangling again.

'Dykes,' City boy slurred and stumbled sideways off down the bar.

'Loser!' Corinne yelled unheard into the thumping sound. 'Coming on to the Ministry Ave?' She indicated Vauxhall with a jerk of her head and slipped down from her stool, beginning to dance to a silent tune.

'No but I'll share a taxi with you then go on. Come on, this lot have made enough out of us for one night. Let's see if we can split without paying,' Ava made for the Ladies as Corinne ducked below the bartender's radar, then turned at the door with W on and made her way through the furthest edges of the noisy crowd to the pavement outside.

'Taxi!' Corinne yelled.

'What about the bill?' the bartender made it to the door just in time to see them ducking into the cab.

'Next time! Bye!' the girls waved at him, slamming the door and collapsing on top of one another, braying with laughter.

But after the cab had dropped off Corinne, Ava sobered. Why hadn't she mentioned, made a joke even, of meeting Ma Wilkes?

This felt like the last time she'd do anything reckless. She must be getting old. In her lunchhour next day, she bought new underwear to prove she wasn't. Black, of course. And stockings.

Buckingham House was rather less imposing than Ava had expected. A modest Victorian villa with bedrooms built on in a modern wing, it seemed well-kept if overheated. There was a security phone on the door and a small, bustling woman ushered them in. 'Nice to see you again Mr. Wilkes. Mrs. Wilkes is in her room and I'll bring some tea. Unless you'd prefer coffee?' She looked questioningly at Ava as she locked the front door.

'Miss Hanson is a colleague. We've a rather complex valuation – needs two heads,' Jon laughed. 'I'm combining business with pleasure.'

'Tea will be fine thanks,' Ava smiled, the phrase not lost on her. This game made her feel trapped behind that securely locked door.

The faint smell of urine as they made their way along the corridor was not, thankfully, evident as they opened the door and entered Mrs Wilkes' bedsittingroom.

'Ma, this is Miss Hanson. Ava. She's come with me. There's a valuation to do on that great old monstrosity behind the cinema in the Old Town. Needs both of us to work on it.'

'How do you do?' The old woman's hand was skeletal, the skin like tissue paper, but her grip was firm. 'Miss Hanson.' She looked Ava in the eye.

'Ah here's tea,' Jon sounded slightly relieved as the housekeeper wheeled in a trolley with a small plate of biscuits, a stainless-steel teapot that had seen better days and cups and saucers.

As the door closed behind her, Mrs. Wilkes sighed. 'I have told them over and over that I cannot lift that pot. They broke my little china one you know, Jon. And it poured so well …'

'I think they did warn us the kitchen here was no respecter of bone china, Ma,' he looked apologetic.

'Perhaps I might pour?' Ava offered and instantly regretted it. Milk first? Probably not. There was a strainer, so she made use of it and offered Jon's mother the milk jug as she placed the cup in front of her.

Gratifyingly, there was a smile on the old girl's lips.

They made small talk over tea. The journey from London, the way the town here was benefitting from London buyers, the possible uses that the place they'd come to value could fulfil to maximise its potential. Mrs Wilkes was well informed, if a little out of date and Ava knew she was being observed as well as heard. She mentioned being taken when a youngster for a treat to the ice cream parlour on Broadstairs seafront and it made the old lady sigh and smile.

'Ah yes. Lovely. Do you have many brothers and sisters?'

'No. I'm an only child I'm afraid.'

'Oh, like my Jon. Well. All the more ice cream for you then I suppose…'

Jon looked at his watch. 'Well better be getting on with things Ava …'

'Yes. Shall I wait for you at the car?' It seemed reasonable to give him time alone with his mother.

'No. Actually, I need a word with Matron before I leave. There was a mistake on the last bill. I'll see you out there in about ten minutes,' and his long legs made short work of the distance to the door.

There was a silence between the two women.

'So it's you he's fallen in love with this time?' There was an age-quaver to the voice but it still carried authority.

Ava looked up and couldn't stop the blush. Her nerves were strained enough by the encounter without this challenge. 'We work together Mrs Wilkes.'

'And a great deal more beside I imagine.'

'I'-

'Let's not pretend. He's a shockingly bad liar. Always was, even as a little boy, I knew exactly what was going on with him. Just like his father who couldn't tell the truth if his life depended on it.'

'Oh. I'm sorry.'

'Jon should never have married Margaret. I told him, so did everyone he knew. He thought he should have a wife and she fitted the bill – good family, well-known in the town and so on. The child just settled it, as so often happens. But Margaret's dreadfully ill-suited to my Jon. You, on the other hand, seem rather better fitted.'

This was going faster than Ava could manage. 'It's been very good to meet you Mrs. Wilkes. I'm afraid I should be going now,' and she held out her hand.

Instead of shaking it, the old woman clasped it between both her bony palms. 'Look after him for me. And do call me Edith in future.'

Well I won that round, Ava thought making her way back along the corridor to Jon. But it left a nasty taste that surprised her, as if she'd been playacting to get in her good books when really she'd liked Edith.

'Well how did you two girls get on?' Back on his home ground in the Saab, Jon was less of a rabbit in the headlights, more the man she'd go to bed with that evening.

'Very well. Although I hadn't realised she and your father hadn't been happy.'

'Whatever gave you that idea?' He swore at the driver overtaking them. 'Bloody idiot. Must be doing a

63

ton. No, he worshipped the ground she walked on. Always did. Left her well provided for. That place isn't cheap you know.'

'No, well they're not.'

'They were very close, very close.'

And Ava, hearing the lie in his voice, wondered. Families are funny things.

He drove on quickly, following the coast road, the sea on their left in the twilight. As the fields became flatter, the towers at Reculver were silhouetted against a moonlit sea.

'Jon this is beautiful – I never saw it like this as a child, always had to be in bed by now,' she laughed.

'Well, I had something rather along those lines planned, I must admit …' His hand slid up her thigh and found the flesh at the top of her stocking. 'Oh my god, Ava.'

So she had other things on her mind when eventually he pulled up onto the gravel drive past high wooden gates.

'Halcyon,' she read the painted sign. 'Halcyon days eh?'

'No,' he shook his head. 'It's some silly myth about nesting. Ma's idea. They moved in after they married.'

'I suppose she was thinking about raising a family,' Ava said, wishing she hadn't but he was concentrating on parking. She'd look it up when she had a moment.

Before she could get out, he reached for her overnight bag on the back seat, then came round to open her door.

She glowed at his touch. This was how men were supposed to make women feel, wasn't it? It was at once old-fashioned and very, very sexy. Or perhaps it was just how she was feeling. They climbed the steps up to the front door at the centre of verandas which stretched either side, welcoming them in.

The inside of the house, though, felt uninhabited, with a mustiness in the air. Their footsteps echoed on the tiled floor and he dived under the stairs to find the mains switch.

As the light went on, Jon disappeared down the steps to the car again and Ava looked around at the bare bones of a solid Edwardian home largely emptied of belongings; a couple of pictures on the walls, an occasional chair were all that was left of the home it had been.

It didn't matter to Ava, who had spent her working life seeing through the detritus most people filled their homes with, the better to describe them to new buyers. Potential, that was what she could see and this house had it in abundance. Ava guessed the best pieces had been sold to meet Edith's care fees but in any case, what it needed now were new things, clean lines and colours. She pictured the effect of pale carpet all around her and stretching up the staircase.

Jon came back in with a bag of logs and a couple of bottles of red. 'This way,' he opened a door.

In the sitting room, there was a hard-looking sofa and little else. Jon drew the curtains and set about laying a fire in the tiled fireplace, calling over his shoulder to Ava to find glasses for the wine.

Here she was again, in another woman's kitchen. A tap dripped noisily into the sink. On the hunt for glasses, she cautiously opened cupboard doors, as if gremlins might hurl Mrs Wilkes' cut-glass to the floor with malicious glee. She shook her head to clear it and on a low shelf in the corner cupboard found a few wineglasses, looking until she found two that matched which seemed to matter. She rinsed them out and was wiping them round with a tea towel she'd found when Jon came in to rummage for his mother's corkscrew. 'Everything all right darling?'

'Yes – did you get the fire going?'

'I bought firelighters when I stopped for the sack of logs.'

'You've thought of everything,' she smiled.

'Well I wanted this evening to be right for us.'

'And it is.'

'Find everything you need?'

'Well I wouldn't mind freshening up.' What an archaic phrase but it suited the house. And Jon, who looked gratified.

'Of course. The bathroom's upstairs. Oh god. Towels-'

'-Don't worry. I packed one.'

'My room … is the big one in the front.' He was less assured now, boyish almost. 'If you wanted to put your things in there, I mean.'

Endearing.

'Be back soon,' she grinned. 'You concentrate on tracking down the corkscrew.'

As she climbed the stairs, there was a clatter of things falling in the kitchen and Jon cursing at something. Ava had tried opening the dresser drawer but it had stuck. She guessed he'd used brute force.

Upstairs, things seemed slightly worse. The bathroom was horribly cold and of course there was no hot water yet, so Ava made do with brushing her teeth – that stupid thing women do when they hope they're about to go to bed with a man - and checking her hair in the mottled mirror over the basin.

Her holdall was lost in the huge bedroom. She stood in the wide, bay window, transfixed by the moon on the sea. Far out, a line of waves broke in a random hypnotic pattern.

'Looking at the Knoll eh?' He was behind her, his arms enfolding her before she knew it.

'Knoll?'

'Hmm. Sandbanks. Like the Goodwins. More than one's come to grief on them.'

'Oh.' A bedroom with a view of tragedy wasn't what she'd come all this way for. 'Let's draw the curtains shall we Jon?' And then she showed him what she was wearing.

It had been a long day what with meeting Ma and the drive on to here, but she wasn't going to miss this opportunity.

They made the most of it.

Thought Ma had spilled the beans for a minute but it's really all gone very well. Very well. That underwear … those legs … gripping me … that bloody drawer … have to get a man in to see to that.

Every shop seemed to have Karen Carpenter warbling about logs on the fire filling her with desire.

Ava had wound up more or less everything at the office and just had a couple of things to get. Corinne – now what would she enjoy among the shelves and shelves of things nobody needed? Their tastes had always been similar so she should just look for something she'd like to unwrap but there was the complication of posting it to Abu Dhabi, where surely no luxury was in short supply, so it ought to be lightweight. She settled for a black silk teddy, had it gift-wrapped and wrote on the label *Hope there's someone there to wear it for.*

At Customer Services they were happy to deal with the international delivery which more or less doubled the cost. Oh well, she could afford it.

That just left Jon. Difficult. *I could have myself gift-wrapped and delivered to his house so I'd be the first thing he'll see on Christmas morning. Not something his wife would appreciate. You give men jumpers or golf balls or ...* Ava's hand trailed over the glass-topped counter beside her. Yes, a pen. Something he could carry around and use and if questioned say it was a gift from a client. She spent a long time deliberating, settling in the end on a Montblanc classic.

'Would madam prefer the 14carat nib ... or the platinum?' the girl, trained to upsell, did her job well she had to admit and Ava happily dented her bank balance by a little over four hundred pounds, wondering why she was so sure Jon was worth it. How did anyone ever know such things?

Only a few people were dedicated enough to commute in for Christmas Eve and so she could walk with the parcel through the open-plan desks, without anyone seeing her head for Jon's office. He was on the phone when she stuck her head round the door but beckoned her in with a big smile and she placed the present carefully in front of him, smoothing the satin bow to look its best. His eyes opened wide.

'I'm going to have to go. I'll leave that to you,' he ended the call at the same time as glancing up at the open door to see if anyone was watching.

'It's okay,' she smiled, 'we've almost got the floor to ourselves as far as I can see.'

'Oh. This is really for me?' he looked up at her.

'That's what the label says,' she nodded.

'For putting your name to all the big deals to come,' he read and slipped off the ribbon. The box lid snapped up crisply and he stared down, taking in the details.

His head dropped. 'I haven't … haven't got you anything like this. I'm sorry I … didn't …'

'Jon,' she came to his rescue. 'This isn't about Christmas really, it's a thank you, for all the wonderful times you've given me. Honestly. I'd like to take advantage of the fact that we're almost alone darling, but …'

'Oh god, absolutely. Security'll be round soon. I'll sort out some time as soon as all this is over, I promise.'

When she got in to the flat that night, there was a ring on the doorbell. 'Delivery,' the intercom told her.

The roses, fifty of them, cellophane crackling between the Moyses' wrapping, were finished with an extravagant red velvet bow and so big they almost obscured the delivery boy. Jon must have ordered them on his way home and paid god knew what to get them to her this late on Christmas Eve.

Lying alone in bed later she remembered they had the contract for the displays that filled the City Road atrium.

Just got that in in time I think. See? –
throw enough money at a problem and it
goes away I've always said. It's like
having an expensive hobby – racehorse or
boat or something. They cost money
while you're having fun and then you trade
them in for a new one. A chap's got to
have an interest. Dad did it after all.

Wind buffeted the shutters, rattling Jon and Ava out of sleep as they stirred in the unfamiliar room. Dampness seemed to be in every corner of this house, she thought, making her way carefully down the open stairs, holding two tea bags. There had been milk in the fridge too but it was never in her experience the same as at home. Still, all part of the adventure.

She looked doubtfully at the embers in the grate then, as the kettle boiled, made her way over to the darkened fireplace. There was no life, no glow. She used some of the post which had accumulated behind the door to try and coax life into it, but the papers and adverts were damp too.

'We'll need firelighters,' she told Jon. 'And smokeless fuel – it'll stay in all night that way. Logs look romantic'- she saw the look on his face, reminded that logfires had been a dominant feature in this dream '-and we'll burn them at night when we're here, then make the fire up with the fuel. Easier than laying everything out each morning.'

'Really? Mother always used to have the grate swept clean each day.'

'Well, it's the maid's day off here.'

'How do you know so much about fires anyway?'

The inglenook at Coastguard's cottage passed fleetingly through her mind.

She shrugged it off. 'Chilly childhood.'

In the night, Ava lay in the darkness of a village without streetlights, no cars driving by and passers-by only in summer. She had been put into suspension, away from real life. The only way to make a telephone call was to slip down the cobbled street to the little square outside the Mairie and feed coins into a slot. Near enough mediaeval.

Still it gave her a chance to think.

Corinne had asked what it was with her and married men. To be fair, there had only really been two, although she could see neither wife would see it like that.

Ted's wife Sal had been a mystery. There were few signs of habitation simply because the place was Ted's showroom and while the kitchen often had a bowl of fruit or flowers, they were literally window-dressing. Until she saw those Marigolds. *She lives where she works most of the time ...* Still she was there to be worked round, a reason not to meet, to be discreet.

And Margaret. Well Ava knew her well enough by now to agree with the generally-held view that she and Jon were incompatible. Away with the fairies, someone had said and that seemed right, completely at odds with Jon's cool precise approach. 'She could never be on time,' he said once. 'Syd was always late for school so she just grew up thinking that was normal. Drove me mad...'

There was some truth in Corinne's theory that married men saved you having to make the one big commitment, simply because they weren't free to commit to. Truth was, Ava thought in the darkness, she simply hadn't thought she needed a husband. Only children were a bit like that, growing up on their own, they just weren't very good at compromising all the time.

But she would make this work.

Well I've been sold a pup and no mistake. Bloody place is freezing, just have to sit it out. Need a list of everything that's wrong – Ava'll do that. Then we'll sue when we get back.

And always here, he closes the door behind him. To keep the heat in, he explains. 'Willy-shrinking cold,' he said one evening after the second bottle of red had been despatched and he couldn't manage an erection.

That sounded like something a schoolboy would say. This can't seriously mean we've had proper sex for the last time? Already? Things will look up when we get back to England I expect. I hope.

This house, which was to be their escape, became a series of cells. Why did her psyche protest? Was it years and years of Tube doors closing in on her? Or simply that, at heart, she was a gypsy?

The snow that fell overnight a week before Christmas meant convoluted arrangements, conducted in Jon's poor French, for log deliveries and ankle-threatening slides on cobbled hills. Ava would have fared better with the language but knew better than to usurp what he clearly saw as his responsibility.

On Christmas Day, they loaded a picnic, baguettes and cheeses, into the car and the Saab came into its own, negotiating steadily up the winding, ice-packed mountain roads of the Cévennes. Once out of the shadowy valley, the sun shone and the countryside sparkled.

'This is utterly beautiful,' Ava breathed out in relief at not having to pretend. Jon parked and carried the bag as, muffled up, they tramped through snow to the lookout point where the champagne cork was popped. It was a highlight.

In January, a letter came from the plumber saying that he'd tried ringing the number Jon had left without success. The boiler needed replacing and while he was doing that, they should consider new radiators and while he was about it, the pipework could do with upgrading. Modern thermostats being what they were, the house would be noticeably warmer he said.

Seeing an opportunity, Ava said she thought it should be the priority call on their budget.

'Well,' Jon seemed to take an age to consider this. 'Well.'

He was a long time buying the wine for dinner and when he came back said he'd phoned from the antiquated box by the Mairie as there were a few things from the office that needed tidying up. Would she mind going back? The weather had been atrocious, cold and wet. This side of the mountain was splendidly cool in summer, the owner had said.

'But not quite warm enough for winter,' Ava finished for him.

At last they could leave.

When they got back, the plumber had put the handbasin on the wrong wall and the salad she'd prepared the day of the wedding was a green pond in the bottom of the fridge.

'So how was it? Glad you saved yourself for your wedding night?'

'Corinne you are a clot.'

'I know. But I've met the most marvellous man.'

'At last! Brilliant. What's he like?'

'Edible most of the time. Not there the rest.'

Surely she hadn't done what Ava had done. 'Married?'

'No. Course not. He's absolutely rolling in it but it means he travels a lot.'

'I liked Sam …'

'He's history. Gavin. He's the one.'

'What does he do? When he's travelling.'

'Oh huge contracts, all over the place – Abu Dhabi now but it'll be somewhere else next month. He gets a cut from each one.' It was clear she'd chosen not to go into it in detail. 'Anyway, this gorgeous bolthole you got whisked off to?'

'Well,' Ava began, 'it was bloody awful weather most of the time.'

'Really? So you just stayed in bed and …? You've got to look after the old man, Ava.'

'Oh I do. We got out too,' Ava laughed. 'On Christmas Day, we drove up the mountain and drank champagne in the snow. It was beautiful.'

'Well as long as you're all right.'

'Fine. Honestly.'

Now she was home – and Ava was pleased to realise that was how she thought of the house and Broadstairs itself - she would make it count.

Two months later, Corinne rang again. 'You all right?'

Feeling she should have rung her first, Ava began with the being busy excuses everyone uses. 'Yes, the bathroom's nearly finished. But we've had a terrible wait for the tiles. And the new rad had to go back for a re-spray. It was completely wrong.'

'-Christ I hope it's warmer . I practically had to break the ice for a bath on your wedding day.'

'Yes. Sorry. So how's Gavin?'

'That's what I'm ringing for.'

Oh. It hasn't worked out for her.

'Well, I've been wondering. Would you recommend it, now you've had a while? The being married thing?'

'God yes,' Ava smiled at the memory of interrupting Jon stripping wallpaper and how they'd spent the rest of that afternoon on the bed's dustsheet. Although he muttered something about the neighbours seeing, until she pointed out no-one had a line of sight in to the uncurtained bedroom.

'Only … I've worried about you Ava. With Jon, you know…'

'Oh, that's all in the past.'

'So … you'd recommend it?'

'Corinne, what's all this about?'

There was a long pause. 'Qatar – the place, not the nasal thing. He's asked me to go with him. Gavin. Only we'd have to be married, see?'

It seemed preposterous. 'In this day and age?'

'It's their thing. The company's. They're not UK based, see?'

The repetition in Corinne's words made it sound as if it was a rehearsed argument. 'What does your Mum say? And your brothers?'

'Same thing, all of them. "Oh well, if he's as rich as you say and it doesn't work out, you can always divorce him for half of everything". Did you ever think that Ava?'

'No. Once he'd asked me, it was actually something I really wanted. To be half of a successful marriage. Not easy to do I expect, but ...'

'Yes. That's it. That's what I want too. So we're going to do it on a beach in Bali, just the witnesses, like you had, then fly back to the penthouse.'

'Where's that?'

'The Tower. Doha. It's beyond *everything* you can imagine, Ava. The boys know it. They can't believe I'm going to live there.'

'When's this then?'

'We'll be leaving in four days. I'm sorry there's no time for a hen, but we'll make up for it once I'm there I promise. You'll have to come over. Got to run. Sorry, so much to do. But I wanted you to know, be pleased for me. Us.'

Sometimes, you watch the pages in the book of your life turn over. This is one of them.

'I wish – well, Jon and I wish you every happiness. Send me vids and ...'

'What?'

'Make him take care of you, this Gavin, yeah?'

'Yeah. You bet.'

Not just another page. Another chapter entirely.

147

'Gardening again?' Jon had wandered up the garden and seemed surprised to find her there. 'I thought it might be time for coffee.'

'I'd love one darling, thanks,' Ava smiled up at him from the border, knowing full well that wasn't what he'd meant. Not his fault, he'd had a lifetime of having someone around to do the everyday stuff for him. To allow him to do the important stuff, like men did. Well now it was just the two of them.

When he came back with two mugs, they settled onto the bench. 'Do you know,' she began, 'I thought I might join a book group. Be nice to make some local friends wouldn't it? I've a bit of time to read now and I went into the library and there's a group who meet on Wednesday evenings and'-

'-Well if you think … I thought we might do something together.'

'What Jon?' This was news. 'Golf?' she giggled.

'Well Bridge actually,' he was affronted. 'Mother always played.'

'Gosh. Wouldn't know where to start. You could play though,' she urged him. It looked like an impending row and she dodged it. This life was meant to be *fun.* 'Do you know, they're talking about closing the library?'

'No,' he sounded sure. 'Not here.'

'Yes. Really. There's a meeting tonight. I thought we might go. I think we should go – the more oppose it, the better.'

'Well I really have quite a bit of correspondence …' But later, he turned on the TV and glued himself, as usual, to the news.

So Ava went alone. She targeted the book group, got talking. They'd been reading a Barbara Kingsolver she thought looked interesting.

'You been here long?' the blonde with the millboard asked.

'About a year,' Ava nodded. 'There's a lot to do to the house still but I love reading, to switch off you know?'

'You can lose yourself in a good book,' the woman nodded. 'Our year's been shit and books have been a place to go.'

'Yes,' Ava nodded. 'Sorry to hear about the year though. Was it ill-health?'

'The mother-in-law. Cancer.' There was a long silence.

'Sorry,' Ava repeated.

'Then my husband lost his job. Got taken over. They got rid of all the staff, sold the plant, the land.'

It felt horribly familiar to Ava. 'Sorry,' she said for one last time, then headed into the meeting.

In the stuffy, dusty atmosphere of the civic offices, she sat playing buzzword bingo, listening to the usual phrases which meant the County Council would do what it had always intended and this was not a gathering which was going to make it change its mind.

The speakers against the closure were all aware they were being used as pawns in the fight between local and central government and made cogent arguments for retaining the service. Ultimately, Ava knew, it would make no difference. Across the room, she noticed the butcher from the High Street and one or two other faces which were beginning to become familiar. How sad that just when she was ready to join this community, it was evaporating beneath her feet.

'How's my little crusader?' Jon was in his armchair when she got in. The news was still reeling on.

'Jon, this matters,' she felt teary.

'Yes, yes, of course, I see.'

She saw too, that she had made a mistake.

The moment of lucidity flashed across her vision like a bolt of lightning.

She had rushed – and been rushed – into this. Her tears weren't for the death of retail in a High Street she barely knew, they were for herself. Self-pitying, unattractive. Jon hadn't changed, she had: from the bright, self-sufficient woman she'd been when they met, always up for a challenge or fun. First of all, the sheer grittiness of life in London and battling for her career in the firm had sandpapered her soul, draining the energy out of her, as it did for most people. Then the sudden arrival of a stepchild as Margaret decided Jon was no longer required in her life – that, and what it cost, had been more of a shock than anything.

Once a man's in your bed every night, you begin to mould to what he is and what he wants.

And after all, I was getting something too. The smug satisfaction when it became known you were a couple? Makes me shiver now - disgusting. Yes, the woman in the toilets was right. You, Ava Wilkes, did have it all.

She and Jon had become two creatures scuttling together out from the dark sewers of the City into the seductive sunlight dancing on the sea. *You knew what you were doing, all of it, to make that happen.* Filled with self-loathing, she remembered her conversation with Corinne about marrying Gavin. Tying the marital millstone round yet another woman's neck.

She should admit she'd made this mistake and separate from Jon. Her blood chilled as she thought how Margaret would like that, had probably thought it would happen once Ave realised what she knew. That Jon, once you looked past the initial attraction, was unmarriable. *Don't be melodramatic – it's just the jitters.*

Ava had married him, leaving her past behind, giving her word, committing herself to making it work in reparation for all the damage they'd done.

She could change him, surely? She'd look for something they could do together.

There's little choice if you're honest with yourself, Ava. Corinne will have to paddle that canoe of hers; she had choices too.

And you will have to make this marriage work. Somehow.

Typical woman they marry you, then ditch you for some cause or other attention spans of a newt, every one didn't think she'd be like that. Why don't they teach girls useful things at school nowadays? Too busy encouraging them to take over the world …

'Damn!' The phone rang just as she threw broccoli into the roiling water. 'Dinner's almost ready. I'll get it Jon!' She couldn't remember when it had been agreed that she would cook every night after a full day's work decorating a room or trying to get some shape into the garden but Jon always seemed to have things to sort out in the early evenings. He'd pour her a gin, then lose himself in emails or arrangements with Willow/Margaret about weekend visits. Never cooking though.

Clutching her drink, she hurried from the kitchen to the hall table, noticing through the open livingroom door that tonight, his urgent business seemed to centre on the cricket coverage.

'Hello?' she spoke into the phone hoping this would be short.

'Ava? I've found you. God, you've no idea the trouble I've had.' The voice, dark and deep, was unmistakeable.

So startled that the glass almost slipped through her fingers, she slumped against the cool painted plaster of the hall, feeling the world shrink into the receiver in her hand.

'I've looked everywhere,' she heard the familiar growl. 'Your old office – that was closed.'

'I left.' There was a catch in her voice.

'So I rang the other branches.'

'The cuts'-

'Well yes. And the flat – you sold it.'

'That was ages ago.' *Another life.* But she sounded more like herself now.

'Then I remembered that mate of yours, Corinne, with the place in Lowestoft …' His voice still did what it had always done to her.

Even now, the memory of the weekend there overwhelmed her. Ava's knees finally gave in. She slid until she was sitting on the carpet, back against the wall, cradling the phone. 'I told Corinne – well, everyone – not to say anything.'

'Oh she didn't.'

'So how−?'

'–Doesn't matter. Look. Well, I think – know – I've been a fool. All the time I've been trying to find you I've had this picture in my head, kept thinking of you that night. In front of the fire.

'And you got *married*.'

'Yes,' she said quietly.

'You said you loved me,' he was reproachful.

'I did.' *But you weren't there to love.* Suddenly she was angry. How dare he think he could simply walk back into her life, reclaim his lagan, just when she was sorting everything out?

The tang of burning metal began to waft through the hall. The pan, boiling dry on the hob, had begun to spit and smoke. Annoyed at the disturbance to his viewing, Jon stuck his head round the door. 'Something burning?'

'For god's sake, the pan's boiling dry,' she gestured to the kitchen.

'Not my territory really,' Jon shrugged apologetically. 'Which knob do I–?'

From the receiver in her hand, she could hear the voice ask what was going on. 'I'll ring you tomorrow,' she said and ignoring whatever it was he began to say, hung up.

'Old school friend,' she got to her knees without looking at Jon and raced past him to the kitchen.

The lie made it crystal clear.

She had had an affair with a married man who despite her friends' dire warnings, had left his wife for her. She had re-built her life around him …

The knot tying tighter and tighter in her stomach was strangling, pulling her down. *It's inescapable. A few moments of his voice proved it. What effect might his presence have?*

How could I have done this? Why did I have to say yes? I can't let Jon down now. I married him. He gave up his wife and child and career … What sort of woman am I?

… She had learned the lesson she thought she had taught Ted. She didn't ring him back.

I will not think about him again. I'll make him stop invading my head. I will.

'Another year of wedded bliss. We should mark the occasion.'

Ava looked up. 'Really?'

'Absolutely. Five years isn't it?'

Five years … it seemed weirdly both longer and shorter than that to Ava. Longer like a trek across deserts, no end in sight. Shorter as in where the hell had five years of her life gone?

It was impossible to deny – she only had to look at Syd in the pictures on her phone. The chubby girl was now a spindly teen in shorts that made her father tut.

On cue, it rang.

'Lo Ave.'

'Hello yourself.'

'Did you ask him? About the trip?'

'Well, we'll pay for you to go of course. Milan is a great city.'

'Yes but will he tell Mum I can?'

'They need to talk it through Syd.'

'*Oh.* What's to talk about?'

'Dad's worried about you going'- Almost immediately, Ava knew she'd started a fight.

'-Oh for god's sake!'

'Syd – I've told you. Try saying goodness' sake.'

'Oh get real.'

Christ, no wonder I decided never to have children.

'Tell Dad not to stress.'

Tell him yourself, Ava fumed, stamping around the house to find Jon who had slipped out of the room when he heard it was Syd on the phone.

She had become Jon's interpreter, whose job it was to explain the whys and hows of modern life to a man whose conscious awareness seemed to have ended somewhere in the late fifties, as if social history after Teddy Boys (bad) and National Service (good but bad it had ended) had simply stopped mattering as he left childhood. Ava had, for three or four years now, taken to speaking openly and loudly in short sentences about whatever was happening, trying to engage Jon in the now, but it was futile. Riots, terrorism, atrocities, all the dreadful scenes that reeled along the TV screen, fell unheeded, silent as snowflakes around Jon, sat only a few feet from the set, frowning in concentration.

'Something going on?' Ava asked, seeing him scribble notes as the interview with the Bank of England muttered on.

'Nothing to worry about.'

These days, he seemed concerned only about his immediate surroundings and comfort. If the house and garden were up to scratch, Jon was affability personified. If not, he sulked. For maybe a day or more, there would be the Mount Rushmore Jon, stony and impenetrable and the way round it was for Ava to apologise for upsetting him. In a way, she believed it. *If you know something's going to upset him, why mention it? Just ignore it.* It left fewer and fewer things to talk about, that was the trouble.

This passivity wasn't new to Ava, when she thought about it. She had rehearsed it as a well-behaved only child, and again in tedious business meetings with a client for whom she had no respect at all. *Keep a smile on your face and work through. Put a smile on his face too.*

A few days before, she had made coffee and taken two mugs up to where Jon was working at the top of the garden – his veg plot, he called it. It wasn't much good for growing things because the rise of the land had meant less digging for an Anderson shelter whose concrete roof had made an ideal spot for a bench in the sun after the War. Ava had been fascinated to see inside but Jon said shaken his head knowingly.

'Two hundred and seventy-eight bombs dropped on Broadstairs you know? Dad said this would be the safest place in the town – got a builder friend to build it.' Determined, Ava waited until he went out then, after a long struggle with brambles and ivy had managed to wrench the door open a couple of inches, taken one look at the webs across the door and closed it immediately.

Going through the arch, she was surprised to see his feet then the rest of him sprawled on the bench, face up to the sun, legs apart and trousers undone.

'Aha! Trafficking is it?' she made light of it.

'Eh?' He started, red-faced and pop-eyed, and immediately moved his hand from his trousers to smooth his hair.

'Don't worry,' she said, slightly surprised to find herself turned on. 'Here, let me …'

His head went back again and soon, 'Uh! Oh my god, Ava…'

Sipping coffee after, he asked, 'What did you call it?'

She told him about the English lesson.

'God. Never knew Shakespeare did that sort of thing.'

'It's as old as time Jon.'

'Margaret didn't think so. She always had to wait for some cycle or other – moon or tide or something. Had to see to myself – daily – I mean a man's got to do it more than a woman, right?'

'Not necessarily,' she smiled, took his hand and lifted her skirt.

'Not in the garden, darling. The neighbours …'

No sauce for this goose then. Ava drank her coffee. A breeze ruffled the leaves and somewhere in the house, the draught blew a door shut with a bang.

'Ava,' he tutted, 'I think I've said before about doorstops making sure that can't happen. We don't want to have to get a man in to mend broken hinges do we?' …

So the anniversary loomed. A break would be good. And if Syd could go to Milan, they could go … somewhere. 'Where were you thinking of going?' she asked, dreading another return trip to some haunt he'd enjoyed as a young man.

But Jon it seemed had learned that lesson at least. Last year, they'd re-visited a hotel where everything had been 'simply marvellous' when Jon had stayed with Margaret/Willow. 'We rowed the whole time – it was completely wasted on her,' Jon had shaken his head sadly. 'Lovely place, great staff, couldn't do enough for you. She hated it. I want them to see how happy I am with you Ave.' Well, he should like it, Ava thought as they registered at the desk. It was apparent that nothing had changed for some years. Tired decorations and outdated menus. Beds rutted with use, plates whose patterns had worn away. 'Bit disappointed with all this Ave,' he'd admitted eventually. 'Standards fallen. No place like home eh?'

It had sounded like a prison sentence. She had created the walls around herself by making his home into exactly what he wanted.

So with a chance of a break-out, where would she suggest they went?

'Like the look of this place Jon?' she pointed at the screen.

'*Long Hill* … yup, well, if you're happy, I'm happy,' he was all bonhomie. 'Our anniversary, let you decide – just point me in the right direction as we're going.'

She cut his hair before they left. It was a habit they'd got into after he'd stomped out of the last barber in the High Street outraged at the cost of what was essentially, he

158

pointed out, nothing more skilled than lawn-mowing. 'Well if you can …' he said when she offered to trim his hair.

She sat him on a kitchen chair, yesterday's Times laid to catch the soft thin wisps as she worked methodically around his head from the neckline up, just like the way she'd watched hairdressers do.

When had his sleek, smooth head lost its thatch? As the steely colour left it, more and more of his head was revealed and she combed carefully so as not to scratch the scalp, blue-veined and smooth. It was a head she was fond of, often stroking it as they made love but that didn't happen as often now.

'Well that's saved us a lot of money Ave. You've got the job,' he beamed as he inspected the results.

For life.

As they turned into the hotel gates, Ava's heart lifted. This place actually looked like the website, historical and imposing enough for Jon and with a modern wing incorporating *The Orangery Spa* clearly signposted. Ava would have liked one of the newer rooms near it, so that she could slip easily along for a morning swim, but for Jon's sake, she'd booked a room above the great staircase in the main house, so that he could play lord of the manor when they made their way upstairs and to be fair, when they plonked bags down and took in their surroundings, it was great.

'Bed looks jolly comfortable,' Jon was appreciative.

'Not so comfy we fall asleep straight away I hope,' she smiled back.

Later, they showered and dressed for dinner and walked into the bar and it felt as if all the years had gone. Jon was still a head-turner, tall, slim as ever and smartly dressed for once, was the man she'd felt giddy for, that first time in the office. And putting on a dress, with time to do her hair and something to look forward to had put sparkle back into Ava's own eyes. This was going to be good.

The maître d' hovered over them. 'Your table is ready for you Sir, Madam.' And they drained glasses and stood, following him across the great hall, shoes sliding on the shiny flagstones. 'Please mind your head sir,' he murmured with a practiced motion of the hand and Ava held Jon's hand as they ducked together into the oldest part of the hotel.

Deep black beams glowered over fiercely starched tablecloths and candlelight flickered on the uneven walls as it had for four hundred years. At the table before the inglenook, Ava lowered herself into the proffered chair and allowed the man to unfurl her napkin with a flourish and tender it over her lap, a gesture so curiously without intimacy she decided he was gay.

'Bats for the other side eh?' Jon whispered too loudly as the maître d' retreated with a slight stiffening of the back.

'He'll hear,' Ava giggled.

The wine waiter appeared, cradling the bottle Jon had chosen and Ava watched her husband revel in the ritual; the nod of acknowledgement at the label, the pulling of the cork, the sniff, the gentle splashing of deep red into generous glasses and the first appreciative sip. After allowing a second's delay, Jon's nod indicated that the offering was indeed up to his high standards.

'This reminds me of the first night of our honeymoon darling,' Ava smiled at him.

'Yes, yes.'

Don't look back Ava. There's a rule against it remember?

Then it happened. Advancing towards them, the waitress bore unsteadily down, white cloth draped over the arm holding the steak knife for Jon on a slightly worn silver tray.

'It's Julie Walters look,' Ava giggled again.

'Julie who?' Jon's brow furrowed.

'You know – that TV programme we watched last week. Best of Julie Walters? We really laughed …'

Jon just shook his head.

In place of the actress' unsteady walk, Ava could see now the real woman wore the signs of congenital deformity, a curved stoop, which projected from the black dress and yes, white apron in the candlelit room. 'Oh,' she muttered.

'You're sitting here,' the waitress said quietly with no trace of a Brum accent.

'Well, yes, obviously,' Jon frowned.

'You wouldn't rather be in the window?'

'This is the best table surely? Do you mean my wife will be in a draught?'

'Listen.'

Up beside their heads, they became aware of a faint sound, then silence. There was a scratching, then silence again from the chimney.

'I've told them,' the woman shook her head sadly. 'The best table and it happens all the time. Needs a thing on the roof. To stop it.'

'What is it?' Ava was fascinated.

The woman looked at her. 'A bird. Young probably. They fall in and can't …'

The maître d' arrived, leading a waiter bearing two plates. Too late. And they sat and ate in silence as the sounds from the creature in the chimney gradually stopped.

I simply will never understand them take them somewhere nice throw money at them and what do you get very little. Time was she'd have her legs round me and there was that time she had it in her mouth. Oh my christ. Now what do I get? Nothing I couldn't get for a tenner in a back street. Bloody disappointing. And bloody expensive.

Since the summer, Jon had been talking about having a quiet Christmas.

'Suits me,' Ava didn't look up from her book. 'Syd'll go to her mother. We had her last year, didn't we?'

'Er..'

Annoying he didn't remember more clearly. Ava had gone to a lot of trouble but Christmas lunch had been delayed while Jon had to go and get Syd back after she'd walked off down the road when he'd found her smoking outside the kitchen door.

'Right. Good. And … look, Jon. Don't spend a lot on me eh? I've really got everything I need you know. In fact, why don't we leave presents until the sales?'

'Whatever you like, Ava.'

He'd spent a lot of money on her over the years. Well, to be honest, more in the early years. Hotel rooms, restaurants. There'd been a lot of perfume, she remembered. It wasn't as if she needed anything much these days although a few new clothes would have been nice. Her wardrobe still held suits and high-heeled shoes but there wasn't much call for them. Most days – well, all of them – were spent in jeans and trainers, either doing housework or decorating or gardening. Ava didn't mind that, it was just as if he'd run out of enthusiasm for her since they'd left London and moved into his mother's house. There had been some sort of contest for her and he had won. A contest? She considered Jon and Ted squaring up and smiled at the picture.

But on Christmas morning, he disappeared into the back bedroom and returned beaming, with her present, excitingly large and wrapped by someone other than Jon, she was fairly sure, so Syd probably. She tore the wrapping paper and revealed a cheap lightweight hovermower.

'Because I watched you using the old Hayter and it's too heavy for you darling.' *Thoughtful.*

This toy looks as if it might last one summer at best. And why can't you cut the bloody grass?

She supposed she shouldn't complain.

Then it was New Year's Eve, but they stayed in as they had done for many years now …

At the end of their first year in the house together, she and Jon had stood under a full moon in a clear black sky in the back garden. It was very cold – colder even than Gornies the year before, although she hadn't thought that possible, so they were under the arbour, watching and listening for the new year bells, while Jon identified the stars.

'That's terribly clever, Jon,' Ava was impressed by his knowledge. 'But how will we know it's midnight?'

'You'll see,' he drew her into his coat and they kissed. Suddenly there was a distant bang and crackling noises. 'There! Midnight. You see?' His turned her around to see the tops of fireworks visible above the hedges. Distantly, church bells joined in.

'Oh! How lovely!'

'They do it every year, on the beach, weather permitting. Bit of a waste of money really but children like it.'

'*I* like it Jon.'

'Really?' He looked down at her and a red shower of light illuminated the surprise in his face.

'Can we go? Next year?'

'Well it gets rather crowded … rowdy.'

'We'd be all right surely?'

'Have you made a resolution?' he changed the subject as silver and gold rained over the town.

Ah, now here it was. This surely – this moment in this garden, with this man, without the spectre of work looming, represented everything she'd hoped for – so why not just wish for more of the same? And so that was the resolution Ava made, to continue as they were, for as long as they could …

She had got what she had wished for. It didn't include fireworks though. No wonder they said *be careful what you wish* ...

She's let herself go rather I mean it was good of her I suppose, taking down the old fence the way she walloped at it with the hammer she found in the shed no idea how really took it out on the wood, rotten as it was, giving as good as she gave it still as I said to her when she came in, look at your nails Ave just look at them your hands used to make me feel- but those wellingtons, they still do it but she's gone, like the last time, off to clatter around in the kitchen.

Jon had said it quite often – three or four times this year at least. 'See I might be getting a bit forgetful sometimes but I don't let my wife's birthday slip by unmarked now do I?'

Well I sometimes forget things too surely? Don't I?

He drove, having insisted on a day out, a birthday lunch in the country he said.

In the car she glanced at his profile. He looked like himself, sideways on, the occasional emptiness in his eyes she had forced herself to acknowledge was less apparent. To be honest, the last time he gone up to town with some report or other, his suit had looked too big, his shirt gaped at the neck, like the old boys you saw in the High Street when they were dressed for a funeral.

Today, low October sunshine made him drive carefully or he would not have had time to spot the sign half-hidden in the hedgerow.

'Ah good. Farm shop.' Jon wrestled the Saab over the bumpy dried mud in front of a thatched barn, oblivious to damage being done to the suspension. He always winced and sucked his teeth though if she bounced into a pothole.

'I don't think we need anything Jon,' she started but he'd hauled up the handbrake and was already unfolding his long legs out into the sunshine.

She had to walk quickly to catch up with him and warn him to duck as they reached the black-framed door. Inside the barn rose above them, a sparrow flitting between the beams. The smell reminded her of Harvest Festival, of earth and chrysanthemums and, as her hand brushed over them, she breathed in the delicious scent of real tomatoes. 'We could take some of these,' she lowered a vine of five or six into a brown paper bag, relishing the trace they left on her fingers.

But he was following the sparrow's progress from beam to beam.

Apple crates had been laid out to display a bright-coloured slope of gourds. Shiny mustard and speckled bottle green, custard and orange, smooth and ribbed, knobbled and speckled, wobbly, warty and deformed.

Gloriously autumnal. 'How lovely – I haven't seen these for years,' Ava exclaimed.

'We grew 'em ourselves,' one of the two girls, young and pink-faced, said proudly. 'Said to Dad to sell 'em'-

The barn filled with Jon's howl as, turning to see what Ava was doing, he tripped on the uneven flagstones and crashed against the display.

'Frogs!' he screamed, real terror in his eyes. As the tumbled display thundered, rolling and bouncing on the stone floor, the gourds seemed to come alive. 'Frogs Ave! Get them off me!' and he ran, sliding on the squashed flesh and smacking his head on the doorframe, into the sunshine.

'*Jon.*' There was a road out there. '*Come back.* Mind the cars.' She dumped her bag and ran to slow him. '*Wait.*'

They brought him a battered chair to sit on and a bowl of water and some kitchen roll for Ava to mop the scraped skin on his head. Jon sat whimpering, a scared child, for a bit then fell silent.

'They're only gourds mate,' the farm girl began tentatively once she was fairly sure he wasn't going to need an ambulance. 'Not frogs. I'm sorry about your head and all that but, you know, there's a lot of stock there,' she gestured to the pulpy mess her friend was scooping up 'and I can't sell 'em now.'

Jon pulled himself up. 'It was an accident. My wife's terribly sorry. Here,' he scrabbled in his jacket and pulled out a bank card. 'Please cover all your costs.' But when the girl came back with the card machine, he couldn't remember his PIN so Ava had to fish her own card out.

As she folded Jon into the passenger seat she heard one girl say to the other, 'Poor old thing.'

'He's off his trolley.'

'Oh *he* is, yeah. No I meant the old girl. Fancy having to cope with that.'

Fancy was right. Ava didn't know which hurt more – her feelings or her bank balance. How ironic. Her husband, who had spent all his life scrutinising balance sheets, had lost his own balance.

Frogs. She'd been married to him all this time without knowing this secret fear. She wiped her eyes, the scent of tomatoes still on her fingers and drove home, the lunch forgotten.

He was watching her – she could feel his gaze on her back. Once upon a time … and here, she was talking a couple of years only surely? … maybe it was more, now she thought about it … that would have been a prelude to sex.

He would have suddenly been close, pressing, his hands under her clothes and her response would have been happily automatic.

She preferred it to be dark, or behind drawn curtains. Her body seemed to have dropped by an inch each time she caught sight of it in a full-length mirror but it didn't seem to stop Jon wanting it as much as it stopped her wanting him. What had been joyful, instinctive, something to delight in, somewhere along the line had turned into something more studied, dutiful. With more clothes kept on.

Today, he remained seated at the kitchen table as she chopped meat, browned it, seasoned it, turned it into the casserole which would make dinner for three nights if she threw in all the root veg on the board in front of her.

Then, he'd have taken her before she'd got around to them but those days it seemed were over and it felt as if he too acknowledged the need for all the veg to be added. The sad thing was that she felt no loss for those heady early days, just a sort of vacuum.

'What are we having?'

Jon's voice had once been something she revelled in, smooth and controlled in the office but in a domestic situation it seemed to come from on high. More and more, he sounded like royalty meeting and greeting subjects with the open-ended question to put them at ease.

'Kangaroo, I thought, for a change.'

'Good, good. Plenty of gravy.'

She smiled and turned, paring knife in her hand to tease him but the phone on the wall rang, saving him. She wiped her hands and lifted it to her ear, clutching it between shoulder and chin to carry on with the veg. 'Hello?'

'Ave? That you?' There was a pause. 'Oh good. Look – is Dad there?'

'Yes – want a word?'

'No.'

But it was too late and Jon had commandeered the phone and was asking how his favourite daughter was. You never knew whether he'd want to talk to her or not. More than once, Ava had held the conversation because he had frowned, head shaking when she offered him the receiver. And then there were times when she talked to Syd, hung up ready with a precis for Jon only to find him sulking because women never let a man get a word in edgeways.

Ava just heard Syd say *Shit*, then the conversation was one-sided for what seemed a long time. There were pauses between the noises she was making as if she was unsure of something and Jon, listening with his head down, frowned and just said *Oh* and *I see.*

'Well,' he said with a deep sigh. 'You'd better come round. We need to talk obviously Syd,' and put the phone back on the wall.

'Whatever's the matter?' Ava tipped the last mushrooms into the pan, scraping the wet wooden board with the knife, which always set her teeth on edge. 'Is she okay Jon?' She started on the carrots.

'She is not okay.' He sat back down at the kitchen table. 'She is pregnant.'

The knife sliced deep into Ava's finger.

Syd was there within the hour. The kitchen was starting to fill with the stew's redolent steam and Ava had finished wiping the surfaces and replaced the bloody plaster on her finger. The questions she'd fired at Jon were without answers, so she'd busied herself to let him absorb the news. In case Margaret was coming with her daughter, Ava ran upstairs to drag a brush through her hair and put on some lipstick, guiltily aware of vanity on a day like this.

But the child stood alone on the doorstep, soaked to the skin.

At only just seventeen, she couldn't be described as an adult and certainly today looked more like a rangy twelve-year old, her hair dripping and with deep rings under her eyes. A large spot flared on her chin making her face lopsided. 'Lo Ave,' she muttered and set off, head down, for the kitchen.

'Hey – no hug?' Ava asked.

The girl turned and ran back to her with a blurted sob. 'Oh Ave.'

'Come on now, cheer up. We'll be all right, you'll see,' Ava held her wondering how exactly she could achieve that. 'Dad's through there.'

Syd sniffed. 'Is he …?'

Ava shook her head. 'I don't really know.'

Jon had retreated round the kitchen table and stood as they came in. For a moment, it looked as if would extend a hand to his daughter, ask her to sit and discuss her cv.

'Come and sit down, Syd love,' Ava pulled her out a chair at right angles to her father. 'Cup of tea?'

'No milk,' Syd grimaced.

'Oh? Oh I see.' Filling the kettle, Ava remembered something, then shut it back away where it belonged in the locked box at the back of her head.

'Now,' Jon began. 'This is a family crisis and I don't think there's anything to be gained by raised emotions. I propose we set out all the facts, calmly discuss the options, then take a vote.'

For God's sake. He was in shock obviously. 'Well …' Ava began, 'perhaps Margaret should be here too?'

'Why?' Jon's fist connected with the table making their mugs jump. Automatically, Ava got up for a cloth. 'She's allowed this to happen. She's supposed to take care of my daughter. I think she's forfeited a seat at the table.'

'Jon darling. This isn't the time for democracy. It's Syd's future we're talking about.'

'*Lack* of future unless we deal with this sharpish.'

'You sound as if you've decided already Dad.'

'You,' he pointed at Syd, 'Are barely old enough for this to not be a police matter, just remember that young lady.'

'And, there's someone else involved, surely?' Ava suggested quietly, putting refilled mugs of tea in front of them both.

'Huh?' he looked up.

'Who is it Syd? The boy you were seeing last weekend? I thought you weren't eating much. Robin wasn't it?' She vaguely remembered a small nondescript lad waiting awkwardly on the doorstep.

'*No.* He's such a drip. I think it was at that rave I went to? In the field outside Chilham back in the summer. It was such a *great* night. Hot.' The girl shrugged 'I just don't … know. I don't care. I just want this baby. It's mine.'

The summer seemed a long time ago now, so it was too late for Syd to take any advice Ava might offer. The conversation came round to planning the arrival and Ava saw a glint - of triumph, could it be? – on her face.

Jon's head slumped.

And who the fuck's going to pay for this? So now the thing to do is not to panic not that I would obviously this all went to plan before even if it's spotted there's nothing nothing at all to connect it with me or Ava of course let's just say it's such a fundamental error you could drive a coach and horses through it let alone a cheque can't believe the bean counters missed it before and now it's time to do it all over again they pore over the accounts year in year out adding and checking and cross-checking and counter-cross-checking and they've never seen this it takes a certain type of mind analytical you could call it although I must say I thought I'd trained Ava better than that thought she would have spotted it… all frogs and no toads … anyway Syd needs somewhere to live with the child

A shelf shine *child*

Steve watches Ava walk past, beyond the neatly aligned chops and the ribs of beef and the endless chains of sausages. Alone…

In the beginning, his first year here – that was the first time.

Even on the opposite side of the street, she had been incandescent, glowing with happiness, her slender wrist through the crook of her tall, older man's arm. It was summer, he remembered. He had not long finished playing rugby and was at his peak. Mid-thirties, so maybe, fair enough, a couple of years younger than she was but oh she was lovely. *Smile if you had it last night* they used to say to the girls in the bar to make them giggle and you could just tell from looking that that was exactly what had happened.

She was a lot smaller than the man and it made Steve bristle to think of her being under his grip but when she noticed the new shop and pulled the man to cross the road with her for a look, he followed like a puppy. Like all men, his gaze focussed on the steaks and they bought two large fillets.

'Are they large enough, Ava darling?'

'They'll be fine,' she reassured him.

Steve's own mouth watered as he sliced down through the flesh, weighed and bagged them, thinking of her cooking them later that day.

'You have a lovely shop,' she smiled as he bagged and handed them over. 'Everything looks delicious.'

He mumbled thanks, too tongue-tied for more.

Were they married?

Somehow, Steve doubted it. They looked too fresh with one another to be shackled. He sighed as he thought of Pauline waiting at home. She would be disdainful when all he produced was a bit of sirloin but Ava had taken the last of the better cut. Too bad.

Maybe they were down for the weekend and he'd never see her again. Viciously, Steve slammed three or four lamb chops into the bag on top of Pauline's steaks. She hated cooking mixed grills but he liked them and today he felt like having what he liked.

'Not chops again,' Pauline groaned that night, making his heart sink.

'All there was. You should be grateful,' he grumbled back.

But Ava was back the following Friday, alone this time. The fillets had been good she told him, smiling at the memory but they had visitors on Sunday and she'd need ribs, four she thought. He had exactly the joint he told her, diving into the cold room and proudly bearing the cut back to her like a loyal labrador.

She paid in cash and there was plenty left in her purse, he saw. The meat was heavy though – he could deliver it later today? No charge, of course. She thanked him and told him the address. He couldn't wait.

But the house was a surprise. Old-fashioned and needing work. 'Nice place,' he nodded, laying the meat on the kitchen table (he had taken care to use the side door out of courtesy).

'Well,' she laughed, brightening his day, 'one day perhaps. It's not really mine to change. Yet.'

So they weren't married.

Then the man bustled in, grinning at the bagged joint and actually rubbing his hands together and it was time for Steve to go. He trudged down the path thinking some blokes had all the luck. And that he would never, ever, love anyone more than he loved Ava …

For the first few months, there were visitors. Ava and the man enjoyed Steve's produce and even though sometimes she'd have a bag from the fishmongers over her arm, she'd still glance over and wave cheerily at him.

He couldn't put his finger on when things changed. Suddenly he realised she was wearing a wedding ring and he just had to face it, he stood no chance. Then one day he couldn't remember the last time Ava had bought much more than mince and the man – Jon she called him in conversation – didn't come in any more but stayed outside the door, hands in his pockets. Well, there was a recession. Why should they be immune? It was a surprise though, given the house they'd bought. So hard times then Steve thought, adding a bit more mince for a good customer, he told Ava. Actually, now he looked at Jon, he could see he stooped a bit and even he saw, as he watched more closely, was he actually talking to himself? Steve's heart went out to Ava, wondering what she had to cope with and wishing he could help with more than a bit extra now and then. She looked drawn, hair scraped up like an urchin and in clothes he'd seen her in a hundred times.

Then today, this unforgettable morning he spotted her and had to look twice. Her old man was pushing a pram. As she parked him and the pram outside the window Steve felt his throat strangle his words.

'How's that house of yours coming on?' he managed. Lately, there had been no need to deliver the shrinking packages and he missed seeing the slow but steady progress she was making.

'Oh,' Ava nodded. 'Okay. The garden's lovely this year.' She seemed amused. 'That's Daisy,' indicating the tiny sleeping bundle.

He should try to say something. 'Well now.'

'My husband's granddaughter.'

Thank Christ for that he wanted to say but another customer, an older woman, had come in.

'After you,' Ava gestured.

'Oh that's so kind dear. I don't want to miss my bus …'

When she had left, Steve could think of nothing to say but to take up where he had left off. 'Big gardens those. You have help I suppose?'

She looked at him. 'No. I'm happy to do it. Better than being in an office all day.'

Another piece in the jigsaw. 'Well if you do need someone, my nephew's a good lad. He's learning the trade

176

with that lot.' He nodded over at the Garden Guru's shop a little further down the High Street.

'Oh I couldn't afford them,' Ava shook her head sadly. 'We're having to help this little one's mum buy a place in Whitstable. Things are a bit tight right now.'

'No, he'll do it private. Tenner an hour for cash, you know.'

When she looked up, he was horrified to see tears in her eyes. 'Now then, no need,' he reached across the counter to pat her arm.

'Thank you though,' she passed a fiver, the only note in her purse today, to him.

'I'll get your change.' He would have given her the bloody mince, just to see that smile he'd seen the first year one more time but knew he couldn't insult her.

She threw the coins into her bag and left, beckoning Jon to her side and hurrying him and the pram away.

Steve felt like a good cry himself.

Bloody butcher always in my house

Ava doesn't mind the long quiet evenings. It's the pattern set by that long, late, only-childhood; trainee adulthood, after all. So it must be what all married couples become, silent bookends of the life they have created.

After working in the garden, making dinner, engaging Jon in conversation, an early night – just that, nothing intended - seems like a good idea.

But she wishes he wouldn't always stand between her and the window, whatever window in whatever room. It's just a habit. He would do it when he walked into her office remember? To block everyone else out.

But because he's so tall, it does make it dark.

A shorter man wouldn't blot out so much sunlight.

But isn't that just it? She could remember a wedding on TV – a silly film - and being distracted by the phrase *keep thee only unto him.* It stuck with her because deep down, she knew that if he walked into the room now …

Better not to go there.

What about the others? All right, *all* the others. The man on the Yorkshire moors, the fitness freak in the lift, Josh – no, not those two – but plenty of others. That man in the office that time … their names, their faces, their bodies were a blur now, bar one. She knew well enough not to trust herself. It was lucky that he wouldn't walk into the room.

She had known what she was doing – the married ones – was fun but wrong. It had made Jon's marriage long-term collateral damage.

'Jon! Look at this! On the front page,' Ava rattled the paper under his nose. 'Pension freedom! Didn't see that coming. There was nothing in the Sunday paper was there? I can cash in my annuity, do the house up – we could live on your income instead of firefighting all the repairs all the time, it'd work well. They say it's something no-one in the industry saw coming – had to keep it quiet or investors would have skewed the share prices of the pension funds. But it's marvellous for us.'

For a moment he said nothing. 'You don't want to do a thing like that Ava. Most unwise. It's not for us.'

Puzzling, she read the article again in case she'd misunderstood. The capital would fundamentally alter their standard of living, mean Jon could keep this house he loved so and they'd hardly miss the annuity income it would buy her in a few years' time because she was so comparatively young. The actuaries would determine she'd live another forty years.

A group of women calling themselves WASPI were lobbying because they'd just missed their chance to access their own money. The arbitrary date chosen by a faceless Whitehall mandarin simply locked some people out of the opportunity, like missing a lifeboat on the Titanic. No wonder they were mad – some had only opted in to annuities the day before the announcement.

But why isn't for us, like Jon said? I don't understand. I'll google it, check again tonight when he's had a chance to read some more.

That night was the first time he hit her.

It was a thumping, swinging slap like a two-year old in a paddy, frustrated because they couldn't do something they wanted to do. Hurting more though, from a man over six feet tall. Shocked, neither of them spoke. Jon turned on his heel and Ava walked into the bathroom where she could lock the door with shaking hands.

It had never happened to her before but now she had to admit she had half expected it, watching him daily losing a battle with himself over so many things.

That won't be the last time.
Perhaps it will. Just a one-off.

To give him a chance to apologise, she didn't say anything when they bumped into each other on the landing. In a high, slightly shaky voice, Jon asked what was for tea.

Perhaps he doesn't know what he did ... but he was careful not to touch her shoulder where his fist had thumped into her.

She dabbed arnica cautiously onto the bruise, thinking perhaps it was a sign, using the healing power of a daisy, all things considered.

Christ fucking bastards

On the night Daisy was born, he opted to stay at home 'to let the women get on with it'.

Ava, beginning to recognise it was better this way, went alone to the hospital, recoiling from the smells along the peeling corridor. Was it true, she wondered as she made herself concentrate on the signs for the maternity ward, hoping not to bump into Margaret and Aggie, that babies were waiting to be born and if for some reason a birth went wrong, their soul just sat patiently for another mother?

She found Syd sitting in bed with a glazed smile on her face. 'No Dad, Ave?' The smile disappeared. 'This is my sort of cousin, Jojo, Ava.'

The girl cradled the sleeping baby, smiling and humming low, then handed her over.

As Ava looked into the tiny face, she recognised this as the baby she hadn't had. This little one had been waiting for her. Ava hadn't wanted any baby – not many women would be brave enough to say that, she knew though it was right. Oddly, now this little scrap was in her arms, face puckered at the scent and rhythm of an unfamiliar body, Ava felt the first twinge of what would grow into an alliance with her. Both of them weren't supposed to be there – Ava should have left Jon to his marriage with Margaret and Syd should have protected herself from the hardship and difficulties that lay on the road ahead of her.

When Jon did visit, he returned apoplectic. 'She wants to call her *Daisy*. A common or garden weed. I thought …'

'What? That it would be a boy?' Ava smiled, noting the baby's weight and time of arrival in her diary for posterity.

'Well if it *had* to be a girl, she could at least have called her Edith after Mother.' There she was again, Edith, gone but not remotely forgotten.

'She's our granddaughter Jon.' How strange it felt to be labelling oneself with that. 'Doesn't matter what name Syd gives her does it?'

His eyes narrowed. 'Well, technically of course, she's only mine.'

Not wanting to provoke him, Ava murmured, 'Ah well.' Since then he had shied from any 'nursery talk' detail and took only a detached interest in his granddaughter and more and more, in life. And she had come to realise that Jon had no intention of blending the two parts of his life. Somehow she would have to build a small silent bridge between herself and Syd, helping with Daisy in any way this life allowed.

The mornings were becoming dewy although the 'lawn' was still the colour and texture of a used teabag. In his annual pattern, Jon became more and more anxious that they should have days out 'somewhere nice'.

'Tenterden today I thought,' he munched toast and Duchy orange and grapefruit preserve.

For nearly a year, Ava had been refilling the jar with the cheapest marmalade she could find.

'Splendid stuff this,' Jon's open mouth offered a view of its progress as he talked. 'Just like Mother used to make.'

'Good. Jon'-

'Tenterden then old girl?'

When did that start? At first she'd been *darling,* then for a brief and hateful period *Mrs. Jon,* and now *old girl.* What had she done to cause this slithery slope from mistress to … what? It felt horribly like she'd become a replacement mother and it was true that if he hurt himself in some way, she was moved, like the skull-cracking incident at the farm shop. It stopped her sniping at him for ignoring jobs around the house and softened her attitude, immediately resuming the role of carer. Perhaps that became too reassuring, made life too easy for him. Perhaps, she thought and immediately acknowledged that it was too late to do anything about it now, just possibly Jon had reached the peak of his maturity into adulthood and was beginning the slide downhill to second childhood.

'I've quite a bit to do here,' Ava pictured the ironing pile and the hedge that looked like it was wearing a crinoline.

'Hedge is it, you're thinking of? Don't worry about that. Get a man in,' he waved an arm expansively.

'And Syd wanted me to babysit.' It wasn't a prospect she was relishing, although she was getting better at it. And she knew there was no point asking Jon for help.

'Look, is it too much to ask that I have a day out with my wife?' His face was reddening, she could see the familiar defeat, her regular climbdown.

Ava crumbled. 'I'll need a bit of time to doll myself up of course … the older I get, you know …'

He looked grateful for the admission. 'Long as we're away by eleven.'

She caught herself replying with a simpering smile. And hated herself for it.

As they drove into the pretty Kentish town, Jon headed for the Waitrose car park. You stood a chance of someone apologising there, he said, when they smashed their door into the Saab's bodywork, not like at bloody Asda.

He relished these encounters, bridling, barking until he'd established their credentials. And today, as if he'd planned it, it happened. When Ava was scrabbling in her handbag for a comb, there was a hard metallic thump near the boot, rocking the car.

Jon was out in a trice and the well-spoken blonde in the Range Rover was utterly charming, so he was right. Whose fault? Neither seemed to care. It was as if they were players, taking well-rehearsed parts but Ava despaired. The cost of doing anything to the Saab was always astronomical, but it would have to be ironed out, nursed along. There was no question of a new car.

Then, he discovered he'd been to school with the husband of the offending woman. 'Not *Hugo* Greenhalgh-

Black?' his fury had turned to a silly smile. 'Lancing boy? His parents used to live here …'

Confused, the woman agreed that her husband had indeed gone to the school 'a long time ago now, of course. And sadly, the parents were no more.'

'Same house as me,' Jon swept aside any further discussion of the dented rear wing. 'How's old Hugo doing?'

As Ava cringed it became apparent that old Hugo was in fact doing very well indeed and was now something big at Lloyds.

'Well, lovely to have met you,' Jon took Ava's arm. 'Off to treat my lady wife – her birthday you know. Remember me to old Hugo.'

He struck off down the High Street and, where it widened to a pan-tiled forecourt, indicated a bow-fronted shop with a mannequin in the window. 'Let's have a look in here, shall we?'

Inside, the smiling saleswoman made a fuss of him, sitting him on the little gold-legged settee outside the changing room's satin curtains while Ava stared miserably at the price tags attached to floaty, strappy bits of nothing.

'It's the end of the season I'm afraid, madam,' the woman was at her shoulder now, murmuring, 'so this stock is marked down. Our winter party stock will be coming in soon.'

Marked down or not, it was nevertheless all very expensive. 'It has to be today, I'm afraid,' Ava grasped at the chance there might in fact be nothing she could arguably squeeze into.

'What about that one, old girl?' Jon pointed from the sofa until they identified his target, a strident yellow chiffon number with a sequin-encrusted halterneck. It was so laughably wrong, she found herself smiling.

'See? I know what you like. Let's try it on,' he urged.

Behind the padded curtains, she stripped off clothes, back deliberately turned to the mirror. The halterneck meant no bra. Ava considered the cost of a new backless one which might somehow hoist her breasts up to where they once had been. What was she thinking? Even if she found one, even if the yellow thing fitted, where the bloody hell would she wear the thing?

'Come on. Let's see you,' Jon boomed.

'Splendid,' he said, immediately she stepped from behind the curtains. 'We'll take it,' he told the saleswoman whose implacably professional face betrayed no thought at all.

To get it over and done with – and God only knew how he was going to pay for it – Ava ducked back in, stripped down again and holding the curtains together with one hand, held the yellow thing, as she knew he wanted her to do, out with the other, naked arm.

Sometime later, and she could picture the circumstances without difficulty, he'd mention that naked arm.

And then, to her horror, she overheard him begin to pick over the outfit, haggling. A seam was, apparently, looking strained. There was a loose thread at the hem. And finally, triumphantly, Jon pointed out that one strand of the sequins on the collar had begun to unravel.

She knew how it felt.

By the time she had brushed her hair, Jon was signing the credit card slip with a flourish and the saleswoman had shifted a practically worthless piece of last season's stock at a modest discount on the sale price.

'Tea now I think?' he held out the substantial glossy carrier, tissue peeping from the gold ribbon handles for her to take with the required gratitude.

'Lovely,' she murmured, not catching the woman's eye, as Jon made a show of tucking his card and the receipt into his wallet. 'Thank you so much darling,' she added because she had been taught to.

She loathed the mirrors that lurked in every nook of this place. As she walked out, trying to hold in her stomach, the very last one, a reproduction cheval by the door, reflected the smirk on the saleswoman's face.

They had tea in a low-ceilinged, dusty place, where the bored girl took an age to bring a battered silver pot and a bowl of elderly sugar lumps that had long since lost their crisp angles.

As Jon finished his teacake, task completed, he mellowed. 'Well, that's that then old girl. See, I might be getting a bit forgetful, but I never forget my wife's birthday, do I?'

'… No.'

'So – better be getting back? I know you were worried about that ironing …'

They walked back to the car, Jon insisting on holding her hand in a display of affectionate gratitude.

When they got in, she headed for the utility room and the ironing.

It wasn't her birthday.

It's the stupidest thing but I couldn't remember why I was there *Excuse me what is the name of this place?* The woman driving the other car looked at me, eyes narrow Tenterden, she says And you have just driven into my car don't you remember takes a bit of managing that Of course I say I remember but you reversed out of that parking place right into my Saab that'll cost quite a bit to put right then Ava takes over gets all the details down on paper names addresses insurance companies. You sit down Jon she says and then the other woman says Greenhalgh-Black I say Not Hugo? Hugo GB? And she says yes and of course once I've explained we were chums at school everything goes well, all sorted both cars driveable everyone happy whose birthday? Right I say to Ava see? that's what going to the right school does should have sent Syd to one she'd have turned out differently I can tell you now shall we go home and she says I'd said something about looking for something for her to wear while we're here fine I say where is this again? Yes, he was a good sort, GB, and that wife of his now she's a stunner doesn't look like she messes around in the garden…

Ava was halfway through putting on her face when the bell rang. It was mid-morning and the time had evaporated in getting Jon up and dressed. She wanted to walk him to tire and help him sleep, so a bit of make-up was called for, but she hadn't got as far as mascara.

The woman at the door was very thin. Her burgundy spiral-permed hair had the pan-scourer look of the over-dyed. Ava thought she might be collecting for something. 'Can I help you?'

The woman smiled beatifically extending her slender hand. 'Fay. I've just moved in next door.'

'Oh?' Ava shook it, surprised. The hedges were so high she'd no idea the old boy had gone. In the years they'd been here, neither Jon nor she had ever exchanged words with their neighbour.

At once, all the usual suburban anxieties crowded in. Did this woman look like a developer, set on pulling the house down, ruining the privacy of their garden? Or a profit-bent landlord, set on filling the house with undesirables?

How protective she felt about the house that used to be Edith's and was now hers too. 'Sorry – I hadn't realised we'd new neighbours.'

Despite the hair, the woman's face was unlined. It was hard to tell what age she was. She wore little make-up and, Ava now saw, open-toed sandals, in December. Tiny beads on a delicate thread wound tightly round her throat and a tattooed butterfly peeped from the deep vee of the dress billowing around her calves in the brisk Channel breeze on the high doorstep.

'Do come in,' Ava said praying she wouldn't. The house was its usual chaotic self and she'd no idea where Jon was or what he was up to.

'Well, if you're sure I'm not imposing?' And she was in, bobbing slightly as she entered in a deferential dance.

'Come through won't you? The kitchen's warmest at this time of day. The sun you know.'

'Oh I'm a real sun-worshipper,' Fay assured her. 'It's one reason we chose the house. Privacy in the garden. And the moon too - so important in our lives don't you think?'

Ava set the kettle to boil and reached for cups. Or was Fay a mug-user? Hard to say but betting she was a hippy, Ava stretched for the tall coffee mugs and found the real coffee at the end of the shelf behind the cafetiere. She'd no idea how old it was but if she made awful drinks, Fay wouldn't bother them again. As she spooned the fragrant grind Ava couldn't stop herself wondering when she started worrying about cups or mugs.

'This is lovely,' the woman lied, glancing round at Edith's kitchen.

'It isn't,' Ava laughed. 'But perhaps one day …'

'Oh, we've so much to do over there,' Fay's head nodded next door. 'But Kris won't start until we've had the feedback from the consultant.'

'I'm sorry. You're ill?'

'Oh no. *No,*' she threw back her head and long silvery earrings flicked in time. 'The Feng Shui consultant. It matters terribly to us to get that right. He was with us on all our property searches that felt like they mattered, you know?'

'I don't, to be terribly honest,' Ava filled the cafetiere. 'I'm more of a practicalities sort of person when it comes to houses. Drains, rewires, new boilers …'

'Really?' Fay looked around her.

'Well, not this house admittedly. I – we – inherited it. From my husband's mother, so we took early retirement and came to live here.'

'Lucky you,' Fay looked at the coffee. 'Don't suppose you've herbal tea at all?'

'No,' said Ava. 'Afraid it's builder's or nothing in this house. Chris did you say?'

'With a K. Like Kristofferson.' There was that smile again.

'Oh. Oh no – wait.' She dragged a chair over to the cupboard beside the fireplace and scrambled on to it, sliding a hand along the top shelf. Here,' she brought down a box of camomile she'd got in when Margaret-Willow had finally appeared on a visit to discuss Syd's pregnancy. 'This any better?'

Fay looked relieved. 'I find coffee so … alien … since I became vegan.'

'Mm, I imagine.' *How do people contrive to lead such self-centred lives? Fay would get on well with Willow.*

The small talk trickled into the room. No Butterfly Fay didn't have children. *Good – less noise.* Yes they were from London which had become intolerable and they were seeking a quiet life here on the coast where they could meditate and run a small yoga retreat, encourage wellbeing and mindfulness. The *energy* of the town had hit both of them as soon as they'd started to look round.

'A retreat? In the house?' Ava could imagine Jon's reaction to a steady stream of orange-clad hippies tripping up the front path banging little cymbals and chanting like they did in Oxford Street.

No, Kris had taken a lease on the old Toy Museum which had closed when the owner retired and ironically moved to London to be nearer her grandchildren. That was a relief.

'And there's a call for that? A retreat? I'm afraid it's not something I've ever gone into,' Ava sipped her coffee. It wasn't bad. Actually now she thought about it neither was the idea of a retreat – going to one, disappearing.

'Oh huge. People will pay hundreds for a few nights of peace and tranquillity. That's what we're calling it. The Sea of Tranquillity. It's all greens and blues inside, Kris is stripping the woodwork to look like driftwood and we're putting the most amazing chandelier made of shells in the entrance hall.'

'Well.' Ava had rather liked the untouched fustiness of the rooms and moth-eaten toy exhibits now all stripped away no doubt. She couldn't think of anything to say. DFLs were all like this, splurging their property windfalls on wacky start-ups, bringing the spending power parameters they've been used to in London to this slightly faded resort then being surprised when customers didn't materialise.

'*Three pounds fifty* for a loaf of bread?' Jon was incredulous outside the new baker. 'And I don't want sour anything, let alone dough.'

Too bad. Let them learn.

'You must come to our launch party,' Fay's top gaped and the butterfly wobbled slightly as leant forward to grasp Ava's hand. 'I sense tensions in your face. You'll benefit enormously from a few sessions I just know.'

'Well my husband's ... ill.'

'Is it cancer?' Fay sounded almost excited. 'There's been a lot of discussion about the merits of holistic diets.'

Thinking about the cheap ingredients she often resorted to made Ava feel newly guilty. 'No actually well, he gets confused a lot – a bit - I'm sorry to say.'

'Oh *yes.*' Fay was off again, babbling about wellness meditation and the link between mid-life stress and later dementia. 'I'll drop some of our essential oil round – it's made with local seaweed – Kris is really excited about it.'

Alarmed, Ava pulled her hand back. 'I'm sorry, I don't think I could afford'-

'-Oh, special rates for neighbours you know.' With a little tinkly laugh, Fay stood and made for the door just as Jon stepped into the room. 'Ooh you must be Jon,' she was effusive. 'Heard so much about you. Fay. From next door. Ava will tell you all about us. We've had a lovely chat and you must meet my other half Kris – with a K you know – and come to our launch party.'

'Yes,' Jon grinned unexpectedly. And she was gone past him and out of the front door before they knew it.

'Goodness, she talks a lot,' Ava got up with the mugs noticing Fay hadn't touched her tea. 'Says I've got tensions in my face.' When she looked in the mirror she realised her face had been only half-painted all through the conversation. Tensions? More like completely drained.

That butterfly though ...frogs toads frogs toads

And this, Ava sees now, is how it is in places like this town. People are washed up here, borne on tides of love, luck, sheer chance and gather into the flotsam and jetsam that floats through the streets, buying houses and demanding obscure vegetables, selling unwanted possessions that do not fit here. Gradually moulding the town to suit them with their expertise in marketing and the internet and their bulging wallets. Free now to 'give something back', which they all seem to want to do, making Ava wonder, but not dwell on, what it was they stole away in their city jobs. Enjoying the days here as they never could before when their noses were to different grindstones. They are not all from London. Some come from the north, sure it's nearly the South of France and that they're living the life they always envied. Some are from further afield, entranced by the Englishness of it all.

Trade prospers on these incomers. Estate agents naturally, the buzzards of the High Street, always ravenous but never hungry, and those niche shops which can adapt to whatever the new tide demands. Where once, when she came here, everything dazzled white in the sunshine, now it is Farrow and Ball Elephant's Breath. A few bolder owners have painted their houses Drainpipe, but passers-by mutter (darkly, naturally) that it looks like an undertaker's.

Surprisingly Fay becomes a friend to Ava. They have supper at Kris and Fay's. He cooks, pours drinks, flirts gently but without serious intent with Ava and cajoles a few laughs from Jon. Fay, a ghost in her own house, flits around making very little impact on the room except for the faint trace of patchouli that lingers when she brushes past.

In the new year, Ava agrees she will come to pilates at The Sea of Tranquillity. Kris has offered to host Jon in one of the quiet rooms while the instructor leads the group.

It leaves Ava exhausted which she is fairly sure is not the intention but she has revelled in being in charge of only her own body during the hour of stretching and bending.

When she collects Jon though, for a moment, she's fairly sure he can't remember who she is.

The very next day, she thought an undertaker was needed when she walked into the livingroom, and Jon looked waxen and utterly still. She dreaded this coming and acting only on what she'd seen in films, Ava felt his wrist for a pulse, squeamish at the feel of his bones under the thin skin. There definitely was one. The ambulance was soon at the gate and as Jon was admitted to hospital, Ava following, her heart in her mouth.

'Best to take him in love, just to be safe. They'll do some checks. Soon have him right as rain,' the paramedic said comfortingly, filling in forms as he spoke.

She couldn't believe how much she hoped so. She muttered under her breath so many times about him, about how he was driving her crazy, now all she wanted was him home and well.

In a few days, he was indeed home, no real harm done, just the change in medication for his blood pressure hadn't suited him, said the professionals. Life carried on. In a way.

Not a way that resembled their first heady days together though.

Mornings often start with a scratching, pawing somewhere behind Ava, often her neck because once, just once, he massaged there and it turned her on. Now, like a cat insisting on being let in from the cold, this persistent, dry-skinned movement breaks into her precious sleep. These are not the smooth-skinned fingertips which have brought her to climax in the past. *Horny-handed son of the soil* always comes into her mind but he doesn't do much in the garden. She tries to be fair and just tell herself these are old man's fingers. It doesn't help.

Often she pretends to sleep but he doesn't stop, so in the end, muttering about needing the loo, she throws back the covers and stalks off to the bathroom, leaving him to his own devices. Traffick.

let me in Ave my wife let me in

Nowadays, Fay is a constant and untroubling presence in Ava's life. If Ava wants to tell her something, unburden herself of the weight she faces every day Fay nods, listening. If Ava simply wants silence, Fay seems to recognise this and the two women sit side by side in the summerhouse, watching Ava's garden as summer turns to autumn, then winter, then spring once again. More and more, Ava hears about Kris' shortcomings. Perhaps every marriage is like this.

When she woke, Ava was worrying about money, her head filled with piles of notes that, as soon as she stretched out to touch them, tumbled and blew away. That bill? Had it been for hundreds or thousands?

As she came to, she knew it had been a dream but the unease – and the bill for £540 to see to the wiring - lingered. Ah well, Christmas – how could it be time for another one already? - heightened anxieties all round.

The letter, thick and with shakily hand-written envelope, so probably one of those self-congratulatory family circulars from an ex-colleague arrives in early December and gets piled with others in red envelopes, some in gold or silver, small square ones, long narrow ones to be opened later so that she can send replies on their own modest cards which Jon has chosen because he liked the Three Wise Men in silhouette.

'There's no religion on most of them,' he stated loudly in the shop, 'no Christ in Christmas.' A couple of passing teenagers giggled but a woman more his age muttered in agreement. Ava had quite liked the simple white one with the star, thinking it would satisfy them both, but the camels won.

After she has fed him lunch and cleared away and the fire is lit, she settles Jon in his chair, passes him the pile of envelopes and it is his job to open them all, telling Ava who each is from while she scribbles their reply, scrabbling for addresses. Each year, she has meant to put together a database but it hasn't been a priority and now Jon can't put faces to all the names and the numbers are dwindling anyway. Very few are for Ava – a couple of ex-colleagues, a girl she shared rooms with at Uni, the ageing neighbour of her parents who must herself be a centenarian surely?

Intriguingly, this last – Violet – adds in wavery copperplate a line about a caller she had in the summer – an old school friend she thinks? Apologising for poor recall, she adds that she hopes they managed to get in touch.

Ava writes Violet's card thinking that it will probably be the last and makes a special effort to sound upbeat wishing Violet a great New Year.

The last letter at the bottom of the pile on Jon's lap, looks different and by the time they reach it under all the sales rubbish, Ava is tired of the effort of getting Jon to remember all the relatives and relationships.

'Oh. Now. A *letter*,' Jon extracts pages from the envelope with pleasure. 'How nice. Now who's this from Ave?'

A typed address, A4 and thick contents conveyed with an expensive franked stamp.

It certainly won't be for her – some old business organisation of his perhaps – she gets up to make tea, taking her completed cards to the hall. A letter will be something he can savour. Something about the font rings a bell, but she must finish the washing-up before she can sit down.

Sliding the tea tray onto the table she starts to pour. 'Who's it from darling?'

He shakes his head and as she puts the mug beside him rumples the pages into a clump and flings it into the flames which catch immediately. Her first worry is that it will fly up the chimney, which hasn't been swept this year, and catch fire, then she sees the envelope still in his hand. Before she can peer at the postmark, it joins the rest and is soon blackened flakes.

She'll get down to writing the rest of their own cards soon, but it will have to wait, because Jon's hospital appointment is at three and they are already late.

matters arising from an internal audit eh well
I invented internal audits let me tell them and
they can just fucking fuck off like me to
answer questions to assist their investigations
fucking piss off I say why should I help them
burn in hell that's what they can do find your
own fucking bloody frogs

More doors close around Ava. To keep the bills down, Jon says. Except he says, 'Keep bottles down.'

One thing's certain. She doesn't usually like what she finds when she opens them. And with interest rates scraping along the bottom of the barrel, they have to make economies, she can see. Everyone does.

It would be months before another proper letter came.

Ava stamped down from the top garden, kicking off her shoes in disgust before she came into the kitchen. 'Oh god that's disgusting!'

Even Jon raised his head and sniffed the air. 'I say Margaret …'

'I'm AVA!' She threw the shoes into the sink and wrenched the hot tap on as the room filled with a stomach-heaving stench. 'There must be a dog that's got into our garden. I trod right in it – it's disgusting!' She used an old rag to wipe the slimy brown mess away, holding her head back to avoid the smell. 'No-one round here's got a dog have they?'

'Fox, most likely,' he said, getting up and leaving the room.

'Some fox,' she muttered, able to draw breath at last. It was like that night on their honeymoon, the same shitty smell – no, this was worse - had pervaded their marriage.

There was a rattle and slap as the letter flap clattered on Halcyon's front door.

'A letter Ave? A lovely? I'll go.' He pottered purposefully to the mat. For a couple of years, Jon has raced to see what the postman has brought like a child hoping for presents in the mail. Almost always, it was adverts for things he didn't need, couldn't afford and didn't understand.

What a tumbled world this was, Jon in his spiral of decline, Ava clinging to any rock of normality to try to anchor him on it.

She dried the shoes on kitchen paper then followed him quickly into the study, in case any mail got lost as he made his way through the hall. He stood, holding out the only letter. A proper letter, one with handwriting on the envelope, even a red one like this, was something that might work. Ava tore carefully to destroy nothing that might pay re-reading or scrutiny. The thick paper gave way to her fingers and she pulled out – in June – a trail of choirboys trudging through thick snow to a candlelit church.

Inside the card, she was urged to enjoy the best Christmas could bring her and hers. 'Oh it's from Sue. And Phil.' Underneath, below the signatures, a couple of scrawled lines in a different ink admitted they'd found this when clearing out before putting their house on the market. They'd completely forgotten to post it when the news broke about the firm going under.

On the spur of the moment, they were proposing to visit. 'They want to come.' Her stomach tensed. 'This weekend.'

She sliced a banana onto his Special K. 'Sue and Phil,' she looked at him. 'Remember?'

'Yes …' *No then.*

What did it matter if there were gaffes? It might be a laugh.

Some grown-up company would be very welcome and she'd ask their opinion of Jon if it didn't make itself painfully obvious. But he could be okay – you never knew. Sometimes she felt she was wishing him into his oblivion.

She wrestled with the ironing board determined to finish while the day was still cool and hauled one of Jon's shirts out of the basket. Only when she was gliding hotly down to the last cuff did she notice the mess. Seagulls? She crumpled the shirt into a ball and drop-kicked it into the unsavoury pile awaiting today's hot wash. Jon was not a tee shirt man.

But the bruises from the time she'd argued over it had taken a long time to fade. Perhaps soon, she would simply dress him in whatever he chose. In the meantime, she'd give in to the tantrums and slip another perfectly-ironed shirt off its hanger after she dried him off. *He's right in a way. A shirt makes him look a bit less ... deranged.*

'We'll need shopping Jon.'

'Carrots. Can't go wrong with carrots.'

'Well ... yes, green stuff, you know.' *It wasn't just salad... I could please myself in those days – what I ate and if I ate at all. Remember that night Jon turned up when I didn't think he was coming? The look on his face when I offered him half my raw veg and mung beans. Hadn't I got any steak in the fridge? No, I hadn't.*

I was a ten in those days. Sue got down to an eight.

What would Suzanne's first words be when she saw her old flatmate? Knowing her forthright friend, it might well include a reference to elephants but she'd always been able to make Ava laugh at the same time.

Jon slurped cereal. 'Remember that bloody thing of theirs. Wally or something? We looked after it for a fortnight while they went hiking.'

'Camping. In the South of France.'

'Bloody thing ran away from us, belted home, waiting for us on the doorstep when we got back.'

'Olly,' Ava laughed, pleased that this memory had come back for him. 'Old English sheepdog, hair everywhere.'

'Will they bring it do you think?'

'Jon,' she said kindly, 'he won't be alive now. He wasn't young then. That's fifteen years ago. More, must be.'

His face crumpled. 'Poor Olly.'

To divert the tears that looked likely, she turned to the kitchen window and pointed to the Saab on the drive. 'That's lasted longer, hasn't it? How long have you had that now? Can you remember?'

J80 JON looked balefully back at her. Too long it said. The car and its registration plate had been Jon's indulgence, the dashboard array of dials said pilot not driver, ace not average. Not long after he'd bought it the company had stopped trading. *Never mind* he'd said, *it's good for two hundred thou, a car like that.*

His frown deepened. 'Old Jumbo? Dunno.' He munched on and the distant look in his eyes told her something was coming.

'Tell you what Ave, when her time comes, we'll give her a proper Viking burial. At sea. Fire, flames. Well, on the beach?'

They went to bed early that night, Jon furious at his laptop's inability to connect with the internet, ready to chuck the thing through the window. He'd taken his frustration out on Ava, who simply apologised as she usually did, because it defused the rant. After he'd stamped upstairs, she'd gone round turning off lights and in the study had stared at the laptop, screen blank and charging cable severed neatly, scissors lying guiltily between the two halves.

Bloody man and his bloody temper. That meant another trip to the hateful computer place at the shopping centre. And the *money.* The blades of the scissors glinted up at her, taunting. It was a good thing he wasn't there.

She wouldn't sleep alongside him. She just wouldn't. She was entitled to a strop too. But the spare bed was cold and furiously bone-tired as she was, it had taken her ages to get off, head boiling with anger at the unfairness of it all. So as 2:22 blinked from her phone she got up and headed to the kitchen. At the lounge door, she stopped dead.

In the silence, in the moonlight, Jon knelt, face so close to the french doors that the glass misted rhythmically with each breath.

They were moving across what he insisted on referring to as the lawn although the obsession with weed suppression and stripes had long since disappeared.

Two hedgehogs, in a sort of distracted dance. One would go to one corner, the other following, then they separated and split again, coming back together to – what was it hedgehogs did? A constant quest for food probably. People were always doing research on things like this. Finding out that really, hedgehogs had social mores, tribal etiquettes. Fancy spending your time in a job like that, Ava marvelled, free of the drudgery real life consisted of.

'Don't get cold Jon,' she whispered automatically. 'I'll get your dressing gown.'

He was after all, stark naked, his long, smooth back like moonlit marble.

He spun at her voice, eyes wide and furious still. '*Cow.*'

How easily love dissolves into hate.

dyb best be prepared incineration put kerosene on the bill no not bill haven't paid for it list able to burn everything that way

As soon as she'd rung them (her prayers were answered and they were out, so she could leave a brief message rather than go into details) Ava was assailed by doubt. What had she been thinking? Any therapeutic benefit Jon might get from meeting old friends could just as easily be wiped out by one of his accidents with the degrading rigmarole they entailed. And with their jobs vanishing, according to the money pages, these two would be nursing their own wounds.

She spent most of the week cleaning the house and cutting the grass. If it was fine, they'd walk along the cliffs but if it was wet they'd be stuck indoors looking at one another and the shabby paintwork. Why had she ever agreed to this visit? Why not suggest taking Jon to them instead – no, no that wouldn't work either with the car on its last legs. What if it broke down in the middle of London? God it didn't bear thinking about. No she'd have to hope things-

'-Ave. Here.'

She looked down in amazement at the fistful of notes Jon was pressing into her hand. 'Where did this come from?' They burned her fingers.

He looked reproachful. 'Thank you.'

'Oh yes, yes of course. But it's so much. We've no money Jon, nothing in the current account.'

'Ah.' He actually tapped the side of his nose.

It was quite possible she was joining him in the loopy world he inhabited. She glanced again. There might be a couple of hundred pounds in her hand. Even more, she thought, seeing a couple of red fifties.

'Jon, you're worrying me. It's really kind of you, but …'

'You leave things to me Ave. You wobble too much.'

She couldn't choose between laughing and hitting him. She was exhausted yet again with all the housework, had been mentally juggling a tiny bit of cash to produce some sort of meal for the four of them and here he was distributing largesse from who knew where?

She smiled and lowered her voice. 'Where did it come from? You must have been saving really hard.'

He beamed. 'Not silly now?'

Her heart ached for him all over again. 'No Jon. Never silly. But a bit … unpredictable sometimes.'

What she was burning to say was, is there any more stashed away somewhere in this great place with all its nooks and crannies? Were they actually so hard up now because he'd been wildly overdoing the saving for a rainy day? And it had rained an awful lot, metaphorically speaking, lately. Well at least she could put a couple of bottles on the table on Saturday now.

'Darling it's a really kind thing to do.' At last she remembered to say thank you.

He seemed better over the next couple of days even reminiscing about their life in London. 'Remember that time the four of us hired a boat for the Boat Race? Blinding hangovers from that night on the river …'

She'd consigned the boat to history, but there she bobbed again, Syd in shorts sprawled on the ... foredeck probably, who knew? And the grown-ups drinking. When had that slipped from sight? There was no landmark, no visible turning point, no catastrophic event that she could blame. Ava knew the question too well to find an answer any more, so she just pushed relentlessly on, one day at a time.

The Mercedes nosed through the gates and pulled up nose-to-nose with Jumbo. The man and woman getting out were blurred versions of the images Ava remembered, like looking through hammered glass. As she made her way out towards them, she knew they were both doing the same fleeting appraisals.

'Look at you!' Sue embraced Ava with real affection. 'Christ it's years.'

'Ten I think.'

'Oh my god. I'm so sorry about that card but when I found it, packing up I thought, well, send it anyway. How are you? How's life in tees and shorts beside the sea – that's what you said when you left, remember? God I was so jealous. Anyway, we're going to do it now. Grab whatever cash is left in the till and run. We've booked tickets for Rio – you know I always wanted to go? Well we are!'

'Shut up Sue, stop talking and let me at this woman. Ava old love. Gorgeous as ever.' Phil's hug, like his wife's, was something Ava had forgotten. The sheer human warmth made her teary.

'Liar,' she laughed, pushing him away. His hair had gone but he was still easy-going old Phil, smiling brightly, just as she remembered.

'And Jon old mate. Good to see you,' Phil pumped his hand.

'Yes, yes,' Jon answered but looked as if he'd no idea who Phil was.

Ava had prepared for this, guessed it would happen. 'Come on in, let's have coffee and then get out while the sun's shining eh? I've got something to show you.'

'Lovely house Ave. You can't possibly keep all this up on your own? You do? Wow! How many bedrooms have you got?'

Embarrassed that she hadn't offered to put them up overnight, Ava muttered, 'Five on the first floor, then there's'-

'Sue. Stop nattering.'

'Oh pay no attention to him.' Sue took Ava's arm and let herself be propelled quickly through the kitchen and into the garden. On the table, under a paperweight, photos spilled out. Real photos printed onto paper that you could pick up, peer at, stroke with pleasure and hold - not images on a screen. 'Jon, why don't you go through these with them while I put the kettle on?' She prayed he'd be able to make the link between the strangers on his lawn and the workmates he'd been close to.

As the visitors began to examine the photos, laughter rang out. 'Oh my god, look at that blouse. *So* Dynasty. What was I doing?'

Ava walked back into the house with her fingers crossed.

Sue followed her, not commenting on the state of the back door which stuck so Ava had to kick it open. 'Good old Jon eh? So … still as keen on him as ever?'

Ava just smiled. 'Well you know, you get older…'

'And wiser … Well it was never that important to us to be honest, the physical side as they delicately put it these days. Not like you two. The minute my back was turned there you were at it again – shagging away … in the office that time, remember?'

'God yes and you knew the chairman was in the foyer on one of his flying visits so you rang my phone, again and again.'

'Truth is Phil's idea of foreplay these days is to put his teeth in. No I can't be doing with all that.'

'But you're still so – you look …' Ava had to give up. Suzanne's arms were still smooth and taut, her legs brown. She looked like a magazine illustration of how to look at sixty but the glow had gone, there was an androgyny now. Perhaps that was Phil's preference, which was a surprising thought given the strength of his hug which lingered around Ava like a cloak.

'I bought a salon – it's been quite a good investment. Well, the bricks and mortar. And I get all the treatments free naturally. There's nothing more depressing than being in the gym now though. All those gorgeous bunnies around me.'

'Well, it's paid off. You've lasted, you two.' Ava poured coffees. 'Shall we go back outside?'

They settled back at the table, watching the two men heading up the garden.

There was a silence then Suzanne said, 'We've hit our rock Ava.'

'How do you mean? You … met someone?' Ava thought her livewire friend the more likely to flirt, to enjoy the game but then as she'd just said, sex had never been that important to her.

'Not me. Phil. Had the most normal of midlife crises you could imagine.'

Ava thought she caught the glint of a tear behind her friend's sunglasses. The sun emphasised the downward turn of an unhappy mouth, creating lines which hadn't been noticeable before. '*Phil?* I ... I didn't know.'

'Well you don't put it on a Christmas card.'

'But *Phil*. Who with? Why?'

'He said because he could. He wanted to do it before it was too late. He'd been talking to a bloke who'd said Viagra hadn't worked for him. It played on his mind and some little girl at work fluttered her eyelashes – false ones mind – and that was that.'

'Oh Sue. I'm so sorry.' At the top of the garden, Jon was boring Phil with the lawn's shortcomings and it looked as if Phil was steering him back to the house. Ava was desperate to finish the conversation before they came back.

'Well actually that wasn't that as it turned out.' With an ironic smile, Suzanne stirred a sweetener into her drink.

So Ava had been right, she had had a fling of her own.

Her friend's voice was quieter now. 'Someone else came on the scene. In the Leeds office, back up home. That was the one that worried me.

'Two affairs? What was he thinking?'

'What was he taking, you mean.'

Ava couldn't help smiling at the familiar earthy realism. 'You don't really mean two ... affairs? At the same time?'

They caught each other's eye and laughed out loud.

'Bloody hell. But you and Phil. You never seemed that ...' she had to choose her words here.

'Bothered? No. We weren't. Still aren't that much really. But it's just a child's eye view. If you don't play with your toys you'll lose them. Some other kid will take them.'

'God. What about you? How did you cope? I wish I'd been there to ... talk or something.'

She shrugged. 'Well it was always going to come, sooner or later. It's going on all around you, so sooner or later it'll hit you too. Well it hit you and Jon didn't it?'

Ava nodded. 'Like a hammer. I couldn't, *we* couldn't, turn it off, ignore it.' They were two strangers, the Ava and Jon from those days.

'Bet you still feel the same way, don't you?' Sue nudged her.

There was a pause. 'Not really. At least I'- She was going to say *I would but he can't* but it was hardly light pre-lunch conversation.

Sue picked up the hesitation. 'This must be little Syd? And she's a Mum now?' she collected a framed photo from the sideboard. 'Lovely. You're not really Granny material but it must be nice to have another generation coming up. You put a lot into her I know. You used to look exhausted after you'd had her for the weekend – oh sorry, I didn't mean how that came out.'

'I was exhausted, you're right. I never wanted motherhood but it just came with Jon. A lot of people would say it was the best of both worlds? No pregnancy, no giving birth, just the fun bits?'

'Is it fun?' Sue looked wistfully at the photo.

'No.' Ava's voice was firm. 'You haven't missed much at all Sue if I'm honest. Let's get out into the sun eh?'

They'd brought a litre of Bombay Sapphire and the first round quickly disappeared.

'Ave. Another drink?' Phil boomed from the kitchen as ice tinkled in glasses.

'Oh yes please Phil.' It was marvellous to have someone else in the house, doing something without causing mayhem. Jon always got in a muddle and Syd would just sit back and let Ava take the initiative and do everything.

When their glasses had been replenished, Phil took Jon to look over the Merc.

Ava asked, 'Did you, I mean have you got over it?'

'I'm really fond of him. I count myself lucky at my age to have him around.'

Her friend's pragmatism winded Ava. Sue's priorities had always been different from hers. A smarter house, a newer car, watching every ounce she put on and losing it immediately. A man at her side meant more to her than the space that her dignity would have achieved. 'I'll get the lunch. Just a sort of ploughman's,' she added apologetically. 'But there's some good wine.'

'Lovely.'

'Salad Sue?' Jon, remembering his manner, moved the bowl across the table. He watched fascinated as Sue's long manicured fingers delicately held the glass servers and recovered dressing from the bottom of the bowl before lifting it to her own plate.

'Jon?' Ava nudged him. 'May I have some too please?'

He hadn't heard her.

'Telling the truth. Now there's an unfashionable thing to do,' Phil helped himself to the cheddar. They were discussing the latest intake of interns, how each CV over-emphasised their abilities.

'Blame The Apprentice,' Sue bit into a stick of celery.

'Oh surely there's little choice,' Ava asked relishing grown-up conversation.

'You can't blame them. Everybody does it now. *Full consultation* means you've got ten minutes then we'll do what we wanted in the first place. Transparency means exactly the opposite. I was offered a bank loan the other day. Advantageous rates it said. Advantageous to them maybe not me with base rate at a quarter percent. And look at the pensioners, or rather non-pensioners I should call them. There's nothing left in the pot. You knew where it was all going. All been shifted sideways into the Caymans and wherever else it can't be got at.'

'Your own included Sue? Oh my god.'

'No, not us. We did what Jon did. Cashed in the very second we could. It probably won't last us but it's better than nothing – valueless share options, non-existent bonuses. That's how it was going, we could both see. And of course once it was all in Private Eye …'

What Jon did ... 'Was it?' Feeling sick, Ava sees Sue's slight shake of the head at Phil. 'What did they say?'

'Nothing much love,' Sue reassures her. 'No names anyway.'

'It'll still have been clear who they were talking about.'

'Well, only to those in the know.'

A lot of people in the City then. 'What did it say?' she asks again.

'Ava, you know the Eye. They've always thrown lots of rumours out there, some ridiculous, so they can't be sued. They invented fake news. It was just about the takeover, who moved out and why – remember old Hatton?'

'Yes of course.'

'Died.'

'Yes. But what did they say he did?'

'Well like I say, they were never going to be specific about what anyone *did*.'

'They just close that loophole and wait for someone to find another.'

'Fiscal retrenchment,' Sue quoted with her fingertips in the air, 'that was in the last annual report. The press tore it to shreds. All smoke and mirrors. Lies in other words. Everyone's doing it. *"Collateral damage"*– classic example. Means people get killed in wars,' she finished her wine, 'and business.'

Ava was silent, remembering the twin towers.

Phil topped her up. *'Care in the community*. Remember that? That's where it started and what have we got now? All sorts of loonies wandering around. Everything dressed up with words.'

There was a silence while everyone considered the elephant in the room. Jon had hardly spoken all through the lunch despite prompting from all of them.

'But then,' Ava tried to keep it light, 'How can you sign off audited accounts if you know they're full of lies?'

'Easily,' Sue and Phil said in unison.

'Things *have* changed.'

'No.'

Everyone turned to stare at Jon.

'Say hello to Rio for us!' They waved Sue and Phil off and turned back indoors.

'Shame they had to go early,' Ava murmured. As she began the washing up, she couldn't wait any longer. 'The money Jon? Please try to tell me what you can.'

'Money?' The light had gone from his eyes and her spirits dipped – he'd lost the grip he'd had in the company of visitors.

He left the kitchen – and the work – to Ava.

To her surprise, he came back almost immediately. 'Aha the money.' The theatricality made her grit her teeth. She steeled herself.

'Well Ava your clever old man took a bit of a long view there were too many debts black holes unsolved equations I did what folk have done since banknotes began.' On a good day Ava would have been pleased to hear this many words strung together but this didn't feel like a good day any more. The rumbling avalanche of words meant he'd be asleep soon, she knew.

'Hoarded them?' She couldn't believe this. Like an automaton, she carried on washing up.

'Not as such didn't leave it to the buzzards circling to pick up and fly off with not me no indeed it's here Ave most of it.' He tapped his temple and folded himself into the chair in the corner of the kitchen.

'So … where did the money come from? And *go?*'

There was a smug child's smile as his chin lifted. 'My money.'

Stupefied. That was a word she'd never used before. It entirely summed her up. Made to look stupid, gaping like a goldfish in her own kitchen.

Always waiting for the post – all the pages of that letter he burned. Then something else - the sudden escape to that god-awful house in France, made sense now, keeping low until he thought the thing he'd done had gone undetected. That must have been it. Why did he marry her? She hadn't asked for wealth – if anything, the reverse. Just for the two of them to be quietly happy beside the sea.

When she turned back to Jon, he was snoring.

'Christ Ava. How long's he been like that?' This isn't starting like a standard, polite thank-you call.

'I don't know Sue. It just feels like forever.'

'Jesus. We didn't know. How could we? He seemed so … *himself* … when he …'

'When he what?'

'He came in to the office. You knew that though?'

'Well he was doing consultancy commissions.'

'No – well he could have emailed the reports.'

'So what did he do? What happened?'

'He asked us to sign things off.'

'Things?'

'Pension transfers – like we did before, you remember. The Plan Fund. And then another time – last year - the mortgages.'

'And you did. Sign. Last year.'

'Well yes. It was Jon Wilkes. *The* Jon Wilkes. Why wouldn't we?'

'What else Sue?' There was a pause.

'Phil and I will be in Rio next week. Leave it till then? For old times' sake?'

'What for?'

Her old friend sighed. 'It might be better perhaps Ava if you spoke to a solicitor.'

"Earn money from home … easy income … £10000 a month. All you need is a phone."

But who would look after Jon while she was out selling double-glazed conservatories?

Ava's head pounded. *I don't know why I didn't do it years ago. Perhaps we wouldn't be in this mess now. And who'd give me a reference?*

Ava dialled the number and a man answered. But Ava it seemed was overqualified and had very reasonable expectations of a salary, given her experience, which sadly the conservatory people would not be able to match.

The next day the only post was a wedding invitation on the mat … a date in September that at the moment, was so far off as to be able to convince herself that it might never happen. A handwritten ps gushed

So looking forward to seeing you all again. It'll be nice to catch up. Tania

Ava hadn't seen or heard from Tania since Edith's funeral and doubted she'd recognise her if she passed her in the street but something else had begun gnawing away in the back of her mind.

A wedding. Husband and wife.

It had been on Woman's Hour while she'd been driving Jon to the specialist in Canterbury last time. A change in the law. Ava simply hadn't paid it much attention. Spousal something? Privilege? Something about a wife testifying against her husband.

Was that why Jon asked her to marry him?

I can't remember what I can't remember
frogs? toads? frogs? toads?

The garage forecourt is icy and Ava treads gingerly, placing each foot where it looks as if there might be a foothold. The distance between the car and the cash machine seems to stretch and a passing driver sounds his horn, making her jump. Typical that today the Pay at Pump wasn't working. She'd get her hundred out, pay for the petrol and have enough for the shopping

The vile weather - leaden skies for months now – has turned, snarling at everyone. The house is so cold, Ava goes out because the shops are warmer. She leaves Jon tucked under a duvet and crosses her fingers he doesn't start any more fires. Edging up behind the woman using the machine, Ava breathes a sigh of relief.

'Bloody thing's not working,' the woman mutters and sweeps past, heading for the shop.

Remembering the skating rink she's just crossed Ava thinks she'll give it a go anyway, feeding the plastic card into the blinking green slot.

YOUR CARD HAS BEEN RETAINED

PLEASE CONTACT CUSTOMER SERVICES

'Oh for God's sake,' Ava says loudly in case anyone is watching and thinks she's overdrawn her overdraft then spins to stalk back to the car but the spin, the one thing she has walked so carefully to avoid this morning, takes her off her feet and crashes her instantly onto her left knee which hurts more than she has ever known anything can hurt. 'Christ almighty,' she screams in agony ashamed of blasphemy and outraged at the blinding pain she has so stupidly caused herself.

All at once, she is surrounded by concern – this is a nice town remember, with kind people who volunteer to call for an ambulance, ask if her if she can move and at the same time tell her not to move. Bloody bank. Slowly, gingerly, she feels how much she can move and is gratefully aware it doesn't cause more pain, so she must be okay. Without knowing how, she finds she is standing and the people who have apparently helped her up melt away until only one man, a fireman he tells her, is left checking to see if she can carry on with her life.

'I feel so stupid,' she mutters crossly, face crumpled.

'You won't be the only person to have gone over this morning,' he grins, teeth very white against his Asian skin. 'Just be glad you didn't do more damage. I think the pavement will be all right.'

Despite herself, she manages a laugh and says yes, she thinks she'll make it back to the car. The fill-up can wait. 'I can drive – it's automatic.' But the first step she takes squeezes another little scream from the back of her throat. She can't move.

'Here,' the fireman offers her his arm, 'Push onto this and support the bad side. Let's see if we can get you home.'

He is so solidly reassuring – training probably – that her panic subsides and slowly, they inch-hop their way back to the Saab. 'Are you local? I can follow you home, make sure you get in?' His eyes are very brown and his hair is expertly cut and gelled into a quizzical Tintin flip at the front.   But he seems genuinely willing to help and after making sure she's in and the car starts, he moves across the forecourt to a van signwritten with a local plumbing firm.

Their two vehicles leave the garage and people who have been politely patient, waiting for this little emergency to clear, can get back to doing what they came here for and the rest of their lives.

True to his word, he follows her as she drives down the ice-glossed High Street, past Steve's shop where she had been intending to stop for sausages (Jon's favourite), to the sea and left onto the Esplanade. When Ava has pulled onto the drive, the van follows and the fireman/plumber comes to her before she can even open her door. 'Take it easy now – you've done well to get home – let's see if we can get you up those steps,' he nods at the five which guard the front door. Jon has always liked this arrangement. Already taller than most of his visitors, he looks haughtily down at whoever has rung the bell. Which works well with cold-callers, not so well with friends.

At the foot of the steps, Ava wonders wildly if the fireman will do what firemen are supposed to do and hoist her over his shoulder, but instead, one firm arm goes round her waist and he half-hoists her on her good foot up to the door.

'Oh god, thank you,' her voice wavers and she's suddenly very conscious of his powerful aftershave. Perhaps you need it, dealing with plumbing, to block out other smells.

'Delayed shock,' he frowns. 'Let's get you in. Is there someone home who can make you a cuppa? I know it's what people say, but it does help, hot tea.'

'Yes. No. Sorry,' she shakes her head wrestling the key which sticks as usual. 'He's in but not … well. Yes tea. I can do it.'

'But you shouldn't. Can I? Look,' he props her against her bannisters and fishes inside his coat for a business card, handing it over with suitably Edwardian propriety, a belated introduction. Considering how close they have been, how strong she already knows he is and those dark brown eyes, this is … *Mo Collins*. 'See? Plumber when not fighting fires. So now we know each other …?' His eyes enquire.

'Oh yes, of course. Ava. And thank you. Really.'

'Come on. Kettle.'

Once he has got her sitting in her own, glacial but thankfully fairly tidy kitchen, Ava watches him. He's adept, doesn't waste time. It reminds her of someone she hasn't thought of in a while.

'Cups in here?' he asks in his confident everyman voice and points to a cupboard.

'Good guess.'

'Just see a lot of kitchens in my jobs.' He pours water onto the teabags.

'Of course. You must do, one way or another, flooded or on fire I expect.'

'Well it's not always that dramatic,' and they laugh together, Ava and her rescuer who is really a plumber but sometimes takes risks and is a fireman.

'Any paracetamol?' And he follows her gesture to the other cupboard, popping two onto the saucer he passes to her.

Then the door opens and in dishevelled pyjamas, Jon shambles in. He seems to take in what Ava recounts of her fall and rescue but you can never tell and Mo, draining his tea, says he'll see himself out, not waiting to be thanked again.

Alone with Jon, Ava can only remember Mo's aftershave and the easy, overpowering sensation of strength that emanated from the arm round her waist. *Get real, you are – literally – old enough to be his mother. He's in the pub with his mates now, telling them how he saved an old girl who'd gone over on the ice…*

'I'm hungry Ave. Are we going out?'

She opened the cupboard for beans which he'd usually eat, but there was a gap. She'd been going to buy them this morning.

That left the bank to sort out as soon as she could hobble to the phone dreading the interminable muzak, because their High Street branch, along with the other three banks, had closed.

not the butcher, the plumber then or maybe as
well christ tart it's those wellingtons what
man can resist them bend her over and oh my
christ

'I'm sorry Mrs Wilkes, I'm afraid your account is overdrawn.'

After the never-ending security questions, the girl sounded about fourteen and had no real grasp of English beyond the training session's standard answers. Ava could picture a delicate, dark-skinned girl, self-esteem boosted by the status her job conferred. This was going to be slow.

'I have an overdraft facility,' Ava tried to keep it formal to help her understand.

'Yes ma'am but I regret to say however that you have exceeded that amount.'

'How? I'm very careful to keep my outgoings within the limit of my income.' Ava was indignant. It was the way they'd agreed to split household costs, with Jon handling the bigger bills to keep it simple. The annuity she'd bought had provided a small lump sum which she'd been happy to plough into the house and the Saab's clutch rebuild. It was the price she'd cheerfully pay for freedom from work and commuting and stress.

'I regret I can only discuss details of an account if you are a named account holder.'

'I'm not asking you to. Surely my money went in this morning, to this account of mine - ours?'

'I regret to say *What a godawful job, being paid to regret everything you say* ... that no payment has been paid into your account today.'

'Oh well that's it then. It's just a mistake. I'll ring them.' With a sigh, Ava hung up and swivelled her chair to the box file where she kept the slim clutch of Sun annuity papers.

She shuffled to the living room door and checked Jon was dozing.

At least this lot were in Surrey. More security questions. Her policy number, her age, place of birth, mother's maiden name, favourite teacher, favourite food ...?

A delay. Could she check the policy number? Some had been updated with new prefixes...?

Ava eased her knee up and placed her foot carefully on the desk. She'd need to take more painkillers soon, the throb was deepening. Outside it was already getting dark and there'd be no chance of getting Jon out for fresh air although she'd be happy to let that one go, the way she felt. But that meant he'd be awake most of the night.

'Hello, sorry to keep you waiting. I think there's been a mistake of some sort. We've definitely got no policy of that number.'

'But I've been receiving payments for nearly ten years – no, more. Every month.'

They checked and re-checked her name, bank account details and the reference on the original forms she'd received. No.

There was not, nor ever had been, such a policy to the best of their knowledge.

Ava hung up and stared at the phone. The last thing she wanted to do was use it again, listen to the interminable tuneless music and apologies, but she rang the bank back. It was getting colder now and she wanted the comfort of the throw on her chair in the other room but it was too far away. How would she cope if this knee didn't get better soon? Overnight?

A different voice, but equally lilting despite the headset she was using, told Ava they would endeavour to ascertain the source of the monthly payments paid to her account. There was another long bout of lift-music. As she waited, Ava tried to imagine the baking heat at the other end of this call. They wouldn't know what icy ground meant, would always be pleased to get to their air-conditioned office every day.

She was, Ava thought, always cold in this house. Even in summer, because it faced north-east, it was at best pleasantly cool, never hot.

'Hello ma'am? I am so sorry for keeping you waiting but regret you do appear to have been regrettably misinformed. The payments have been paid to your account

direct from an account held in the name of Mr Jon Wilkes
of the same address as yourself ma'am.'

'What? Not Sun Alliance?'

'Yes ma'am. Precisely.'

Perhaps it was a tax thing.

She hobbled into the living room and eased herself into the
chair with the footrest, wrapping the throw around her, the
voices she'd just heard replaying in her head … mistake,
misinformed, regret. And then *no further credit facility.*

Jon snored gently and from his open mouth, drying
saliva formed a tidy white line in the crease to his jowl.

'What did you do Jon? What did you do?' She spoke
aloud without meaning to and the familiar voice stirred him.

'Who are you?' He was a toddler jolted from sleep.
Then his focus returned and he grunted, 'Going out?'

'No. It's icy. Dangerous. I fell, remember?'

'Are we going out?'

This endless repetition is so wearing. Surely she's
entitled to have a grown-up conversation with the man she
married? What the hell has he done? She's staring at a
betrayal so immense it's incomprehensible and so keeps
making excuses like *misunderstanding, oversight,
misinterpretation.* The truth is-

'-No. Jon listen. Sometimes, when you try, you can
remember things that happened a long time ago. Like when
Suzanne and Phil came, you know?'

He looked willing to try it, closing his eyes to
concentrate.

'Good, that's good. Now – when we left work and came
here to live, we sorted out … an *annuity* for me, do you
remember that?' Vaguely she felt using the correct term
instead of childspeak might jog his memory.

There was a long, too long, silence. Then, from
underneath his eyelashes, tears began to wash down his
face.

Ava sat on the shabby carpet, legs splayed and back protesting. The front room with the sea view, Jon's study, was in chaos. She had pulled every file out of his cabinet and stared appalled at the disarray. Instead of the accountant's approach to their life, lay MoTs, insurance policies going back to before they first came here, council tax bills, bank statements (which she refused to read), bills for everything imaginable from every trade – plumbers and more plumbers, electricians from the year the lights kept fusing, tax codes … as jumbled as a deck of cards which had just been shuffled. It would take months to sort out, and she doubted it would be worth doing. Everywhere she looked there was nothing about income, the lifeblood she and Jon were scraping by on. 'Must be another box file somewhere. Two I suppose, one each,' she muttered, hauling herself up from the mess with an involuntary groan.

She checked he was still snoozing. He sprawled, his old gardening trousers making it look as if he'd had a hard morning digging when in reality he'd not moved from the chair since breakfast. She went upstairs, glancing upwards and, pointedly not looking at the damp mark, considered the loft hatch. Could he have put them in the attic, thinking they were matters which were settled? Anything was possible.

She loathed the heavy loft ladder, always fearing it would amputate her fingertips as it crashed down, but before she had a chance to wrestle with it, Jon wailed for her.

Needing fresh air, she settled him then suggested a short, slow walk. It was a windy day and the sun was fickle so she dressed him carefully, layering sweaters and with a hat folded into his pocket. Then she threw on her own raincoat, collected Edith's walking stick from the stand and they set off down to the clifftop. Before long, he was shuffling as usual, just behind her. The bay curved out beneath them and they leant against the railings soaking up any sun there was going, the breeze sending clouds flying along.

'What can you see darling?' She was intrigued to see him focused on the water, high tide bringing it up to spray over the jetty, but his gaze was on the deeper water where one or two kitesurfers practised and fell in regularly.

'They'll be all right, don't worry.'

'No.' His head shook vehemently. 'Ava.' His eyes narrowed. 'Water.'

It was hard to know which was more tiring; the relentless repetition or the detective work needed to try to follow his thinking. It was bound to be as frustrating for him as it was for her, she supposed and set to trying to follow his gaze.

'Ava. Ava.'

'I'm sorry darling, I can't see anything. Just the waves.'

Suppose he was right and there was something – or someone – in there? Someone drowning? One of the surfers? But they all looked unconcerned, falling off, disappearing under the waves, then hauling themselves back on again for another go.

Or something? A marker of some sort? Bobbing in and out of sight as the waves obscured then revealed it? But try as she might, Ava could see nothing. Nothing in the sea. And nothing in the bank.

When they got home, Ava wondered how many passers-by had seen the long dark stain down the legs of his chinos.

A day later, she'd exhausted all the possibilities, so she'd have to face the loft. Somehow she had managed to persuade the bank to agree a temporary increase of their overdraft, but it wouldn't last beyond the month. It was a beautiful morning and she shrank from the idea of the ladder and the cobwebs which hung in the roof, but there was nothing else for it.

Looking around, there was actually very little of hers – most of the boxes contained Jon's mother's stuff plus the sort of thing everyone puts away on the basis it might be useful one day. The kettle, its handle broken, still worked but the plug fizzed, each time she had used it. She took it to the traphatch and dropped it, with some pleasure, onto the floor below where the lid bounced off then rolled along the landing and teetered on the top step. One thing she could control.

But still nothing about pensions at all.

So that left the Anderson shelter. Mildewed, spider-infested and overgrown. She heaved the treacherous ladder back up through the hatch and set off up the garden. Bloody Jon.

She pulled ivy off the door until she could drag it open and the smell of damp earth met her as she shone a torch round the web-hung interior, at the tools hung in a line on the edge of a shelf on the dank wall. An axe, a shovel, an auger, a club hammer to dig them out with, if it came to that. A shiver ran down her back at the thought of being incarcerated in there with the spiders.

Ava was used to dealing with everything on her own but the endless weight of problems, illness, mess, worries had built into a black mass that hung over her awake and invaded her sleep. This couldn't go on. Could no-one help?

The office. She would ring, speak to HR, then follow a trail of phone numbers until she found someone who knew something about it.

Before she could get started though, something happened.

The next day, mid-afternoon, the doorbell rang breaking into the Ava's precious free time while Jon slept. She checked him on her way through the hall, but his nap looked undisturbed.

'Yes?' she knew she was scowling at the pin-striped man on the step below the front door.

'My name is Patrick Howell. Good afternoon.' He handed over his card. 'You may know our offices on the High Street? Howell Homes? Are you the householder by any chance? Ms …?' he glanced at her left hand on the door jamb and she remembered her wedding ring on the kitchen windowsill.

'Yes. Wilkes. But …'

'I would really appreciate the chance to talk over a proposition with you. If you're free that is? No time like the present is there?'

Normally, she'd have sent him packing but on the other hand, since this chap was on the doorstep, perhaps she could at least discover if her finger-in-the-wind guess at the house's value had been anything like near the mark.

'I can give you ten minutes,' she waved him into the hall, 'Mr Howell.'

'Pat,' he had shaken her hand before she had time to stop him. 'My friends call me Pat,' and he passed by her on a wave of deep, expensive aftershave.

Leading him into the kitchen, Ava was suddenly aware of the scuffed paintwork that she had been meaning to tackle. Come to that, she felt scuffed too. Washed-out and only half there.

Well, let him earn his money. The house would surely be marketed as having potential and he'd have to tackle any haggling that arose.

'My husband hasn't been well,' she jammed her ring back on. 'And he's asleep at the moment but I can tell him of your interest as soon as he's up to it. Actually, what *is* your interest in this house?'

'Your husband…' He looked taken aback. 'Well it might be better if I spoke to you both together …'

Now that he was in the house, Ava didn't want to lose this chance. 'No, you've got my full attention now. And I'm not inexperienced with property. He and I worked together at BHM – it's SRZ now, of course, in the City? You'll be familiar with the name I imagine?'

Pat Howell looked at her and she could see the decision being made. 'Right then. I'll put my cards on the table.' He opened his briefcase.

The conversation flowed smoothly, leaving Ava with an uneasy feeling that if she nodded at the wrong time, it would be like bidding without intending to at an auction. She'd find she'd acquiesced to something that would not be to her advantage.

In the end, it was simple enough. Once cleared, the land the house stood on would enable Howell Homes to develop a gated estate, 'cutting-edge design for discerning buyers' he assured her, by allowing access to the gardens of the three houses in the quiet cul-de-sac behind them. All the existing houses would be demolished, he explained, and he had been assured in discussions with local planners that the draft layout he was showing Ava now would meet with no opposition.

She watched as he worked through the papers. For an office worker, his hands were rough and large with dark hairs that glistened alien inside the crisp pink cuffs. His suiting was pin-striped, the chalky pattern confidently broad and so *obviously* she thought, a man like this would choose a loud salmon and garnet tie. With his immaculately-cut steely blue hair and the deep tan of his neck and wrists, he was a glorious peacock in the faded sittingroom…

There was a memory inside Ava of watching someone else's hands – *not* Jon's, she prickled slightly - doing something with a pile of papers as they stood side by side a long time ago. She had become hotly aware of the physical reaction sparked high inside her, had lost the thread and smiling, had to ask him to go over it again. Which, with a grin, the hands' owner had been happy to do. Well, at her age, at least she was safe from such diversions now. When had that happened?

In fact, just after she and Jon had got together, when he was in America, she'd worked briefly with a man certainly ten years younger than her and was astonished when he'd made an urbanely elegant pass. Her initial reaction was to feel flattered, thanking him before declining. When Jon flew home, she told him about it and he said it seemed very odd behaviour in a young man. Which wasn't what she had meant but she was too tied up with sorting out her father's estate then.

In the beginning, her relative youth had made Jon seem younger himself. Lucky bugger, she looks like she could go all night. Can he keep up? Keep it up?, the laughter rolled behind her back.

Now, she looked and felt at least as old as Jon. The age gap had whipped around and slapped her in the face. Ava had never thought to question how long he might retain his vigour in bed. He'd never mentioned it. Both superstitious perhaps that, just by talking about it, the affliction would be brought down on them. Keep it up? No not now. In fact, not for most of their marriage. Christ, somebody up there was nodding with satisfaction.

She made herself concentrate again…

He had chosen to approach Ava first, Pat Howell explained, spreading plans and brochures on the table, as Halcyon's plot would allow the best access but if she wasn't interested, he felt sure approaches to her neighbours on either side would be successful.

In other words, if she didn't sell, she'd find herself living in the middle of a housing estate. The 'little boxes' that Jon had always railed against would be crowding in around him, driving him even further into himself, she could imagine.

And demolishing Halcyon certainly solved the issue of haggling over what they could afford to do to it.

As she shut the front door behind Pat Howell, Ava felt the weight of the house pressing around her, a reproachful silence falling tight-lipped over the cool air in the wood-panelled hall.

How could you think of doing this to me, Ava? The house's innate masculinity seemed indignant. Its air of faded paternalism was the thing she battled every day. Like an Edwardian gentleman, the house needed a private income and staff.

'I'm sorry,' she spoke aloud. 'God knows I've tried to keep up with you. But I can't keep you going any longer. I'm tired. And broke. And you're too damn big for me to manage. I've had enough.'

In the living room doorway Jon stood, stricken. 'You're not going to leave me are you Mummy?'

Like a woman with a secret lover (and Ava knew how that felt) she could hardly wait for him to slide into oblivious sleep that night so that she could gorge on the project. But when she did, the numbers were hopeless. They simply owed too much.

Ava was awake. Rain was splashing against the window from the blocked gutter.

How could she have been so stupid? Imagining the technicolour Pat Howell was some benevolent Good Fairy who'd be able to turn her life around in thirty fortuitous minutes? Her euphoria disappeared with her breath in the cold bedroom and the cloud of her surroundings settled around her, heavier than ever.

And anyway, how had Pat Howell discovered she needed to sell?

In the study, she flicked on the laptop and cursed at the blue bar's grindingly slow progress. Finally, she could search BHM. *Did she mean Roberts Wilkes?* Of course not, she knew the name of the firm that had drawn her blood for all those years.

She shook her head and searched again. There'd obviously been changes. Good thing probably. And Hatton, thank goodness, was dead.

She typed in Financial Actuaries and saw SumnerRobertsZakaria. A smart new logo with the Z twisting around the S and R. The office was where she'd left it, at the bottom of City Road but the old name had disappeared along with the old people.

Priti Zakaria. Imagine that tiny girl who she, Ava, had brought in to the firm as an intern, in the big office with the view now. Astonishing.

But why should it be? Priti had worked harder than everyone, was studying when Ava left and wept copiously at the thought of losing her mentor. She deserved whatever she'd achieved, Ava thought with a tinge of almost parental pride.

thought I hadn't seen him did you tart well let
me tell you I saw him all right and I'll punch
him if I ever see him again

'Ah. Post.' Jon made his insistent shamble towards the doormat where frozen food and life insurance fliers jostled for his business.

'Oh let's leave that. Get out while it's still nice.' Ava took the letters from him, trying not to notice that at least two had carefully typed addresses – not the bland computer-printed sort, but the type which would begin Final Notice and end darkly warning that their home would be at risk if she failed … blah, blah.

Jon trundled down the path as she shut the letters in the kitchen drawer with the others and struggled to shut it. What was she supposed to do? Go on the streets? What could she possibly do whilst watching Jon like a hawk? Their income had flatlined with yet another year of minimal interest rates, the bank had written last week to ask what were their plans to address the overdraft situation.

They were close to the junction now and she steered him away from the turning that led to the High Street. Walking that way was depressing, like watching slow motion car crashes. When she and Jon first came here, there had been four banks, two grocers, two butchers, a real baker, a shoe mender. The hardware store had been the first to succumb becoming a Costa and even that had put up the shutters now. The gaps were filled with hairdressers and beauty salons. Charity shops and estate agents were all that was left of the town's old businesses.

Jon stopped. 'Tart's boudoir.'

'Mm,' she could see what he meant, chandeliers and velvet upholstered sofas gave the nail bar a louche air. 'Let's go down The Vale, Jon' and he obligingly swung to follow her.

He'd taken to walking a little behind her, requiring her to glance back every so often to make sure he hadn't taken it into his head to veer into someone's garden. Looking back was what she did best now, she reasoned with herself, since the future held what looked suspiciously like a yawning void.

When they reached the promenade, she let him choose east or west, knowing it would please him to do so and after he had raised his nose like a dog and sniffed, sure enough he broke into a small smile, a child with a secret and they headed round the bandstand until the harbour came into view. Dark clouds had rolled in now though, the sun had gone and a squall blew inland threatening to drench them.

'Oh hell.' The last thing Ava wanted was Jon to catch a chill. She grabbed his hand and they turned up the side street and ran into the only thing open.

From the outside, the place hadn't altered in all the years Ava and Jon had walked past. The Gingham Kitchen looked forlorn, but the threatening deluge overcame her reluctance. A small, very old man took his time to potter towards their table which like all the others, was covered with a slightly sticky gingham-patterned oil cloth. Tutting at the rain that ran from their clothing and puddled on his shabby floor, he offered a menu.

'Just tea please. For two,' Ava said and he returned behind the counter. 'I've never been in here before.'

'Wheels,' Jon shook his head disdainfully.

'Wheels?'

The inside was bland, plain white walls relieved with pictures haphazardly dotted around. Not pictures, but paintings, she realised, peering at the nearest. Two people, a man and a woman, shown from behind, sat at the very table where she and Jon sat now. Hunched forward over teacups, they stared out of the window in front of her, where rain smashed ferociously onto the glass, threatening the structure of the whole café. In the picture too, the street outside was rain-sodden. The only difference was that the picture's interior was festooned with every beach apparatus imaginable. Underneath, beside a modest price, the title was 'Mustn't grumble'.

'I really like this one,' she smiled as the owner returned with cups and teapot.

'One of my son's.'

'He's talented.'

'He wants to get a proper job. Don't pay the rent does it? Being an "artist".'

'Oh. I'm sorry.' Ava knew how that felt. 'What a shame.'

'This place'll have to go soon. My legs are bad. I can't keep it up.'

Ava bit her lip to avoid repeating herself. It was a shame really. The shop needed – well she hated to say a 'woman's touch', but it was spartan, not welcoming.

'Do you live upstairs?'

'Up there?' he nodded upwards. 'No. They were building that Wimpy estate when I married his mother. It was her idea. *A bungalow to retire to* she said. Three grand or so it was back then. Mind they said we were mad, moving out of the town to the country like.'

Ava nodded, picturing the estate leading up to the new shopping centre that was responsible for the High Street's dip in fortunes. 'Not the country now though is it?'

'No,' a snort of laughter made him cough. 'Not three grand neither.'

Soon, they finished their drinks and the downpour had turned off like a tap.

When she lay in bed that night, Jon snoring securely beside her – she couldn't sleep, but at least she knew where he was – the idea came into her head.

The house said she and Jon were an upstanding couple but right from the word go it had changed him – he was no longer the attentive lover but a householder. What a shame he couldn't be both.

And all Ava's time, all her energy, went on maintaining the bloody house, not her and not their marriage. As if the outer appearance being kept up meant all was well within which it most definitely was not. What did it matter, she argued with herself, if the front garden needed mowing? Her hair needed cutting just as badly, and styling, and colouring so that the grey didn't show. And she yearned for the demonstration of affection that their love-making had been. *Silly girl, bed doesn't mean affection to a man. It just means sex. You of all women should know that.*

But what I wanted was love. What a farce.

It was time to cash in. She would ring Pat Howell when the office opened and see what, if anything, she could realise.

The streetlights were still on when she slipped out of bed and went downstairs carefully avoiding the squeaky third tread. Lifting her coat from the hall stand she put it on, padded quietly into the study and flicked on the computer.

She began by listing the things it would need, the money which would go out before anything at all would come in. Then she spent a ridiculous amount of time doodling alternative names. She knew why *The Sea Garden* was something she was trying to avoid but she settled on it for now. It made sense. The business was limited by its physical size but anything larger would be more than she'd be able to handle alone in the winter months. In the busy summer months, she'd be able to use the space in the walled garden for more tables and find students willing to clean tables and take orders. The menu would be small, serving anything from coffee and cake in the mornings to early suppers. It was, after all, what she did now every day, just on a bigger scale. And the flat above would be a shoebox to keep Jon safe in.

Allowing herself to daydream through a paint website Ava settled on the slatey blue of the Channel for the walls which would be a perfect backdrop for the paintings she had already decided on selling, reckoning that the prospect of more customers would encourage the man's son to agree to this. A small percentage of his sales would provide her with another revenue stream and she might supplement this with some work by other local artists from time to time.

She'd caught sight of the kitchen as they'd waited for their teas and it looked a workable enough space – she'd be able to park Jon at the table where she could keep an eye on him. That pulled her up short with a shiver. How long would that last for? One summer? Two? Two summers ago, he'd seemed no worse than forgetful, now look at him.

Life was a series of constant adaptations. A lot of time had passed since her childhood. The school they'd sent her to taught 'get' was common and now everyone said they wanted to 'get' this or that off the menu. And Ava had once been smacked for 'grabbing' but now even Sainsbury's exhorted you to Grab Your Bags. Not that Ava could afford to shop there, but she collected Jon's prescriptions from their pharmacy on the way to Aldi.

The bottomless void of uncertainty filled her with dread but then she chided herself that no-one knew what lay in the future anyway. She was probably just cold. It was 6.04, still an hour before the heating was due to come on. She pulled her coat tighter and began to play around with a website before deciding social media would be just as good, more current and suited to the artistic community that washed around the coast. Gradually she forgot the cold and lost herself in the plans. How delicious it was to have this world where she was in control.

Then she flicked through the estate agents' pages. It was impossible to tell though what the house was worth simply because it was such a one-off and she wasn't going to take Howell's word for it. Ava settled for the lowest price in what looked like a band of houses of the same age and with roughly the same number of rooms.

When Jon ambled downstairs and into the kitchen she realised with a start that he would be the first person she'd have to convince of the idea's worth. Or was that right? Might it be better to make all the enquiries then present him with the sort of resumé she would once have produced at work, with a summary and recommendations?

Perhaps that was what he had been missing in this new life, the scaffolding of structure, of decision-making and analysis. Being cut adrift in early retirement was maybe what had tipped him over the edge from chronically careful decision-making to chronic indecision. And worse.

She made her way out to the kitchen, filled the kettle and began the routine of feeding, shaving, showering, drying, dressing and settling him down, not in a playpen, but in the sunny corner of the living room with his Telegraph which took up most of the rest of her morning. The Sea Garden evaporated from her mind like dew.

'The Boy' was significantly older than that, she could see as he brought two cups of tea to the table and straightening the long black pinny round his waist, sat, straightened his neck and folded his hands on the table. He had, she saw, perfect oval nails.

'So'- they both began at once.

'No, sorry, you first,' he said.

Ava began as she had rehearsed, picking up the threads she'd woven into the phone call she'd made the day before, complimenting his art and how the café looked, then adding, 'It's just a shame …'

'…there are no customers.' His lips pursed.

'Well I'm sure there often are, but when I pass by, it's more often'-

'-Empty.'

She hoped he wasn't going to be difficult then thought she probably would be in his seat. 'Look I'd love to offer you a partnership. I've very little (*no*, she thought) capital, but I could do the catering side of things and leave you to concentrate on your art. It must be really hard doing both and your father'-

'Isn't getting any younger.'

'And with a bit of PR, we could build up the footfall, focus on attracting customers interested in art, maybe set up a couple of exhibitions a year- '

'Tried that.'

If he had, it was the first Ava had heard about it. 'I hoped you'd at least consider the offer.'

'Oh,' The Boy sighed, stretching that long neck again for all the world like a swan, 'I'll consider anything, me.'

242

'I don't think,' Ava gambled, 'either of us has much choice.'

Under finely-shaped brows, he narrowed his eyes at her, 'You wouldn't be the first bored wife thinking she can do this better than I can. Helped out by a cash injection from a husband who works in the City and wants to keep her amused.'

Ava could only laugh. 'Boredom and for that matter, cash injections, don't come into this, believe me. I need to earn money, not spend it and my husband needs – and is going to need – care. He needs to be somewhere I can keep an eye on him while I work.'

'What's wrong with him if you don't mind me asking?'

Their teas were getting cold. This would be the first time she'd told anyone else what she knew was true. 'Early onset dementia.'

'Christ, I'm sorry.' Colour flooded over his face. 'What I said about'-

'-Shall we just move on? I didn't explain myself very well, so let's start again. Christopher, isn't it? Can I call you that?'

'My friends' and Ava crossed her fingers under the table, hoping that meant she was going to be one, 'call me Chrissie. On nights out,' he stared at her intently, 'that is.'

'That's both our cards on the table then,' Ava said. 'So how about it?'

'Well,' he stretched his long neck again like a ballet dancer. 'Better give you the guided tour I suppose.'

He flipped the sign over to Closed and took Ava through to the back door, warning her to take care of the rubbish bags piled at the foot of iron stairs leading upwards. Once they'd made it to the top, Ava gasped with pleasure at the sea glimpse the flat roof gave, down between the houses to the bandstand on the seafront.

The flat was topsy-turvy, done for the builder's convenience, plumbing all on one side of the Victorian building, so the lounge was small and they'd put the kitchen in a spacious room, big enough for a table and a sofa, with a fireplace. Past the bathroom, a tiny staircase led up into the two attic rooms.

'And I'll suppose you'll want to 're-brand' the place – they all do. Call it Christopher's Corner or something equally saccharine.'

'Well I did think about … because I think it's a bit under-used at the moment … how do you feel about *The Sea Garden*?'

'Oh,' he glanced past her, at the door to the garden which even on this sunlit morning was closed, looking surprised. 'The garden's not something I really think about at all, not my thing you know.'

'I guessed. But it could double your number of covers in the summer. And the takings with it.'

'I'd have to have a word with the old man – the lease is in his name – but he'd be glad not to have to do as much here, I think. I'm not promising anything mind.'

'I understand.'

'When,' Christopher's long, artist's hands unfolded in supplication, 'were you thinking of making a start?'

Ava stood in his shop wearing a dress that looked as if it had been washed too many times. Like all butchers who need an analytical eye to gauge quality, Steve recognised he was a perfectionist and not the easiest to live with perhaps. He longed to plunge his big hand into the till and pass her a fistful of notes *Go treat yourself my love* he could say. *Get your hair done too – I don't mind the silvery look you've got now, don't change that. But it could do with a bit of a smarten-up.* Or whatever women called it. If he could bear to listen to Pauline in the evenings, he'd probably know the right thing to say, but the last time he tuned in, she was cracking on about having an artistic eye, the carpet needing to go and a wood floor instead and just look at the state of this kitchen. Dimly, he gathered she was on about refurbing it and felt so deeply that it hurt, that if he was going to pay for anyone's kitchen to be done up, it had to be Ava's. If only her bloody husband would do the decent thing and die

244

like Steve thought he'd done. He'd make her a merry widow all right.

'Eh?' He looked at Ava.

'Well,' she carried on, 'I said I'm opening – re-opening -a little café, calling it The Sea Garden and well, at the beginning, I won't pretend I'll be your biggest customer, but I hope it'll build up over the first few months. I thought I'd do casseroles through the winter months. And lasagnes. Then in the summer, roast chickens – do a whole one as a sharing dish, you know? And your gammon's always proper ham so I'd like to use that. I don't think I'll be able to buy a lot to start with but I'd really like to use you. If you don't mind.'

He would have laid down on the floor so she could use him as a doormat.

'Well,' he swallowed. 'That sounds great. If you're not buying a lot to start with, why don't I extend you some credit, just to get things going? We'll keep a tab, so you don't lose track, then look at it after a few months?'

At first he thought she was going to cry but she swallowed hard, extended a hand over the counter and accepted. Perfect. They chatted for a little while, he made notes in his delivery book and promised that if she ever needed anything, he'd do his best to help. He'd mention The Sea Garden at the next Chamber of Commerce, make sure everyone knew how good it was going to be.

There it was again, that little flutter of self-doubt in her eyes but she squared her shoulders and thanked him, shaking his hand again. She would ring when they'd finished decorating, about a week before they were due to re-open, so she could get cooking and freezing.

He would never forget the feel of her hand in his.

Wait. *They* were due to re-open? Was that the husband then? Surely she didn't have someone else? Well if so, he'd see them off.

'Is there much to do?'

'Well the Food Health people think so,' she smiled ruefully. All the budget's going into a new steel kitchen.

But I can paint the tables and chairs – shabby chic, you know – and the garden'll come into its own once the bulbs are up. Christopher says there are loads.'

Something stirred in Steve's memory bank. 'Oh. Oh, wait a minute, I know the place don't I? Down Cliff Road?'

'That's it,' she grinned. 'It used to be really popular when his mother ran it but it's gone a bit downhill – he's just been using it as a studio really. Any customers coming in have been a bit of a nuisance to be honest. But he'll be able to work in the outhouse in the garden and we hope his paintings will sell when people see it's been done up. And the flat's going to be nice once it's had a lick of paint.'

'Perfect,' Steve beamed. And it was. Christopher – yes he knew him. And his alter ego Chrissie, the one with the long blonde wig who sometimes turned up in the pubs down by the harbour. He'd be no competition at all. 'Perfect.' So that just left the shell of a husband. No competition at all, he reckoned.

Out Ave done things arewegoingoutAve
things done now

She had stared for a long time at the bank's form, until the boxes were floating in front of her eyes so that where she had ticked a Yes, the box appeared to be answering nothing. No question before or after. Just Yes. Urging her on.

Ava was not naturally a gambler. She had worked too hard for too long to get what she had had before Jon to risk what was left of it on a whim, a gut instinct. Now, with no choice, she was pushing all her chips out onto the table for this single roll of the dice. If they lent her the money she was asking for, it would mean she could refurbish The Sea Garden to the standard she wanted and perhaps she would make a success of it and it would be at once her refuge and her future. But her equity would all be at stake.

If they refused her application and she couldn't blame them for doing so – she had no commercial catering experience and this was a vicious recession – she would be trying to make a rundown café into a welcoming destination (much like home, she shuddered involuntarily) and she wouldn't be able to blame customers for walking by.

But she had, she reasoned, no choice. Jon would contribute nothing financially to their lives for the rest of his days on earth. His pension was only enough to ensure that they were ineligible for any of the meagre benefits on offer. Ava had completed every form, studiously answering in explicit detail. The reply regretted the fact that her income was too much to mean she qualified for help. Glancing at her surroundings, she laughed out loud. Too much income, but even more outgoings.

This house he had been so insistent on keeping after his mother died was too large for them, too run-down to offer as B&B or even foreign student accommodation and was doomed for demolition. The silently rotting veranda that underlined the ground floor of the once-elegant Edwardian structure would fracture easily at the bulldozer's onslaught and the eroded red bricks would be reduced on site to crumble. Ava wasn't surprised to find the plans Pat had shown her had been 'superceded' and now comprised rows of featureless, cramped boxes which would soon cram onto her precious garden. Patios and decking would obliterate Ava's beloved plants and Jon's nemesis, the lawn. She could remain here in one of them spooning baby food into her husband or walk away, freed at least from the memories of what had once been.

Poor Jon, once her lover, now her overgrown child.

His endless spreadsheets of their spending patterns had not been enough to stop him slicing off chunks of their capital to 'invest' in what he was sure would turn their situation around.

This gamble – and she should stop thinking of it as such, as if she had an alternative – had to happen. She had to impose her will on the situation she was in, turn it around and if her business plan was to be believed, in say, two years, she would be the owner of a viable café.

She went back to the start of the form, to check it so they could not reject her for a formality.

The final box was the one she had left blank, mystified as how to answer.

Marital Status

Single/Married/Legally Separated/Divorced.

All of those and yet somehow none.

For heaven's sake, they give loans to complete imbeciles who don't even need them.

She picked up her biro and in a steady hand wrote N/A.

In a few days, the reply, too slim to contain forms to sign and return, arrived. She realised with a sinking feeling that the recession had stopped the flow of the business she'd known all her adult life.

'I wondered if you'd like to go to see Kent play Derbyshire?' Ava tried to make it sound like a thing they did a lot.

Licking the butter off his toast and humming contentedly but tunelessly, he didn't seem to have heard her. She waited.

'Mmm,' he nodded and she wiped the butter from his chin.

'It's on Wednesday. You haven't any appointments,' she added dutifully meaning hospital ones but sounding as though she were his secretary which, along with all the other things she had become, she was now. 'It starts at eleven, so we'd have to leave after breakfast to get to Canterbury, get parked.'

'Mmm.'

Was he in favour or dreading it or considering it? You couldn't tell. Thinking it might help, Ava added, 'And we'll soon have a bit of money left over from the house, so we can do it more often, if you like it.'

That did it, tears welled then spilled down his face.

Sod it, she'd miss the house – well the garden - too. Life in the Sea Garden flat was going to be very cramped indeed – and on one of the few days she could take off, she wanted to be as out in the open as possible. She could hardly bear to walk up the garden path with the washing now, trying not to look her plants in the eye, knowing what awaited them. Watching men play cricket was hardly her first choice but she had reasoned it was a controlled environment where Jon would relish the rules and etiquette. It might, just, be the compromise she'd been looking for. She hadn't expected tears and felt like crying too, not least for him, an overgrown toddler sitting amidst the breakfast detritus, shoulders shaking. Her heart ached for him. He'd never get over losing the house and she'd been stupid to bring it up. *Don't ever mention it again.*

'Come on Jon,' she wrapped her arms round him kissing the top of his head. Which would need a trim before he could go anywhere that mattered. Suppose one of the 'old chums' were there – quite possible, after all. 'Let's look forward to a nice day out. You'll love it when we're there. It's only two sleeps,' she echoed Syd's words when Daisy had been fractiously waiting for Father Christmas and miraculously it seemed to work.

With a big wet sniff, the sobs stopped. He wouldn't eat any more though, pushing the plate so hard away that it slid off the table and crashed onto the floor.

'Never mind,' Ava consoled. 'Silly old plate, falling off like that, eh?' Blaming inanimate objects seemed to work for both of them and it was one less to pack.

Her prayers were answered and the forecast was good – not too hot, but she made sure he had his battered cotton sunhat in his pocket – and no rain due anywhere in southern England that day. Showing the tickets at the turnstile, they wandered around the stands, drinking coffee from plastic cups.

Their seats were right on the boundary facing the parked cars on the far side of the ground. The game began, the visitors bowling. A fielder came and stood quite close to them but Jon dismissed the idea of his autograph as he wasn't *one of ours.*

Ava began to feel her shoulders unknotting in the warmth of the day. The cloudless sky was a rich blue backdrop to the immaculate emerald field dotted with players in pristine whites. Her eyelids drooped as she tilted her face to the sun and held Jon's hand so that she would know if he stood.

There was a shout, an appeal and a ripple of applause as, head lowered, the batsman made his way off the field. 'Fishing around outside offstump,' Jon muttered. 'No need for that at all.'

Ava had no idea, but it was good to hear Jon sounding lucid and the man beside him agreed. Perhaps this was what Jon needed, the company of men with whom he could exchange the sort of remarks that made them both feel … what? Part of a club, Ava imagined. She'd be happy with that, it would leave her free to work at the Sea Garden, if there was somewhere she could leave him.

She smiled grimly. Ironic that after all the years she had spent working childless, devoting every effort to her job, she was now the one considering putting her child into a nursery.

They drove home at the end of the match. There had been no rain, the right team had won, they'd had a day out of the chaos at the house and little in the way of tantrums.

'Nice day, darling?' Ava put her foot down as they cleared the city, pleased with how things had gone. 'Jon?'

But he was asleep already and the next day couldn't remember what she was talking about when she chatted about it, hoping to jog his memory as she spooned breakfast into his mouth.

'Ave? That you?'

Who else would it be? Your father can't remember what a phone is for. 'Syd darling. Lovely to hear from you. How's little one? And you of course?'

How bad she was at this, Ava thought. She had spoken articulately and to great effect with clients on the phone for years but these days her foot and her mouth seemed connected by invisible string. *It's just tiredness. And frustration. And-* What was Syd saying?

'So I said obviously it'd be great to go but you know, with Daisy and all … so I thought I'd come and pop in on you and Dad and see what you said.'

This wasn't making sense – why would fixing a babysit need a personal visit? Still it might be a good chance to explain about the move. They fixed for the following day but Ava and Jon were rarely out, so it wasn't a surprise when Syd and the pushchair appeared on the doorstep as it was getting dark that afternoon.

'Oh. Hello,' Ava hugged her.

'Lovely, lovely,' Jon squeezed his daughter's shoulder as he bent to his granddaughter. He began unstrapping the toddler and by the time they'd rescued her and him from this activity and with a disjointed two-year old level of conversation, had jostled awkwardly together along to the kitchen, Syd had been talking for some time without anyone being able to take in what she was saying and Ava made her start again.

As she filled the kettle, Ava half-listened. She didn't mind having Daisy for a while now and then. It was only really like two toddlers in the house, with two lots of soft bland food to make rather than just the one. There'd even been a couple of sleepovers which had been, she was pleased to feel, moderately successful by dint of having 'forgotten' the pushchair and walking the little girl along the beach until she could hardly keep going. She had slept through, right round to six, beating her grandfather by an hour both mornings.

'We thought you were coming tomorrow,' Ava pushed the mug towards the girl. 'Nice hair by the way,' she nodded at the blue and green streaks which seemed to be a new addition as far as she could remember. 'That your friend Josie's work again?'

'No way,' Syd laughed. 'She's ok for a trim but I got this done at Cuts Inc – they're top.'

'Top price too.'

'Model night,' Syd said quickly and Ava thought she was as poor a liar as her father. What was this about? A date? Well, good luck to her. She may have 'chosen' to have a baby as she so often said, but Syd needed someone to be with and to share Daisy with and Ava fervently hoped this individual would turn up sooner rather than later.

'How's that lovely cottage? Coming along?'

'It's very small,' Syd shrugged and Ava bit back the comment that it was bigger than the Sea Garden flat was going to be. She and Jon had bought the cottage – Syd had insisted on staying in the close narrow streets of Whitstable among the shops that were filled with impossibly expensive things, with her mother nearby, which did make sense even though property was a lot dearer there. Margaret's part of the deal was to oversee the renovations, then help Syd decorate. Ava doubted secretly that Margaret was capable and her doubts had been borne out when a lot of money had been spent on making the whole thing open-plan with big glass doors but there were no funds left for a new boiler to keep the space warm so that had been Syd's Christmas present from her father last year.

'It'll teach her,' Jon had commented unsympathetically.

Spooning sugar into Jon's cup, her back to the table where father and daughter were sitting, Ava began to stir. 'Did you say Sydney? You've heard from Marg- Willow?'

'That's what we said, isn't it Dad, see?' The girl was intent on her father's face, despite his oblivion. 'We'd meet up at Cairns, she could show me where to go from there down to Sydney – I mean I can't not go, can I? Not with my name – and then I can just link up with that lot from school and see where they're going next and I might go with them or I might not, you know ...'

Ava placed the mugs on the table, carefully stepping over Daisy who was crawling out from under it with something dark and sticky on her hands. Syd ignored her and while Ava rinsed out the dishcloth and mopped the little fingers, the conversation continued.

'I can earn as I go then. Everyone does. Willow picked watermelons.'

'Who's Willow?'

'*Dad.* Mum.'

'Did you say air fare Syd?' Ava wiped the child's chubby face, cuddling away the protesting squeal. 'Are you going on holiday?'

Syd nodded. 'Well sort of. With Mum and Aggie. It's just a really great chance.'

'You're going to Australia? It's a long way for a little girl.' Ava hugged Daisy protectively.

'I can pay my own way, once I get there, Mum says, she's been living on watermelons'-

'-You said.'

-'for her fare on to Bali.' The idea was so improbably romantic to Ava as to be barely credible.

'Once you get there?' It looked as if she was asking Jon to buy her ticket. Couldn't Margaret, who'd been so keen to lose her daughter ever since Ava and Jon had been together, pay for her now, she wanted her to join in the fun?

Ava's heart sank thinking of Jon, head bent over his Telegraph, reading it over and over again, twisting his hands at the picture of a young girl very like Syd, behind bars in a Thai jail for acting as a carrier. His anxiety levels would go through the roof if she was actually travelling.

Perhaps she could keep it from him. 'Oh I know lots of people do it. I'm sure Daisy'll be okay but oh I don't know. Won't it be hot, really hot there now?' She studied the top of Syd's head, bright streaks bowed intently over her mug.

'Well, no Ave. That's it see? She could stay here. With you and Dad. Then she wouldn't have to put up with the flight and the heat and the spiders and'-

'-Stay here? *Here?*' Ava was incredulous. We're moving in a few weeks, she wanted to say, but stopped herself. Well, she'd managed sleepovers. A sleepover was one thing but this ... 'How long for Syd? How long are you going for? A fortnight?' Surely, she thought, it was hardly worth going all that way for less but ... 'How long Syd?'

Jon was ruffling the toddler's head, not looking up either.

'How long?'

'Six weeks,' the girl added in a rush, 'or longer maybe.'

Aghast, Ava could only manage, 'When?'

'Quite soon. Well it'll have to be, see. While she's there.'

'When Syd?'

'Next week.'

'*Next week?*' Ava clutched at a straw. 'You need visas though? Vaccinations?'

'Well actually,' Syd coloured up, 'I've done all that. So I'm all set. Mum said you wouldn't mind and so I just went for it. I thought Dad would have said by now. He got the ticket for me ages ago'-

'*Ages?*'

'Well last month. In Canterbury. In Trailfinders. They're really good.' Now, Ava remembered the elaborate arrangements for a train ride so that 'the child would know trains' Jon had said. 'They got me connections all through. Dubai'-

'-is a long way from Whitstable, Syd.'

She would deal with Jon later. When does wrapping your father round your little finger turn into a mugging? Didn't she even question whether or not Jon could afford it? Or is a Daddy a bottomless money pit? Her own had never been that was for sure. Ava earned what Ava spent from her days in the corner newsagent onwards.

'Daisy's ever so easy to look after Ava. She loves sleepovers with you and her Grandpa,' she blackmailed. 'I could write down everything she likes and there's a nursery here in Broadstairs – they'll take her for another hour in the afternoons. It's only another twenty quid a week.'

'Oh is that all?' *Will they take your father too, I wonder?*

'So you had to say yes?' Christopher had been listening to the tale. He and Ava were clutching coffee mugs as the café's heaters battled with the overnight chill that always greeted them on unlocking. This 'meeting' – the only time in their day when they could both sit down at once had begun as a means of identifying issues but, as usual, the agenda was personal rather than commercial.

She hesitated. 'God knows I don't begin to know how I'll manage it but …'

'Oh it's the blackmail thing. If you don't agree, she'll never speak to you again.'

'That. And I suppose I think – well I suppose she's very young and it'd be a great experience for her. And … I want to see if I can make a difference.'

'To Daisy? She'll grow up regardless Ava.' He sipped coffee and smoothed back his hair.

'But maybe I could make her grow up better – you know, start her counting and looking at books and learning things. Better than that nursery are doing anyway. And there's Jon too. Wouldn't it be worth seeing if somehow, it might make him better? Or slow down at least.'

'That's wishful thinking, love. Dementia isn't cured. One day, maybe.'

'I know Christopher. But somehow I feel I owe them this.'

'Jon and Daisy?'

'Jon and Syd. Suppose it's right, what she said when we were arguing once. That all of this wouldn't have happened if he'd never met me.'

'Well how about you? He didn't have a gun held to his head. Are you trying to tell me you'd have ended up in this café coping with the big baby if he hadn't pulled out the charms in that office of his?'

'It was my choice. I was a grown-up too. And … it was my choice not to have a child with him. I thought we'd be better without.'

'Dangerous. What if you found you were really rather good at it, the mother thing?'

'No chance. I'm Mistress material me.' *Was, not am.*

'Well, you're making a good job of being married.'

'Obviously the timing couldn't be worse, with us moving upstairs in a fortnight. I just need to do it. Christopher. Make the effort.'

He tipped up his coffee, draining it. 'Make the sacrifice you mean. You and your guilt complex Ava.' He stood up. 'Well how hard can it be for a gay and a scarlet woman to look after a two-year old for …?'

Ava swallowed. She hadn't told him the sentence yet. 'Six weeks,' she whispered. 'Or so.'

'Oh well, that's all right then,' he smiled as he took his cup out to the kitchen. Then his head reappeared through the hatch. 'No. You're not joking are you? Six weeks …'

And together they laughed, 'Or so.'

She had practiced this, rehearsed it in an attempt to immunise herself from the unbearable pain to come.

Ava slipped quietly out of bed, twisted her hair up in the clip she used every day and pulled on a tee shirt. Now, standing in the farthest corner of the garden, so early that the birds were all still singing, her feet felt rooted in the soil. But she had to go – there was no choice, no possible compromise, you couldn't half move out of a house. And the money had long since run out.

Every single thing around her hurt to look at and even closing her eyes didn't help as the jasmine's fragrance invaded her senses. She opened them again.

The eight-foot fence Jon had insisted on – trying to keep intruders out or her in?

The roses – recovering again from Jon's secateurs. 'What's the matter?' he'd asked perplexed at her tearfulness over the shredded stems. 'Have to prune roses, Ave.' He'd been reproachful, talking to a child who should know better.

Not in full bloom in July.

The grass – his lawn he always insisted, patchy now, no longer striped by his relentless mowing, sometimes twice a day. The cheap toy mower he'd given her as a Christmas present had given up the ghost the first season, so she just had to trust him with the Hayter.

A couple of months before, Ava had relinquished control and gone for an early night. If he didn't make it to bed, sat watching TV without her chiding him to turn it off and come upstairs, well, his loss. Perhaps he'd sleep the next day and she might have a few precious hours to herself she'd thought guiltily as she dragged up the stairs.

The drone of the mower - back and forth always before up and down because you got better stripes that way - had woken her just in time to hear a neighbour's muffled expletives hurtle across the dark gardens. Horrified at what injury Jon might inflict on himself, she had run as fast as she could down the stairs, out through the kitchen and up the path, ignoring the swathe of damage through her flowers and only grateful to find him uninjured.

Years ago, on the day they had moved the last of her things in to his mother's house, she had stood in this very spot for the first time – the corner where what she now knew were mahonia and abelia made a deep green nook – and felt the garden take her hand. *Look after us and we'll be here whenever you need us. You'll see,* she had heard them say.

She'd willingly invested hours of hard labour, watching it grow from season to season in ways she could never have guessed at, marvelling at how nature rampaged if you let it.

They'd briefly discussed the possibility of selling the house early on. But he was adamant. If only she had insisted, might Jon have been jolted out of the spiral down to second childhood? After all, this was where he had been that boy in short trousers and long socks, on the end of the second row in the school photograph he kept on the sideboard, where his mother had placed it.

When she was little, Syd had raced into the house, demanding to see it (a week before, Ava tired of dusting it, had mutinously placed it in a drawer).

'She likes it, reminds her of her grandmother,' Jon had thumped it back into place.

He'd argued for staying at Halcyon. Yes, the exterior needed attention most years. In winter, rain and frost would peel off more of the pebbledash, like the shell of a hard-boiled egg. The house's murderously expensive, forever rotting wooden balconies were, he said, designed for an Edwardian gentleman, an ideal he aspired to, with values and manners and standing in the community. It suited him very well, now he had made an honest woman of Ava. She could still feel her own slight frown as he said the words, their implications brushed aside by her own subliminal desire to become half of a respectable couple where no one knew their past.

Maybe that child, a child of their own would have altered things? It had never been something Ava had wanted, Syd had been more than enough to deal with. But suppose she had gone ahead – would Jon have come back to her? Been different? Who knew?

Leaving the inside of the house wasn't a problem. These rooms held too many tormented ghosts for her now – arguments, anger, accidents, the gradual realization of his deterioration. Like the carpets, her memory was stained and she could walk from room to room for the last time without a tremor.

But here, outside, (and now even the sun came out from behind a cloud as if to say Not going, are you?*)*, this had always been her sanctuary, despite the damage Jon had wrought sometimes, making her cry hot tears of rage and sorrow.

This crying thing wasn't her at all. As a child, there'd never been any need since they'd given her everything their limited budget could afford and there were no spiteful siblings to punch her when the grown-ups weren't looking. As a young adult, nothing, nothing at all, made her cry, even exam questions she hadn't revised. Now when a mouse drowned in the watering can, she wept freely, grieving for its lonely, desperate death. It was as if these years in this house were eroding her ... well, were eroding *her*. Perhaps it was karma.

Today though, she could breathe deeply, see clearly. This ground she was standing on was her bankroll. What was left of it ...

Ava drew a deep breath. She'd better get back inside before Daisy toddled in to her grandfather and who knew what she'd find?

She reached out to pat the hollyhocks who nodded peachy heads as if to say *There, there. You have to go. We understand. Perhaps the bulldozer won't hurt too much.*

If only she hadn't gone to bed with Jon that night after *Tosca* – and the nights that followed – this was payback, her penance. Another woman's husband. A common mistake.

Tomorrow, she'd re-visit the scene of the crime, get things straight.

When she rang the office, she'd been put through to unfamiliar names. Civil to start with, then curt when they rang her back after a day or so. Then the letter had come and it was clear they'd found something unexpected. Her stomach churned.

She could only plead ignorance then scuttle back to Broadstairs – Fay would only be able to cope with both Jon and Daisy for so long ...

Of course it mattered what she wore to meet Priti. She should look herself, but herself *retired.* At ease with life. Everything she wasn't until this silly pension thing got sorted. She dug out an old suit which, to her amazement, still fitted. It was a bit dated but would do.

The journey itself – late trains, crowded Tube, and dirt everywhere, so little changed from her commuting days - took its toll on her and when she reached the familiar building, anxiety was shredding her thin veneer of confidence. She longed for sea air and promised herself a walk on the clifftop as soon as she got back...

'You'll have no objection to this being recorded, I assume?' Priti looks her in the eye.

Surprised, Ava tries for nonchalance, realises too late it'll sound wrong, tries to switch to honest openness and ends up squeaking, 'No.'

'The matter has been very closely examined, as I'm sure you can imagine.' Tension is drawing lines on Priti's face as she switches on the machine.

Ava realises she's guilty of having condescendingly believed the girl would have grown taller by now. At a small table in the corner of the room, a boy opens a laptop, flips a pad open, as the meeting gets under way. *This room's narrower somehow*, Ava puzzles, taking in the once familiar surroundings. The walls display qualifications with coats of arms, degree certificates with crimson seals, grad photos of Priti in cap and gown. *Well, good luck to her.* It dawns on Ava the room's been partitioned. *Sensible. Will show a saving in the accommodation numbers. Should have thought of it myself.*

'Ready,' the boy nods. *He's not a boy. Showing your age, Ava.* Priti has her own intern now, tapping away. *If all this is being recorded, what's he writing?*

Priti opens her folder. 'Your enquiry prompted a lengthy examination of the arrangements put in place when you and Mr Wilkes, then Head of Acquisitions, left the firm. It's unfortunate he's not able to attend today. Analysis of the financial arrangements at the time has revealed irregularities of concern. It would appear that considerable misappropriation took place. The conduct of more than one senior member of the firm has been scrutinised and certain criticisms will be made.'

This is all a bit strong, isn't it? A bit of manipulation of the rules, that's all.

'Considerable misappropriation?'

Priti nods at the boy again, who taps a key and the screen on the wall behind Priti blossoms into life with a rainbow, backlit spreadsheet. Ava scans the columns as Priti takes several minutes to read aloud. The figures are eye-watering.

'Surely, Priti, it's just a mistake … You can't seriously believe my husband would have …'

She can't find the words, her vocabulary has not had the exercise lately. *Stolen* is far too crude. Repeating their word, *misappropriated,* makes it all sound preconceived.

Perhaps Jon's mental state had begun its slippery slide long before she recognised it, but someone else did and took advantage. *Oh my god, she means Sue and Phil.*

Realising she has hesitated fatally, Ava struggles to finish, '… would have done anything wrong.' But it sounds weak.

'As you can see, it was important to look at all aspects of the case.'

So it's a case now.

If this goes badly, for her as well as for Jon, they could ask for a custodial sentence, to make an example. The headlines bounce in her mind. Fat Cat and Wife Fiddled Firm's Pension Fund …

There'd be no sea air there. A long time ago, Edith said something about him never telling the truth, didn't she? Just like his father. Jon and I never discussed honesty, only accuracy.

'And how,' Ava crosses her hands and looks her old pupil in the eye, 'can I help?'

'We've prepared a report.' Priti is handed a folder which she pushes over the desk for Ava. 'The FCA will come down on this like a ton of bricks.'

'Well, obviously, I'll need time to consider your findings.'

She has switched back to Business Ava, as if all the years of housework and beach walks never happened.

'The matter is very serious. In view of the scale of the possible fraud, I'm sure you'll agree we have to proceed on the assumption that funds have been … mis-directed. These are not sums which might have been accidental.'

'How is that?'

Priti looks uncomfortable for the first time. 'It looks very much as if your own not inconsiderable pension fund was inappropriately handled.'

'How exactly?' *Oh shit, they know.*

The woman Ava taught flicks back through her copy of the file. 'A firm called Buckingham Holdings.'

'Buckingham?' She's never heard of it. 'Buckingham?' *Oh wait.* 'But that's where …'

'This wasn't the first significant transfer of funds to the account.'

'Whatever does that mean?'

Priti looks down at her hands. 'We believe Mr. Wilkes' own pension funds were also transferred into the account on his retirement from this firm.'

The boy's fingers are flying now.

'And what is this account exactly?'

'This is the difficulty. The normal procedures do not seem to have been followed on the retirement of either Mr. Wilkes, or yourself.'

'What do you mean?'

After a pause, she goes on, 'It appears the funds were… irregularly transferred in both cases.'

Ava thinks for a long time. 'You mean the requirement that they be transferred into new pension funds was not complied with?'

'In your husband's case, exactly that.'

'But he set up a new company – I was a director, he transferred them over. And anyway,' here's that defiant child again, 'the law's changed.'

'Now. Yes. Not then.'

'So … where did the funds go?'

Priti looks at her as if to say *don't you know?* 'It appears an account in the name of Jon Charles Wilkes. We are unable to say what happened after that.' The room falls silent.

What did you do, Jon?

Fight back. 'How? How could that happen Priti? How could the firm's procedures allow that to happen? There are regulations to be complied with. Laws, for goodness' sake. How could he do it? It can't be right. There must be another explanation.' *Bit over the top.*

'Can you provide any documentation?' Priti's turn to scribble now, in the margin of the report, just the way Jon used to. Not in pencil though. In ink. 'Other than what we already hold copies of.'

Ava thinks about the loft ladder and the money dripping steadily each month from Jon's account. 'I'll need to see what you hold, Priti.'

'It's all in the appendix,' Priti nods at the folder. 'The important one is the charge on the deeds of the Broadstairs property twelve - no, thirteen years ago.'

'What?' *No no.*

She begins speaking in a measured, precise way that reminds Ava of the caution the police have to give when they're arresting someone. If it's not right, their case is screwed. 'It appears there was an arrangement at that time, with the Managing Director, concerning the transfer of equity to compensate for the shortfall in an account Jon Wilkes had signed off ...' and ends, slightly rushing, 'with effect delayed as the property was Mrs Edith Wilkes' home at that time..'

She was dead by then. He must have forged her signature. Oh Jon. 'He mortgaged the house when interest rates went down, I clearly remember.' *You don't, you know, remember? Too busy making pastry to read it all through.*

'On the contrary, he signed the property over as soon as Mrs Wilkes Senior had died.'

So that's what it said. He came into the kitchen. 'Don't you trust me Ava?'

Write it off. Don't let her see what you're thinking.
'And the pension funds that were accruing?'

'Well the new pension freedoms have allowed for customer choice, as you're aware. Perhaps you could look into that, provide the name of the financial advisor you appointed, between now and when you've had a chance to consider the report. There may, only may, be some leeway there, but ...' Priti frowns at the file, shaking her head as if mystified how someone so clued-up could get herself into this situation.

'How long can you give me?'

'We are anxious to come to a conclusion, as you can imagine. Ever since you rang to enquire about the whereabouts of the funds, the firm has expended considerable time and resources on looking into the matter. But we have managed to keep it in-house. So far.'

So Ava blew the whistle on herself.

If Jon was here now I'd – what? What would you do Ava?
Actually, what would he do? Old Jon, I mean. He'd smooth it over of course.
Do it. Smooth, Ava, smooth. But how? Think. Think. Think.

Priti is gathering up her papers, readying to draw things to a close. 'If evidence is forthcoming about irregularities, the authorities will have to be informed. I'm sure nobody wants that, but you can see the company will have little choice.'

'Well I can see you won't want your reputation dragged down by being ripped off by a pensioner suffering with dementia, yes.' *That'll do for a start.*

There's a pause. 'You would be able to provide medical corroboration of his prognosis?'

'Yes. My husband is going mad. Yes. And … *careful* … one last thing, Priti. This arrangement he reached with the firm regarding the property charge. A sort of early form of equity release, I think we can agree?'

'I wouldn't say that.'

'No. I can see why. Now it's become more common, I think we're all aware of the checks and balances that have been built in to protect the homeowner. Whilst I'm grateful Mrs Wilkes senior was undisturbed at her advanced age, what exactly were the terms my husband agreed to after her death that allowed him, us, to continue living there?'

Priti turns over pages. 'They don't seem to form part of this report.'

Ava sits up straighter. *One last shot.* 'It seems to me that the firm is far from blameless in this.'

'Hardly. Given Mr. Wilkes' … the discrepancy found.'
She's wobbling. 'Notwithstanding' *it's been a long time since I used that word* 'your findings, which I have yet to read, the firm's performance leaves a lot to be desired.

There seems to have been more than one departure from accepted procedures with no oversight. Furthermore, I think the firm's actions could be construed as coercion.'
Ava isn't a card player, but she thinks that's called an ace.

The room chills. Priti stands, snapping her folder shut. 'You have until Friday.'

'That's three days.'

'Friday at 10 am.'

In the lift back to the ground floor, a thought hits Ava so hard she can hear blood pumping in her head.

Is this all Jon did? She thought she knew everything, but how many other times had there been?

Had he been on the take all the time?

If so, she's implicated…

On the platform, Ava stands looking down onto the tracks where a grubby mouse, town cousin of the slippery cadaver in her watering can, scuttles in the dust. There's a delay. The next train to Victoria will be twelve minutes. Twelve minutes in which to decide. But you don't do the dramatic, the bad things, any more, do you? You just get on with things. Do the good you can do.

Why she thinks of it then, she'll never know. But Jon's tall back disappearing out of her office one day when Corinne rang, comes into her head. *Is everything ok there? Only there's a couple of rumours going the rounds …*

Reassuring her friend that this takeover was going very well indeed, Ava watched Jon move smoothly through the desks back to his own room. Very well.

Blinded. The train is coming, the rails are singing their signals.

That's when the deepest, darkest thought hits her. Hits her so hard, she reels, gasping for breath, knees buckling, onto the platform, falling back against the curving, tiled walls.

'You all right love?' A woman her age offers a hand. 'Only this is my train.' *If only she'd just grasp my arm, haul me up and whirl, hurl me to the tracks.*

Ava struggles upright, makes her feet move, one, then the other, toward the platform edge, the rush of air in her face.

She has to accept this. This would be the easy way out – but it's an option she doesn't have.

If she doesn't go back, who will look after Jon?

Or Daisy?

Green, gullible Ava. Who knows what you might have achieved if he hadn't been there on that audit?

You would have done better, achieved more.

But perhaps not. Maybe you never were as good as you thought.

A week later, the bulky package came and Ava's eyes slid over the dancing words. This has been written by the boy, because the words are not quite as polished as they would have been in Priti's concise style. *Concentrate. Don't misread this.*

It was over two hundred pages long, copies of every document – Ava skipped over the ones with her signature on - *Too late to read that now* and verbatim records of interviews with members of the firm they'd managed to drag out of retirement. *Wonder what they were paid?* But there's nothing from Sue and Phil in sunny Rio. Some had died in the interim, like Hatton, excusing themselves from the proceedings. Even the old IT guys were harried but reported no evidence of Mr Wilkes ever having asked them to adjust records on the firm's back-ups, then iCloud storage. *Not sure he'd have known there were any – he only just grasped floppy discs.*

By the time she read all of it, a change of tone had become clear. At a guess, Priti has stepped back, handed it over to someone, somewhere and a prudent decision has been made. A lot of criticisms were thrown in all directions but for Ava only one sentence mattered. It seems her ploy worked.

'In light of the financial disadvantage suffered by Mrs Ava Wilkes and the advanced ill-health of Mr. Jon Charles Wilkes, the firm considers that nothing would be gained by pursuing the matter since the sums in question form part of Mr. Wilkes' estate to be released on his death or the sale of the property Halcyon, Eastern Esplanade, Broadstairs, Kent. Should Mrs Wilkes choose to take civil action, that is a matter for her.'

They've weighed it up and decided there's so little equity left, there's no point in pursuing the matter which will only lead to poor PR for a firm trumpeting its skills in financial analysis.

They've not found, or have chosen not to find, evidence of anything more.

She clenches her fists. '*Yes.*' She will move on.

So now it's Ava's turn to stand, pen in hand, offering it to Jon. 'Just sign this darling.'

At the solicitor's, handing over the documents, she smiles and says, yes, they are looking forward to downsizing. 'Aren't we darling?'

And Jon, bless him, smiles back and nods.

Sometimes in the small hours, wakened by his snores she'd ask herself what it was she really did want nowadays but the truth was she'd stopped wanting and couldn't even remember how to switch on the motor that had driven her once. It had got her a long way, that instinct, into jobs, into more beds than she cared to remember and best of all, into *fun.* What a long way off that all was. She could remember sitting at a desk, aching and glowing all at once on more than one morning after. It had all gone because she had married Jon – oh, and probably it wasn't his fault, whoever she'd married would have reined her in. So what did she want? A couple of days at an exclusive spa? And who would look after him while she luxuriated in creams and serums and seaweed wraps? Not his daughter, that was for sure. Syd was always in denial about her father's condition and even when she brought Daisy in for Ava to babysit, would scuttle out again before she could become embroiled in the daily confusions of his life.

That wedding invitation was still there, on the kitchen shelf, the date getting nearer and nearer. She should have done the wedding list first thing, when the deep pink envelope had first arrived. All the cheaper presents would have been bought long ago. It would have to be a modest cheque written at the last minute, once the sale of the house had gone through. Then she'd splash out on a haircut.

She'd have to dissuade the hairdresser from anything too radical. Jon wouldn't recognise her at first, which would mean a couple of days of reassuring, like when there'd been a ring at the door and she'd wound a towel round her hair and run, in her dressing gown, out of the shower and down to the front door.

Jon, fumbling through a bowl of cornflakes while she was upstairs, had looked up alarmed as she dropped the parcel onto the table. 'Who are you?'

Did Jon see her, really see her at all? He often called her Margaret and she was fairly sure he now thought of her as a loyal staff member, if anything.

Pampering was such an industry. Ava couldn't believe how long women had been gullible enough to believe that, plucked and glossed and finished down to their toes, they'd be irresistible. Ironic when most men were put off by too much polish, only too aware how expensive a hobby such a woman would be.

Looking back, some of Ava's best times had been when she was least prepared for them. She and a colleague had been on a training course in Leeds together, then as the weather had worsened, going over the moors, they booked into a pub with rooms. Ava tried not to listen as he rang his wife. Yes, the weather was dreadful. Oh it was on the tv was it? He sounded relieved to have his excuse backed up by the BBC. He'd probably be home the next day, snowploughs permitting.

Ava hadn't shaved her legs, her hair could have done with a wash and there wasn't a toothbrush to be had, let alone hours of effort by a team of beauty professionals. But what man worries he hasn't shaved before making his move?

Ava knew she should have said no, should have stopped what so easily happened next, have feigned a headache or scruples or brought up another man in her life, but she was motivated by simple physical need and knew that it would be, for both of them, not mentioned again. She used to think, she realised now, like a man. *If you can't be with the one you love, love the one you're with.* Oh, the glorious freedom that had been her generation's gift. And now she couldn't remember the name of that one-night stand. She could hardly criticise Syd. But then she'd been caught and much as she loved Daisy, would never recover the giddy years.

Had it really been deliberate, Syd's pregnancy? A teenaged, look-at-me move to get her own back on the grown-ups who'd turned her world upside down with their self-centred love lives?

Everything about Facebook depressed Ava and the last thing she wanted was to be seen on it, so she persuaded Christopher the pictures to go on the café's page should be only of her hands, holding different dishes of food. Although she actually liked the one he sneaked in, which shows her from behind, just half her body, so she looks just the size she used to be. The café's refit has brought a 5star rating from the Council at the top of The Sea Garden's page and Christopher has done whatever was necessary to get it hundreds of likes within no time at all, which apparently matters. Customers have even been found who are willing (and able) to post kind reviews.

Soon, Ava gets on quite well, posting photos of functions and food and reading the comments customers post. She has even started furtively to look around, like a shy guest at a crowded party.

If he's still dealing in antiques, he's probably got a page on here too. Her finger itches over the search bar but she mustn't. *Things are going well, mustn't jinx everything.*

'It's true you know,' Christopher pushed the laptop at her to see the latest review, 'about your food. It's great.'

She shook her head. 'Nah,' and laughed. 'Nice though.'

She's let Christopher get on with it, only nagging when he omits to post his own work, his pictures. 'They make this place, Christopher, they have to be on here.'

Blushing a bit, he said 'Well if you're sure you want them with your food ...which is lovely by the way.'

Without realising it, she sighed, a deep, saddened gust of despair as she chopped walnuts for the salad.

'Oh come on, nothing's that bad is it?' Christopher looked into her face. 'Jon again?'

'No, no,' she was quick to defend him on one of his better days. 'He was good this morning. Same old questions, but I just agree with him all the time. No, no it's me, I suppose.'

'You're not ill?'

'No. Don't worry. Old workhorses just plod on and on,' she smiled. 'But that's it really. It's what I feel like, an old creature who's been in the field all winter, except,' she looked at her feet, unkempt and uncared for in flipflops, 'I haven't been to the blacksmith's.'

'What's brought this on?'

'Wedding. Family. I barely know them, but they should know Daisy.'

'Ooh I love a wedding,' Christopher said dreamily.

'Well this place can manage without you for the day,' Steve coming in with a delivery, thumped a parcel of carefully wrapped and labelled meat down on the counter. 'And it will, really do you good, like they say.'

'Even if it did, there's all the dolling up I'd have to do …' she looked down at her hands. 'I look like I've been doing forced labour for a year.'

She does not bear comparison with the polished and toned women who tilt their heads upwards towards their phones for Facebook. (Christopher told her they do this to lose their double chins and it works. All she needs is a counter set below the level of the café and she too would re-define her jaw). Not only that but the time they must spend on themselves, gossiping away … Hours and hours with personal trainers in gyms – or somewhere.

Worst of all though are the teenage girls who feel they must publicise themselves at what is obviously the apex of their appearance. Do they think they'll always look like this? Don't they know gravity will exert itself on them too? How depressed will they be then?

'Ah well I can help you there,' Steve pulled the local paper from his jacket, unfolded and pointed. 'See at the top?

> *Pagoda Pretties*
> *Hello, one lucky reader*
> *Win top prize in our competition*
> *and you can be walking on air.*

Simply tell us in twenty words why you deserve to win this exciting prize and we'll treat you to a manicure or a pedicure at our new luxury salon.

'It's that new place in the High Street? With the chandeliers? Go on – what's to lose Ava?'

She looked at him with a laugh. 'I'd need a new wardrobe just to walk in the place. And it'll be a fix anyway. They'll give it to someone from the private estate with friends with money. Would if it was my business anyway.'

'You never know …' and he was gone, back into his van and roaring away.

The more she thought about it, the more it made Ava despair. Of all the things that she needed, a wedding was way off the scale. She looked down at her feet, dwarfed by Christopher's crocs she always wore to wash this floor. Without knowing why, she tore out the form and wrote

I'd like to win because my floor gets more attention than my feet

She'd push it through the door on the way home, after they'd closed. It had been a diversion, kind of Steve, but now she had to get on.

As she worked, her mind wandered. *Suppose, just suppose, there was a man, a man without strings for the night, as she would be, at this wedding. Just to abandon herself for a while, feel as she used to do…* she considers the prospect with no sense of guilt whatsoever.

And of course, because she had given it no more thought and because it was the last thing in the world that was a priority and because, quietly, like he had with Pat Howell, Steve had a word, Ava won.

'Would you really? You're sure it's no trouble?' She hated the doubting tone in her voice. And knew at the same time Jon would be a lot of trouble even on a good day.

Fay looked at her. 'I said I would and I will. Kris and I owe you – for agreeing to Pat's scheme – it's saved our lives. This is the very least we can do. I'll cope, honestly.'

'Is Kris … here? With you?'

'At the moment. He wants to do some more travelling. Wants some space to think about a book he wants to write. I think it was when he heard about Syd.'

'You don't want to go though?'

'Plenty to keep me occupied here.'

It doesn't sound as if he'd ever planned to include her. Ava likes this new, practical Fay more than the airy-fairy one and feels a tinge of sympathy.

'Anyway,' Fay dismisses any more discussion, 'we managed fine that day out you had in London didn't we?'

It wasn't a day *out* in London, Ava wants to say, but she can't tell anyone about the little difficulty with the old firm, so she just nods.

'The only thing …' Ava's reluctant to jeopardise the chance of relative freedom for a day. 'Don't leave him near any books – valuable ones.'

'Okay…?'

'I found him and Daisy on the floor tearing pages out of one yesterday.'

'Oh. Shame.'

'He looked so cheerful doing it I couldn't be cross …'

Of course there's no money to buy anything new to wear, but what does it matter? She'll dig out that bloody birthday dress from Tenterden. At least she'll have perfectly painted toenails. She will admire them, tap-dancing on the Faustian compact she and Jon made.

First there is money to be spent getting Syd ready for her great adventure; a backpack, new Timberlands. Then a send-off.

In the end, they settled on the fish restaurant down by Whitstable harbour, not least because Syd's leaving do was on a Wednesday, two-for-one night. In the morning, the car would come to take her to Heathrow, so they couldn't be late. Then it was back to Halcyon to pack and move in next day. Ava would ring Syd to say they've moved when she was settled into having fun somewhere.

'What about Daisy though?' his daughter set Jon the challenge, used to him tutting at children in restaurants.

'She'll be fine I'm sure,' Ava was surprised to hear herself say, 'there'll be three of us after all, to keep her happy won't there?' Well what did it matter? 'And then,' she took a deep breath, 'we'll swap the child seat over to our car and take her home with us, tell her it's a big sleepover. Keep her mind off you not being there.'

'And I've asked Jojo to come too.'

'Oh right. Four of us then. She'll be delighted with all that company.'

The day had been sultry and overcast but at six the sun broke through the clouds. Somehow Ava made time to get ready. They strolled down the pretty High Street towards the sea, molten in the setting sun, Ava pushing the buggy, Jojo making Daisy chuckle at her reflection in the upmarket boutique windows, Jon and Syd following. A happy, slightly lopsided family.

'Monkey!' Daisy's chubby arms reached out. Bending to stroke the little girl's head Ava looked for whatever had attracted her behind the glass. A breeze ruffled Ava's skirt as she bent to Daisy's eye level and inhaled the smell of fresh paint.

In the display of antiques, china, glass and sparkling silver, a tanned, square-fingered hand was carefully placing a very old, jointed monkey, one simian arm raised in salute, blue bow tie at a raffish angle.

Behind him, smiling down at Ava and Daisy, was the unchanged face, grey eyes twinkling as they always did, alive with amusement. The path her life had not taken. *So* alive. And the well-preserved blonde beside him laughing at something he said, was also, definitely, very alive.

In the Crab and Oyster, what with Syd's chatter about the flight *only a few more hours now, can't believe it* and Jon and Daisy both needing to be fed, Ava's kept occupied.

Her body is still tensed as if that hand had burst through the window and grabbed a handful of her flesh. The bustle and voices bouncing back from the tiled floor are obliterated by the white noise in her head about what he looked like. She thought he might have aged but hardly and who was she, the blonde, and why did Ava have to have all these people with her and why couldn't she think for the life of her of an excuse to go back on her own and anyway why would he be interested after all this time?

Then, she reminds herself, she has promised not to think about him again.

I'll make him stop invading my head. I will. Somehow.

No-one seems to notice that she hasn't touched her own fish.

On tiptoe, she pushes back through the heavy swing door, thankful that the Ladies on this floor is better kept than the one in A&E, as if to reflect the special work in this unit. This darkened ward has an elite air – there's more space around each bed and calm reigns. Everyone here is either near death or clinging so perilously to life that they have no time for buzzers and chat. Ava counts ten bedstations each in a pool of muted light, five offset against the opposing five so emergency teams have room to do whatever they have to do. The five beneath the windows are all occupied by bodies linked by wires and tubes to the technology around them. After a heart-lurching scan of the faces she identifies Jon, in the only occupied bed on the opposite side. He'd like that, she thinks. Being set apart from the common herd. This feels like retribution for the thoughts that have filled her head since she walked down Whitstable High Street that evening.

When they were carrying Jon in the sitzchair down the metal stairs to the ambulance he looked like the overgrown toddler he was in her daily life, only ominously still. *He'll be fast-tracked if he's lucky,* the green-overalls had said, *unless there's an emergency.* Wasn't he one then? *Don't worry if he's not in A&E, they'll be doing tests.* She would follow, she told them, as soon as she'd locked up. In truth, she had dallied. First, after watching the flashing lights recede into the distance then turn the corner, she had stood on the doorstep feeling the warmth of the sun on her skin for a moment. Then before anyone alerted by the blue lights could call over, all concern, she had quickly shut the door and gone from room to room straightening things, collecting up paint cards and her measuring tape and sketches. Ava's fingers were itching to get started but the solicitor had tutted that she would just have to wait until completion.

What more could go wrong, she asked? What with getting Syd ready to go, keeping the move a secret from her, having Daisy almost every day so that when Syd had gone it wouldn't be so unusual, this bloody wedding looming all the while she'd been taking Jon with her every day to the Sea Garden flat to get him used to it, her mind was whirling even before she'd found her husband slumped forward where she'd left him.

It would be too much for Jon, the move to this doll's house. It was no smaller than her old flat had been but the contrast with Edith's house was stark. Would Ava ever have thought of it as her own house? Probably not.

Anyway, too late now. Once she got it sorted, divested the rooms of all the things they had no further need for, the little place would be adequate. One bedroom for Jon, one bedroom for her and Daisy, for now.

Daisy.

Ava had quite forgotten her in the crisis with Jon. Guilt flooded back, colouring Ava's cheeks.

The nursery said they would be happy to keep Daisy until Fay came for her. Of course they would. Ava could see their bill inflating like a balloon. Well she could hardly take a toddler to A&E.

'I'm so grateful Fay,' Ava said over the phone. 'Children are a bit of mystery to me at the best of times, I don't know how you cope.'

'Well, you seem to be managing really well. As for me,' Ava could hear the shrug in her voice. 'I've tried with the Centre but it's not working. Kris was saying last night that our last six months have been disastrous and since I've had Daisy a couple of times, I've been thinking it might pay to have a change of direction.'

'Oh?'

The wellness centre is not taking up quite as much of Fay's time as she had expected. She has adapted two rooms near the toilets and is fast filling them with children whose parents are too busy to look after them, and so park their accessory child while they yoga. It's not a bad plan. After all, it's what Ava's doing with Jon, so she can go to Amanda's wedding with Daisy and stay overnight.

'A creche. With the emphasis on well-being, of course ...'

'It'll be significantly less calm,' Ava pointed out with feeling.

'Well, needs probably must. Good luck at the hospital. Go on you go.'

Luxuriating in the unbroken silence for nearly fifteen minutes, Ava packed a few things into the overnight bag for Jon then reluctantly found the car keys. Perhaps it wouldn't start again? There'd be no choice but to call a taxi which would mean explaining to a kindly driver why she needed to go to the hospital and Ava really wasn't sure she'd be able to go through all that.

No, better to make the car go by rolling it gently down the hill and bump-starting it.

But of course, it coughed into life at the first turn of its key. She flicked on Radio 4 and relished the bliss of a short story, but the traffic was light and she reached the hospital car park before the end. There was a space right up near the entrance so she could not even dawdle to the ticket machine then pace herself up the hill in the warmth to the automatic doors. The sun was doing its Indian Summer thing, golden at this time of the afternoon and she knew she had to turn her back on it and hurry indoors to see what had happened to Jon.

The rest of the sunlit day passed in a chaos of faces and indefinite waits while she pretended not to watch what was going on to those around her. A bedside curtain offers no privacy. Other patients' loved ones muttering mutiny seemed to get fast-tracked but Ava had more respect for the staff and sat quietly beside the high-sided cot, nodding at the various medical interventions and diagnoses Jon received. Her scalp prickled with guilt. These people are bound by oath to do their best for this man they have never met. She, Ava, had stood in front of a minor local government official a long time ago and promised to … she could hardly recall the words now but *in sickness and in health* had surely been part of it, despite the anodyne surroundings of the Register Office?

Talking of whom – family that was, she should be ringing someone – it was what you did, the right thing to do. Ava slipped out into the corridor. What time was it in Australia? Syd's phone had been in her jeans pocket when at last she'd found a hostel with washing machine, so Ava would just have to wait until Syd rang her, which might be too late. How about Margaret-Willow? Ava should at least leave a message. If she rang now though, it would be four in the morning, she calculated, and it would seem terribly urgent. No, better to wait until there was something definite to report.

And Tania, doubtless in a last-minute whirl of pre-wedding frenzy, what could she do? If she knew Jon wasn't coming she'd be frantically re-doing the table plan again. Ava could only wait to see how this turned out. The green lines on the heart monitors were looking ominously feeble – perhaps that was a good thing? Surely an erratic pattern would be worse? Suppose Jon … she had to confront this … suppose he didn't make it?

Except that this wasn't Jon, not any more. Not the tall, slim man who'd bent over her desk pretending to read the work she was pretending to show him while static fizzed between them so vividly surely everyone in the office could see it. Or perhaps it had just been she, Ava, who had been giving out signals. Poor Jon, now a man who was a stranger to himself. So muddled and messy and diminished that if he were a dog, a vet would be shaking his head over him. What hope had he had once Ava had set her sights on him?

'Mrs Wilkes? You can go back in to ICU now, they've got him comfortable.'

In the peaceful darkness of Intensive Care, Ava considered the lines that fed in and out of the supine body, air and fluids in – all essential surely? Fluids and vital signs out. Which of these could be disturbed for a short time – and surely it would only take a short time – for all the struggling to be done with? And then she'd be free to go to Whitstable, walk past that antique shop …

A nurse flitted by without acknowledging her but bringing her back to reality. What a betrayal of trust it was to even think such things.

Or was it?

As Ava's foot stretched for the oxygen line trailing on the floor, Jon's eyes flickered open and caught her gaze.

pursued pebbledash prejudiced jurisprudence
jeopardise jalopy

going out are we going out Margaret

Then the nurse comes back with the test results and says he'll be fine, it was just another blip with his medication but they've definitely sorted it out now and he'll be fine to come home tomorrow, but not first thing because the consultant will have to see him first. They'll let her know the results of the CT scan but it'll take a while.

His dry lips part under the mask. 'Hello Margaret darling,' he croaks.

So Scarlet Ava has a morning free …

'Are you sure you don't mind Fay?'

'Look I've said, anytime. She's no trouble.'

'I think it'll only be a couple of hours …'

'You take your time Ava.'

'What you need first, darling,' Christopher's eyebrow arched, 'is a trip to my friend Marie. Total overhaul, hair cut, brows threaded – chin too possibly, let's see … No, no need for chin yet, so you're a spring chicken under all that straw.'

'I know,' her head dropped. 'I know really but there's the money and Jon can't be left and I – I'd feel such a fool in some salon with doll-like young girls who think I'm a granny. Which I suppose I am, aren't I?' she could hear the surprise in her own voice.

'Leave it to me,' Christopher's surprisingly firm, speed-dialling. 'My friend Marie is *very* discreet … and I'm owed a favour …'

Discreet and six feet tall, Ava thought, shaking the hand of his friend and looking in wonder at the best make-up job she'd ever seen.

'Lovely to meet you Ava,' a deep voice murmured, air-pecking at her cheeks. 'Now why don't you come through and take a seat.'

This part of the High Street, the unfashionable end, had funny little shops shoehorned into the spaces between post-War developments and a car sales forecourt always full of very small cars for people who couldn't contemplate driving anything larger in the packed streets near the seafront. Jon had disparaged them as Chinese junk – another favourite joke – but passing them now, Ava saw the merit of something smaller and lighter than the Saab which weighed a ton and Jon didn't drive any more.

Marie's salon didn't seem to be advertised from the road, but Christopher ushered her up to a door and in to a normal-looking treatment room with a white reclining chair.

'Let's see,' Marie took Ava's hair up off her face. 'Lovely and thick still, so that's good, but you could do with something a bit lighter round here – they're some cheekbones you've got. And here,' she stroked Ava's eyebrow with cool index fingers, 'let's lift these a little. And define. Lift and define, that's the mantra this morning.'

On the way back, bolder now with new hair and brows, Ava popped in to Pagoda Pretties. 'You not want fingernails today?' The tiny dark-haired girl was probably an illegal, Ava thought, who'd paid a lot of cash to earn money in England and send it back to her family.

'No, sorry. I won a free pedicure remember?' she panicked slightly afraid she would after all have to pay for this.

'Ah yes,' Lotus Blossom giggled a tinkly sound, with her fingers to her mouth. 'Newspaper mistake. I have you in diary for mani/pedi. You get both done for prize.'

'Really?'

'Yeah, yeah. It say here. Look.'

Before she changed her mind, Ava said quickly, 'Well in that case ... I don't suppose you could fit me in this Saturday morning? I'm going to a wedding.' She smiled and passed over a fiver, something to be sent back home.

Walking home, she waved cheerfully at Steve, always there behind the sausages and joints.

He waved back then carried sawing down through the rack of lamb, whistling. 'It'll knock ten years off you, my lovely.'

Lagan

anything sunk in the sea, but attached to a buoy or the like
so that it may be recovered.

The silver-haired woman waiting in the sunlit porch gave the nod.

Cutting short the phrase he'd been improvising, the organist struck the cue and chatter hushed obediently as everyone stood.

What secrets were these couples hiding, Ava wondered? Here in a church, they should come clean, tell the truth – about an affair, his dislike of her mother, her attraction to another man. Like this priest say, imposing in a rich cope, and surveying them all from the altar steps with the dark depth of his gaze.

The woman in the pew in front of Ava glanced at her watch. 'She's not kept him waiting.'

'Not likely,' her husband replied. 'No chance for second thoughts.'

Trying not to think of any places she hadn't searched, Ava muttered to the toddler at her feet, 'Come on sweetheart, this is it. Oh your dress.' Stripes of the dust of ages which had been gathering silently under the pew of the tiny stone church shadowed the little girl's skirt.

'Dress,' Daisy's bottom lip wobbled.

'Not to worry,' Ava brushed with one hand. 'Oh.' The same dust had underscored the hem of her own ridiculous chiffon. 'Look, Daisy, look at Amanda – isn't she beautiful?' And she was.

'See,' the toddler pouted, hemmed in by women teetering on towering heels.

'Oh you're getting big now,' Ava puffed, hauling Daisy up to her hip. 'There, here she is,' she leant out of the pew just as the bride glittered past them on her father's arm.

All that money Ava thought. All that hope.

In her wake, two teenagers in cerise satin scowled self-consciously.

'Jojo!' Daisy recognising the nearest bridesmaid, squirmed in Ava's arms, reaching for the older girl.

'Lo, Daisy,' she whispered back, a sudden grin transforming her into a beautiful young woman.

So that was how it was, Ava mused, setting the little one to stand on the pew, anchored by a fistful of sparkly dress, pretending to read the upside-down Order of Service. Perhaps Daisy would be bridesmaid at Jojo's wedding, then it would be Daisy's own turn. Ava could only pray (she was in church after all) that this warm little person would make a better job than she'd done when, *if,* she married.

Daisy marked her days like nothing else she'd experienced. At work, it used to feel like Ava was going forward, gaining, growing, each payday luring her on. These days, every milestone Daisy passed seemed to pile up like stones on a cairn in which Ava was interred.

And a day off, which was what this felt like, always made it harder to go back to work. The Sea Garden flat and the café, closed for the day and piled with boxes, had been chaos when they left this morning. Could she just get into the car and drive away from that life, start again somewhere? Not with Daisy. Perhaps she could just leave her with the childminders at the reception and vanish? Vanishing sounded delicious but oddly, leaving Daisy didn't. And in any case, Ava was tethered here in another way.

She had become someone she didn't recognise in a role she didn't know how to play.

Her head was full of that bloody house. Handing over the keys on completion, all she could think of was that one of the builders ripping it apart would find Jon's stash of notes and quietly pocket it until he could nip up to the casino after work. Finders keepers.

Or maybe, she acknowledged as they began *Immortal, Invisible*, Jon had simply used it all up himself, gambling not at the casino but on stocks and shares. And losing in the same way. Somehow, she had to make herself move on.

'I'm really sorry to hear that,' Amanda had been polite on the phone, making a good job of sounding as if it didn't matter that the seating plan would have to be re-worked. 'Has he had it for long, this cold?'

About five years, Ava thought silently. 'Yes I'm sorry it's such short notice. But Daisy and I are really looking forward to your big day.'

'You know the hotel do baby-listening, Auntie Ava? You'll be able let your hair down, have a few drinks, get bopping, you know.'

Waving her arms in the air, flesh wobbling unrhythmically was not something Ava planned to be doing. She'd always expected to be the sort of forty-year old who exercised regularly, looked toned, like all those French women on the beaches she loved in her teens. Now she was fifty-something - it was hard to remember what exactly when your husband wished you happy birthday most mornings - and the regime hadn't even started. Talk about a lost decade.

The saturnine priest began a laudably fresh-sounding run through the words he must have been able to recite in his sleep.

But she wouldn't have too much to drink despite not having to drive. To keep up appearances for the guests who knew Jon. Or thought they did. Which left the question of what she would be doing.

Tania, the bride's mother, had said there'd be no children *evident* at the reception, so the grown-ups could enjoy themselves. The icy rill of disappointment running through her veins surprised Ava.

One big advantage to coming here with Daisy was that she'd distract whoever they met so that instead of concluding Ava'd let herself go, they'd be evaluating how like her grandfather Daisy looked. Without her, Ava would be laid bare to scrutiny. Still, she looked down at her feet in the sandals she'd unearthed, they looked all right now.

A thread dangled from her blackened hem though, floating in the day's warm air currents. Ava leant down to pull, watching horrified as the hem unreeled raw-edged. She tried to snap it but only succeeded in pulling more out. 'Christ.' Couldn't she just go home?

The woman in front glanced over her shoulder, snapped open her bag and wordlessly, keeping her eyes on the priest, offered Ava a small pair of silver scissors.

'Thanks,' Ava whispered after she'd tidied the hem as best she could and handed them back. That was what women her age were supposed to be like wasn't it, carrying spare this and thats, plasters, paracetamol? Just in case. Ava's life, until Broadstairs, had allowed her to pop into a department store or send a member of staff out for anything she needed. At least she'd remembered the blue rabbit and copious oatcakes for Daisy who was offering her toy to the woman.

Charmed and happy to play along, she whispered admiringly, 'Your granddaughter?'

'I suppose so,' Ava muttered.

Puzzled how anyone could be unsure, the woman turned back.

She wasn't married to Jon.

The 'arrangements' for this afternoon included Cuddles the Clown, along with an indoor bouncy castle, face painting and games. The team of girls would 'see to everything – nappies, even the bedtime stories, then would listen carefully to the baby monitors in the evening'.

What could go wrong?

Sitting to pray – (*does anyone ever kneel now?*) – she felt the cool puff of air under her skirt as it billowed in the light breeze from the door, relishing the soft tickle on her legs. Wearing stockings, that was what it reminded her of, when the bare tops of her thighs met the hands exploring them. Get down, Scarlet Ava.

'Ava.' She looked in her bag for an oatcake and handed it over mechanically, bartering for good behaviour for a little while. Even at the reception, it would be unlikely she'd be able to relax, would instead be waiting throughout the day for a familiar howl that meant Daisy needed her.

Which left her in this hated yellow chiffon and day-long limbo, once this bit was over.

Up ahead, Amanda was repeating, in the clear voice of a still-enthusiastic new schoolteacher, the vows phrased by the priest. Her groom duly followed and across the aisle, his mother lifted the brim of her hat, an ill-advised red straw job and dabbed with a tissue. He might be earning an enviable salary in a bank, but he seemed to be a softy at heart – unless it was an act for the benefit of his colleagues swelling the ranks on his side of the church, each accompanied by a startlingly beautiful, barely-clad girl. They'd all have fun, seated together at the reception, drinking a lot and laughing even more.

Who would Ava be stuck with?

Olive, she wouldn't mind betting. Jon never seemed keen on his distant cousin – too clever, not pretty – but Ava had liked chatting with her at Edith's funeral.

Ava hadn't seen her since. She had nothing against Olive, but nothing in common with her either. She'd be a responsibility, nevertheless. *It's just not meant to be Ava, this day off thing with a spare male on hand.*

There would have been a sigh of relief at the table-planning re-jig. 'Great! – we'll put Olive next to Ava now Jon's not coming – and Ava will be able to help with that wheelchair she's got now.' Two names crossed off, two old birds, one stone.

Daisy was chuntering quietly to her blue rabbit, so Ava concentrated on the priest's homily on marriage, surprised at being drawn by his performance. That was what it was. No humility, just stellar quality and everyone listening was rapt. She thought something she had not thought for a long time. His dark colouring, deepset eyes, reminded her of something. Will you never grow up Ava? He's a man of the cloth for heaven's sake.

Yes, she argued with herself, but *without* the cloth … Perhaps that was why she was always in jeans now? To swathe herself into chastity, away from stocking tops and temptation?

The homily ended, surprisingly, to a brief round of applause from the congregation. With a swirl, he led the couple and their parents and witnesses into the vestry. As the photographer scurried after them, organ music fluttered around the church once more.

'Lucky that rain stopped in time,' the woman in front of them turned to continue chatting. 'It was awful yesterday wasn't it? I went down to Waitrose'-

'-D'you know this Beacon place?' her husband butted in looking first at his watch, then at Ava.

'The Blazing Beacon,' she smiled. 'I'm afraid I've not been but I'm sure'-

He turned away.

A day of endless small talk. Who'd be on the table with her and Olive? Communal dining was something she thought she'd left behind with her job - pushing food around a plate making conversation. Finding out what you needed to know and performing to your optimum to impress, all nothing to do with eating.

It was over. Will and Amanda sailed back down the aisle, a catamaran of happiness, content and relief evident on a triumphant wave of Vidor.

'Go,' Daisy pulled decisively to follow Jojo, now grinning at everyone, but Ava diverted her attention with a ragbook while the congregation filed out in order of importance. Soon Ava and Daisy were alone with only the organist in the church as the noise level grew outside, released from Church-induced propriety to revel in the sunshine.

The music slowed and dwindled to a final, mournful note and a young girl with spiky red hair, definitely not the elderly man Ava had envisaged, appeared from behind the screen beside the altar, cramming sheet music into a case. But it slipped from her fingers and papers floated to the tiled floor.

'Shit!' the girl fell to her knees trying to catch them, then looked up guiltily and caught Ava's eye. 'Sorry. Sorry.

Late. Got ten minutes to get to St. Agnes'. Saturdays are sods. I'll have to run.' She shrugged out of her cassock, bundling music into her case.

As the white folds fell, Ava saw she was in head-to-toe lycra. And trainers.

'What, literally? Run?'

'No wheels,' the girl shrugged.

'I'll drop you,' Ava said. 'We'll be passing it on the way to the Blazing Beacon. Come on – I parked round the corner.'

'I'm really lucky to get the work,' the girl, who'd introduced herself as Tilly, explained as Ava strapped Daisy into her seat, tossing in the book and rabbit. 'If you could hurry …' she added, glancing at her watch.

'Of course,' Ava started the engine and the Saab roared into life as she floored the pedal. 'St. Agnes' in five minutes. We can do it.'

They did too. A new congregation was already beginning to accumulate on the green in front of this second church, all looking remarkably like the crowd they'd left behind. 'Told you we'd make it.' Ava hauled on the handbrake.

'Ta. See you later,' the organist said automatically. 'Nice feet by the way.'

Ava glanced down at her toenails. 'What these?' The girl had massaged a soft tan onto her calves, they did look good. 'I won them.'

Tilly looked confused, made her apologies and ran.

Ava turned on the car radio quietly so as not to wake Daisy and headed inland.

A strand of DNA connected the child to probably half the people Ava was going to have to spend the day with, so it was the right thing to do, she knew.

And one day soon, she also knew, they were going to have to find Daisy's father. Another right thing to be done. She was always doing them, or trying to at least, as payback for all the years of pleasing herself, not having to worry about anyone else.

Roy Orbison was crying again. She needed to be up today, not teary, so she turned him off. It's beyond tears now, her life. There were a couple of years when her eyes would fill at a remark Jon made or the injustice of her situation but it was her own making. Retribution.

Her old life had injustices too, like the time her phone was lifted from her bag on the escalator at Angel, meaning she lost photos of her Dad. But she'd enjoyed searching through boxes of old photos, shiny rectangles of her childhood, finding snaps of the good-looking tall man holding the hand of his little girl. It felt like she'd got her own back on the lowlife who'd robbed her. She found herself wondering why there hadn't been similar boxes of photos among Edith's possessions – obviously, what was now so instant had been bothersome then, a trip with the roll of film to Boots (or later, if you were daring, posting it to some obscure address not believing you'd ever see it again). Then having to make the return journey to collect the envelope with its generally disappointing results. 'You never smile! Why don't you stand up straight? Why do you always make me squint into the sun?'

She could see why Edith might not have been bothered.

Although the only son, surely they'd have wanted keepsakes of Jon? Records of how he was growing? Why was there only the form photo that had lived on the sideboard?

She remembered Caldwell's face when she handed in her notice, showing him the letter about her new job in London all that time ago. From here on in, he could keep his hands to himself. No point in complaining, *no smoke without fire,* they'd say.

Laughing at the outraged, pompous little man, she'd run, buoyed with exhilaration, from the overheated office in the

Canterbury side street, never a backward glance. Well, hardly.

At work, there would be someone listening to your woes. Other girls saying they'd heard a rumour about what that girl in Accounts had told Caldwell to do with his job.

There isn't anyone listening now, hasn't been for a while. She's become hardened to it.

The thing with having Daisy around for these weeks – any child, for all Ava knew - they besieged every one of your waking moments then they switched off, flopping blissfully, suddenly, into sleep. All the thoughts that would have been carefully dismissed, one at a time, if you hadn't been distracted, busy watching out, mopping up, flooded back to confound you. Or got laughed over with someone; if there was someone.

Lonely wasn't a word she wanted to dwell on.

Their London life, their careers, then being catapulted into playing happy families every other weekend, had been exhausting. When they first came to the coast, she'd happily made Edith's house and Jon in it, her priorities. A little surprised that, out of work, Jon didn't prove to be a joiner, she'd watched their life gradually freeze over, like ice forming on water, take on a sealed quality, not unlike the silent spaces of her childhood. And after all, there was always a good book to enjoy in the silence.

Then Jon's illness had taken over and didn't allow for a social life of any sort.

Turning left, she headed for Wraik Hill, the only bit of the directions which had come with the invitation that she could remember.

Ava pulled over to check the directions carefully printed in pink and stared. She'd barely registered the name of the reception venue, let alone where it was. She must take the next right.

Surely not. Not this way. She traced the line with her finger.

This road leads to another. After a couple of miles winding down round fields, you follow a left turn, a single-track lane curving along from the chalk downs until the land flattens into fertile fields and then finally the sea. She could clearly remember the first time she'd driven down here.

Is it still there? Number 1, Coastguards? Of course. After she'd seen Ted in Whitstable, she'd guiltily allowed herself to google it, flying over the patchwork fields, following the sea's contours until she spotted it and zooming down as close as pixels allowed, the cottage definitely still was there, keeping guard over the water at Seasalter, watching for smugglers.

Probably a holiday home now.

So he won't be there in it.

He didn't even recognise you, a middle-aged granny in the midst of a happy family unit.

No, stick with daydreaming, going back in time to a warm sunny afternoon just like this one. Those deep-set eyes watching her undress … goodness that priest and his breeze had unlocked something.

Concentrate.

She changed down, opened the window and enjoyed the peace. There was no traffic, no walkers, just space…

Today, she had to ignore the pull of the coast, but Ava still made the drive last as long as she could because Daisy had fallen asleep as soon as she'd been strapped into her seat. A good thing, she'd need re-charged batteries to cope with the rest of the day. It was only about twelve miles but surprisingly quickly, the urban sprawl of the seaside gave way to cottages in narrow lanes, then simply fields as far as the eye could see.

She passed free-range pigs rooting contentedly in mud, splashed over the ford, then the hotel came into view. A smallholding originally, now the main house was converted to a restaurant and the outbuildings and stables into accommodation. The Saab crunched over the gravel drive and round to the signposted parking, past the marquee on the striped lawn, sides open to let the breeze in. Judging by the cars here, the place was fully booked for a lucrative weekend. Squeezing between a Range Rover and a Cayenne, there was only just room for Ava to contort herself so that she could reach in, unstrap and wake the toddler.

'That was a nice nap wasn't it?' she smoothed the little one's hair and re-tied the sash of her dress. 'Let's go and see where we're sleeping tonight.'

It was a struggle getting Daisy, their bags, the rabbit, the ragbook and the room key all up the stairs but when she'd fiddled around with the keycard, the room was adequate. They were up in the eaves, so sloping ceilings gave it a claustrophobic feel, but Daisy loved it. It was where a princess lived, she decided.

'And we'll put Rabbit in bed ready for you? I've hung his special towel in the bathroom.' Ava hadn't been able to resist buying the bathwrap with rabbit ears and Daisy always loved the velvety feel of its pile.

But there was a moment's indecision etched on the child's face.

'He'll be safe here,' Ava told her.

Daisy nodded solemnly.

The receiving line inched forwards, towards that red straw hat. The voice was husky from years of smoking. 'Darlings – lovely.'

Hanging back, Ava stared at the seating plan, searching for her name among the tables bearing the names of islands Amanda and Will had 'hopped' through on their gap year. Intriguing to see that on Ko Samui, the name below hers was not Olive, but a *Jason*. Jason Argent. She frowned, unable to put a name to the face.

Oh God, that meant he was one of Will's City friends, looking forward to spending three hours beside a

menopausal woman about as much as she was eagerly
anticipating his incomprehensible, exhausting onslaught
about yields and leveraging. Or he'd be the sort you
couldn't wring two words out of, once he'd identified the
fact you were good for neither bed nor business.

Wishing she'd pushed in earlier, Ava edged Daisy
forward more or less at the end of the line.

The young woman in front of them was bare-shouldered
in a strapless dress, making Ava envy her pert figure.

The ghastly yellow chiffon still fitted, but Ava had spent
what seemed to be a fortune in M&S in a moment of panic,
dismayed by the effect of gravity on her own breasts. The
box promised that the bra would adapt to any style which
wasn't going to matter at all after today, but it was the only
one that didn't show beneath the halterneck.

Will's mother, Ava enjoyed the malicious thought as she
shook her hand, could also have invested in a better bra for
her own outfit.

After a whispered cue from Tania, she turned. 'Darling
Ava, isn't it? Marvellous colour, your dress.' The woman
was a complete stranger but air-kissed her all the same.
'And this is your granddaughter?'

'Yes, absolutely. Ava. And Daisy. What a wonderful
day for you both.'

Will's father shook her hand but his eyes travelled over
her shoulder to the bar and Ava took the hint and moved on.

'Tania – you look *great*. Real Mother of the Bride.
Didn't have a chance to say earlier at the church–'

'If I do, it's a miracle,' the woman laughed. 'It was
awful in the house. Such a rush. Those bloody girls all
panicking about something or other. You've never seen
anything — oh and this is Syd's little Daisy? Amazing.'

'Yes. Say hello Daisy.' But the little girl hid behind
Ava's skirts.

'Never mind,' Tania dismissed and Ava bristled. She
had no idea of the effort it had taken Ava just getting them
here.

'Get on with it you two, some of us haven't had a proper drink yet,' her husband interrupted, enveloping Ava in a hug. 'Little one going to spend the day with Mr. Cuddles is she? Come and have a G'n'T eh?' He propelled Ava trailing Daisy toward the bar, gesturing at the barman to make them large ones.

'All these City types, Gray? Are they all millionaires?'

'Probably. No idea really. But the star guest's arriving late. Bagged him just for you, dear. Had to keep it a secret, of course – the paps follow him everywhere apparently. Turns out Will's known him since they were in short trousers.'

But before she could ask what the hell he was talking about, he was spirited away.

Ava squeezed Daisy's warm paw. 'Come on then sweetie. Let's go and meet Cuddles,' but the little girl who stood beside her now, quieter than usual, was overawed by the throng whose volume was growing by the glass.

'Cuddles,' Daisy repeated hopefully and Ava found herself wondering if anyone would notice if she too, slipped into the Fun Club for the afternoon ...

There was a tug on her sleeve and turning, she saw Olive grinning up at her from the wheelchair which had been decorated for the day with white ribbons. A bigger surprise was Olive's waist-length, snowy hair, loose around her shoulders and sparkling in the sunlight.

'Ava. At last. Someone to have a decent conversation with. You remember me?'

'Of course, Olive. At Edith's funeral. And you were our first visitor at Halcyon.'

'Oh I remember your cake dear – scrumptious. And Halcyon? Still as big as ever I suppose?'

Not for much longer.

'Anyway,' Olive beamed suddenly, 'I like the ... outfit, dear. Yellow. Nice to see someone with a touch of individuality. I always loved that high-neck halter look – you look like The Shrimp, Jean Shrimpton?'

'Are you enjoying retirement?'

'It's better than working, my dear.' There was a surprisingly throaty laugh, then she looked down from her chair at Daisy. 'And just look at you Missy,' she beamed, 'How big you are.'

It was all too much for Daisy and Ava dipped to collect her up onto her hip. The high neck was the main reason she'd settled on wearing this thing. It hid the thumb-print bruise on her neck. 'I wondered who'd be here – Daisy's family I mean – who she should meet,' she asked too brightly.

'Well, Tania and Gray, obviously … and Jojo.'

'Yes, Tania and Gray were at the wake weren't they? But I hardly had a chance to talk to them. Jo-jo's been brilliant with Syd since Daisy was born – a real friend to her. But no-one else?' *After all the trouble I've gone to just to get the two of us here, surely there must be.*

'Not really dear. Bit thin on the ground, the Wilkeses. Oh, old George and Mary - I think I saw them in the church. Hardly recognised them. Amazed they're still alive. I must say,' she brightened with a change of subject, 'I like your hair that colour.'

'Grey you mean. Well it's nice to see you, Olive. You look … great.' To hide the embarrassing surprise in her voice, Ava rushed on. 'How are things?'

'Hot, dear. Any chance of you and I sitting over there, under that tree? I've masses to tell you.'

'Of course. Should I get you some water? Then I must take Daisy into see this Clown chap.'

'I didn't mean that sort of hot dear. There's no hurry. You take Daisy inside.'

The room, away from the main reception and marquee, was cool and tall windows let in a breeze. There was a table of drinks with paper straws, cushions in corners on the floor and soft toys scattered beside them. Plates of sliced grapes and strawberries looked undisturbed, but the Haribo packs lay empty, shelled like pea pods. Packets of wet wipes were on every surface. Three or four young women in matching pink polo shirts kept a watchful eye on the toddlers. Soon Daisy was sitting chubby legs crossed, in the front row, her gaze steadily on the clown's over-exaggerated routine.

From the doorway, Ava watched for a while, then turned and made her way back along the hotel's corridor towards the noise.

Collecting two glasses of champagne, she headed out into the sunshine.

The conversation started predictably with an update of Olive's consultant's views, the failings of the local hospital and Council. 'Not that I have to tell you much about *them* I expect, dear. No, the thing is … I actually feel rather good.'

'That's … good.' She certainly had a glint in her eye.

'I'll say.'

It was polite to press for more of this to be extracted, like juice from a reluctant, unripe fruit. 'Come on Olive. Tell all.'

'Well, you know how it is. I was thinking I should get out more. So I joined a night class – they've ramps up to all the doors now – and I stuck a pin in the prospectus and it was Photography. Well, truth to tell first time, it was *Physics and the Psyche* and I simply couldn't imagine staying awake for that. I trundled along and well – you see the photographer?' She nodded to a tall man with a full head of silvery hair in a mustard waistcoat organising bridesmaids and ushers on the lawn, who glanced over and blew a kiss. 'That's him. Marsh. Marshall.'

'Oh.' Ava's voice sounded small.

'Quite. A looker, I think they call it these days.'

'He was a student too?'

'The *tutor* dear.'

'Oh.'

So that was why someone else had to be found to sit next to Ava. She had become the only singleton. The story of the romance continued and, making the right noises in reply, Ava took stock of the company to take her mind off this new status.

There was a sprinkling of blossoming young women either just married themselves, or engaged, or hanging hopefully on the arms of young men and squealing unconvincing protests every time someone said *Your turn next* ...

'I must say it's really rather wonderful. Mustn't count my chickens of course, but ...' Olive remembered her manners. 'Now you dear. How about you? Jon?'

'Oh, you know ...' Ava took a deep breath. 'Yes, well. It's ... odd ... not having him here.' She watched Jojo, unrecognisable from the denim-clad figure she was familiar with, flirting with the best man's younger brother while a black-haired girl in what appeared to be a turquoise satin handkerchief looked murderous beside him.

''Odd?''

'Oh – a sort of sign, you know. I ... well I should have looked after him better. They say diet plays a part now? Well, it's one theory. No'- she brushed aside Olive's protestations before they could begin, '- I always feel guilty I didn't do more. Or perhaps just did what I did with better grace ... One day, perhaps I'll be able to please myself, then I'll feel guilty about *that*'-

'And now Daisy for ... how long?'

'Yes. Exactly. My penance. It's looking like it's going to stretch beyond six weeks.'

Olive's eyes narrowed. 'I don't think you had to pay a penance.'

Ava shrugged. 'It's the seventh commandment – or is it the sixth? I was never sure - adultery.' The girl in the turquoise handkerchief switched her hair over her shoulders with a deft flick of her head and stalked on imperious stilettos into the depths of the hotel.

'Jon and Margaret were so unsuited,' Olive went on. 'I told him so when they got engaged. Never stopped telling him. Wasn't at all surprised he had a fling. He was lucky you came along – so was Syd. You're more of a mother to that girl than Margaret ever could be.'

'Not enough of one to stop her having Daisy. I mean she's a lovely little bundle, but they always used to say the girl was ruined forever and it's still true in some ways.

'Anyway, it's Willow these days – Margaret I mean.'

'*Willow?* Where did she get that from?

Ava laughed shrugging, 'I think it was her … companion's influence. She seems rather earth-mothery.'

Olive was laughing. '*She?* Really? Bloody hell. Lucky old Jon's not going to have to cope with that. Oh sorry, my dear. I didn't mean- '

'Don't worry. He did know actually, some days. Just took it as confirmation that he'd been right to divorce her. It was a sort of vindication for him.'

'Yes I can see him doing that. Are they happy? Willow and her chum?'

'I think so,' Ava nodded.

'And now you've moved, I gather? Tania's just told me. Edith's old place a bit much for you I expect.'

'Yes. Things have been a bit tight … *stop lying Ava …* I left work too soon really. The flat's a lot smaller, less expensive to maintain and Jon'll be fine there. And I thought the business would mean I could look after him and earn my keep again. The café, the business, well I think it might be going to be okay but it's early days. The commissions from Christopher's paintings will help – he's started listing them on Instagram and the most surprising people, all over the world I mean, buy them.' Ava watched Olive's eyes narrow, gauging how much of this was the truth. *She probably thinks Christopher and I are an item.* 'Anyway, Daisy? It's not been as bad as I thought funnily enough. Exhausting though.'

'As if you hadn't been tired out already.'

Oh look – this is the best I've looked for years. Couldn't you be nice to me?

'The shop's been hard work, harder than I thought. Some days I don't feel too bad actually. It's just – oh you know, as you get older, your face seems to drop and everyone says *Cheer up* when you don't actually feel that bad and that makes you feel worse so'- A swell of anger rose in her and she suddenly felt the need for space. 'I ought to go and check on Daisy. Always dangerous to assume no news is good news.'

'Don't you worry about her. Charlie Chuckles or whatever his name is'll soon say if she's squalling. I need you here for adult conversation until Marsh's done.'

'I ken offer canapés you?' The voluptuous blonde offered a tray of vibrantly-coloured confections.

Olive watched as she made her way, weaving between the increasingly voluble guests. 'Eastern European invasion by stealth – always knew the reds would take over. Mm anchovies though – delicious.'

'He's here!' Turquoise Handkerchief had grabbed the arm of a friend who spun on her stilettoes at the news.

'*No*. Is it really him?' She peered into the comparative darkness of the hotel. 'Did you see him?'

Her friend nodded. 'See? With Will and Amanda look! Ohmygod – he's – I can't believe it –Jas Argent's actually *kissed* Amanda!'

Before Ava could see him, he disappeared in an excited crowd.

'Ah! Marsh darling, I want you to meet Ava.'

She spun to look up at very blue eyes. He was wearing his age well.

'Baby girl, I'd love to shoot the breeze with you two, but I've a long list of family groups the bride wants photos of.'

Shaking his hand, Ava could only think she'd never heard anyone addressed as Baby Girl. Olive of all people. Well. 'I really should check Daisy. Will you be okay?'

'Mmm,' her head was back, face turned up to the sun.

Ava made her way towards the hotel thinking wistfully of the paperback she had, at the last minute, stashed in the overnight bag. There was a corner of the courtyard too deeply shaded to be attractive to the guests basking in the sun, where a low bench beckoned invitingly. Why not make the most of the day?

It felt as if she had been parachuted into this company, was floating gently above the new frocks, tight suits. It was a long time since she'd had two glasses of champagne (oh, and Gray's G'n'T she remembered) and no-one to stay sober for. *See? I told you it was going to be all right.*

The Ladies was full of Amanda and her dress and her bridesmaids. 'Lo Auntie Ave.'

Ava could remember as a child agonising over what to call adults who weren't relatives and being told Auntie. She was torn between appreciating a child who'd been brought up properly – difficult when the child was today's bride – and being made to feel middle-aged, which Ava indisputably was.

'Amanda, you look amazing. Really. And you Jojo.' Ava put her arm round the teenager who brightened.

'Not a bit … you know … *naff?* ' she whispered.

Ava shook her head resolutely. 'Completely not naff. Fit? Isn't that the right word now? I don't know how you can manage those shoes though.'

'Actually,' the teenager confided, slipping off a strappy pink sandal then sitting, foot drawn up on her knee as she rubbed, 'they're like *killing* me.' She massaged her foot, head back and her hair shone slippily over her shoulders. 'Did you see him? Isn't he just – well – fantastic? I never thought doing this,' she plucked at the fuchsia satin derisively, 'would mean actually meeting Jason Argent.'

'Er …' Jojo probably thought she was prehistory already, so Ava seized the opportunity. 'Who is he?'

The girl turned, eyes wide with incredulity. '*Who is he? Who is he?* Just the hottest ever, Ave. He's like … *huge.* '

Ava grinned, shrugging. 'Well fine. But doing what? What is it Jason Argent actually does? Films or something?'

'Oh Ave. BGT? He got the most votes ever. Then it turned out he acts too.'

Was BGT part of the gay scene? Ava tried to look impressed as Jojo went on, 'That new thing with the spies? He got his kit off remember? Come *on.*'

'Oh. Him.' Ava did remember that. '*Television.* With the curly hair. On his head I mean.'

'You musta seen it?' The girl's face shone. 'I was like *ohmygod.*' She sighed happily and turned to the mirror, scrabbling in her clutch bag for eye pencil and began re-painting her face.

'I see,' Ava said with feeling. An actor without a script in his hand would have nothing to say and a young, good-looking one would be ten times worse. Still perhaps he'd open up about the nude scene. One thing was sure, he wasn't going to be the missing part of Ava's plan. Too young. Too good-looking.

The space emptied as Amanda followed by her flock of flamingos swept from the Ladies'.

Able now to get to the mirror Ava dragged a brush through her hair. There hadn't been time to tint it last night. Just as she was about to get started, Christopher had messaged for three cakes *Urgent* for the morning and Ava was reluctant to risk the pungent purple toner dripping into the cake batter while she waited for it to work. Wondering how Christopher was doing at the cafe now she reached for her phone then saw the lipstick in her bag. He'd just have to manage without her.

Slipping back through a side door, Ava collected a glass from a waiter and found herself a spot in the sun on the far side of the hotel from the noise.

'Lo again.' Bottle in hand, Tilly stood in front of her, swaying slightly.

'Hello yourself,' Ava was pleased to see her.

You see? Everything's going fine. Plenty to drink, someone new to talk to. Not so bad after all, is it? 'That's a great dress Tilly – looks amazing on you.'

'Heart shop in Faversham High Street.'

'Really? It looks new.' Ava thought Tilly probably hadn't a lot of money for fashion.

'Yeah. They're really good – people with money and consciences live around there. And we can't keep making stuff and throwing it away can we?'

Another shovelful of guilt landed somewhere near Ava's feet. Well, alcohol made her defiant, her kitchen dresser was being re-purposed. 'I suppose not. I'd have gone there myself if I'd known.'

'That dress is fantastic though,' Tilly lit a cigarette nodding at the yellow chiffon swirling on the flagstones. 'Vintage?'

Two things made Ava laugh at that – what Jon's reaction would be and the fact that it had probably been in the shop so long when he bought it, it counted as exactly that.

'I've just had it a long time and … I didn't know you were coming here too,' she changed the subject. 'How did that wedding go?'

'Oh fine. They're all alike really. 'Til you get to your own I reckon.'

'I should think that's true. Or you get one where someone actually says there's a just impediment why they can't get married … Has that ever happened to you, when you've been playing the organ I mean?'

'I live in hope,' Tilly grinned. 'I shall play the Hallelujah chorus.'

'Wonderful,' Ava laughed.

'You won't catch me doing all this stuff.'

'Bet you change your mind when it comes round.'

'Nah. What about you? Did you do the big white dress?'

At least she hadn't added *in your day.* 'Well, it was just the Register Office actually.'

'Cool.'

'We didn't want a fuss.' Ava pictured Syd's furious face wedged tightly beside her father at the front of the small group in the rainy photos.

'Oh is he here, your old man?'

Ava was better at saying this now, had found a form of words that signalled enough for strangers not to probe further. 'He got very ill. They thought it was a brain tumour at first …'

'Oh my gawd, poor you. How did you know … find out?'

'Find out? About Jon?' Ava helped Tilly out. 'How ill he was you mean?'

It was a question people started, then backed away from. What they wanted to know was, what should I watch out for? And she never usually answered in detail, because you could see the fear in their eyes, as they listened to whatever symptoms she recited, just in case something sounded horribly familiar.

'It was like a rope – you know?' Ava looked at Tilly. 'Gradually untwisting, strands snapping and flying out. All the things that had held him together, manners, the right way to behave, the need to *protect* himself – they all just left gradually.'

'Couldn't they do anything?'

'He was referred of course. I went with him. Everywhere, by then. If he went alone, he'd forget why he'd gone, miss the appointment and come home. So there'd be another wait. Anyway, this day,' Ava emptied the bottle into their glasses, 'it was like Alice in Wonderland. This doctor - he *was* the White Rabbit? White hair, big front teeth in a long, pale face, white coat and – you couldn't make it up – a pocket watch. No wonder poor Jon lost it.'

'So … this brain tumour thing? Did it take long for him to … you know,' her voice dropped, 'die?'

'*Die?*' Ava looked at her. 'Jon's not dead, Tilly. Oh god, no,' she laughed bitterly. 'Life's not that simple.'

Ava sat in the garden, allowing the dusky heat to envelop her as the voices rose on clouds of alcohol, watching Tilly sweet-talk a waiter for another bottle.

Coach lamps set onto the stone walls began to glow, casting golden circles of light onto the bench beneath. She had deliberately chosen this seat though, because it had no lamp, as if she might disappear. If possible, she would have liked to simply evaporate. The amount of *words* today had already spilled around her, coupled with the prospect of small talk with Jason Argent, of continually worrying whether her make-up was standing up to the warm moist air, of sitting up straight in a dress rather than the habitual jeans, of pretending to enjoy the ridiculous food because it would be rude not to, of spinning out the evening with sips of wine alternated with water, of … *everything* made her head tighten. *Be grateful*, she reprimanded herself, to be part of a social occasion. *Invited as almost-family to such a jolly, forward-looking thing as a wedding. Why was it such an ordeal? I mean, it's not so bad here after all. Is it?* She felt herself begin to thaw.

'You still with Greenfields?' A man's confident drawl came from the other side of Ava's wall.

'God no. Greenfields Homes is long gone actually, yeah. No, best thing that ever happened. Set up my own agency with the payoff?' Ava guessed it was a couple of the polished-face men at the bar earlier. They both laughed loudly, grown-up versions of the City boys she used to meet. Not very grown-up at that.

'Yeah, definitely a good move. Good spot on the high street and top properties will always sell,' he added implying he wouldn't deign to handle cheap houses. 'You just have to persuade the seller a lower ask value is sensible in current market conditions. And frankly,' the voice continued lower, 'some of them are very *attractive* clients, you know?'

'Yuh? Lucky you. Haven't the energy myself, not after the commute and getting back for bath time which Angie insists is quality time, though for the life of me, I can't see why. I prefer it when they're tucked up in bed fast asleep. Little angels then.'

'Two is it now?'

'Four.'

'Christ, no wonder you're exhausted old lad. Good thing you are knackered if you ask me. Four's enough eh?'

'Well, you know, still fond of things in the bedroom department on a Saturday night, if you know what I mean? Ange looks pretty ok I reckon, for her age. Getting ready to come this morning, I said to her, let's just leave it at the fascinator shall we, when we get in? That and those heels that cost me a packet eh?'

'Good for you. Me – well you won't catch me getting hitched again. That bloody divorce nearly did for me. Still, then Greenfields went down, I started up the business and my very astute numbers man makes sure the ex only sees the books the taxman sees – you know, the ones where we're making no profit at all to speak of.'

'Good man,' the voice said wistfully. 'So, up for any opportunities that present themselves eh?'

What simple souls men are, thought Ava, programmed to make money and have sex.

'You bet. Matter of fact, there's a girl been giving me the eye looks like she's up for it.'

Her skin began to prickle.

'Yeah? Which one's that?'

'Short red hair, black bodycon dress looks like it's sprayed on? She was talking with that couple of old girls – Wattle and Daub I call 'em – Wattle's the one in the wheelchair, when she laughs, everything below her chin flaps. Daub's the one in the lipstick. Wattle and daub – couple of period properties, get it?'

The sheer bloody cruelty of it, of the pair of them, pompous self-congratulatory oafs believing Tilly could possibly fancy them, being so unkind to Olive despite all the problems she was facing and … worst of all was the fact that really they'd a point. Ava wasn't used to lipstick now and had been stupid to think spending money on one would magically wipe away the years. Wasted money, wasted years.

Eyes filled with hot tears she didn't know she had left, she stumbled to her feet and headed away to the far side of the garden as fast as she could in the dusk across the flagstones in these ridiculous heels. She moved so quickly that she missed the rest of the treacherous conversation on the far side of the wall.

Another forced laugh met with silence, then, 'That one in the yellow though – Daub? Yeah. Quite a looker I thought. Under that lipstick, I bet she'd know how to give a chap a good time …'

'There you are. Sorry I took so long,' Tilly had found her again, champagne bottle in hand but there was no time to enjoy it.

'Ladies and gentlemen! The wedding breakfast is about to be served!' The toastmaster, red-faced and red-jacketed, boomed over the champagne-fuelled excitement.

But it looked as if people weren't going to play as the toastmaster boomed again, 'Please take your seats' and nobody made the move out of the last of the sunset.

Across the lawn, the hotel manager was whispering earnestly at Tania who shrugged helplessly, then gestured to Ava, pointing to Olive.

'I'll have to go, Tilly. See you later?'

'You got it.'

'Come along now folks,' a new voice sang out, 'let's not keep the happy couple waiting! This way now!' Everyone turned to see who'd called over the hubbub, whose arm it was beckoning them all in.

'Ohmygod. It's him – come *on.*' The girl beside Ava grabbed her friend and, leaving their men trailing, joined the stampede towards Jason Argent who by positioning himself just inside the marquee's draped entrance was luring them all in, asking their names and pointing to their table on the plan.

That's clever of him, Ava thought, returning to steer Olive into the line. *Kind? Or just egocentric?* Well she'd soon know. The filling marquee was buzzing now, everyone exchanging jokes about meeting the famous one, not washing the hand he'd kissed or being sure he'd taken special note as a girl had given him her name.

'Hello there.' Jason dropped to his knee and took Olive's hand. Close up, he was smooth-browed and over-groomed. Ava would never get used to shaped male brows. Watching Olive's face light up, Ava thought *Now that really is over the top.* 'Let's see. Where are you...?' he peered up at the plan as Olive pointed. 'Ah, yes. Here, shall I?' and he took over the handles from Ava and steered Olive between the tables to her place, a wake of murmured admiration behind him.

How to milk an audience Ava thought walking, as unremarked as if she were transparent, towards her own seat. Hide Family, it had said on the plan with her own name and Argent's. And Tania's aunt and uncle who she vaguely thought must be nearly ninety now. She couldn't place the Hides though. Must be groom's side, she decided, reaching the table just as Gray shepherded up a small man, his wife and their two small children, all with shiny black pudding basin haircuts from short to long, each of whom bowed solemnly to Ava before perching decorously on the little gold chairs. 'Ava'll look after you,' he said loudly. 'Sorry. Got to dash.'

Across the table, Uncle George muttered something about the War, took out his hearing aid and switched it off.

'Now dear. Don't spoil it for everyone,' his wife admonished and turning to the small boy, beamed, 'You can call me Aunty Mary. What's your name?'

Startled he jumped to his feet, bowed again and looked at his father.

'Please excuse,' the man began diffidently. 'I working in London at bank with William. He extreme kind invite and family heeday.'

'Today dear?' Mary looked puzzled.

'Family heeday,' he pointed at the place name. 'Heeday.'

Not Hide then. Heeday. And they all turned as Jason Argent pulled out the chair beside Ava. 'Good, that's everyone in I think.'

The room rippled as people craned to watch him and Turquoise Handkerchief actually stood on her little gilt chair to get a picture. 'Jason,' he said unnecessarily to Ava. 'Hello. Pleased to meet you. Ah – showtime.' And leaping up, he helped Ava move her chair back first, then moved quickly to see to Aunt Mary and Mrs. Hide, as everyone stood, then applauded as the bride and groom made their way to the top table. It was exhausting just being in his slipstream.

'Sorry,' he said, peering down at Ava's place name. 'I can't quite …'

'Ava,' she said, slightly surprised. 'Ava Wilkes?' she turned the card towards him. Was he dyslexic? 'Distant family.' There, that pigeonholed her well enough surely.

'Great,' his voice dropped to a whisper. 'Actually I'm blind as a bat and I dropped one of my contacts down the toilet this morning. Couldn't ask you to be my eyes today I suppose? Not supposed to wear specs in public –image thing, you know,' he shrugged apologetically.

'Oh. I see. Well, yes, of course,' Ava reassured him. He was somehow more human sitting down. 'I don't think you'll have to do much reading here. How did you manage that business with the table plan then?' she asked, curiosity aroused.

'Practice,' he said grimly. 'People recognize their own names faster than anyone else's, you know. And I've got the speech off by heart I think.'

'You're speaking? But you're not the best man …'

'No – shame really. Will and I were good mates at Chatham House… Prize exhibit though,' he brightened. 'Sort of cabaret. Later.'

Because you'd have stolen the limelight as best man. 'I'm sure you'll be brilliant. It's your job!' *And I suppose you couldn't come to the church for the same reason.*

'Actors get scripts. I had to write this one myself. Childhood scrapes, teenage indiscretions, first love flops?'

Alarmed by faint twinges of sympathy, she reminded herself sharply what fee Jojo had said he'd negotiated for his latest contract. She leant to one side as the waitress placed a plate displaying three prawns on an artistic squiggle of pink in front of her and caught the scent of him. The Hides looked at their own plates with consternation.

'Ah,' Jason squinted down at his own plate. 'Sorry. Shellfish. No. Reaction - you know?' he looked apologetically up at the girl.

'Oh that's *great* – I mean, no problem, Jason. Sir. I'll get you the melon,' she beamed, scarlet. 'Be right back.'

'I bet they drew lots,' Ava smiled. 'To see who'd get your table ...'

She was surprised at first by his downward glance, seemingly modest. *Don't be stupid,* she re-interpreted. *It's because they're not his type, girls.*

As the waitress proudly placed a melon boat in front of her idol, the Hides pointed excitedly and Mr. Hide began negotiations to have the prawns in front of them replaced too. Something to do with the violently pink sauce they were surfing, Ava gathered from the gesticulations.

'Now look what you've started,' she nudged Jason's ribs. 'Any minute now, there'll be a tsunami of rejected prawns flooding the kitchen.'

'God,' he glanced guiltily at the top table. 'Hope they've got enough melons to go round.'

Ava gingerly nudged a prawn towards the pink blob on her plate. As she speared it with her fork, it left a gelatinous ruby smear. 'I *think* it's only beetroot. Oh look,' she reached for the card hidden among the flowers at the table's centre. 'A menu. Don't worry, I'll read it to you. *Deepwater langoustines ...* well, hardly ... *on Chef's own beetroot and vanilla foam.* Why do they mess around like that I wonder?'

Munching on melon, Jason shrugged. 'Well they've got to colour it with something, or it'd look like cuckoo spit. And to satisfy the public's appetite for saying things like ...' and he adopted a falsetto, 'of course, we served beetroot foam at my son's wedding in our artfully draped marquee ...'

'You're right,' Ava laughed and pushed the plate away. 'I can see why you're in show business. Was it something you always wanted to do?'

'Absolutely. Not the office type.'

'You've been lucky – done well. Oh – obviously, you're talented, I didn't mean it was just down to luck.'

But he said, 'No, you're right, it is luck. For every audition where I've got a part, twenty didn't and probably two hundred didn't even get seen. And luck breeds luck. Your face gets known and people want a bit of that success in their next production.'

'I suppose that's the downside too, though. Your face getting known. Bit hard to have a ... private life?' she winced at her own euphemism.

'Too bloody right.'

'Madam?'

Ava started as a different waiter balancing plates on one hand, placed one in front of her. They'd obviously worked out a rota so everyone got to meet Jason.

Something that looked like rather poor modern art, a cube of pale meat, some squiggles of greenish sauce and three asparagus spears criss-crossing one another. Lucky she wasn't the hungry sort, Ava thought.

'Looks fairly grim, doesn't it?' Jason whispered.

Before she could agree, he went on, 'Bit like old Will there, eh?'

Glancing at the groom, Ava realised with surprise he was right. Will's face was set, his eyes staring. 'Just pre-speech nerves, don't you think?'

'Either that or he's realised he's been caught,' Jason laughed.

'Surely … I thought they looked happy enough at the church?'

'Ask me, I think he's begun to realise just how clever Amanda's been.'

'I did wonder when her hobbies had included rugby, I must admit,' Ava said thoughtfully, adding, 'and sailing, actually.'

'I think,' Jason pushed the food around on his plate, peering at the end of an asparagus tip on his fork, 'that he was hunted like an animal. The trap was prepared, baited and in he walked. Caught. For life.'

'I do know what you mean. About being a hunted animal. Why does it happen? Why aren't we willing to live alone? I know you can be lonely in a marriage. And then there's all this 'The One'. What *really?* In the whole *world?* It's so unlikely to work, this commitment.'

'You have thought it through,' Jason nodded admiringly. 'Excuse me−' he caught the waiter's arm, 'I'm afraid my friend and I aren't meat-eaters. Suppose you couldn't rustle up say, some organic salmon perhaps?'

Overwhelmed at actually being spoken to by a TV star, the lad stammered about seeing chef and clutching the arm he had touched rushed away.

'Naughty,' Ava reproved, smiling.

'My agent,' he said ruefully. 'My diet's not mine to determine.'

'Tough deal,' she couldn't feel too sorry for him. Before long, the waiter had come back with two plates of fish, butter sliding invitingly over the steaming pink flesh and they ate, laughing like conspirators, ignoring the envious glances around them.

The toastmaster bellowed above the sound of cutlery being cleared, 'Pray silence for the father of the bride,' and Gray, tugging his waistcoat, got to his feet ostentatiously tapping his glass. As he began to speak, Will appeared to be lost in his own thoughts, staring at the notes in his hand.

Trapped. Hunted and trapped. Well, Ava knew how that felt… but he was soon in control, almost corporate.

And now, strawberries and cream all gone, it was the best man's turn. A mere shadow of his brother, he stuttered and stumbled through a series of unsuitable and poorly-timed one-liners, thanked the bridesmaids and sat down, relief evident.

'Wasn't quite right up here,' Jason tapped his temple, 'as I recall.'

'I see. Poor boy, with such a dazzlingly successful sibling.'

'Yeah.'

Then it was time to clear the tables before the dancing. 'Thank you,' Ava said, gratefully to Jason. 'I've enjoyed your company.'

'Likewise. First dance is mine, right? Soon as they've cut the cake and I've performed.'

Ava wouldn't hold her breath for that dance. Dropping a kiss onto her head, he nodded to the bride and groom who beamed back. The videographer zoomed in.

A murmur of anticipation breathed across the room as Jason took up the microphone.

'Ladies and gentlemen, everyone, I'm delighted to announce that Will and Amanda will now cut their beautiful cake.'

There was a dutiful cheer and the ornate knife sliced dramatically down through the soft white icing. It looked like a gesture of violation, an echo of days when girls really were entitled to wear white, making Ava shiver. As the camera flashes died down, Jason made a show of taking a folded script from his pocket, fanned his face with the sheets to a good-natured ripple of laughter and began.

It was a good performance, affectionate and not quite as professional as she had expected, calibrated to entertain without overshadowing his schoolfriend. Word-perfect, Jason made a point of congratulating the groom's hapless brother on a job well done as best man. Faces beamed, everyone toasted and glasses were drained. As the applause rippled away the happy couple got up to sway to Adele.

'Just right,' Ava nodded to Jason as he took her onto the floor. 'Everyone loved it,' she said. 'I can only stay for one dance though, it's past bathtime.'

'Yours?'

'No. I've a little one to put to bed.'

'Ah. I see,' he nodded but obviously couldn't guess at Ava's complicated life.

He slid an arm round her waist, took her hand with the other and bending her slightly backwards, began to swoop around the floor to the music. It was *easy*. How odd it was to be dancing again and to be doing it with him was surreal. This blend of bodies, not formalised, just following the rhythm - how long was it since she'd felt like this?

How did she feel actually? Just … tonight, not old.

It reminded Ava of someone and then she knew who.

She slipped out to the Fun Club. It was bedtime.

Daisy had not missed her. Had eaten up all her tea, made lots of new friends and been well-behaved all day. Well, Ava thought, it was like putting a dog in a kennel and going on holiday – the dog wasn't going to complain of maltreatment, was it?

She plonked the toddler in the bath and let her splash as much as she liked. It was the hotel's problem, not hers for once, if water seeped into cracks and dripped below.

But the mirror was a shock again. All that eating and drinking had made the lipstick disappear and an older, more tired version of herself stared back. For the first time, Ava realised this was the Ava Daisy knew, not the painted version of earlier in the day when she'd felt more like her old self.

'Let's get you dry and find Rabbit. Look, there he is, in bed, waiting for you. And there's your little nightlight for when the big one goes off so you can sleep …'

As she read the bedtime story she read every night because Daisy asked for it, Ava's mind wandered. She should re-do her lipstick before she went back…

Sandwood. Dior. Twenty-five pounds something. More than she could afford but perhaps wearing it would lift her into well, if not the same league as most of the women at the wedding, then at least out of the unpainted comfort zone she inhabited these days. All these young females were delectable, toned, glossed, waxed, exfoliated, honed down to slivers of themselves whereas all the women of her age had become their own caricatures - chins, noses, more Punch than Judy. Even the ones who were obviously able to afford limitless pampering could no longer pretend to compete.

She took spiteful pleasure in reminding herself that the exotic flock of young birds on parade here would probably be in their nineties by the time they got a State pension, the way things were going. *You dismal old trout, pensions would never have crossed your mind once upon a time. Now they're always on it.* What a fool she'd been to think she could just stop work when he did. Despite the difference in their ages, she had taken him at his word that his investments would keep her without working.

The Telegraph's Frock Bit, as Jon used to call it, full of stick insects in clothes that cost more than the Saab was worth these days, had said this lipstick was the latest colour from a line of cosmetics promising perfection all day. The glossy toffee-coloured stick appealed to Ava and she had gone to Canterbury to buy it because the local shops wouldn't get it for ages and anyway she couldn't bear to be served by someone who might recognise her and think *Poor old love.* It had been strange being back in the City, seeing that the old office and its car park had been swallowed up by a block of apartments.

Bolstered by perceived anonymity, Ava walked across the department store's sepulchral marble floor towards the counter, praying she wouldn't trip.

Perhaps just buying this lipstick could transform her. You never, Ava reflected, saw anyone lovely sitting at these counters being made-over. Only women of her age, family wedding in the offing, desperate for a passport to the glamour that pervaded everything these days.

Presiding over the counter, all black glass and gold tubes and big prices in small writing, was a slim man with immaculately contoured eyebrows and a touch of mascara in an improbably unwrinkled face. One eyebrow lifted slightly as she neared so maybe it was just good genes, not botox. He actually sounded quite excited when she said what she was looking for and insisted she sit on one of the white leather stools while he fetched the new tester.

With her back to the shop floor and thanking her judgment in getting out of her own town, Ava took in the display of glistening powders and liquids set out temptingly before her. They all offered magic. If they could really rejuvenate to that extent, why did anyone ever look old, she wondered.

What on earth was she doing here, captive audience to the sales patter and worse still, so obviously in need of much more than lipstick? Trying to avoid her reflection ambushing her from the mirrored surfaces, she concentrated on the testers. Her finger itched to blur the quilted patterns of the pristine shadows, gouge a nail deep into the bronzer's embossed surface. She pictured herself freeing the foundation bottles from their platform and squirting them wildly into the air, covering the black gloss with flesh-coloured trails.

A posse of rake-thin schoolgirls with long black legs beneath pelmet skirts made its way through the counters, while gimlet-eyed assistants watched for light fingers. One girl with hair the colour of chestnuts saw Ava and said something to the others who laughed back.

'Sorry. Took forever,' Ava's man was back. 'These Saturday girls never refill anything. Now let's try this, shall we?' About to say she'd just take it and run, Ava found her face being cleansed with damp cotton wool as if she had arrived fully made-up.

'I must say,' he dabbed colour onto a disposable brush and began to fill in the line of her mouth, 'you've good bone structure. Hair too for'- he stopped before *your age.*

'This is just my hair,' she shrugged. 'I don't mind the grey – with this tint on anyway. Marie said it's fashionable now.'

'Not Broadstairs Marie? Really? How's he doing? Haven't seen him for ages.'

'Oh sh- he's fine. Very good at … the job. I've never been able to do anything but this style anyway. So this is how it's stayed.'

'Mm,' he smoothed the fringe down and flicked the sides behind her ears. 'Suits you. You're lucky. Give Marie my love next time you're in.'

'I will.' *You see that's another new friend you've made. It's easy without Jon.* Refuelling the guilt tank, she relaxed and, marvelling at such intimacy with a stranger, she let him fill, blot and re-fill her lips...

Daisy was asleep, cherub-like and clutching Rabbit.

Ava twisted up the lipstick and tried to copy the salesman's expert touch then switched on the baby-listening monitor and slipped back downstairs.

Yes, Reception assured her, they could hear Daisy's snores loud and clear, she would be fine.

In the courtyard, Tilly, glasses and bottle in hand, sought her out. 'So if life's complicated,' she continued their conversation as if the meal hadn't happened, 'you'd better begin at the beginning.'

Ava watched the young girl whose music had filled the church, tap the packet and extract a cigarette then offer her one. 'No thanks. He was just there one day at work.'

'What did you do?'

'Property, estate management, investments, valuations. Don't look like that. In the 90s, it wasn't everyone who was making loadsadosh. It was just a small family firm, got taken over when the banks wanted a slice of the action and suddenly there were money men crawling all over us, picking over files, questioning valuations … Jon was one of them. He was assigned to City Road, where I worked.' *And saw me. Gullible Ava.*

'Lust at first sight?'

'Something like that. It all sounds so obvious really. A cliché.'

'Go on, I'm hooked.'

'Well I thought I was for the chop too. So many people lost their jobs. But turned out I'd made myself useful enough to warrant being kept on in the brave new world.' In the distance, the disco was thumping. Stubbing out her cigarette in the flower bed, Tilly urged her on.

'They made me manager of the branch then I got a seat on the board.'

'Good for you,' Tilly nodded encouragingly.

'Yes and no. All the responsibility. None of the perks. They'd gone with the new brooms.'

'And that was when you and Jon got it together?' Tilly was lighting up again.

'Yes. Later, we got it together. Should you smoke so many by the way? You play beautifully. I never expected the service to be so moving – and it was largely down to your music.'

'And The Archbishop,' she laughed. 'He's a very high opinion on himself, that vicar. Still it wasn't bad. Considering.' Tilly drew on the cigarette. 'Anyway smoking's not going to stop me playing, is it?'

'Well … in the long term it might,' Ava warned. 'I know middle age seems years away, but it'll be here sooner than you think.'

'Yeah, yeah,' Tilly shook her head. 'Whatever. So go on, you were telling me about you and Jon. Hammer and tongs stuff was it?'

'Pretty much,' Ava laughed. 'We went out a few times, it was fun. I didn't think it was doing any harm really, but Jon was taking it more and more seriously, I could tell. But I didn't expect anything to come of it. You don't. Married men, you know …'

'Yeah,' Tilly said with feeling.

'… then suddenly he was there, in my flat at two in the morning.'

'Sounds like a stray cat.'

'He was rather …' Ava remembered the wounded look on Jon's face.

'So – happy ever after then, was it?'

'It was a surprise – something I hadn't considered. There were compromises – well, for both of us. I was used to having my own space, he was used to being a father.'

'So you got used to having him around?'

'It's a long story.' And this wasn't the time and place to tell it.

'But you love him, so that's all right isn't it?' Tilly tugged up the top of her strapless dress and reached down to the champagne bottle at her feet, revealing a tattoo snaking up the top of her shoulder to her hairline.

It was very hard to say. How easy it is for love to slip to indifference when you've had things happen. Easier to lie. 'Yes. Quite.' Ava mused, wondering why girls scarred themselves now. In church clothes, Tilly had been sombre, her cropped red hair the only rebellious sign. Tonight, in this tight black dress, her long legs ending in ridiculously high platforms, she looked free and rather glorious.

Tilly hiccupped into the dark air. 'Did you think you'd have kids with him?'

'No. They were never on my agenda.'

'Just wanted it all to yourself, did you?'

'That's a funny thing to say.'

'Well you weren't saving anything for future generations, you banker-wankers.'

'It didn't seem like that. And there was money to be made.'

'S what I mean, 80s earth-gobblers – huge hole in the ozone, global warming. Not much of a legacy to leave is it?'

'Christ,' Ava felt herself tearing up. Yet another bloody thing to feel guilty about. 'I'm not saying you're wrong but maybe it's easier to see, to be wise, after the event. When you're my age…' and that was a phrase she never thought she'd use, 'I wonder what your generation will regret?

'Our aim was to make money, so we could buy anything. And,' she rose to her own defence at last, 'I chose not to have children, add to the world's burden.'

Sensing the sore point, Tilly mused, 'S'funny, isn't it? How it's the one thing some women really want and the one thing some other women don't want. Such a big thing. Whether you do or whether you don't.'

'Yes,' Ava, glad to get on to something on a scale she felt she could handle, agreed. And she'd heard plenty about the tormented agonising, compressed by a ticking clock, some women felt.

'*Huge,*' Tilly emphasised with an expansive wave, forgetting she was holding a glass which tipped into her lap. 'I'd love six kids,' she shrieked with laughter and hiccupped again.

'Do you think …' Ava struggled to her feet. She'd been matching Tilly, glass for glass and her foot caught the bottle and sent the last bubbles foaming over the uneven flagstones. 'Do you think maybe we've had enough, Tills?'

'Never,' the younger woman was emphatic. 'Can't ever have enough. Out of all the people who've been at this wedding and that other one I done at St. Agnes'—'

'—Did,' Ava corrected automatically.

'S right. The one I did at St. Agnes – well, do you think *anyone's* sober?'

'Not likely.'

'There you are then. Now. Games. Spin the bottle, yeah?' The girl leant forward and whirled the neck of the empty bottle with her forefinger. 'When it stops, truth or dare, yeah?'

'Whatever,' Ava felt herself slipping backwards in time to when life could be carefree. And of course, the bottle stopped pointing directly at her.

'Ha! 'Ere we go, then. So,' Tilly cupped her chin and stared. 'What 'appened? He just made an honest woman of you?'

Ava frowned. 'Why do we still say that? I wasn't really worried about marrying. It mattered to him though.' She drew a deep breath and watched the moonlight outlining the shape of the green glass at her feet. Confronted by Tilly, she had to acknowledge that it had all been … *steady* … after that.

'And what did he say? One knee job was it?' She shook open a packet of cigarettes and lit another.

Ava wasn't that drunk. 'That's two questions. Spin the bottle first. Go on.' And this time, the bottle revolved on its label until the neck neared Tilly's bare feet. 'Ha! See! My go. So … men.' Slightly sobered she got her head together. 'Who are you in love with Tilly? Truth now.'

The girl blew smoky, boozy breath from puffed cheeks. 'I gotta tell the truth?'

'You have,' Ava nodded solemnly.

'No-one. Ever again. I done three years at the School of Music. Last year, there was a new tutor. He played so, so beautifully. I loved, really, really loved him and it's got me nowhere. At all. No. Fucking. Where. Married, course.'

First love. World-shattering. That, Ava could cope with. And Tilly's story reminded Ava that Jon could have stayed with Margaret. 'You won't ever forget him, I promise you that. The way you felt when things were good.'

'You're the only person to say that. Wish my mum was more like you. She and all of them are all like I'll forget all about him, plenty of fish.'

'Then I bet they all say they remember their first love, don't they?'

'Actually yes.'

'It's what I mean. You remember what that first love made you. Stronger. More, oh I don't know, more grown-up. And sometimes, in your head, aren't you sitting watching him, listening to him and just loving it?'

'Yes, yes.'

'That's what you never forget.'

'Christ I do wish my Mum was like you. She's been like, mad. Wanted to go and see the Dean, have him kicked out of his job. I said that won't make him love me Mum, will it?'

'Well I think it's fear – that you'll be damaged. And anger of course. That someone's hurt her baby.' Ava heard her own surprise at the realisation.

'See? You'd have been a great mum.'

'Well it's a bit late now, but that's fine by me. Why not,' she bucked up, 'have a dance with Jason Argent? He's gorgeous, isn't he? I sat with him at dinner – he's lovely, very chatty, very nice. I wouldn't blame you for fancying him. I could introduce you if you like,' she said generously. 'He'd be happy to have someone more his own age to talk to. I'll tell him how beautifully you played the organ today. That Vidor was masterly.'

'Oh,' Tilly let out a shrill laugh. 'I know Jason, Ava, he's my brother. Well, sort of. Half.'

'I didn't know'-

'S complicated. My Mum and Dad split. We never saw him for years, then next thing, he's got a girlfriend and she's got a son. Jason.'

Ava could only manage 'Oh …'

Then their heads both jerked in unison as thunder rolled around in the heavy night air and a shard of light lit the countryside around them.

'In!' they both laughed together.

Gradually the sound of rain on the marquee roof grew, the steady percussion getting heavier. Oh well, someone said, at least it had been sunny for the photos.

Guests crowded back in from the garden, shaking rain off and laughing at one another. The staff were frantically closing the sides down. As rain began to beat horizontally against the plastic windows, there was thunder, making the ground shake and lightning followed almost at once.

'Come on everyone! Let's drown it out!' the DJ yelled and switched tracks to It's Raining Men.

I'm gonna get ...

There was another clap of thunder.

...absolutely soaking wet

And just as Ava remembered Daisy, asleep in the room in the eaves, a flash of lightning slashed the sky and immediately, deeper thunder rattled the glasses, lights went out, somebody squealed with excitement.

Above it all, a distant voice cried 'Fire!'

Flying past Olive being pushed by the young waiter through the melee at reception, Ava takes the stairs two at a time scrabbling for the key card in her bag. She should go back for her, but Marsh will be looking after her surely and she has a tongue in her head. Daisy, on baby-listening in the room, can't do that.

Her stomach heaving with anxiety, Ava swallows bile as she gasps for air. She's on the final flight now – and can she smell smoke? Christ, don't let anything happen to her, God, I know I've been bad, but she doesn't deserve this. *The sins of the fathers ... and non-mothers.*

Jamming the card into its slot, she takes it out too quickly and the red light flashes. Jesus how hard can this be? What happened to keys? These things must have some sort of failsafe thing for powercuts. She pulls herself together and tries again. Further along the corridor, a couple are emerging from their room, the man pulling on his jacket and dragging a wheelie case while his wife hops from foot to foot, trying to put on her shoes. Finally, at last, Ava hears the door lock click and bursts into the darkened room.

'Daisy, Daisy I'm here darling.'

'Nightlight.'

'Yes, there's no electricity to make it work because the hotel has been struck by lightning- *Oh leave that out, she doesn't have any idea what you're talking about, stupid.* 'We have to go darling, nothing to worry about, we have to get downstairs. It's another adventure.'

'Where's Charlie?'

If he's any sense he's a million miles away from here.

Ava is trying to wrap Daisy in the quilt from her bed, find the toy rabbit, bundle things into her bag, telling herself not to be stupid, she just needs to get out. *Why did I drink so much? God where's Tilly? God why did I ever come to this stupid wedding?*

'Off we go darling,' she tries to sound grown-up.

With Daisy in her arms, bag on her shoulder, Ava feels her way down the corridor – *careful, mind the stairs – I think they were here, on this corner.* Cautiously she probes the dark landing with one foot in front of her until, at the curve of the wall, she finds the top step. 'Here we go, sweetheart. Just one more flight after this.'

And what about Jon? If something happens to me, who will look after him? She makes an effort to move even faster. As she turns down past the first-floor landing, she can follow the flight of stairs by clinging with her free hand to the handrail and below her, voices and phone torches are within reach.

Except for that treacherous little half-landing she had forgotten about…

Falling and desperate to cushion Daisy from whatever impact is to come, Ava folds her in her arms just as her foot hits something very hard and pain sears up through her body.

Then there is only blackness and pain.
And all she can think is *Who'll look after Jon now?*

As Ava tries to open both eyes, her vision is filled with flashing lights. There is movement – jolting and sliding, then there are voices – Jojo and Tilly and Jason -and with Daisy still in her arms, she loses consciousness again.

Rain slews horizontally across the wipers' ineffectual arc. She hurts from her toes up to her hips, her whole leg throbs. The relentless thrum of the car's suspension jolting up tracks and round corners matches the percussion in her head. Everything hurts more than she would have thought possible. A knife is thrusting up through the sole of her foot, searing and twisting around her shin and carving into her kneecap. Keeping awake for Daisy, who is snuffling fitfully in her lap, Ava can only pray that the lunatic driving this thing knows where he's going and wherever it is isn't far away. There is a strong smell in here of tobacco – not, perhaps, cigarettes but something else, scented and heavy. Combined with the fall she's taken, the LandRover's diesel fumes and a neckful of champagne which she's not used to, it's a nauseous mix.

'Uh!' The sound is forced out of her mouth before she can stop it as the vehicle plunges, bucking again to begin a stomach-churning, wheel-spinning ascent up the mud before racing down what seems a sideways, vertical slope.

'Oh my god!' Jojo, squeezed between Tilly and Ava with Daisy, panics. 'We're going to roll!'

But the car settles, the headlights' main beam picking out trees, a lot of mud, what looks like a crop of wheat and at one stage, everything slithers to a curving halt to avoid a sheep whose face looks out of the darkness. The hard door handle catches Ava's funny bone as she slides forward, unable to hold anything to steady herself, so intent is she that Daisy must be cushioned. It would help if she could brace her good foot on the floor, but the space is filled with something squashy and lumpy - from the stink, something to do with a farmyard.

With the next lurch and a crunching of the gears, something from the space behind her, something soft, wet, and very smelly, topples heavily between Ava and Jojo. It has animal qualities.

'Oh my god it's a *sheep*, a *dead one!*' Jojo screams.

'Don't be ridiculous, girl,' the driver who seems to Ava to be too old to be driving this vehicle, growls above the engine, wrestling with the gear lever, 'it's a sheep*skin*. I 'ad a newborn lamb on that this morning. Mother wasn't interested in the little beggar. Only meant to have lambs in spring but it's been that sort of year.'

'Sure it's not still in here?' Tilly clutches at the back of Jason's seat to distance herself.

'Daft girl. Moans a lot, don't she?' he yelled at Jason. 'Nearly there.' Ava can't remember what relative of Tilly's this man is, just that a tent in the middle of nowhere with a darkened hotel and a deluge was no place to be in her state, Tilly had said, wrapping a blanket from one of the bedrooms over her shoulders as the flames grew, crackling, oblivious to the rain.

They bump and slide along the top of the ridge the car has managed to scramble up. Outside, there is only biblical black night. Water is seeping under the door cills and the unmistakeable feel of wetness that should be outside, not in here, is creeping into the one shoe Ava has at last managed to get on the floor. If this rustbucket breaks down, they'll be nowhere until morning, with lightning all around them.

'Ava,' Daisy mews tearfully.

'Nearly there.' Ava cuddles her under Jason's jacket.

Now and then, the car swerves as a tree, a hedge, another obstacle looms up in the headlights. The car is steamy, but so cold that she can watch her caught breath, exhaled in fear. Another burst of thunder, right around them it seems, and lightning turns everything into day for a second, then there is only the blackness until a second, closer bolt lights the countryside. Everyone jolts and slides in the deafening, crunching chaos as the diesel fumes thicken.

Even in her throbbing, confused brain, something hits Ava's awareness, a lucid picture of a field, a line of trees and cottages in the distance. *A cottage with a line of trees to break the north winds.* Well, how many of those are there in the countryside?

But, as they bump down the last track, she sees it in a final, apocryphal burst of electricity. Rain slewing across the catslide roof, cascading over the gutters and splashing into the gathering levels of water in the yard behind it.

'Quite a night eh?' Jason yells over his shoulder at her. 'Here we are though. They're expecting us. Let's get in.'

Lowering his voice not to frighten the child, his arms stretch out. 'I'll take little'un.' The rain on the car roof is an incessant drumming. Ava lets him haul Daisy between the seats and the child, tired into comatose limpness, rolls onto his lap.

'Tills, Jojo, wait there – I'll get coats.' And he and the driver have gone.

'Tilly,' Ava's teeth are chattering with cold now. '*Who* did you say this place belongs to?'

'It's a bit complicated,' the girl begins, shivering now still only wearing the tiny black dress. 'My Mum's sister was married to our Uncle Pat and then when that all went pear-shaped…' but the convoluted lovelives of Tilly's family dance and wash around Ava like waves, as the pounding in her head at last begins to fade and her eyes slowly close ...

A faint whiff of kerosene permeates her brain. One eye opens slightly, the other following. A room comes into focus, a low room lit by the lamp which is making her nose twitch and the cracking wood fire in the inglenook's log burner.

'Thank Gawd for that,' Tilly breathes out relieved. 'Thought we'd lost you Ava. Now, I don't know about you but I'm busting. Where is it, Jas?'

He nods to the door. 'End of the corridor, turn right by the back door.'

'Left.'

Everyone in the room – and Ava can see now that there are several human shapes around her, turns at once, surprised to hear her speak. 'It's left,' she repeats in the darkness.

She knows where it is because she's been here before.

'It's on the right. Then put her in my bed, Tilly,' a surreally familiar voice instructs. 'We'll get her to a doctor in the morning.'

In the morning … it sounds like a lifetime away. Now the painkillers they've given her are beginning to dull things and she loses her grip on everything.

The door opens, a flashlight picking its way over to her. 'Hello Ava,' Ted bends over her and kisses her cheek. 'How are you feeling?'

She slides an arm out from under the duvet, wraps it round his neck and pulls him down to her, breathing in the scent of him. 'How can this be happening?'

'Mmm. You've missed me then?'

'So much.'

'Be careful. I don't think you're in a fit state to find out just how much I've missed you.'

She groans and nods reluctantly. 'Just what has happened? Why am I in your bed?'

'Can I come in too? It's a bit cold out here.' Soon he's undressed and is slipping in beside her, sliding his arm carefully under her to fold her into a hug and that scent, his odour of heat and musk that she has dreamed about, is still there. 'I think for now, we better just give up trying to work it out. The others have all got places to lay their heads. Young Daisy's asleep in her cousin's sleeping bag. It's three in the morning and I'm knackered as well.' His warm bulk in bed is so different from Jon's cool sinuous presence. And listening to Ted's steady deep breaths, Ava falls asleep.

When you have lived in a house for fifteen years, its noises are your familiars: creaking pipes remind you of plumbers' bills, rattling sashes balloon wind into gas bills and they all curl around your waking head. Lately, she has got used to Daisy's first wailing call to check if the grown-up is awake.

If you're lucky, there are no cries because Jon has fallen and no unpleasant finds on the bathroom floor.

The gulls have woken Ava as usual.

But this house has different sounds, a chair being pulled out across what sounds like a stone floor, a fire being poked and raked out, saucepans meeting the hob but not catastrophically with things being dropped and broken.

And voices. Two. More possibly.

Whose house is this then? Like a dizzy heroine, she thinks Where am I? then shakes her head because it looks like Coastguard's but then again, it doesn't, so it isn't. Ava slips back into sleep and only wakes when trying to roll over, pain inhabits her whole leg in a stabbing gripping vice.

Then thankfully, Daisy's voice is laughing.

But no Ted and so it was just the fevered imagination of a menopausal woman who had too much to drink.

Although the sweater Tilly put her in last night looks like it might be his. The dishevelled yellow chiffon bundle on the floor won't be any use now though, she can tell.

Then the door opens in the half-light and Ted's carrying in two mugs.

'Tea and more paracetamol,' he tips two into her hand. 'Take those first. Christ it's cold but I've made up the Aga and I think the sun's going to be out later, so it'll warm up. There's no electricity yet.'

'Ted?''

'Yes my love?'

'Just checking.' First things first, she needs to pee. 'I have to get up. Bathroom.'

He helps her to the door then leaves her. Everything hurts but she can manage she tells him. 'Go back to bed.'

The skylight is letting in a dawn the colour of stainless steel.

Her face is a mess. Raking her hair with her fingers, she splashes water, wincing as it stings in the scratch down one cheek as Daisy clutched at her and that leads like a pointer to the bruise. What might even be the start of a black eye turns out to be smudged mascara. That she has waited so long for Ted and this is how she looks is actually funny.

Supporting herself on the furniture, she makes her way back to bed and crawls in beside him. Yes, she is all right. No, not too cold. Well, a bit. She finishes the tea. 'Where do we start? What's?'-

The door pushes open again and Daisy totters in, her frown turning into a giggle as she sees Ava and scampers towards her.

'There she is. Told you didn't I? Hey, careful,' Tilly runs in after her and just collects her in time to stop the toddler landing on Ava's leg.

'Want Ava,' Daisy wriggles out of her arms and runs up to Ava who holds her, thinking how good it feels, a child in her arms and Ted beside them.

'Well Ava's not very well. Come with me, we'll find some breakfast. She needs to sleep. Or something.' One eyebrow raises as she shoots a look at Ted and with Daisy under one arm, she closes the door behind her.

'Where we start is easy,' Ted puts his arm back round Ava. 'We never stopped. A lot of things got in our way, but I never felt any different about you. And now you're here. When they brought you in last night, Tilly told me a bit – and Jason - and that's all I could think. She's here. Home. I couldn't believe it at first. Now … what about this husband of yours? Christ, I don't even know his name.'

'His name,' Ava began, 'is Jon and for now at least, you only really need to know two things. He is very ill and ...'

Ted looked down at her and frowned. 'Bloody hell. What's wrong with him? Cancer?'

'Well three days ago he was dying, but it turns out they'd cocked up his tablets. So it's just dementia. Quite advanced.'

'Oh Christ, Ava …'

She shrugs. 'It sort of grows, you don't see it at first, then it's mild cognitive impairment, then you don't want to see it and then it's impossible to ignore and not possible to give it any other label.'

Ava sees Jon now as an egg timer. For years he has been emptying gradually. Now, answering these questions, Jon has flipped but the sand that is steadily filling the space where he was is a quite different colour. The Jon he was, she loved. The Jon he is, the stranger, she doesn't.

'Does he still have good days?'

She shakes her head. 'No just better bits of bad days. There's very little left of him.'

'And where is he now?'

'God. With Fay. I'd completely forgotten – can we ring?'

'Broadstairs? The signal's really poor. I doubt it, but she won't be expecting you yet? Tilly says you were going to be at the hotel overnight. The last phone call I had was from their Mum worried about 'her babies' at a wedding at the Beacon, then the signal went dead. Pete set off for them and came back with you too …'

They both consider that. Ava speaks first. 'Yes, but I'll have to get back …'

'We'll see when it's properly light. And? You said and. When you were talking about Jon in the beginning. And what?'

She will tell him, but first there is something she can't leave. 'I've got to know,' she whispers, 'what you did?'

'What I did?'

She searches for words. 'The burglaries. Antiques. It was in the paper.'

'Oh *Christ.* That was years ago. That wasn't me, Ava. I mean, yes they pulled me in, the police. But I didn't do it.'

'They must have had a reason.'

'There were … links. Yes.' There is enough light now to see anguish furrowing his face. 'I couldn't tell them what I knew, but I had alibis. The things – well the ones that weren't sold – found their way back to their owners.'

'And you said you were going away for a bit…'

He lets out that gust of laughter she loves. 'To Belgium. Not bloody Belmarsh, Ava.'

'I didn't think anything of it at first – you being away, I mean. And then you weren't back.'

'I was in Belgium,' he repeats, 'at the big Salvation Army warehouse first – it used to be so good for stock, but they'd stopped doing it. And I had Tommy with me for lifting and carrying, the truck and a pocketful of cash, so I thought, we'll just go and look for stuff. Went into every old farm building, disused factory. It was a brilliant trip, just a lot longer than I'd expected because other dealers I met up with kept buying my stock to save themselves the trouble of looking for it. So I kept on, into Eastern Europe, all over. Didn't worry me, I was glad to be away from her. Missed Owen, but I was making money.

'Sally had been nagging me for a shop, I told her it wouldn't pay and it never has much but I keep it on ...' he shrugs.

Ava remembers Christopher's dismissive comment about the wives of rich husbands wanting a hobby as Ted goes on, 'She wanted it as part of the divorce settlement and I take a share depending on what's sold there. She put in a manager, local woman and I go in to keep an eye on it.'

'When I saw you ... I thought I was dreaming. You looked so .. you. I thought you'd made yourself scarce because you didn't want to know me. It was all too much trouble, fitting me in to your life. So I left. Got a job in town, moved there.'

'Never gave me another thought no doubt.'

'I believe,' she says deliberately, 'that I thought about you every day. Even the day we married.'

'And decided you were well shot of me.'

'*No.*' This is all so hard. And there is one last question unanswered. 'I'm sorry, I don't understand ... I can't just leave it. Can't you tell me? It wasn't you, the burglaries. I don't think I ever believed it was. So who then? A friend?'

The deep-set eyes fix on hers, gauging her reaction. 'Tommy. My little brother.'

'Why is everything back to front?' As morning light begins to fill the room, Ave puzzles at her surroundings. 'Did you change everything again, surely not?'

'Oh,' he laughs that deep warm sound. 'No, you think you're in number one but we're in number two and number three's through there,' he nods. 'The cottages are mirror images. That's why you thought the toilet was on the left of the hall last night – I see.'

'You did buy the other two,' Ava's delighted. 'All for antiques?'

'No. Boutique B&B they call it. I'm just a seaside landlady now.'

'Hardly,' she chuckles. 'Don't see you in a pinny.'

'Quite right. I had to do something to keep Tom out of trouble. He went off the rails, grew light fingers. Silly sod thought he was being clever, clocking stuff when I took him to see people who were selling. I said you'll throw your life away if you carry on like this. You have to work for what you want. He and Owen trained together as chefs.'

'What's he doing now?'

'Back at sea. He'd been in the Navy.'

'Yes I remember you saying.'

'He started off catering on yachts. Then the Navy but ... he came home on leave and I took him round with me. Which turned out to be a mistake. Now he's on the cruise ships.'

'Sounds a good life.'

'He's all right now. I think. But he's a grown man – just has to get on with it.' He doesn't sound confident.

'And Owen?'

'I gave him this,' he nods at the walls that surround them, 'to make a go of it. It's his business and it's doing very well and so is he.'

'How marvellous.'

'No, he's getting bored with it already, I can tell. You do when you're young, don't you? Want to move on?' The silence grows. 'If you're thinking about Owen's mother ...'

'I am rather.'

'Gone. Found another man – someone she could boss around. O goes to Wales to see her now and then. They've got land, horses and she's queen of the castle. I pity the poor bugger.'

'Oh. When was this?'

He looks down at her. 'She left about ten – no more, years ago – when I rang you, remember? I've been waiting for you to come back ever since.'

The door opens and Tilly, Daisy and Jojo come in with toast and butter and coffee.

'Careful you three – Owen'll give you jobs,' Ted laughs and gets backchat for it. Daisy's come round to Ava's side of the bed and clambers over her legs ignoring the winces she bites back to wriggle somehow between her and Ted.

'Now,' Ted begins when the big girls had gone downstairs and the three of them started on breakfast, but Ava interrupts him.

'I couldn't ring you back, Ted. I wanted to more than anything but I thought, you'll just bugger everything up. You're married, he's married. And I was just going to be … inconsequential again.'

'I didn't ever think of you like that,' he frowns.

'But how did you get my number?'

'Oh,' he laughs. 'Got Steed to ask around. Remember him? He found the cottage obviously, but Corinne had sold it, gone to the Middle East somewhere. But he made friends with the new owner – *good* friends as it turned out.' There's a sad chuckle. 'She was just his type. So he eventually got Corinne's number off her.'

'And I'd told her I was determined to make a success of being married.'

'She said that. But she said, all right, here's her number now. I leave it up to her.'

'I'm glad. But you said was. Steed's all right, isn't he?'

He shakes his head. 'Gone I'm afraid. Overdid everything, Steed. It caught up with him.' He took a deep breath. 'Now, suppose you tell me about this little one.'

Daisy is snoring gently on Ava's lap and he pats her pudgy arm without waking her. 'Your granddaughter.'

'Yes,' Ava says emphatically. 'She is. I'm really sorry about Steed though. You'll miss him.'

'Yes.' Very gently, Ted's finger brushes her neck. 'This didn't happen last night Ava. Bruises start off black then turn yellow.'

Her head drops so that her hair covers it. 'He doesn't realise he's doing it. I can cope.'

Downstairs the girls are sitting at the long table while Jason, who's forgotten his agent for once, eats bacon and eggs.

Owen cracks two more eggs onto the griddle. 'So Dad's in bed with her? Really? Wow. The woman from the wedding?'

Tilly nods.

'Gross at his age.' After a while, he looks up frowning. '*Why*?'

'They go back apparently. And why do you think? The usual reasons.'

He slides the perfectly fried eggs expertly onto her toast. 'Bloody 'ell. Thought he'd gone off all that when Mum went. Said he wasn't into women, they were trouble. Another one for you Jas?'

'It's heaven, forbidden fruit, but I'd better stop, thanks all the same.'

Owen shrugs, 'Suit yourself mate. Just say if you change your mind. There's a freezerful of stuff defrosting in the outhouse, all got to be eaten.'

There are heavy footsteps in the hall. 'You cooking? I'll have anything.' Sniffing appreciatively, last night's driver appears from the hallway and sheds his battered Barbour as he helps himself to toast.

'Right you are, Pete.' Owen drops more rashers onto the griddle and cracks another egg.

Now the back door slams open and a lad, denim legs caked with mud, slams it shut again. 'Look at the state of me.'

'Davey! Well I didn't expect to see my kitchenhand today.' Owen slaps his back. 'So the lane's ok, is it mate?'

'Would I look like this if it was? No I walked over the fields. They say it'll be midday before you can drive it, there are trees down and the pigs escaped when the fence got broken. They've got to be rounded up first or there'll be an accident. Me mum's got mud up to her knees in the house. I said I had to go to work, Ted won't pay me for staying at home.'

'Well you can just turn right round and go back and help her,' Ted appears from the hall. 'I'll pay your money for today, just help me clear this lot up here, then I'll get out and see what damage we've got.'

'Looked all right to me when I came in,' the lad casts another glance at Jojo who's still in her bridesmaid's satin.

'Well, get something to eat, then I'll see about getting the car out of the mud,' Pete wipes bread around his plate.

'Gonna give me a hand Ted?' He nods upstairs. 'She'll still be here when you get back, I reckon.'

'Yes Dad. I reckon.'

Ava watches him rummaging in his wardrobe. The sandy hair and that square, open face haven't changed – oh maybe laugh-lines at the sides of those deep-set eyes.

She sits on the edge of his bed, dressing from the bag Tilly rescued for her. The white linen is crumpled but all she has here. As it slips down over her shoulders she can feel his eyes on her as she zips it up.

'It's good on you. I'd rather it was off you though,' he muses.

What is she thinking of? She's become Miss Havisham, still in her wedding dress at over fifty, a physical wreck, even with painted toenails, with an urgent need to earn as much money as she can and get back to the husband who needs her.

Perhaps it's a reaction to all that's happened since she stood in the church and this, least of all was where she thought she'd be after the wedding. Ted, of all things, of all people. What is she doing? She buries her face in her hands.

'You're quiet,' he's back beside her with a thick sweater. 'Try this. Oh Ava, what's wrong?'

Her voice won't work properly. 'Ted. Jon has to have someone to look after him and that has to be me. I promised.

'I should never have gone to bed with him – he'd still be married to Willow and Syd wouldn't have had Daisy and I wouldn't have had ... I just fancied him for a while and that turned out not to last and so you see I shouldn't have done it?'

'Ava,' he says gently, 'some people are made to enjoy sex and some aren't. Yes, it alters their lives but that's what happens. We can't be in control of everything. I knew the minute I met you, when you looked over your desk at me, remember? I thought yes, we'll go to bed together. You didn't make him – and he could have said no, but he didn't did he?'

'And then Margaret wanted rid of him, threw him out. I had to go and pick him up. That was something else he lied about,' she remembers, thinking how pleased she'd been when she believed he'd chosen to be with her. And how disappointed she'd felt recognising the truth.

'There you go. If she hadn't, do you honestly think he'd have married you? Oh sorry, didn't mean that the way it sounded. He's a port-in-a-storm man by the sound of it, looks out for himself.'

He is, was, that's right. 'Then there was work and the takeover ...'

'None of which was your choice.'

'And anyway, there's Daisy and Syd when she gets back from Australia and Christopher. I can't just step out of that life.' *Don't say 'and into this one.'*

He folds her into his chest. 'Don't worry. We'll make it work. This time yesterday I didn't know where you were. Now you're in my bed. That's progress I'd say?' He smiles at her laugh. 'One thing at a time. We'll get you back to Jon somehow, then you can see how he is. Then we'll make some plans. Daisy's having a lovely time in the kitchen eating everything, she's happy. This Sid though – who's he?'

And just like Jon did, that day in his office, she spells out *S.Y.D – it was her mother's idea.* 'She's Jon's daughter, the little one's mum, and she's in Australia with her own mother and her girlfriend at the moment.'

'Christ. This is going to take a while, I can see,' he laughs.

And that, in the end, is what undoes her, how he takes everything, every flip-flop life throws at him and rides it like a surfer. 'Whether it's bad or not, I love you Ted,' she says very quietly.

'Bad? Whyever is that bad?'

'I told you once before and that was what you said.'

After a pause, he nods, 'I remember. Because you didn't want to get married, you said. I knew it wasn't going to work out, me and Sal, but I couldn't see how loving me was going to be good for you if you didn't want to settle down. I didn't want you torn over me and your career. When I was away buying that time - I thought about you all the time. How I might be able to make it work, us I mean. You'd mentioned working in London if you qualified and I could see why,' he nods. 'So, could I work in London? Not ideal business-wise – huge overheads - and there was Owen. I wanted to see you to talk it through as soon as I got back, but the police were waiting for us at Dover. Stripped the truck – everything we'd bought, all over the Customs Area. I thought they were looking for drugs but then they started to ask questions about places I'd bought from before the trip. It went on for weeks, what with them thinking Owen was the one who'd come with me, lifted things, so we had to prove alibis for all the dates, all over the place. Then I knew I had to make it clear it had been Tommy. And he was at sea by then, so it had to wait until he could be put ashore. The Navy loved that.'

'It must have been a nightmare. Trying to prove you were innocent, proving a negative.'

'When I realised what Tommy had done it got even more complicated, because he'd left some of the smaller stuff at home to sell when he got back on leave. When he told me, I did what I could to return it to the owners or compensate them, whatever. Christ, it was a mess.' Ted runs his hand over his face.

'You took them back? Explained? That took guts.'

'One or two were so impressed they let me buy more from them, actually,' he laughs. 'I did all I could. None of this was what I wanted to land you with. And if I'd rung and said I couldn't see you, you'd have wondered what the hell was happening.'

'Yes.'

'So, finally, it was cleared up. Tommy got a suspended sentence, got discharged and he was lucky, went back to sea, cheffing on cruise ships. Dad wouldn't talk to me because I'd been honest and shopped him. I talked him round in the end, but it all took so much time. *Finally* I felt I could ring you.

'And then you were gone. Nowhere. I went all over, the offices you were running, your flat. You'd just vanished, deliberately I thought and … I understood. You were young, obviously going places. What would you want with a chancer like me with all that going on?

It makes her gasp.

'Then I got your number and the night I rang, you were cooking dinner. I heard you say about turning the veg down and I thought that's it, I missed the boat.'

'I couldn't, just couldn't, ring you back. The consequences … I thought about them and I realised I never

344

did that before. I just rushed into it. And I saw it had been wrong. Wonderful, but wrong.'

'And then I saw you all. In Whitstable.

'You looked such a family. But like I say, Tilly told me it wasn't, isn't, quite like that.'

How appearances can deceive. 'Oh god. I looked at that monkey in the window and thought, Ted's laughing at me.'

'But we've got it straight now though?' For once, Ted looks worried. 'You love me, don't you? I feel, like I did when I met you, the same.'

Then he's up, a forcefield moving round the room, pulling on jeans, socks, shoes. 'Let's sort out how things are going to work. I'm going to go down and dig out the LandRover, see if I can get you back to civilisation and that husband of yours, poor sod.'

'I'd never have believed,' Ava looks into his eyes, 'that it's possible,' she said quietly, 'to love two men at once. In different ways obviously. Not living with them both though, of course. No one man, let alone two, could cope with that. Ménages a` trois are always two women and one man aren't they?'

'But … you still love him then?'

'The trouble is, he isn't the same man. I can't not ... feel concern. Not feel sorry for him. This is a horrible end for anyone.'

Ted swings out of the door, 'We'll talk it over on the way. Now I'm going outside. Don't for god's sake, run away again.'

Soon, her ankle bound and cushioned, Ava is back in the LandRover. They got it out of the mud, Ted and his dad and lifted her into it, strapping her in and adding a hot water bottle for good measure, because the smell means the windows have to be open as they ride the country mud.

In the cottage doorway, Jojo holds Daisy, cheerfully waving goodbye as they pull away. 'See you soon. Soon as the trains are running.'

'So tell me about Jon and you,' Ted swerves round a fallen trunk in the lane and the branches squeal across the paintwork. 'I don't want to ask, to know. But I have to. In the beginning,' he saw her wince. 'I'll tell you anything you ask *me* Ava.'

'Right. Well.' Relishing the breeze coming in the open window, Ava shrugs, 'God knows. Men in positions of power, you know? They ooze it, even the ugly ones. It's almost like a challenge they issue to women. *I'm important - are you attractive enough to hook me?* I don't know why it works that way – maybe after all this time, women just want the alpha male to make their babies – for survival of the species? But I think I saw something I could respect too, admire, he was very, very good at the job. He had such a good brain. I suppose it just burnt out.'

'Pity he didn't put it to better use. What was it actually, this job?'

'Asset-stripping – or at least advising the scavengers. He spotted the obvious everyone else missed. So assured. But that,' she made a grab for the door handle as the car skidded then settled, 'that turned into a sort of blustering stubbornness rather than sureness, a sort of mild bullying – oh not physical, but just ... well, the other day, Daisy wouldn't let me put her shoes on to go to the park. There was a set to her jaw that was pure Jon. *If you don't stop going on at me I'm going to make a scene then you'll be sorry* ...and of course I backed down. I haven't the time to,' her fingertips made quote marks, 'talk through issues' like the therapist say to do.'

'No. You just want to say look, let's get on with it, enjoy the day.'

'Exactly. It was a side I hadn't seen to him – or maybe just the dementia, for the last few years. But there was no way out. I worked round it to start with, then made it so things didn't rile him and it was easier after that. It wasn't me really, but …'

'Why didn't you leave him? Oh I suppose you're going to say because you felt responsible for him and he needed looking after.'

'I did think that, yes. Responsible for his divorce, Syd's damaged life. I'm not proud of myself – in fact, if I'm going to be honest, I don't like myself much these days either.'

'It's not you, it's what you're having to deal with.'

She flexed her back. 'It's getting old. I sometimes think I've become Margaret. Perhaps that's what being married to someone does. You get moulded into their type over time. But what I look like and how I feel …'

'We are all older, Ava. But I want you as much now as I did that first day in your office- '

Oh. 'You made me wait,' she laughs.

'-we all get older,' he repeats. 'But you're still you.

'And there's another thing Ava. You've been good for so long, you've forgotten how to have fun without feeling guilty. I bet you, oh good, this bit's clear,' he turned up onto a slightly wider lane 'you'd feel guilty if you won the lottery. Think it should have been someone more deserving.'

'I feel guilty about one thing or another,' Ava reflected gloomily, 'about once an hour.'

'See? That isn't the real you. Oh, it's very worthwhile but it's draining you. Jon is ill. And that could have happened – would have – whoever he was married to. He'll need care soon, if he's started to get unpredictable.'

'That won't happen – the care I mean. No.' Ava said. 'Do you know how much it costs? I took him to see one place, because the time will come when I simply can't cope with it all and he'll need regular medicating. Some of the episodes have been a bit frightening. But Ted, it was so expensive. I came away feeling like I'd got a life sentence. I couldn't leave him there, no matter what it meant doing. If I had the money, I'd start a business, a care home, to keep him in it.'

'There's something else you haven't told me. You said *and …*' back in bed. Tell me I'm prying if you want.'

'It's money,' she sighed. 'And it's way beyond complicated.'

'Go on, if you want.'

'He stole.'

'Woah.' Ted glanced into the mirror then pulled over. 'Who from?'

'Companies who could afford it, like the one we worked for. It's going on all the time, all around the City. And people get away with it. Blind eyes are turned because that suits.

'And, it turned out, from me too. It's not a nice thing to say, that your husband has made off with your pension fund.'

'He *robbed* you? What sort of a man would do that?'

'It's complicated. I should never have given up work. And that bloody great house of his eats money. But I didn't go without, not really,' Ava says quietly. 'He paid me. Until the money ran out.

'I don't suppose I'll ever really know everything. But there's very little left. Of the house, his pension, *my* pension. My best guess,' she sighs, 'is that he was living the life he wanted and the life he wanted to give me. Not thinking about the consequences. He chose a path didn't he? Remember that poem? It's all we ever do.'

'So it was a Ponzi. He paid you your own money. And then couldn't remember what he'd done I suppose.' Outside, the sun was filtering through the last clouds of the storm, the countryside radiant with the colours in the trees blazing with the last life of autumn.

'I don't know. I won't get my State pension now for years and it just feels so long, so I've got to stick with the Sea Garden to pay the bills. The flat needs work – oh, it's a home but it could be so much better and I don't know why I bother because all he ever wanted was that great big pile because it was his mother's, but she had a woman come in

348

twice a week and a gardener and no husband doing awful things all over the place- '

'Steady on, Ava love. Fight your battles one at a time …' he patted her knee and she could feel the warmth of his hand. 'All right to go on?'

When she nodded, he put the car into gear and drew away.

She pulled herself up. 'When you marry, you say *for better or for worse*. I heard myself say the words and honestly it was the first time I'd thought about that but you can't back out half way through the ceremony. I grew up in a split second.'

'It's a big promise. But everyone can only do their best. You can't be superhuman. All the modern dream stuff about having it all – careers, house, cars, holidays'-

'-and it's even worse now for girls, the young ones like Tilly. They have to have it all and have perfect children.'

'They'll get old too Ava. I can't stop you getting older… I can't stop me getting older.'

'That's a comforting thought,' she laughs. 'About them getting older I mean, not us.'

Isn't us a big word? Only two letters but it carries so much volume. It falls into the car like a boulder. 'I'm talking too much. It's just so lovely to be able to *converse* not just deliver baby phrases.'

'I see,' he laughed. 'So, I'm just here for a good chat?'

'*No.*'

'So, you'll try?'

The paracetamols were making her drift again. Just as well because all of this would be impossible to manage unmedicated. She winced as she flexed her foot to test it. 'Try?'

'To unlearn being a saint.'

'Okay, but to be honest I think you're the saint around here.'

'Believe me,' he stopped at the crossroads, held her face in his hands and kissed her then reached for the gear lever again, 'I'm just waiting 'til you feel better … now do you feel up to going through the figures? In round terms?'

'I told you,' she sounded sharper than she intended, 'There's virtually nothing. Jon did what asset-strippers always do. They fillet off the prime stuff, feast on the meat then throw the bones to whichever jackal gets there first.'

'And the prime meat was you my love. Young, beautiful.'

'Was I?' she was surprised.

'I used to dream about you in between getting my hands on you,' he grinned happily.

'I didn't know that.' There's a pause while Ted circumnavigates fencing which has blown into the road, swerving the car up and along the hedgerow bank, making Ava cling on to the grab handle in the roof to keep herself from sliding.

'Anyway, now, there's no cash anywhere, only the house when the contracts were exchanged and the charge on it from the firm ate most of that and … really there's going to be hardly anything.'

Ted pushed back from what used to be Edith's kitchen table and linked hands behind his head. 'So that's it? Nothing else anywhere?' They'd spent three or four hours on the Sunday evening going through everything.

'Sorry,' Ave shook her head. 'Believe me I've scoured all the papers. There's no more money to be had.'

'Okay. State Aid no use to help with care costs?'

'No.'

'No surprises there then.'

'They'd only cover the basic sort of places. I've got to top it up and I don't know if the café can support that. But it's my problem, not yours. Being here in this flat cuts outgoings and with time, and when Syd comes back to look after Daisy again, I'll manage.'

'I don't want you to manage,' he said carefully.

A week later, Ava was in the café kitchen before Christopher came in, getting soup on so that the customers and Jon would have something to eat. In her head, Ted's words bounced and echoed – different things he said, how he sounded. He was still the man she remembered, something for which she was very grateful. *Really though, can he actually be this wonderful? Wouldn't it always be the case that the Ted I've dreamt of is unreally perfect? Aren't all men?*

But the thing she's surprised by is that she's no longer tired. Instead, she burns with energy. She can consider things, plan.

Christopher's first question – after wondering why her ankle was strapped – was 'Well?'

It meant did you have a good time? Tell me all the gossip. What did everyone wear?

What he hadn't expected was the blush that crept up Ava's neck. 'Oh my god. You got lucky. Ava you did, didn't you?'

She couldn't stop smiling. 'Not the way you think, no. But yes. I did get very lucky. I met someone I used to know, a long time ago.

'Lucky cow.' Christopher's admiring glance reminded her.

'Thanks for getting me scrubbed up. It helped, honestly. But we didn't .. you know.'

'Give it time. Anyway, my pleasure ducky. I'd do it every week to see you smile like that on a Monday morning.'

'Well. Time Cinderella got back in the kitchen. Work to do….'

Think. Think. She chops onions then sweeps them into the oil. *You fell in love with him, fancied him, went to bed with him, then believed he was a burglar who'd done time.*

So you ran away, didn't you? To London and to Jon. And if it hadn't been Jon, it would have been another hapless pair of trousers.

The radio was on Radio 4 for Daisy to hear grown-up words instead of the endless repetition of toddler talk she and her grandfather shared, but so far it just seemed to lull her to sleep, so she was upstairs in her cot, napping. The headlines came on.

Ava heard something she couldn't believe.

'What?' she shouted. *'What?'*

They raised the retirement age for women. Again. Now she couldn't stop hot tears of frustration. Nearly two more years until she got her pension.

'You heard that,' Christopher came in from clearing tables in the garden, filled the sink with hot water and dumped cutlery into the bubbles. 'I saw it on a customer's Sun, the headline. They're bastards, this government.'

He went off to collect the last used china from tables in the café. Rain was pelting against the windows, mirrored by condensation on the inside.

'All governments,' Ava muttered grimly, adding them to the water. 'However old am I going to have to be to actually stop working?'

'I thought you liked it here,' Christopher sounded affronted.

'Oh I didn't mean that. It's just all so relentless. Because we're women with more important things to do than head up multi-million-pound companies, just *so* many things to do, and we're all different ages and we're spread all over the country and we're affected in different timescales, the mandarins have calculated, rightly, that we'll have no electoral impact whatsoever at the election. Cynical. But right.'

'Have you ever thought about standing for something?'

For a giddy moment, she considered doing just that, making a difference.

'You mean local politics or something?' But in warming to his theme, Ava came back to earth. 'When?' she collected a palmful of soapsuds and pushed it, despite his laughing protests, down the neck of his tee-shirt unable to stop herself joining in with the giggles. 'In my spare time?'

Two old girls, regular customers, in the café's corner table were exchanging their own jokes at the horseplay visible through the kitchen's serving hatch. 'Go on, you tell'im,' one encouraged Ava.

Then the café's door, always a sticker in wet weather, slammed back, jingling the bell and crashing into a chair.

'Steady love,' the old lady admonished the slim, tanned girl in rain-sodden shorts.

'*Steady*? I'll give her fucking steady. Where is she? Ava? Ava? You here?' She was yelling at the top of her voice and Christopher's shocked face appeared at the hatch, towelling off his neck.

'I'm here Syd.' Ava emerged from the tiny kitchen. 'What a lovely surprise – when did you get back? Dad's … fine. He's not here'-

'-Well he's not at home is he? Because THERE IS NO FUCKING HOME.'

Taking a deep sigh to give herself time to work out how to put this, Ava tried to put an arm round Syd's shoulder but was shaken off.

'AND MY DAUGHTER? AND WHO'S HE?' Syd's furious glare landed on Christopher who blanched.

'She's fine of course, absolutely fine. She's upstairs – a nap. She's fine honestly Syd. Look, come up and see for yourself. When did you get back sweetie?'

'Last night. Tried to ring you but it just said unavailable.'

Ava could picture the telephone wire dangling loose as the demolition men began.

'Yes well, there's lots to tell you, but come and see little one first. Christopher – you'll be okay if I just'-

'Oh absolutely. Do. Go. Er … nice to meet you,' he held out a hand to Syd who swept past.

'And I always thought this was a nice place,' one old girl muttered to the other.

Unlocking the door to the flat, Ava said 'I'll go first. See who's awake shall I?' She sniffed surreptitiously, then, tiptoeing up to the livingroom door, she listened for snoring. 'He's fine, well away. Let's find Daisy eh?' and she led Syd into the room she'd painted – the only room she'd managed to paint since they moved in – the colour of buttery lemon curd.

Pushing open the door, she stroked the warm, sleeping bundle. 'Daisy? Daisy darling? Look who's here – a lovely surprise.'

They sat around the kitchen table patching together the pieces of news.

Toying with her mug, Syd's story came out. 'I loved it, really loved it, but I … I missed Daisy. Thought what am I doing here? I'm missing every little thing she's learning to do, every day. She's grown so much and,' she sniffed, 'I don't think they really wanted me there. And Aggie's *awful*. Just *awful*.' Syd drew Daisy into an even tighter hug. 'I missed Mum when she went, then I missed Daisy when *I* went.'

'So your mother's still travelling? But you feel better being back home – here?' Ava probed gently. 'You're sure? It might be a while before you can get back there you know.'

Syd lowered head shook. 'No. It's like not me, you know? Travelling? But,' she shrugged, 'you have to go to know.'

People tell you things, they sell you things. She really had grown up.

On her mother's lap, Daisy wriggled happily.

'She's grown, hasn't she Dad?' Syd looked at Jon.

'Yes. Yes.' But his gaze was somewhere else, beyond the bookcase.

Syd frowned and lowered her voice. 'What's wrong with him Ave?'

'He's … getting forgetful. You remember how it was before you went. Muddling up words, where he'd put things.'

'Yeah, I s'pose,' she looked doubtful.

'It's stopped raining at last,' Ava said gratefully. 'Let's wrap you both up and get some fresh air. Dad will stay here I expect, won't you darling?'

But he sat silently.

On the way out, Ava said quietly to Christopher, 'Could you – you know – keep an eye?' and glanced upstairs.

'Course.' He stalked through the empty shop, flipped the sign to Closed, looking glad to get out of range.

are we are we going out Ave are we going out Margaret are we lucky Ava always been lucky haven't you? So here I sit where I'm safe and they can't get me and you've done it all, catthatgotthecreamLucky Ava we going out now? Ava? Margaret?

'You must be feeling the cold. Here'- Ava unwrapped the scarf from her neck and wound it round Syd's golden goose-bumpy shoulders as they headed down towards the seafront. It was a quiet day, what with the rain, which made talking about things easier.

'Oh Ave, what's happened to everything? When the taxi dropped me at the house and it was half-demolished I thought there'd been a gas explosion or something. Course I could see the bulldozer and the building site stuff but … And that builder said where to find you.'

'We couldn't ring you Syd.'

'I know, I know. After I put the first one through on the hot cycle, I got another, but I dropped it down the toilet in Surfers' Paradise but I thought I sent you a message with the new number. Sure I did. No – wait. I sent it on Mum's phone. Ran out of credit and there wasn't anywhere to top up.'

'Well, we never got a message, I'd have rung her if we had.'

They pushed on, Ava taking the buggy to help support her leg and it bounced over the pavements rocking Daisy back to sleep. Good, it'd give them a chance to talk. And Ava a chance to think.

'There must have been some good bits?' she asked. 'The weather?'

'Oh yeah, yeah. Really hot. But they just wanted to stay in backpackers' places and they didn't have aircon and I wanted, you know, a bit of luxury.' Then we went on a bus trip into the outback and that was so awful I just can't tell you. No signal and really uncomfortable, you know?'

'Well,' Ava smiled, 'you've got the accent, the lilt.'

'Yeah, well. So, the house?'

Ava'd been trying to decide on the truth, the whole truth, or just bits of it but if she was going to regain Syd's trust, it'd just all have to come out. Apart from Ted, obviously.

'Put simply love, your Dad's lost his grip on things. When you look back it's been going on a long time, but you just put it down to getting older, a bit forgetful.'

'S'funny you say that, that day in Canterbury, he kept saying the wrong word. I just thought two bottles of wine at lunchtime had been a bit much. But you know Dad. The County's always been his favourite.'

Ava kept going. *Two bottles of wine there. About what I'm spending on housekeeping in a week.* She could picture the fawning waiter and could only hope he heard Syd call Jon Dad, or else the conclusion he drew would be well wide of the mark. 'Well, going back, you know Granny had to be in a home?'

'Yeah, Mum said no way was she going to do all that carer stuff.'

'Well this is the price we're all paying now. Dad re-mortgaged the house when he and I got married. He really always loved it, didn't he?'

'Yeah but it was worth millions.'

'Well not quite. We know the first mortgage was a repayment one, so that was keeping the cost down, then he borrowed more.'

'But you two, you've always earned a lot.'

'Yes but when I stopped work to be with your Dad, we had to live on something so we decided to take our pensions early and they didn't last.' Ava was praying Syd wasn't quite following this because part of the reason for all the borrowing had been to buy Syd a house of her own. And guilt was not the legacy she wanted to pass on – it was too heavy a burden.

Plus of course, the way Jon extracted the pensions from the firm was fraudulent; signatures, 'financial advisers' who never existed. Probably. She'll never know.

'So I saw the Sea Garden and met Christopher – he's a painter, did you see? And gay obviously,' how guilty it made her feel to dismiss her friend that way. 'And I thought, well I could work there, we could live in the flat over it and I can look after your Dad, Syd.'

'God. *Catering.*' Syd made it sound one step up from drain-unblocking. 'Anyway, Dad doesn't need looking after,' she bridled. 'Well, perhaps a bit, I s'pose.'

They walked in silence along the promenade for a moment, seagulls keeping up with them along the cliff, just out of reach. Ava drew a breath. 'I'm afraid he does need quite a bit of care darling. The consultant says he's going to get more and more frail – he already finds walking really tiring. I'm sorry darling, I know he's your Dad and you love him, but there's really nothing we can do except take care of him until'-

'-Until he dies you mean?' Syd stopped and turned to stare at Ava. 'Just like that?'

'Well no, he'll not be able to do things for himself and I'll – well I already do a lot – washing, dressing, that sort of thing you know. And sometimes he's … difficult. He's a big guy Syd. Takes a bit of handling. And that makes him do things he … well, he isn't himself.'

'Oh God I didn't know.'

'Well it's hard to accept at first, but the specialist has been very good at explaining it all.

'I thought I could manage – no choice really – but to be honest with you I've been tiptoeing around him for about a year or more.' *Definitely more – thinking exactly how long's the really frightening bit.* 'Perhaps you could come along for his next hospital appointment, ask any questions.'

Syd looked wretched and Ava's arm went round her shoulders. 'He has good times too, don't forget, so we need to make the most of those … but,'

'But he isn't going to get better.'

'No.'

Syd looked about twelve as she drew her arm across her nose and sniffed again. 'What will happen to him?'

'Well, very often, it's a heart attack. Or a stroke.'

'Oh *God,* poor Dad.'

At the deserted bandstand they stopped. 'He loved it here this summer Syd. We three walked down and listened to the music in the afternoons.'

Daisy stirred with a whimper. 'Tea for three at the Sea Garden then?' Ava squeezed Syd's arm but as she turned back with her and the buggy, the one huge unspoken thing she hadn't told her weighed heavily on her shoulders.

What has she been thinking? Ted rode in on his white charger offering to make everything right. How would that ever have worked? As badly as she wanted to be with him, Ava could see that there was no easy answer to this. In fact, there was no answer. She would just have to do what she promised. Stay with Jon, caring for him, for the rest of his life.

'Ave? You all right?' Syd peered up into her face. 'Aw, come on. Something'll happen. Won't it?'

What happened was that a mud-caked LandRover was parked outside the Sea Garden as they made their way up from the seafront. So many things were racing round Ava's skull that her instinct was to turn and run but Daisy, wide awake now, was waving happily at Ted who, leaning against the car, wiggled fingers back at her.

'Syd, let me introduce Ted,' Ava said weakly as they got level.

'Ah, so you're Syd,' he grinned, shaking her hand. Ava knew how that felt. 'I've heard a lot about you, but I thought you weren't back for a month or so? Popped in to see my mate Christopher and he told me about you getting in earlier today. Quite a surprise. Come and tell me all about Oz. I've never been, always wanted to go. You okay with the buggy, Ava?'

He had taken her breath away time and again over the last week. All she could do was nod and wheel through between the tables, hoping that the sceptical look on Syd's face would go away.

'He's fine,' Christopher jerked his head up to the flat above them as the kettle boiled. 'Took him some tea a while ago.'

'Was he … okay?' Ava didn't want to ask.

'Well – just a bit of a mess to clear up, you know?'

'Oh,' she nodded grim-faced.

'Nothing I couldn't handle. Don't worry. He said he couldn't find the - somebody had moved the bathroom … you might want to replace that waste-paper bin though.'

How's this going to end? There's only one way possible. As soon as I can, I'll tell Ted that he's no place in this life. And her heart had never felt heavier.

Going out in the hall, the tide tables sat ready to be consulted for a long beach walk at low tide.

Or a long walk off a short pier at high tide.

Then for the second time that day, Syd whirled in, banging the door against the nearest table.

'He's gone. Dad's not there.'

Christopher followed her in. 'He was upstairs …'

There were now so many people in Ava's line of vision that her eyesight felt blurred, like a kaleidoscope gone wrong. Fay had turned up because Steve the butcher, who'd been delivering to the Sea Garden, heard Jon was missing and went round to her first at the Wellness Centre that was now a creche. Owen had come to see the Sea Garden's kitchen when he heard his Dad was heading this way and Tilly, who seemed to be joined to Owen at the hip, got in the car too. Jojo had still been at Coastguard's, so came along with Pete in a second car.

Ted was organizing everyone into groups. There had to be a local, a mobile phone that was fully charged and someone in each group who would recognise Jon and more importantly who he would recognise if (*when* Ava assured Syd) they found him. Ironic that so little time ago, she was contemplating the pier, now it was where at least one group set off towards, down the esplanade, past the little amusement arcade, onto the steep slope that leads to the boats …

Ava wanted to go too, but Ted told her that she'd do better taking care of Daisy, who was quiet, bemused by the adrenalin and urgent whispers going on around her. While the bath was running, Ava took the little one onto her lap and began humming. How many wheels can a bus have? It never failed to surprise Ava how her own body responded when she was cuddling Daisy. It seemed to warm, mould itself round the toddler, instinctively making a haven.

The bathroom was filled with steam and the bath just the right temperature, with bubbles and every water toy Daisy owned. Just as she lowered her into the water, the door opened.

'Ted! Lo!' Small fat palms slapped the bubbles and a minor tidal wave breached the bath's rim.

'Woah! Steady there miss,' he laughed, pushing up his sleeve to reach for a boat. 'This is just like my boat Daisy. Well, not pink.'

'Is there …?'

'No. Not yet,' he said.

'What can have happened do you think?'

'Where's he gone before?'

'If he's in his pyjamas, usually the beach, but Christopher thinks he was still dressed, so it might be anywhere in the town.'

'God this has been hard on you.'

'I think we should tell the'- her voice dropped to a whisper, '*police*. For CCTV, that sort of thing, it'll be quicker than going everywhere on foot. Oh,' she stopped suddenly, 'the old house.' She grabbed his arm. 'I bet he's there, Ted, I'd put money on it.'

'I'll go. Where is it?'

'*Oh.*' Much as she loved Daisy (something she'd only just realised) she felt trapped.

'Postcode. For the satnav.' And he jotted it onto the back of his hand, turned and ran down the stairs.

Just as well.

She'd have to get used to his absence.

'Ava?' little hands were tugging her jumper. 'Ava?'

'Just soap in my eye little one,' she swallowed and brushed her face with the back of her hand.

When the car tells him he's arrived, Ted pulls up outside the demolition site that is Fay and Kris's old house, headlights picking out the orange plastic barriers festooned with Health and Safety hazard warnings. Not something Jon's likely to have taken heed of. A digger, one of the big ones, is parked in the darkness at the site's lowest point and neatly symmetrical piles of rubble wait like oversized cake ingredients weighed for the mix. The house to the left has been levelled, and Halcyon, to the right stands, dark windows waiting their fate next. Already, someone has begun to use the windows for target practice and one or two blink fractured onto the street.

Clouds race across the night sky and for a moment, the moon illuminates the house's footprint and Ava's garden beyond it.

From somewhere, probably the skip where the rest of the shed's useless contents were thrown, Jon has found the carcass of Ava's hovermower, and is wrestling it across the rutted ground. The mower's cord trails and bounces behind him, no electricity supply to anchor it.

Jon is not in his pyjamas. He is naked.

'You poor sod,' Ted breathes, switching off the ignition and reaching onto the seat behind him for the blanket.

Getting out of the car, Ted makes his way carefully past the barriers and over the uneven ground up the slope that once gave the house its haughty air, round what's left of the garden wall and up the path.

'Hello Jon mate,' he says quietly. 'Ava's worried about you. She sent me here to pick you up. Dinner's ready. We can finish the mowing in the morning. You going to come with me now? How about putting this round you? You must be cold.'

Too late, he realises Jon will not recognise him.

Fight or flight? Jon has nowhere to go. He looks down at Ted and heaves the hovermower in a furious blinding arc.

Dinner'sreadygottogogoing out ...

GoingoutMargaret?
Goingoff?Gettingcough?

Once again, life is going on around Edith's kitchen table. It fitted the old house but here it reminds Ava daily that she has downsized. Tonight though, with everyone squeezing in, it has come into its own once more.

Jon has had his sedatives and is rocking back and forth. Syd has come in from putting Daisy to sleep and is puzzling over the plans spread on the table. Christopher and Owen are heads together, compiling figures although as Christopher readily admits, Owen is way ahead, albeit hampered tonight by Tilly snuggling on his lap. Pete, who wants to invest in this, his son's new business, is sitting in the corner, listening intently.

Olive and Marshall are here because Ava rang yesterday to make sure she was alright.

Olive had chatted happily, assuring Ava that Marsh looked after her very well indeed. He'd driven to the wedding in his campervan and so they'd spent the night in it, watching the hotel's thatched barn burn and collapse in a flurry of sparks, with Marsh naturally taking pictures, which he had subsequently sold to the local press.

'After that dear, it was just like the flower power days all over again …'

But Olive had told Ava about something else.

'I didn't say when we spoke the other day. After all, it's history, it can wait. I didn't realise my dear, quite how bad things had got for you until that nice Tilly and I got talking while you were dancing with the charming actor.'

'Her brother,' Ava says, anxious to make sure Olive doesn't think even worse of her. 'Well, half.'

'And then, next morning, over breakfast'-

'Breakfast?'

'Oh the hotel staff were marvellous. Set up a barbecue – it was so cold – we had bacon rolls and they made coffee somehow.'

'Oh good.' Will Olive ever stop talking about what has admittedly been quite an adventure?

'And I knew you were safe, the hotel said there'd been a sort of rescue convoy.'

Thinking back to waking up in Ted's bed, Ava agreed she too had been lucky, very well looked after and her foot would be fine soon.

'So then Marsh and I just pushed back and chilled.'

Olive's whole new vocabulary brings a smile to Ava's face.

'So, what I was thinking,' Olive got back to the point, 'is that it doesn't sound as if Jon quite told you the full story.'

'About what exactly Olive?' If this is another skeleton in Jon's cupboard, Ava wants to get it over with.

'Edith, his mother.'

'I met her of course. She was very frail. I think she died the following winter? It's difficult to remember exactly now.'

'Well it's not so much that she died, but that she lived as long as she did.'

Not following, Ava manages, 'Well, she was quite a good age …'

'Yes dear, because she was so well cared for in that home. She'd been going quite downhill looking – well at least trying to look – after herself in that bloody great barn. While her husband was alive, he'd never let her have money – and it had all come from her family in the first place. She walked out on more than one occasion, came to live with my parents once for a few weeks – I was just a girl, but I remember I had to tell people she was visiting, wasn't done for a woman to leave her husband then. But he got her back, used the boy to make her come back.

You're not going to leave me are you, Mummy?

'I always expected you'd talk Jon into selling Halcyon, finding somewhere smaller, a love nest for you two.'

God that sounds like a lifetime ago. 'Sorry Olive, I'm not quite following.'

'And so I said to Marsh – oh, I'm not one to gossip, don't misunderstand, but I do feel I can tell him anything – I wouldn't mind betting her son, the little liar, has done exactly the same thing again. He'd married Margaret – no I *refuse* to call her Willow – because he thought her family were well off, but that turned out not so and when she told him the truth, that her father's engineering business was on its last legs, he was furious. Didn't talk to her for days.'

'Olive I'-

'-Yes, yes, I'm coming to the point. Well that *is* it actually. You. He found you. I'm afraid it rather looks as though he decided - oh he said he was madly in love with you – as soon as I arrived that day, the tea, you remember?'

'I do.'

'- and decided to try the same thing again. I thought, what do you take me for? Another foolish woman? I don't wish to be harsh my dear, but perhaps you should have asked yourself'-

'-Olive, I have asked myself questions about Jon until I think I'm going as mad as'- Ava stops herself.

'Well that's it really. Jon, just like his father, was a good-looking man with very little propensity to work.'

'He never qualified formally, I remember him telling me.'

'No well, his father told him there was no need you see? Just taught him the rudiments of double entry book-keeping with that silly jingle thing'-

'Sorry?'

'Put a couple of the creatures in his bed one night as a practical joke to toughen him up before they sent him off to Lancing. The child was terrified, Edith told me. Wet his bed for days after – and got caned for it, of course. Charles forced him to pick them up, hold them, in the garden, to show he'd been taught a lesson. Then, I can see them now, Jon on Charles' knee, being shown the numbers on one side, then on the other, to balance. *Fear of frogs, terror of toads* ... He'd say it over and over again, to make the boy get the point. *Fear of frogs* ...

'Terror of toads,' Ava finished sadly. 'It's such rubbish. What does it even mean? Nothing.'

'Didn't matter. It stuck it in his head. Just keep your eye out for ripe pickings, Charles told me once. It was what *he'd* done with Edith – took every penny she brought to the marriage, bought bloody Halcyon and had a mistress or two. Set up the business and worked his way through several clients' investments, paying them something but paying himself more. Big cheese in Rotary, big fish in small pond, no questions asked, you know the sort of thing.'

'What happened to him? '

Ava heard Olive draw a breath. 'They said it was an accident. A two-bar heater in the bathroom.'

'Oh my god. How awful. Jon never said.'

'One never knows in cases like that …'

What does that mean?

'And at the inquest, they mentioned the trouble the business was in, which was quite a surprise to a lot of people ...'

Ava was beginning to feel sick. 'How could Edith go on living there?' She'd always hated that bathroom …

'So once he'd died,' Olive is back in full flow now, 'Edith couldn't cope with Halcyon. She was determined to get her own back. Made Jon pay for her keep at Buckingham House …'

'And then I came along, just like Margaret had. Only by now Margaret wanted to be with Aggie.'

'And he leapt like a bareback rider at the circus, from one galloping horse to another…'

Last night, when she should have been sleeping, she lay, burning in her bed. A tangle of thoughts, each fighting the others for precedence, filling her head. If this is right, how can that be? He said this, but was that before or after? What did he do when that happened? And everybody saying she was getting on because she slept with him. They were right, then.

Once you open your eyes, you see so many things. Perhaps some are real, some are not. The child. Was that really an accident? Or part of …

Jon, on the take all the time … He kept her on when that first takeover was creating carnage. Promoted her onto the board. An only child who'd inherit a house. Good-looking young woman. Took her to bed. Invaded her flat like a cuckoo. Nurtured dependency in her. Exploited the feminine side; of course she would bring Syd up, so much easier than all the pregnancy thing, just present her with a ready-made daughter. Or would a child of her own bind her even more tightly into this? Worth considering.

So on it wound, the cobweb of transactions, moves, loyalty, wound so tight she couldn't think any more.

Then, once she was snared, complicit, he burned their bridges.

You simply never were as good as you thought…

While everyone is eating, Ava watches the dynamics ebb and flow around the room. When she is not helping Jon get food into his mouth, she enjoys the sensation of being part of the crowd, which is, she knows now, a lot more comfortable than being the only child at the table. What a warm bath of company this all seems to be. Amongst the chatter and the noises of cutlery and plates brought together, she sees each person evaluating their place in the company, watches Olive watching Ted, knows Syd is doing the same and for the same reason. Their relative is being superseded in Ava's life and it seems they understand why.

Ted, nursing the black eye Ava thought she'd got two weeks ago when she woke up at Coastguard's Cottage, is clearing away the dinner plates. There is nothing left of the lasagne Syd helped Ava make when they realised how many were coming to hear what he has to say.

'Dad was never cool, was he Ava? *He* is though, that Ted. *And* Marsh. I like him too.' Syd layered the sheets of pasta as Ava ladled bolognaise, filling gaps with courgettes before the cafe got busy.

Ava had to turn away. 'Just got to stir the sauce to go on top,' she said. 'Yes. Cool. And fun, Syd. I – I've known

370

Ted a long time. Haven't seen him for years. Then – after the wedding – yes. Cool.'

'So it's true what Jason said. You two go back?'

It must make it better for her, hearing that from a TV celebrity. Something to talk about at the Mother and Toddler Club. 'So you like him? Ted? He's going to try and help your Dad, Syd.'

'Oh? He must be a lot younger than Dad.'

'He was my friend, not Dad's.'

'Oh. *Oh.*'

Glasses are filled again, chairs moved back and there is now an air of expectation.

Ted's been busy, crunching numbers, calling people. He and Ava have scarcely been alone together since the night Jon went missing, but they talk, quietly, on the phone each night, when Jon is sleeping. There is no doubt in Ava's mind that she still loves Ted but what is she going to do with that knowledge?

Tonight he is selling. Selling the plan they've discussed, their ideas. In lots of ways he is similar to Jon – what an amazing discovery – driving, taking people with him. But without Jon's slippery smoothness. Ted's rough edges give him a grip on the room without needing a position of power to which people acquiesce. He is just straightforward.

He has already sold one of his buy-to-lets and the other three will go soon. He'll keep Coastguard's because he will borrow against the cottages to re-invest in a bigger property – he has his eye on two which are suitable, providing there are no planning concerns. There will be a gap of months while the legal side is sorted out, but he's confident nothing insurmountable will be found. During this wait, the new house will be enlarged, kitted out to comply with all the requirements for a home for dementia patients and staff will be taken on and trained.

Ava's role will be financial. As Company Secretary, she will keep the books, overseeing the business. It's still a surprise to Ava how much she'd relish this role and she's printed out forecasts so that everyone can see the figures. She watches them, fingers running down columns and knows she's missed this. And why.

Ted's turn again. Syd can be involved or not, as she wishes, in the care of her father. Owen can manage the catering side, if he fancies?

'Yeah, *great*, his son nods. 'I didn't want to say, but I've been a bit bored with the B&B lately. I'll have to get online, look for comparable businesses, see what their costs look like, but it's do-able definitely.'

Now Ted has finished reading out the plan, pushing spreadsheets and drawings around the table as he goes.

'You can't be this kind,' Ava whispers.

'Why not? It suits me to. As a business it's viable. There's a lot of demand. I'll end up there myself one day.' He leans across to grasp her hand, 'Just a joke, Ava.' Everyone, even Syd who has come to understand a lot recently, grins. 'It will work. I've been over it with people who know the business.'

'Where are the places you've seen?' Her old professional interest is piqued.

He takes a deep breath. 'There are a few around, but the trick is to find one where people want to sell. Really want to sell. After the storm damage and the fire, the Blazing Beacon was one. They'll miss the whole of next wedding season.

'And The Seasalter Company is the other.'

'What's Mum got to say about that?' Owen laughs.

'Your Mum's moved on from me, mate. The brewery want to sell the pub of course – it's no good as a business, like a lot now. People not drinking and driving, drinking at home instead. And there's quite a bit of ground around it.'

'So it can be extended,' Pete nods. 'And it's relatively quiet there.'

'As is The Beacon. They've put in insurance claims and it'll take quite a lot of sorting out. They're not earning while that's going on, so they listened when I made them an offer.'

He's already done so much I'd hoped to do. What a difference money makes.

There's no stopping him. Thought he'd stick around with an old flame when there are so many other delicious fish in the sea? And it's not just sexual. Look round this table, they're a little bit in love with him. What a great salesman.

'My preference,' Ted says, closing the folder on the table, 'is The Beacon site. It's a little inland, more accessible for suppliers and visitors. It's on main drainage, gas and electricity. Well when it's fixed.'

'So ...' Owen begins, startling everyone who turns to look at him. 'If you have The Beacon for your old folks' home...'

'*Owen*' his father growls.

'Sorry – care home?'

'Yes,' Ted nods. 'Go on.'

'Can I have The Company?'

Ted puffs out his cheeks. 'Suppose I say yes. What for?'

He looks at his father. 'Gastropub. Saltmarsh lamb. Samphire. Seafood of course from Whitstable. And live music,' he nods at Tilly, grinning.

'Can you do that and the catering for the home?' Ava asks.

'I'll get it up and running. To start with. It'll need a small team that's committed, reliable. Yes,' he nods defiantly. 'Yes I can. With Tills.'

'Oh.' Everyone turns to look at her, watching the blush rise from her neck to her cheeks.

'We'll have to go into it,' Ava sounds hesitant.

'I've got some numbers ...' Owen holds out a hand and Tilly puts a sheaf of papers into his palm.

'Okay,' Ted says. 'It'll have to be on a business footing, no family favours, you understand?'

'Definitely,' his son and Tilly nod.

'Right then, if you think it'll work, it looks to me as if we've every viable business in the Liberty spoken for. Which,' he says, rather proudly, 'is the new name I thought we'd give it, the care home.'

Christopher laughs, 'Well I think we can see the Blazing Beacon's consigned to history.'

'So what?' Everyone's agog.

'Liberty House.'

'But …' Ava shakes her head.

'Why not?' Ted's head is on one side looking at her.

'Liberty – real liberty – is the thing you can't give them. I've spent so long trying to stop Jon going off and doing what he wants …'

'I see that's right. Never mind, a name can come later,' Ted scratches out the word on the paper in front of him.

'I, well, if you think it's any good …'

'What?' he trusts her to have the answer.

'Halcyon. Not,' she adds quickly, 'anything to do with the old Halcyon. But the idea, or rather the myth, isn't that perfect?'

'What myth?' Owen wants to know, but Tilly's thumbs are already flying over her phone.

'Says *A mythical bird identified with the kingfisher said to breed in a nest floating at sea, charming the wind and waves into calm*,' she reads. 'Oh I get it, we'll make a calm place for them, out of all their troubles. That's cool, Ava.'

'It is,' Ted nods. 'Halcyon.'

Christopher is the only one not smiling and Ava leans over to him. 'I haven't given up on the Sea Garden you know. I'll be there for you, I promise. You threw me a lifeline when I was drowning.

'But you mustn't stop painting, that's what matters. We can find any number of people to take the café forward.'

His head drops. 'I'll hardly see you.'

'You bloody well will.'

'The Halcyon … I could do your publicity shots?' Marshall offers tentatively. 'And kingfisher blue would be a good house colour for your artwork. All gratis obviously. The burning barn pictures have won an award, did you hear?'

Olive clasps his hand. 'I'm so proud of him. The local news programme on the box – Action Shot of The Year.'

Amid the congratulations, Pete growls, 'And Coastguard's, Ted?'

'I hope I – we – live there.' Ted looks Ava straight in the eye. 'I've thought hard about this, planned it for you. You're very quiet.'' He takes her hand in his own, 'I hope it suits you my love.'

They all talk at once and suddenly the noise makes Ava's head ache. *I have to get out of here.*

Syd finds her sitting out on the metal staircase that leads down to the Sea Garden.

'Does this really mean Dad's going to be looked after properly?'

'It will, yes.'

'But Ted's making a profit out of it.'

'That's a bit harsh, Syd. Whoever helps us look after Dad won't be doing it for free. Ted's just found a way to do it and cover the cost. What's this about really, Syd?'

'Oh you old people, you're always looking at things that way. It's money this, money that.'

If this is about saving the planet ... 'Tilly calls us wanker-bankers and earth-gobblers,' Ava laughed. 'But money - well it helps with the things we want – somewhere to live, keep warm, get around.' *Like Australia. And a cottage in Whitstable.*

'Dad's done some things though ... I heard you talking to Auntie Olive, I only got some of it, but it sounded bad.'

'Well, he and his father, your grandfather, copied what a lot of people have done, still are doing. It doesn't make it right, but Dad and I knew lots of people at work who got away with it. He wanted to get out, have a quiet life and I was all for it, Syd if I'm honest. He just got carried away a bit, took it too far then couldn't put things right.'

'Mum said to Aggie, 'You can't trust a word he says.'

'A bit harsh again.' *But just what his mother said.*

Syd's voice falters. 'Will he … will he go to prison?'

'No.' *Probably not. But if you say that, or It's complicated, you'll leave her with doubt. Full disclosure they used to call it. Best keep all that stuff inside your head, Ava.*

Her tanned shoulders slump with relief. 'I was so worried – prison's horrible.'

This was a surprise. 'Who do you know who's been, Syd?'

'A boy I met in Oz. Only for a day, but they made him …'

'How well did you know him?'

'Oh it was just on the beach at Surfers''

'So did you know him well enough to trust him? What he said?'

She's silent for a moment. 'He was really nice.'

'Are you going to keep in touch?'

She thinks. 'Don't know. I'd dropped my phone down the toilet so I couldn't give him my number. So how would he?'

She's been on a journey all right. She'll work through all the experiences and learn from them. I hope.

'So now Ted's going to make it all right for Dad. Why, Ava?'

'Between the three of us,' both girls jumped at Ted's voice behind them. 'I want to help Ava, so that means helping your Dad. And I want to help Ava because I let her get away once, years ago and I don't want that to happen again.'

'Everyone's got someone except me,' Syd's head hung down.

'Well you've got Daisy, who's the most important thing in the world,' Ted said. 'And you'll meet lots of people before you decide to stick with one of them. That's the fun bit. Ava and I won't see fifty again and your Dad's next big birthday will start with an eight. You wouldn't want Ava to spend those years trying to cope on her own with him, would you? So you see, you've got ages and ages to enjoy yourself and Ava and I have got to get a bit of a shift on for what we're needing to do.'

The girl sniffed and Ava got a tissue out of her pocket. 'So you and Ava – this thing you've got – is that like, going to last? Or will there be another great bust-up in a few months? Only I'm fed up with it.'

'Oh Syd,' Ava handed her the tissue.

'If I have anything to do with it,' Ted's voice was firm, 'there'll be no bust-up if you're happy to see me and Ava together. You, Ava?'

This had gone a long way, very fast. 'Goes for me too Syd,' she nodded. 'It'll be a hell of a lot of work, but it'll be the best thing we can do for your Dad. And neither Ted nor I can do it on our own. And really there's no-one else I'd rather do it with.'

'S alright with me. Just wish I knew what I was going to do.'

'We can find you something.'

'No, I want to do it on my own, Ava. And straight, no fiddling. I've got friends who are working the system, benefits and that, and they jump every time there's someone at the door. Actually,' she pulled herself up. 'I think I'd like to try looking after other peoples' children as well as Daisy. That Fay was telling me all about it last time she babysat, I might have a go and see if she could give me some tips.'

Being honest. How sensible. Why didn't that ever feature when I was her age? Perhaps if you grow up with a parent on the take, it warns you off. If you grow up in a poor, honest household, taking risks looks exciting. It was on the tip of Ava's tongue to offer to help, but Ted was shaking his head behind Syd's back, so she just said, 'Sounds like a plan to work on. And you'll be with Daisy.'

'Yes.' Syd was suddenly decisive. 'Think I'll go and ring Fay.'

'Well. I wasn't expecting that,' Ava said as Syd went back indoors.

'She just needed space to talk it out. Budge up a bit,' his hips nudge her to one side and his arm goes round her shoulders. 'Noisy lot, aren't they?'

'Bit much,' she nods.

'I know. But it's nice that they're enthusiastic.'

'I'm used to silences – it was always like that. *They're* all so full of life. I can't think straight. And I need to.'

So now.

The warmth of his body on the step beside her, reminds her of the hurdle that stands between Ava and the future.

'Tomorrow night, Ava,' his voice is deeper than ever. 'Are you free?

'To talk? Yes.'

'That. And more. And Fay will babysit?'

'Yes. If she isn't too busy with Syd,' she smiles. 'Kris'-

'He's gone, has he?'

'You guessed. Wants his own space.'

'Obviously.'

'Why do you say that?'

'Because it sounds like a good idea until you try it. I'm guessing he's hankered after this for a while.'

'The Wellness Centre ..'

'Isn't very well?'

'No.'

'Ah well, they gave it a go. Might have worked. So, tomorrow night Ava?'

For god's sake. Only a few weeks ago, she would have grabbed any man who asked. But she only wants Ted. The solid nearness of him, the musky smell and feel of him, wants him as much as she ever did.

Jon, she is ashamed to admit now, was more attractive physically when their relationship burned through the office – all good suits and acolytes and kudos and admiring glances. Without those, she hardly recognised the diminished figure she collected from the filling station that night.

Ted's energy is more self-reliant, his drive has taken him literally all over Europe. It's what she's wanted for so long – the right response to her ridiculous reasoning for going to the wedding. She wants him, around her and inside her. This is something she has done time and again in her life, driven by her own desire. More times, in truth, than most people.

Perhaps she has had her fair share.

But it's ridiculous to hold back now. 'Ted … it's …'

'Mm?'

'It's a long time, we didn't…Jon …'

'Couldn't?'

'No,' she whispers.

'Well I can, I think you'll find. Trust me.'

'And anyway, I didn't want …'

'The man he'd turned into?'

'I suppose that's it.''

'Come tomorrow night, Ava. To Coastguard's. Come and reclaim your lagan.'

There's the same directness she has always loved. 'You're my lagan? I always thought I was yours.'

'You're the one who went off remember? I stayed here, anchored to the seabed until you came back.'

'Oh Ted.'

'Just come Ava. I'll be there. It'll be all right. I promise. Trust me.'

It strikes her that Jon never said what Ted just said. Trust me. 'You're safe with me.' She can still hear him saying it in the office all those years ago.

She will – she does – trust him. It will be all right, just like he said.

And oh my word, it is better than that.

In the morning, there is a cup of tea beside her when she wakes, but it's gone cold and she gets up heavy-hearted, knowing what she must do. On the pile of her clothes, Ted's notebook is waiting, pen slotted into the spiral binding.

Ava takes a deep breath, straightens up and loosens her neck muscles. It feels as if she's been working out all night, which is right in a way. Last night was everything she's missed and she's so grateful to him she almost doesn't begin to write anything.

She will say that - that she's grateful for the night in his bed and for all the things he's offered. She's grateful he's included her in the development of his plan and only too aware that it's built around her husband, which must say a lot about Ted.

But she must also say she has real misgivings that have been lurking unacknowledged through all the talking and planning.

Not about the work that Halcyon would involve. The accounts are straightforward and she has done enough of the caring side in the last couple of years not to be afraid of messed beds and thrown food.

She'll try to put this kindly, she just needs a break from everything. From Jon, his daughter and granddaughter, maybe even from Ted. Space to breathe before or if, she commits all over again.

It's something to do with always having made the biggest decisions on my own. To study, get on – all my parents, who hadn't done that, could say was Well done. The child – of course it was right that it was ultimately my decision but there wasn't anyone to talk to about it anyway. Marrying Jon – well he wouldn't have been very happy if I'd asked for time to think it over would he? And now Ted, who I've daydreamed about for so long. How likely is he to be everything I think he is? And how likely am I to keep him happy for long, never mind the rest of our lives? I know now I was never as clever as I thought I was. But I have learned a lot of things.

And if I tell him the truth, the real truth, how will that change his opinion of me?

Perhaps Ted won't wait. Like me, he isn't getting any younger and he needs to build this business for the sake of his son. He can do it without me though. That would be justice.

She heads for the shower hoping for a clearer head and enjoys the water's heat on her aching muscles. This has just been an interlude, a diversion.

When she's finished, she wraps a towel round her hair, pats herself dry and puts her jeans back on. Her jumper smells of him and for a moment, she wavers. Then, sitting on the side of his bed, she flips open the pad. On the first page, he has written *I love you Ava. Back later. Have the time you need to think.*

She must tell him to his face. When he comes in.

She sets her mind on the garden. If this is going to be the last time she's here, the least she can do is see if there are jobs out there. *Careful though. This isn't your garden, Ava.*

She makes herself coffee and carries it outside.

'Morning love.'

'Pete – it's nice to see you. Didn't know you were here. Like a coffee?' She will miss him. He has his son's directness and a lot of knowledge in his eyes. 'I stayed last night. But Ted's gone into Canterbury I think – did you want to see him?'

'No, no coffee thanks – no, it was you I was hoping to find.'

'Oh?'

'Look Ava, I'm not one for speeches. In fact soon, I won't be one at all. Not surprising at my age. Can't complain.'

'You're … *ill?*'

'I am.'

She takes his hand. 'Ted knows?'

'Well, no. See he's had a lot on his mind lately, with you coming back, so I din' tell him I'd seen the doctor again.'

'I'm awfully sorry to hear it Pete. Can they do anything?'

'No my dear, no. Livers are like that. Thing is, it will hit him hard, Ted. We've been good friends I reckon, him and me.'

'He's always said so.'

'Look after him for me.'

Oh. Same words. Exactly what Edith said. 'I … it … there are things he doesn't know, things I'm going to tell him when he gets back.'

'Oh.' He is downcast. 'You off again then?'

'I don't want to go, but I might have to. When he knows what a fool I've been.'

'How's that Ava? You don't strike me as foolish.' The older man looks at her with the same deepset eyes as his son.

'My husband, Jon.' She plunges in. 'It looks like he copied his father. Olive told me about it and the more I think about it, the more I think it's right. He just targeted me, right from the word go. How I didn't see it, I'll never know. I didn't see through all the stuff that came with him, everything that was going on with us, with his wife. Even when his mother told me he'd always been a liar, long before we got married, I thought *Well as a little boy maybe, but not now.* But it turned out she was right. I have spent fifteen years being conned. Being groomed to do what he wanted. Being coerced and bullied. I thought I wanted my marriage to work, so I stuck it out like a fool.'

Seagulls are floating on thermals high overhead and the day is as beautiful as any, here on the water.

'I see. And you think Ted's going to go off when he knows this?'

'I'm just not what he thinks I am. I don't even know what I am.'

'Well you're no fool, I know that. Oh, maybe had your head turned by a man but that's happening all over the world, all the time. And the other way round, don't misunderstand me. Look how many fellows get caught by women. It don't alter what you are underneath.'

She can hear Ted's voice and recognises where it comes from. 'Pete, he's going to be lost when you're …'

'For a while, I reckon. But if you stick around, I think you can make a real go of this plan of his and I don't want to see him on his own, Ava.'

'Ted? He'll never be on his own for long.' She tries to make him laugh. 'There'll be a stream of women round the coast waiting for a chance to get hold of him.'

'It's you he wants though, love. I know it.'

'What makes you so sure, Pete?'

'He is honest, is Ted. I know everyone thinks of Lovejoy when you say antique dealer, but we brought them up to be straight. All three of them. Didn't work with that silly sod Tommy though.'

'Ted said you didn't talk to him when he shopped Tommy to the police.'

'S'right, at first. I thought well, that wouldn't happen in the Company. But we talked about it and I saw he was right. He's a good boy, Ava. He'll make you happy.

'Don't tell him though, about me. Leave me to do that.'

'Drink?'

It's been another wait for Ted. Not the years of the previous one, but a few hours stuffed with the things bubbling inside her head. The secrets she has kept and the new one she has only found out about today. 'No. And'-

He puts the bottle down. '-and you want me not to either? Am I driving somewhere?'

'No. But I need both of us to be stone-cold sober. Sorry.'

'Christ, this sounds serious Ava,' he half-laughs.

'I… it is. Things I haven't told you.'

He sits, crosses one leg and looks at her.

'It wasn't Jon. *Just* Jon in the beginning.' Unable to look him in the eye, she gazes out of the window at the low tide. 'The Plan Fund, he called it. I knew about it. He told me, said it was our escape route and all I had to do was go along with it, ask no questions.'

'Playing dumb won't have been easy.' Ted's face is telling her something she can't quite fathom.

'The glass ceiling's real. I'd never get to the very top, I was a woman, didn't go to the right schools, know the right people. Well apart from him and with us being together that would always stand in my way, you see? People already said I'd only got on because I was sleeping with him. And maybe …

'So he said, let's just take what will be yours one day and run with it, your pension fund. We can pay off Margaret, help Syd out when she's older and live the life we want.'

'Was it the life you wanted?' He sounds worried.

Ava takes a deep breath then shakes her head. 'No, not really. But then neither was the one I had. I always knew I'd be no good as a mother, far too self-centred. And a wife? Well let's be honest, I made a better mistress. But I used to think I could do my job. People suffered though. Every time you buy out a company, jobs disappear, hopes with them – the owners' and the workers'. I'm not proud of what we did. But we made money for the shareholders of course and, for a time, Jon and I made money with them.

'But then it all happened and I … it really was like those shifting sands out there. You sink before you know it and

384

struggling doesn't help, so you just have to go with it all. But Jon always said he'd take the blame if anyone questioned what we did and I – oh this sounds pathetic – but I wasn't as clever as he was, couldn't think straight enough to find an alternative so,' she shrugs, 'I signed on the dotted line.'

'SRZ could afford it.'

She stares at him. 'You're not surprised.'

'I was waiting for you to tell me. You must have known what Jon was doing – you're too bright not to. We've all got a skeleton hiding, Ava.'

Her stomach sinks. 'Not you - the thing with Tommy?'

'No, no,' he laughs. 'That was just my brother being an idiot all on his own. But there aren't very many businesses where everything, every day, is run by the book.

'You make an offer to buy something you know you'll sell at a profit and if I'm honest, I offered less if I thought the money didn't matter so much to whoever was selling. And selling – well anything's worth what someone's willing to pay. If their offer's daft I'm not going to tell them that. So by the same token, I've overpaid sometimes I expect. But it comes out all right in the end.'

'This doesn't,' she shakes her head. 'Come out right. He was old enough to get his hands on his own pension, could leave anyway, but I still had years to wait before I could get any income from my fund. Then the firm found out he'd ... there were discrepancies. All he could do was resign, put a charge on the house to keep them quiet. I didn't know how much to start with, he just said discrepancies. Then later, after we were married, he told me they'd made him forfeit half a million to cover it. He just said it was a gamble, like a horse race, that they'd never find it, but he'd lost. We'd be all right for money though, he said. Plenty invested.

'There's something else. Olive told me something else. I've been trying to get my head around it but it's even uglier. What his father did. Embezzled. Took Edith's money.'

'Edith was his wife?'

'Yes. I met her. She warned me Jon was a liar but I suppose I thought I knew better. As soon as he got sent in on that audit, when I met him, the first thing he discovered was that the old owner had been on the take – and it felt like most of the City was, too. There's research – they reckon three in four pension transfers may be fraudulent now.

'The very worst thing – I must be stupid because it only hit me recently – is that I think he picked me out. Grooming they call it nowadays – everything gets labelled. I don't know for sure. Ridiculous that in the twenty-first century, men still prey on girls. But I was an adult, I thought. The young all think they're invincible, don't they? I should have seen it, stopped it. I just don't know when that would have been though.

'And now I think about it, that's when I think he spotted me, decided I'd go along with it and he was right. I was stupid enough to be dazzled. He knew I was an only child, knew my parents weren't young. He made me believe he'd left Margaret, but I honestly think the cost of divorce frightened him, so he went back to her. And then I found out – I have to tell you this because I can't bear another secret and if you think it's terrible, I completely understand … I found out I was pregnant.'

The look of shock says it all. 'Christ Ava. What happened?'

'There wasn't much time. He'd gone, left me and gone back to Margaret and I knew I couldn't cope with a child on my own.'

Ted looks down at his hands. 'When Sal told me she was expecting, I tried to persuade her to have an abortion. I knew we'd be a disaster together. Now I'm glad Owen's around, but it was very, very hard going. It must have been so difficult to decide on your own.'

'I suppose,' Ava sighs, 'it was a good thing there was only me. Only myself to convince, no-one else to persuade? And so little time to act. I haven't regretted it, now more than ever. Who in their right mind would bring a child into this mess? I never told Jon when we got back together, he didn't want another child and I didn't want to look back. So we went back to being a couple. We didn't work together all the time, but when we did, he made sure I watched him, so I gradually became complicit without realising. The deals were always signed off by the chairman and I knew Jon would get a cut of the profits.'

'Whose money was it?'

'Companies who didn't miss it, I thought,' she shrugs. 'Now I don't know. I'm going over the last fifteen years of my life and doubting every single day of it. Doubting myself most of all. So when we left, he set up the new company and put me on the list as a director, with Sue and Phil, our friends, so he could transfer my fund over. I thought he'd be able to play the stock market well enough for us to get by. But then, the mortgages he'd raised … I'd no idea.'

'Maxwell and Madoff did it. Stole, then paid out to look like income from investments.'

'Until there was nothing left to pay out from. Oh I knew what he was doing setting up the company was illegal, but not uncommon. I turned a blind eye and signed. And then Syd went and got pregnant because she wanted her father's attention to be on her, not me, and she thought we could afford it.

'And Jon? Suppose the stress of everything tipped him over the edge? Once we'd run out of money, he knew he couldn't go back to work.'

'That's the thing that's been getting to me.' Ted stands and moves to the bottle again. 'I'm going to pour us one each. I need it and you deserve it.'

Handing her the glass, he goes on, 'You ran out of money. Knowing Jon from all you've said, that surprised me when you told me the night of the storm, but there was a lot going on. Kept thinking he'd have planned better than this. Would have known what sort of pot he'd need to keep you both for life.'

The scorched twenty pound note. 'I don't think I'll ever know where it all went. Obviously he hadn't invested it in anything above board – an annuity or something – questions would have had to be answered, not least with the Tax people. But we had clients whose money was offshore, he would have copied them if he could. So maybe there just wasn't that much and Jon knew he was losing his grip – and couldn't … steal … any more. Maybe.

'Money came into the bank each month for a few years, so I was wandering around not questioning it, not working. I closed my eyes and'-

'-then the ship hit the rocks.'

'I thought it had happened when the money I put in from my flat and Dad's house dwindled but he just said it had gone into the Plan Fund. All I can think is that it was, literally maybe, in a tin under a bed somewhere. Or perhaps …' she falters, '… perhaps it was never really there. And as he began to know he was ill, I suppose he panicked, then thought he'd have to get rid of all traces in case the firm came looking. Burning it. I was always finding something smouldering – it was so frightening. He'd say they were papers that were too confidential to go out, even shredded. That was when he started getting violent, when I questioned it, so I just suggested we get an incinerator but he forgot to use it and there'd be that smell of burning when I came in from shopping, or when I came down in the morning and he'd got up before me. He could have killed us.'

She drinks, then says, 'But the real shock was knowing the house capital was all gone. All my life, bricks and mortar have grown, it's been a given. But when Halcyon sold, there was only just enough to buy into the Sea Garden lease and hope to recover the position in time. It was always going to take a lot of cups of tea though.

'So that's it. I've been stupid and I've committed fraud. The word makes me gag. I can't go into any business with you, Ted. Can't hold office or anything. You say you know and don't mind but what about everyone else? It'll come out one day and I can see the look on their faces – the disappointment and the smirks. I've worked so hard … at everything, until I married him,' her voice breaks. 'It's all worth nothing. All because I went with my heart not the sensible, tutting voice in my head. I can't do that again, Ted.'

'Hold on, hold on,' he moves to sit beside her on the sofa, his arm round her shoulders, the warmth and comfort like a spell. 'First of all, I'll put money on you not hearing anything further about Jon's arrangement. They've looked at it. They won't have found anything, or you'd have heard. And they won't go back over it because that would make the guys who looked first time look stupid if they found it. So they won't.'

It sounds logical, put like that.

'I know what feeling stupid's like all right,' Ava gulps. 'I'm so angry with myself and even angrier with Jon for the deceit – he lied to everyone, all his life.' Her stomach knots with fury. 'It's a corrosive, deep anger, like nothing I've ever known. How could I not have seen it?'

'He made sure your hands were too full. Like you always say, he was good at what he did. Shame it was illegal.'

'Bloody man.'

'Get your head out from below the parapet. Tell yourself you'll learn from it. There's a life to be lived. Stick with me Ava, you'll see.' He refills the glasses.

'You still want me around?'

'Yes. Oh yes.'

'Oh Ted. If I sit very still, will all this go away?'

'No. We just live with it. And that's another thing, Ava my love. You need to try and start thinking we not I. I understand you've always handled things alone. But there are lots of us here, all pulling in the same direction, right?'

'It's hard to get my head round after so long on my own.'

'Well, I know Syd and Daisy look to you for a lead, I've watched them. And you do it - bring out the best in them, so they find themselves, whatever that is, make themselves as good as they can be.'

'I suppose it was like that with Priti, my intern. She was so capable. Still is,' she smiled ironically.

'There you go. She won't be pleased at having been caught up in it all. But she distanced herself, from what you've told me. She's carrying on. It's all you can do.'

'Is it that easy?'

'No,' he laughs. 'I wouldn't say that. But you keep it in mind to guide you, I'd say, one day at a time. First of all,' he pours more wine. 'We're not going to do anything much. You and I will spend time doing the things normal people do. You've never been on the boat – can't believe I was too busy getting you into bed. We'll potter out, have pub lunches, talk. Re-jig, Ava. Take a long view. Consider what we can achieve, the people to whom it means a lot that we're together. Because we are that. Whatever else. I don't want to think about what we could have done if I'd stuck at it, not let you get away. But we can and will make up for it now.

'Besides, the Beacon have asked if we'll stall for a while. That's where I was today'

'They're not changing their minds?'

'No. But the insurance company are looking at the claim and if they spot the Beacon have had a juicy offer they'll take a long time double-checking everything. We all need a bit of time. Jon will be looked after – we'll find people. Christopher can concentrate on his work, so can Owen, and Syd can look after her child instead of running away to the other side of the world. And Daisy will know what it's like to grow up part of a big family group.

'Then, when we're ready, you and I, we'll do whatever it is we've decided.

'Now,' he stands and holds out his hand. 'Come upstairs with me. Please.'

In the dark autumn dawn, Ava smiles with pleasure at each little ache that reminds her of what happened last night. How glorious it feels to be used this way again, body and soul – the way she's missed for so long. How long have they got?   She doesn't have to be back at Fay's until lunchtime.

A glance at the red digits on the bedside radio reminds her with a start that this is 1.11. Her wedding anniversary.

Goosebumps form on her neck at the all-too familiar guilt. *Go away.* Eyes tight shut, she rolls quickly over and curls around Ted's warmth. He stirs and the way it does when you don't want it to, her phone rings.

'Mrs Wilkes?'

The bed's warmth evaporates, she shivers and reaches for her jumper. Why's Peacock Pat ringing her?

'Can you come down to the house?'

'Now?'

'Soon as you can. There's something you should see.'

'It'll take a while. I'm … *I'm not in my own bed.* I'm not at home.'

'The police are on the way too.'

'Police?' Her stomach twists. 'What's going on?'

Ted's been listening and is up out of bed, pulling on his jeans. 'Well, that's an interesting development. Wonder what they've got? I'd have thought the houses were down by now. It doesn't take long once all the period bits are stripped out. They were virtually all gone when I was there that night with Jon.'

'So it must be in the garden then. But they were using the garages as workshops – where they could lock away the diggers at night, so they must have emptied them first. I don't want to go there, Ted.'

'Come on, Ava. We'll go. It's not your home, your responsibility now. Just a building site.'

All the way there, she puzzles. *Not the Anderson shelter after all surely? And anyway, what is it they found? Oh god, Jon, is this another shock? Or can there actually be a pile of cash? No.*

In the grey November morning, they drive up to where she used to live and it does look different. Halcyon and its neighbours on either side are more or less levelled. Without the houses and mature gardens, there is more light.

A fresh-faced young policeman is glumly writing in a notebook while his pretty colleague radios in.

'Here goes.' Ted pulls up the handbrake. 'Come on Ava – let's see the body.'

'Not funny.'

He holds her hand as they stand on the pavement looking up at the space where her home used to be. Her home, Jon's home, Edith's home. There's a tang of woodsmoke in the air. Wrecked remnants of Ava's beloved roses and shrubs and trees which sheltered her from the truth of life in the house, are being chewed by a noisy machine and petrol fumes make the air smell flammable. As she watches, the burnished leaves of the mahonia disappear into its jaws.

'Oh.' Ava can't help a gulp of sympathy for living things being butchered.

Ted's arm goes round her shoulders. 'We knew it was going to happen.'

'I know I'm being stupid,' she gulps. 'I'd hoped not to come back until all this was over.'

'We look forwards, not backwards eh?'

'Yes.' She takes a step. 'It looks even bigger now it's clear.' As the digger advances noisily up the plot from the pavement, there is a shout and the engine is cut. The shredder stops chewing laurel and is silenced too and Pat Howell, in workboots and hi-viz, waves them up what's left of the drive. At the top, the steps Jon so admired up to where the imposing front door was are bitten into like a biscuit, exposing a cavity in the pile of matchwood which was the veranda. It looks for all the world like a pyramid broken into in search of treasure.

Here? Really? I've walked over it every time I've come into the front door?

'I think this is yours,' Pat Howell points to a battered Mossman trunk, brushing rubble from the lid. Scratched black lettering tells them it belongs to

Wilkes J. C.

'We had to tell the police. It's just about big enough for a body,' he laughed. 'Can't open it though. You got the key, I expect?''

Ava shakes her head and Ted says, 'There's a tyre lever in the car. I'll go.'

'It must be his school things,' she shrugs, 'but why is it here? I never knew this space existed.'

'Spotted a sort of trapdoor under the decking thing,' the grizzled digger driver offers helpfully. Perhaps he's going to be in for a share if there's something valuable. It'll be a good story for the lads in the pub. He grasps the worn leather handle at one end and hoists it easily out of its hiding place. 'Not very heavy though.' His disappointment's obvious.

The policeman peers over Ted's shoulder as the trunk lid yields and the rusty catches flip up.

'Oh. That all?' He snaps his notebook shut, relieved. 'It's like a joke, right?'

With the windbreak hedges smouldering on the bonfire, there is nothing now to stop the chill sea breeze that dances across the site where three grand houses stood. Something flutters from the lid and they all grab to stop it escaping:

'Oh!'

'Careful ...'

'Mind ...'

But it lands back safely into the empty space.

In silence, they all stare at the solitary fifty-pound note, nestling now in the shelter of the trunk's mildewed base.

'Well that's that,' Ted smiles. He looks up as the sun appears from behind dark grey clouds. 'Tide's on the turn, I reckon.'

The onshore breeze stiffens, blowing away the smoke, clearing the air. Somehow, with it, a weight lifts.

And the blood red pulse that has burned into Ava's vision for so long is still there, but the breeze is fanning it – it's still red, but firey now, pulsating with energy. She turns her back on Old Halcyon, with all its dreams and all its disappointments.

There are things to achieve, to experience, to be challenged by and to win. A company to join and life to be lived with redblooded lust.

'Yes,' she looks Ted in the eye. 'The tide's turned.'

Lightning Source UK Ltd.
Milton Keynes UK
UKHW012101140622
404428UK00003B/486